Patient X

PATIENT X

The Case-Book of
Ryūnosuke Akutagawa

DAVID PEACE

ALFRED A. KNOPF · NEW YORK · 2018

For A;
in memory of Mark Fisher, William Miller
and all the ghosts of our lives.

Kappa was born out of my *dégoût* with many things, especially with myself.

Ryūnosuke Akutagawa, 1927

Contents

Author's Preface

These are the stories of Patient X in one of our iron castles. He will tell his tales to anyone with the ears and the time to listen.

Some days he appears younger than his years, some days older, emaciated one day, bloated the next, the pull and the pain of our three worlds, their spectres and their visions, fragmenting and splintering his features into a thousand selves as he relives the horrors of a lifetime, before he was brought to this place; how he . . . No, no, let us leave such details for now.

He told his stories at great length and in close detail as I listened with the physician in charge. All the time he spoke, he kept his arms tightly clasped around his knees, rocking back and forth, repeatedly glancing out beyond the iron grille of the narrow window, where hung a sky overcast and sombre, threatening an immense and endless darkness.

I have tried to set down in writing his stories—already-said, already-told and lived—with as much accuracy and fidelity as I can collect and command. But if anyone is dissatisfied or distrusts my notes, then you should seek out the source yourself. No doubt, Patient X will welcome you with a polite bow, guide you to the hard chair, and then calmly begin retelling his tales, a resigned and melancholy smile playing upon his lips as he speaks.

But be warned: when he comes to the end of his stories, the look on his face will change; he will leap to his feet, shake his fists wildly, and begin thundering away at you: "Quack, quack! Get out! You coward! You liar! You're on the make, like all the rest! Quack, quack! Get out! You cannibal! You vampire! You voyeur! Quack, quack! Get out! Just save the children . . ."

After the Thread, Before the Thread

—Among the palm flowers, among the bamboo,
Buddha has already fallen asleep.
By the roadside, a withered fig tree,
Christ, too, seems to be dead.
Yet we need to rest,
Even before the stage set.
(If we look behind that set,
We find only a patched-up canvas)—

"The Collected Works of Tock," in *Kappa*,
Ryūnosuke Akutagawa, 1927

1

And now, children, let me tell you a story about Gautama and Jesus.

It begins one day as Gautama is strolling in Paradise by the banks of the Lotus Pond. The blossoms on the pond are perfect white pearls, and from their golden centres wafts a never-ending fragrance. I think it must have been dawn in Paradise.

But as Gautama was strolling he heard the sound of weeping, a most unusual sound in Paradise. Gautama stepped down towards the edge of the pond and there, before the blossoms, amidst the fragrance, he saw Jesus kneeling beside the pond, by the water, staring down through the spreading lotus leaves to the spectacle below. For directly beneath the Lotus Pond of Paradise lie the lower depths of Hell, and as Jesus peered through the crystalline pool, he could see the River of Sins and the Mountain of Guilt as clearly as if he were viewing pictures in a peep-box.

And he was weeping at what he saw:

Down there was a man named Ryūnosuke, who was writhing in Hell with all the other sinners. This man had once been an acclaimed author but he had led a most selfish life, hurting even the people who loved him.

But now Gautama recalled how Ryūnosuke had performed at least one single act of kindness. Idling beside the Shinobazu Pond one day, Ryūnosuke had noticed a small spider creeping along the wayside. His first thought had been to stamp it to death, but as he raised his foot, he told himself, "No, no. Even this tiny creature is a living thing. To take its life for no reason would be too cruel."

And so Ryūnosuke let the spider pass him by unharmed.

Hearing Jesus weeping, seeing his tear-stained face, Gautama decided to reward Ryūnosuke by delivering him from Hell, if possible. And, by happy chance, Gautama turned to see a heavenly spider spinning a beautiful thread atop a lotus leaf the colour of shimmering jade. Gently lifting the spider thread, Gautama handed it to Jesus. And now Jesus lowered the thread straight down between the white blossoms, through the crystal waters to the depths far, far below.

2

Here, with the other sinners at the lowest point of the lowest Hell, Ryūnosuke was endlessly floating up and sinking down in the River of Sins. Wherever he looked there was only pitch darkness, and when a faint shape did pierce the shadows, it was the glint of a needle on the horrible Mountain of Guilt, which only heightened his sense of doom. All was silent, and when a faint sound did break the silence, it was only the feeble sigh of a fellow sinner. As you can imagine, those who had fallen this far had been so worn down by their tortures in the seven other hells that they no longer had the strength to cry out. Great writer though he once had been, now Ryūnosuke could only thrash about like a dying frog as he choked on his sins.

And then, children, what do you think happened next? Yes, indeed: raising his head, Ryūnosuke chanced to look up towards the sky above the River of Sins and saw the gleaming silver spider thread, so slender and so delicate, slipping stealthily down through the silent darkness from the high, high heavens, coming straight for *him*!

Ryūnosuke clapped his hands in joy. If only he could take hold of this thread and climb up, then perhaps he could escape from Hell. And maybe, with luck, he could even enter Paradise. Then he would never again be driven up the Mountain of Guilt or plunged down into the River of Sins.

No sooner had the thought crossed his mind than Ryūnosuke grasped the spider thread and started climbing with all his might, higher and higher, hand over hand, climbing and climbing.

Hell and Heaven, though, are thousands of leagues apart, so it was not easy for Ryūnosuke to escape. He soon began to tire, to tire until he could not raise his arm for even one more pull. He had no choice but to stop to rest, and as he clung to the spider thread, he looked down, far, far down below.

Now Ryūnosuke realised that all his climbing had been worth the effort: the River of Sins was hidden in the depths of the darkness. And even the dull glint of the terrifying Mountain of Guilt was far down beneath his feet. At this rate, it might be easier than he had imagined to climb his way out of Hell. Twining his hands in the spider thread, Ryūnosuke laughed aloud. "I've almost done it! I'm almost saved."

But then what do you think he saw? Far down on the spider thread, his selves, his legion of selves—son and father, husband and friend, lover and writer, Man of the East and Man of the West—had followed after him; his selves and his characters, too—Yoshihide, Yasukichi, Tock and all the rest—his many creations and, of course, his sins, his countless, countless sins: his pride, his greed, his lust, his anger, his gluttony, his envy and his sloth. All had followed after him, clambering up the thread with all their might like a column of ants! This slim thread seemed likely to snap from his weight alone: how could it possibly hold so many of his selves, his characters and his sins? And if the fragile thread were to break midway, then Ryūnosuke would plunge back down into the Hell he had struggled so mightily to escape. Yet from the pitch-dark River of Sins, still the unbroken column of his selves, his characters and his sins came squirming up the gleaming silver thread in their hundreds—in their thousands—and Ryūnosuke knew he would have to do something now or the thread would break in two.

Ryūnosuke raised his head again, looking up the spider thread. He was so close to Paradise, so very near. He could see the light of the water, he could glimpse the face of Jesus, even hear His weeping, now feel His tears wet upon his own face. But no matter how hard he tried to pull himself up, no matter how far and fast he climbed, Ryūnosuke knew his selves, his characters and sins would always follow after him, always catch up with him.

Ryūnosuke let go of the spider thread.

And at that very instant, at that very moment, as Ryūnosuke fell back down into the darkest depths, the spider thread broke at the very place where he had been hanging from it.

Behind Ryūnosuke, all that remained was the dangling short end of the spider thread from Paradise, softly shining in the moonless, starless sky.

3

At the edge of the Lotus Pond in Paradise, Buddha and Christ watched everything that happened. And when, in the end, Ryūnosuke sank back into the River of Sins, Buddha resumed His stroll, His face now tinged with sorrow. But Christ remained kneeling beside the pond, before the water, staring down through the lotus leaves, watching the pictures in the peep-box, weeping, weeping and weeping into the crystalline pool—

In girum imus nocte et consumimur igni . . .

We go round and round in the night, the endless night, consumed by fire, by fire, in the night, by fire—

Fire consumed by fire . . .

But the lotuses of the Lotus Pond still swayed their perfect pearl-white blossoms, and from their golden centres still wafted a never-ending fragrance. Yet I think it must be close to twilight in Paradise now.

Hell Screens

In that suburban house, on the second floor, many times
he asked himself why those who loved each other
caused each other such pain,
as the eerie tilt of the floor filled him with foreboding . . .

The Life of a Foolish Man, Ryūnosuke Akutagawa, 1927

Once upon a time, beneath the branches of a red pine, before a blackened gravestone, the man said to the child, These are the stories you told yourself, tell yourself, then and now, now and then, of scenes remembered, on screens erected . . .

1. Up and Down and Out

A voice comes to you in the dark, up the tunnel, through the waters—

"Can you hear me in there? Do you want to be born . . . ?"

Your father has his mouth to your mother's vagina—

"Please think seriously before you reply, but . . ."

Behind the sliding screen, crouching on the floor, his mouth level with her vagina, as though he is speaking into a telephone, asking you, "Is it your desire to be born into this world, or not?"

And each time, after asking his question, while awaiting your answer, he reaches up for the bottle on the table, takes a mouthful of disinfectant, gargles, rinses and spits into the metal bowl on the floor beside your mother's arse, then resumes his position, his mouth to her vagina, asking again, "Come on! Come on! Do you wish to be born into this world, or not?"

Up the tunnel, in the water, you are shaking your head and saying, "No, no! I do not want to be born. The first act of the human tragedy starts when an individual becomes the child of certain parents. You are asking me if I want to be born, but you do not even know if you want me; you have already lost one child, and now you are both at ill-omened ages. Should I agree to be born, in order to exorcize your own bad luck you already plan to abandon me on the steps of a Christian church, and then recover me from the priest as a foundling. It makes me shudder to think of all the things I will inherit from you and my mother. Insanity alone is bad enough. Finally, and absolutely, I maintain that human existence is evil, and the human condition is hell. And so thank you for asking, but no thank you. I would rather not."

But no one can hear you, no one is listening to you or truly cares what you say, your words drowned in the waters, your words lost in the tunnel, and so, before long, the waters are breaking, and off you go, swept along, down the tunnel, through the curtains, into the room and out, out—

"Niihara Ryūnosuke; Ryūnosuke, dragon-son . . ."

In the year of the dragon, in the month of the dragon, on the day of the dragon, in the hour of the dragon, at the sinking of the moon, at the rising of the sun, you first see the light of the world, and you weep and you scream, alone, alone, you scream and you scream—

2. "Mother / *Haha*"

You are in an asylum, in an enormous, monstrous room. All the lunatics have been made to dress in the same grey kimonos. It makes the scene even more depressing, if that were possible. One of the inmates sits at an organ, playing the same hymn again and again, over and over with ever-increasing intensity, ever greater fervour, as another dances, hopping and leaping about in the centre of the room. Beside a hale and hearty doctor, the very picture of health, you are looking on. The mad have a certain particular smell and in their odour you catch the scent of your own mother—

The smell of earth, a taste of mud . . .

"Shall we go," says the doctor.

Your mother was a madwoman. A beautiful, slender and graceful madwoman, born of samurai stock, who married a parvenu beneath herself, becoming ever quieter, ever more timid and withdrawn until the death of your eldest sister, and then your own birth when, and finally, the spectres and the twilight overtook and engulfed her—

In-trancing her, in-snaring her . . .

Your mother blamed herself for the death of your sister Hatsu, believing the meningitis which killed her had been brought on by a cold she had caught while on a day out together. You were born the year after Hatsu died and so you never knew her, but for the portrait of the little round-cheeked girl with dimples which still stands on the altar in your house. But you and your other sister Hisa were no balm to your mother, no defence against the spectres, the spectres and the twilight—

In-prisoning her . . .

In an upstairs room in the Niihara house in Shiba Ward, day after day, she would sit alone, all day long, puffing on a long, thin pipe, her hair held up in a bun by a comb, her tiny face ashen, her tiny body lifeless, as though already no longer really here, always never really there, emaciated, fading and wasting away, away—

In-shadow . . .

But you saw her, saw her then, see her now: your adoptive mother made a point of taking you to see her, leading you up the steep stairs to that dim room, prompting you to say, Hello, hello, Mother. Most of the time your mother would not answer, would never speak, her pipe to her lips, its mouthpiece white and barrel black, though once, just once, she suddenly grinned, leant forward, tapped you on the head with her pipe and said—

"Conk!"

But most of the time she was a very quiet, placid madwoman. But if you or your sister would ask her to draw or paint a picture for you, then she would take a sheet of writing paper, fold it in four and begin. Sometimes in black ink, sometimes in watercolours. Pictures of plants in bloom, paintings of children on an outing. But the people in her pictures, all the people she drew, they always had the faces of foxes, all fox-faced.

"Shall we go," says the doctor again.

You follow the doctor down the corridor into another room. In the corners, on the shelves, there are large jars of alcohol in which brains and other organs are soaking, pickled—

Preserved . . .

You remember her death more than her life; she finally wasted away and died in the autumn of your eleventh year. A telegram arrived. You climbed into a rickshaw with your adoptive mother and flew through the night from Honjo to Shiba. You had a thin silk handkerchief wrapped around your neck, with a motif of a Chinese landscape, the smell of perfume: Ayame Kōsui.

Your mother lay on a futon in the parlour beneath the upstairs room in which she had lived. You knelt beside her, weeping with your older sister.

Behind you, someone whispered, "The end is near now . . ."

Suddenly, your mother opened her eyes and spoke.

You cannot remember the words, but you remember you and your sister could not help but giggle. And then your sister began to cry again.

Your own tears had stopped, and they would not flow again. But you stayed kneeling before your mother throughout the night, beside your sister in her constant floods. You believed that as long as you did not cry, your mother would not die.

A few times, your mother would open her eyes, look you and your sister in the face, and then endless streams of tears would flow down her cheeks. But she did not speak again. And on the evening of the third day, your mother finally died. And then you cried, you cried.

A distant aunt, a woman you barely knew, put her arm around you, pulled you to her and said, "I'm so impressed by you!"

You could not understand what she meant, why she said what she said; impressed by what, you thought, how strange.

On the day of your mother's funeral, you and your sister climbed into a rickshaw, your sister holding the memorial tablet and you carrying the censer, for the long funeral procession from Shiba to Yanaka. But as you wound your way through the streets in the autumn sunlight, you kept dozing off and then waking suddenly just before the censer was about to fall from your hands. The journey seemed never-ending—

To last forever . . .

"And this one is the brain of a businessman," the doctor is saying, but you are staring out of the window, staring at a brick wall stained with moss, broken glass bottles embedded along its top; to keep people in, to keep people out?

"For some reason I know not," you tell the doctor, "I feel closer to the sister I never knew than to my mother. But if Hatsu was still living, she would be over forty, and maybe she would look as my mother looked, in that upstairs room, puffing on her pipe, drawing fox-faced people."

The doctor nods, smiles and says, "Please do go on . . ."

But you do not go on. You do not speak. You do not tell him that you often feel there is a woman in her forties somewhere watching over your life; a phantom not exactly your late mother, not exactly your dead sister. And probably it's just the effect of nerves wracked by coffee and tobacco, but perhaps there is the ghost of a presence somewhere, giving you occasional glimpses of itself and a world beyond this world—

Some-where, over-there . . .

The anniversary of your sister's death is the fifth of April. The anniversary of your mother's death is the twenty-eighth of November. Her posthumous name is Kimyōin Myōjō Nishin Daishi.

You cannot remember the anniversary of your birth father's death, nor recall his posthumous name.

3. "Father / *Chichi*"

You are eating spoon after spoon of ice cream in the Uoei restaurant in Ōmori, and your father is saying, pleading, "Come back, Ryūnosuke. Leave that house in Honjo, and come back home with me. You will want for nothing, Ryūnosuke. Here: have another bowl of ice cream . . ."

Your mother mad, your father busy, he gave you away. He gave you away to your mother's brother, Akutagawa Dōshō, and his wife Tomo, a childless couple. And you are glad he gave you away, you are happy he gave you away. But he does not leave you alone, he does not stay away; he tries to take you back, to steal you away, with bananas, pineapples and ice cream. "Here, son, here: have another bowl, and another . . ."

Your father was in the dairy business and, apparently, quite successful, "able in word and ingratiating in manner," as Confucius said. But he was also a very short-tempered man, a man who had seen military service, who had fought in the Boshin War of 1868, fighting with the Satsuma rebels against the Tokugawa at Toba-Fushimi, who had fought and won; your father was not a man accustomed to losing, to accepting defeat—

So much gained for some . . .

"One more time," he bellows, face red.

You are in your third year of Middle School, and you are playing wrestling with your father. You have thrown him easily with your speciality judo throw, the *ōsotogari* outside thigh sweep, and sent him sprawling. But your father springs to his feet again, his arms spread and squaring up, advancing towards you now. Again, you throw him too easily, much too easily—

So much lost for others . . .

"Another go!" he shouts.

You know he is angry. You know if you throw him again, you will have to wrestle him again, endlessly until he wins, all the time his temper rising, his attacks becoming more aggressive. And sure enough, he comes at you again, and you are grappling again. And so now you let him wrestle with you for a while, a little while, before falling, deliberately falling back onto the floor, deliberately losing, deliberately a—

"Loser," your father gloats. "Loser!"

As you get back to your feet, as you dust yourself down, as your father struts about the room, you glance at your mother's younger sister, the woman who is now your father's second wife, who has been sat there watching you both wrestle, and she smiles at you now, and she winks at you now, and you know she knows, she knows you let your father win, you let your father have this day. Just this day, one last day—

"Father hospitalised . . ."

You are twenty-eight years old and you are teaching in Yokosuka when you receive the telegram. Your father has the Spanish flu. You travel to Tokyo. You sleep in the corner of his hospital room for three days. You are bored beside his deathbed.

On the fourth day, you receive a call from your friend Thomas Jones. He is about to leave Tokyo and he invites you for a farewell dinner at a geisha teahouse in Tsukiji. You leave your father, hanging onto his life by a thread, and set off to the teahouse.

You have a most enjoyable evening in the company of four or five geisha. Around ten o'clock you leave, and you are heading down the narrow stairs to the waiting taxi when you hear a soft, beautiful, feminine voice calling after you, "Ah-san . . ."

You stop on the stair. You look back up towards the top of the staircase. One of the geisha is staring down at you, her eyes fixed on yours. You do not speak. You turn back, going through the door, out into the taxi.

All the way back to the hospital, you are thinking of the geisha's fresh, young face, her hair set in a Western style, and her eyes, her eyes. You do not think once of your father, dying in the hospital.

He is waiting impatiently for you. He sends your two aunts outside the two-panel decorative folding screen by his bed. He beckons you towards him, gripping your hand, caressing and stroking it, and he begins to tell you of things-long-past, things you knew nothing of, of the time when he first met your mother, of the years they had been married, of how they had gone shopping together for a tansu storage chest, of when they had ordered sushi to be delivered to the house. Inconsequential things, trivial things. But as he tells you these things, as you listen to these things, you feel your eyelids becoming hotter and hotter, and you see the tears flowing down his cheeks, his emaciated and wasted cheeks, your own eyes filling with tears; confused and delirious now, your father is pointing at the folding screen—

"Here comes a warship! Here comes a warship! Look at the flags! Just look at all the flags flying! Banzai! Everybody, banzai!"

Your father dies the next morning, without much pain, without much suffering, or so the doctors assure you.

You don't recall your father's funeral at all. But you do remember that when you were accompanying his body from the hospital back to his house, a great, full spring moon was shining down on the roof of the hearse as you crossed the city.

4. Tokyo: A Mental-scape

You hate the parents who gave you life, who gave you away, twice gave you away. But you love your adoptive family, who took you in, who gave you a home, especially your mother's elder sister, your Aunt Fuki. You are happy with your adoptive family, you are happy with your Aunt Fuki; you are happy here, happy here in this happy house, this happy house next door to poverty—

You love the streets around your house, the streets of Honjo, on the eastern bank of the Sumida River. There is not one single beautiful street, not one single attractive house in all of Honjo. The shops are drab, the road a swamp in winter and dust in summer and leading only to the Big Ditch. The Ditch floating with weeds, the Ditch stinking of shit—

But this is the place you love: the Ekōin Temple, Halt-Pony Bridge, Yokoami, and the Hannoki Horse Ground; these are the places which will haunt you for the rest of your life, your thoughts and your dreams, their dusty streets, their flooded streets, their shabby houses and their open sewers, and their nature: roof-top grasses, spring clouds in puddles, the tall trees by the temples and the willows along the open sewers; this is the nature you will always love the most, the nature which lives faintly, subtly amidst all the artifices of our so-called human civilisation, blooming and flowering, with all its beauty, with all its brutality—

With all its mystery . . .

Every morning you walk through Honjo with your adoptive father, you walk and you talk, your heart bursting with joy, so happy and so curious, so filled with love, so filled with wonder, until, until—

Until one morning, the early glow fading in the sky, you and your adoptive father are walking towards your favourite place, the Hundred-Piling Bank of the Sumida River. There are always fishermen here, and you like to sit and watch them fish as your adoptive father tells you stories of the fox-spirits he has seen on his walks, fantastic stories, magical stories. You reach the Hundred-Piling Bank, but this morning the place is deserted. The only things moving are the sea-lice crawling in the gaps of the stone walls of the broad bank. You start to ask where the fishermen have gone, why there are no fishermen today. Your adoptive father points down at the river, towards the water, and he says, "Look at that . . ."

And you look, and you see—

Below your feet, between the pilings, among the garbage, among the weeds, a shaven-headed corpse bobs up and down upon the waves, rising and falling, falling and rising, up and down, with the current, on the tide.

You look away, you turn away, turning away into your adoptive father, hiding away in his coat. But he takes your arm, and he takes your face, and he says, "Look, Ryūnosuke! Look! You cannot turn your face from horror, you cannot look away from death. You cannot hide, you have to look. So look, Ryūnosuke! Look and see . . ."

And now you look, and yes, now you see, see this place for what it really is, see this world for what it truly is: corpses floating in its rivers, hanging from its trees, bodies falling by its wayside, burning in its fires, the factories on both banks, these rows upon rows, the shacks upon shacks, these endless shacks, the railway tracks and the utility poles, its affluence and poverty, the satiated and the starving, all crawling in its gaps, bobbing up and down, rising and falling, pretending and pretending, pretending everything is fine, pretending everything's all right, nothing wrong, there's nothing wrong: there's no deceit, there are no lies, no lies, no lies. No smell of piss. No smell of shit. No smell of death. No cheap cake in a fancy box. No low-grade sake in an expensive bottle. No patched-up clothes, no patched-up screens. No chipped wooden desks, the baize worn thin and varnish gone. No faded red cushions, all threadbare and darned. No artifice, no pretence. No self-deceit. No fathers who are no fathers, no mothers who are no mothers. No scars, no scars across your heart, your broken, broken heart; all lies, all lies—

And now, now you turn; and yes, yes, you run; faster than you've ever run before, faster than you'll ever run again, down these dusty streets, past these open sewers, to your house and through your gate, through your door and up your stairs, to your aunt in her room, always in her room, behind her screens, always behind her screens, your face buried in her breast, your tears burning through her clothes, her arms wrapped around your back, her hands running through your hair, she is whispering, she is whispering, "There, there, Ryūnosuke. There, there, my dear, dear child. This is the world of men, this is their world of lies. But I am here, I am here. And I will never leave you, never leave you, Ryūnosuke. Never, never let you go . . ."

Your face still buried in her breast, your tears still burning through her clothes, Fuki opens a book: *Uji Shūi Monogatari*. Fuki turns its pages, their oral folk tales. Not looking, not reading, Fuki says, "*Mukashi, mukashi*, three sisters lived in the Old Capital in their family home. Strangely, against all custom, against all tradition, the middle sister married first, the youngest next, but the eldest of the sisters never married. Why, we do not know, she would not say. But people whispered, as people do, of honour lost, of secret shame, a drunken uncle, a forced encounter. A child, was there a child? Given away, and lost to her? We do not know, she would not say, would never say. But with no husband of her own, the eldest sister lived on in the family home, tending to her father and her mother, her elder brother, too, her younger sisters marrying, her younger sisters departing, leaving her alone, alone in her room. And so in time, her father then her mother died, and her brother took a wife and brought her to the house. But still, still the elder sister lived on in the family house, alone in her room, in her room, alone in her room, until, in time, she too fell ill and died.

"Her body was left in her room until her younger sisters returned, and with the rest of the household they then took her to the burning ground. But when they reached that place of smoke and ash, when they were about to unload the coffin from the carriage, in preparation for the usual funeral rites, then they noticed the coffin was strangely light, its lid ajar. Yes, the body was gone! All were shocked, for the body could not possibly have fallen out on the way to the burning ground. Yet still they retraced their steps to make certain. Of course, all the way back to the house, they found not a thing, not a trace. But on reaching the house, on entering her room, there she was, lying there alone in her room, lying there as though she had never moved.

"Throughout the night, the family and the mourners discussed what best to do. At dawn, they put the body back inside the coffin and carefully sealed the lid, waiting then until dusk and another chance to proceed with the cremation. But when night finally began to fall, again they found the coffin lid open and the body lying on the floor in its former room. Now the family and the mourners were terrified, and still further frightened when they tried to move the body; they could not move her body. The body simply would not move. No matter how many tried, no matter how hard they tried. The body would not move. For her arms were roots, for her legs were roots. The bones in her ribs, the bones in her back. Planted in the floor, rooted in the ground. Her hair now twine, her hair now vine.

"So there she was, where she meant to stay. You like it here, asked one of her younger sisters. All right then, fine; if that is what you want, then this is where we'll leave you. But we are going to have to get you out of sight, at least! And so they took up the floor, and they made a hole, and yes, she was as light as air when they lowered her through the hole and into the ground.

"And so here they buried her, under the floor, building a good-sized mound over her. But then the family and the servants all moved away, since no one wanted to stay on in a house with a corpse. And so, over the years, the house fell to ruin and eventually disappeared. Only the mound remained. But not even the common people seemed to be able to live near the mound. For people began to claim awful things happened there. And so soon, soon, the mound stood all alone. But in time, in time, a shrine was built upon it, and they say the shrine still stands there, over her rooted corpse."

In her room, always in her room, behind her screens, always behind her screens, your face still buried in her breast, your tears now drying on her clothes, her arms still wrapped around your back, her hands now smoothing down your hair, Fuki is whispering, she is whispering, "These are the stories you should know, Ryūnosuke, these are the tales I will tell you. To teach you of the world of men, to warn you of their world of lies. For all men are demons, Ryūnosuke, this world their hell. But don't cry, Ryūnosuke, don't cry, for I will protect you, I will save you. Protect you from these demons, save you from their hell. For I will never leave you, Ryūnosuke, never leave you, never, never let you go . . ."

You love your Aunt Fuki. You love her more than anyone. She will never marry, she will live with you for the rest of your life. You will argue with her, you will quarrel with her. But you will never stop loving her—

"I will never, never let you go, I promise, I promise . . ."

Never stop loving her for the rest of your life—

"And so do you promise me, Ryūnosuke? Promise you will never leave me, never leave me for the rest of my life . . ."

In her room, always in her room, behind her screens, always behind her screens, in her arms, always in her reach, you nod and you say, "I do."

5. The House of Books

In her room, behind her screens. You are a weak and sickly, cosseted child. Often constipated, often feverish. You are subject to convulsions, you are plagued by headaches. To constant convulsions, by perpetual headaches. A nervous child, a frightened child. Always frightened, always afraid: afraid of the dark, afraid of the light. The sun and the moon. The stars in the night, the clouds in the sky. The sky and the sea, the water and the earth. The ground beneath you, the land about you. The air you breathe, the very air you breathe. Afraid of the living, afraid of the dead. Always here, always there. The people who came before you once, the people who come before you still. The living and the dead, the dead and the living. People, people. Afraid of the people, so afraid of the people. The people and the world, their world and it all. Afraid, afraid, afraid of it all—

Don't be scared, Ryūnosuke . . .

In the house, its other rooms. You are afraid, even more afraid. Afraid of the doors, afraid of the floors. That open, that tilt. The dust from the ceiling, the dust on the floor. Afraid of the tatami, afraid of the lamps. The old tatami, the dim lamps. The family altar, its mortuary tablets with their blackened gold leaf. The family shrine, its two earthenware *tanuki* sat on red cushions. They sit in a dark storage room, a candle lit before them. Every night, every day. You are afraid, you are afraid. Afraid of the screens, their peeling paper. Afraid of the windows, their looming shadows. The shadows and the whispers, the whispers outside and in—

Don't be scared . . .

But in one room, in just one room. Upon the walls, above the door. There are prints and there are scrolls. From another time, a better time. And in the alcoves, and on the floor. There are books, so many books. From a different world, a better world. And in that room, in just this room. You are less afraid, much less afraid. First curious, intrigued. Then summoned, now seduced. By the pictures, by the scrolls. And by the books, by all of these books—

Don't be scared, they whisper. *We can bring you to another time, we can take you to a different world.* In their piles, in their rows. *A better time, a better world*, they whisper. *Come closer, Ryūnosuke. Come closer and see.* You walk towards the piles of books, you walk towards the rows of books. *We will be your guard, we will be your shield.* And you reach out your hand, now you take up a book. *Your guard and your shield.* And you open up the book, open up the book and see. *Another time, a different world.* You see, you see. *A better time, a better world.* This is the start, *the start of it all . . .*

In the dim light, on the frayed tatami. First there are the pictures, the lurid illustrations. In the *Kusazōshi*, the Edo storybooks. So vivid, so magical. With their pictures of ghosts, with their pictures of monsters. Your eyes wide, your heart pounding. In the dim light, on the frayed tatami. Then there are the words, the cryptic signs. In *Saiyūki*, in *Suikoden*, these Chinese classics, in abridged translations. So intense, so spellbinding. With their legends of heroes, with their tales of adventures. Your eyes wider still, your heart pounding faster. In the dim light, on the frayed tatami. Word after word, sentence after sentence, paragraph after paragraph, page after page. You read and you read. In the dim light, on the frayed tatami. Becoming these heroes, living their adventures. In another time, a different world. A better time and a better world. That dim, dim light, now pale moonlight. The frayed tatami, now forest floors. The dripping tap, a thunderous river. The steep stairs, a mountain pass. Your bedding, now a bearskin. Reading and reading, learning and learning. You learn all the names of the One Hundred and Eight Heroes at Liangshan Marsh, you learn all their names, their names by heart. Your heart steady now, your eyes narrow now. Your toy wooden sword, a cold metal blade. You are battling with the fierce warrior beauty Ten Feet of Steel, you are duelling with the wild, brash monk Lu Zhishen. Against merciless bandits, against night witches. With bloody cudgels and with whistling arrows. Living characters, true heroes. These characters your friends, these heroes your teachers. They teach you bravery, they give you courage—

Don't be scared, they shout. *Be strong, Ryūnosuke! Be strong . . .*

So you read and you read. Page after page, page after page. You read and you read, on and on. Legends and tales, stories then novels. Book after book, on and on. You read and you read. Not afraid, not afraid. No longer afraid. You read and you read. In the house, then at school. At your desk, on the street. You read and you read. Bashō and Bakin. Izumi Kyōka and Kunikida Doppo. Mori Ōgai and Natsume Sōseki. Japanese books and foreign books. The Bible and Aesop. Shakespeare and Goethe. Pu Songling and Anatole France. Book after book, character after character. Living each book, becoming each character. Hamlet and Mephistopheles, Don Juan and Julien Sorel, Prince Andrei and Ivan Karamazov. Each book a revelation, each character a transformation. So many characters, so many, many books—

We will guide you, Ryūnosuke. We will help you . . .

They keep whispering to you, keep calling you. Inside the house, now from outside the house. So many books, so many more books, but so little money, so very little money. Your adoptive father is a cultured man, yet a frugal man. But there are the libraries, always the libraries. And your own frugality, and your own guile. The public libraries across the river are too far, too far for an elementary schoolboy. But by the Big Ditch, so near to home, so close to hand, there is a commercial Rental Library. The sweet old lady who runs the place, she smiles at you, the sweet old lady who runs the place, she calls you "Sonny Boy." So day after day, for hour after hour. You pretend to hunt, you pretend to search. Day after day, hour after hour. She never realises, she never suspects. Sonny Boy is always secretly reading, Sonny Boy is only occasionally renting. Day after day, hour after hour. With your own frugality, with your own guile. Day after day, hour after hour. The sweet old lady making her ornamental hairpins at her counter, the sweet old lady calling you "Sonny Boy" as you enter. Day after day, hour after hour. Reading and reading, book after book. Thanks to your own

frugality, thanks to your own guile. For day after day, for hour
after hour. Until you have devoured all of her books, until you've
eaten all that she has. By your own frugality, by your own guile.
Until there is nothing more for you to read, nothing more for you
here. Until the day arrives, now the hour comes—

You must cross the river, Ryūnosuke . . .

Calling to you, calling you. Over the bridge, over the river. Your
school notebooks under your arm, your packed lunchbox under
your arm. Crossing the Ryōgoku Bridge, crossing the Sumida River.
After school and on holidays, over the river and along the streets.
You are twelve years old, and you are on a mission. Mobilisation
orders have been issued, lanterns outside the police stations. First
to the Ōhashi Library on Kudanzaka Hill, then to the Imperial
Library in Ueno Park. Among marching boots, under waving flags.
Through the inviting used bookstores cluttering Jimbōchō Avenue,
the blinding sun rising over Kudanzaka Hill. With the dawn, back
by dusk. Two hours' walk there, two hours' walk back. Under sun
and under moon. Whatever the season, whatever the weather.
Through the spring winds, plum blossom then cherry petal.
Through the summer rains, blooming hydrangea then flowering
lotuses. On carpets of leaves, on carpets of snow. With returning
boots, under victorious flags. In the Ōhashi Library, in the Imperial
Library. They keep calling to you, keep calling you—

Waiting for you, we are waiting for you . . .

On your first visits, you are afraid. The high ceilings, the large
windows. The iron stairways, the catalogue cases. The basement
lunch room and the reading room. The numberless people, on
numberless chairs. But on your next visits, you start to read. To read
and to read, turning page after page. Turning and reading, book
after book. In library after library, for year after year. The Ōhashi
Library and the Imperial Library, then the Higher School Library,
then the university library, the Tokyo University Library. Library

after library, for year after year, borrowing and borrowing, book after book, hundreds of books, loving and loving, loving these books, these borrowed books, these borrowed books all loving you—

Please don't take us back, Ryūnosuke, please . . .

The parting, these partings, tearing and tearing, tearing you apart: you want to keep these books, keep these books with you, these borrowed books, to hold and to cherish for the rest of your life, reading them over and over, again and again. Never taking them back, never letting them go. Never parting, never parting. So with your frugality, and with your guile. Your devotion and your discipline. You stay away from the cafés, and you teach part-time. Mathematics, even mathematics, for three days a week. You earn and you save. Then you buy, and you buy. On Jimbōchō Avenue, in its used bookstores. Book after book, second-hand book. Loving and keeping, cherishing and holding. Owning and possessing. Book after book. Your own books, your own library. Book by book. Building your library, your very own library. Book by book. But there are still so many books, so many more books you want. On Jimbōchō Avenue, the used bookstores. So many books, many more books. Inviting you, tempting you—

Take us home, take us, please . . .

Always so many books, still so little money. And so, but so. All else having failed, as the last resort. With your heart filled with pain, with your eyes filled with tears. Deaf to their protests, deaf to their screams. After all they have taught you, after all they have given you. Deaf to their protests, deaf to their screams. Your victims smothered with cloth, your victims strangled with string. As though to a funeral, an ancient tragedy. You cross the bridge, you cross the river. Tripping on a stone, falling in the road. You dust yourself down, you pick yourself up. With heavy feet, with slow steps. Along the streets, to Jimbōchō you go, you go, you—

No, Ryūnosuke, no. Don't . . .

Enter the bookstore, the second-hand bookstore. You place the bundle on the counter, untie the string before the owner. You open up the cloth, take out the books. And you ask the woman, you ask, How much, how much for these? She offers you less than half of the price you paid for these books, even for books that are still quite new. You sigh, you nod. You accept her offer, and take her money. And you turn, you hurry. Deaf to their protests, deaf to their screams. Away from the crime, the scene of the crime. Their protests and their screams—

Why, Ryūnosuke . . . ?

Because still there are so many books, so many more books you want. On Jimbōchō Avenue, in its used bookstores. So many books, so many more books. Inviting you and tempting you. So many books, now so many regrets. Regrets and lost loves:

Ryūnosuke?

Two months later, in the twilight. You are back on Jimbōchō Avenue, you are back among the used bookstores. Lightly dusted with snow, wrapped in your cape. From shop to shop, you've been making your way—

Remember me, Ryūnosuke?

On Jimbōchō Avenue, lightly dusted with snow. In your cape, stamping your feet. Outside each of the stores, the books on the street. Inviting you and tempting you. But before one shop, now among their books. This shop you know, these books you know. You find a copy of *Zarathustra*, but not just any copy of *Zarathustra*. A book well read, a book well loved. Read by you, loved by you. The very copy you sold not two months ago, the very copy still smudged with the oil from your fingers. Your former book, your former lover. You pick it up, you open it up. Standing out front, rereading and rereading. Passage after passage, page after page. And the more you read, the more you miss. This book, this book, you—

Ryūnosuke, please . . .

Enter the bookstore, the second-hand bookstore. You place the book on the counter, and you ask, you ask, How much is this? One yen sixty sen, smiles the woman who owns the shop. But for you, I'll make it one fifty . . .

Take me back, Ryūnosuke. Please take me back . . .

You had sold it to her for a mere seventy sen, and can only bargain her down to one forty. But you miss this book, for you love this book. So you sigh, then you nod. And hand over double the amount you had sold it for. It always happens, you never learn . . .

Thank you, Ryūnosuke. Thank you . . .

Outside the store, back on the street. The buildings now dark, the streets now white. All very quiet, so strangely quiet. Jimbōchō covered with snow, you are wrapped in your cape. The steel-grey cover of *Zarathustra* pressed against your chest, a self-mocking smile upon your chapped lips. You walk and you trudge. Through the night, in the snow. Back to your house, back to your library, your very own library, your very own . . .

House of Books . . .

Book after book, book by book, pile by pile, shelf by shelf, screen by screen and wall by wall, you build and you build a house of books, your house of books. Made of paper, made of words. A house of books, a world of words: everything you know about the world, everything you learn about the world, you know and you learn from books, through words. You cannot think of anything you do not to some degree owe to books. First books, you believe, then reality; "from books to reality," your unchanging truth: you do not try to improve your knowledge of life by observing the passers-by in the street. No, rather you read about the life of mankind in books, in order to better watch the passers-by in the street. Yes, real-life people are merely passers-by. In order to understand them—all their loves, all their hates, their lives and their deaths—to truly know them as they pass you by, you sit in your house of books, in your world of words, and you read and you read, book after book, observing and noting peculiarities of speech, of gesture, facial expressions, the line of a nose and the tilt of an eyebrow, the way they hold their hands, rough outlines and sketches, in Balzac, Poe, Baudelaire, Dostoevsky, Flaubert, the brothers Goncourt, Ibsen, Tolstoy, Strindberg, Verlaine, De Maupassant, Wilde, Shaw and Hauptmann; you will be the most well-read man of your generation. But every book you read is a textbook for life, an instruction in the art of living. You will find yourself in love with certain women. Yet none will show you what beauty truly is; only thanks to Balzac, thanks to Gautier, thanks to Tolstoy, only thanks to them do you notice the beauty of a woman's ear, translucent in the sunlight, or the shadow of an eyelash, falling on a cheek. If you had not read of such beauty in books, then you would have seen nothing in a woman except the female animal of your species. Without books, without words, life would be unbearable, so unbearable, so ugly, so very, very ugly—

Not worth a single line of Baudelaire . . .

But your house of books, your world of words, with its screens and its walls, with its windows and doors, is built from other people's books, other people's words, borrowed and bought, always, already stolen and used; in your second-hand house of books, in your second-hand world of words, your life is always, already second-hand, second-hand.

6. A Bridge, a Gate; on the Way to Work . . .

One day, at school, you are daydreaming, looking out of the window, not thinking, just dreaming, the wind so very, very strong today, the wind moving through the branches of the trees today, the leaves rustling, the leaves trembling, each leaf, each leaf, halting your dreams, holding your gaze, enchanting you, bewitching you, making you see, making you feel, see for yourself and feel for yourself, the beauty of nature, the wonder of creation, this secret, this mystery, a current, a light; you will always remember this day, this moment, for this is the day, the moment, you know what you want to do, to do with your life, the rest of your life—

You will devote your life to literature, to the *creation* of literature, the rest of your life to writing.

In the Japanese language you have the word *kaku*, which means "to write, to draw or to paint," in other words "to compose or to depict." The characters with which *kaku* is written consist of "the hand" radical on the left and the character for "seedling" on the right. The character for "seedling" is itself a compound of two radicals: one for "grass," the other for "field." When you put them all together you get *kaku* or *egaku*: a picture of a hand planting a seed. For you, all art originates from the germ of an idea, then the seed has to be planted or sown, then cultivated and nurtured by hand. This is what writing means to you, and this is what you are going to do.

You put down your wooden sword, you pick up your thin pen and you begin to scratch, you begin to write, copying down the old tales Fuki tells, scribbling down the stories the maids share, tales and stories of ghosts and of fireballs, widows obsessed with their late husbands, old ladies tortured by their daughters-in-law, filling notebooks with these stories, making little magazines with your friends, telling and retelling, composing and depicting, writing and writing, story after story, learning and learning, learning your craft, building bridges from these stories, these other people's stories, bridges to your stories, your own stories, that gate you seek, over these bridges.

You translate one page of Poe a day, first studying the composition of the stories, then the construction of the sentences, all their hidden secrets, their occluded mysteries; their balance of beauty and truth, of passion and terror, humour and sarcasm, the melancholia of their dreams, the alchemy of their poetry, the precision of these sentences, the concision of these stories, the wonder of all these elements, the effect of this totality; his dedication to craftsmanship, his devotion to his craft. This is what you learn from Poe, this is your education, your apprenticeship.

It is a never-ending apprenticeship, to writing, and to language. For literature is an art of words that depends on language for its expression. And so you work ceaselessly to improve the quality of your language, the quality of your writing. And the quality you seek most in other people's writings is the same as the one you seek most in your own: clarity. You want to write as clearly as possible. You want to express in precise terms what lies in your mind. And so you try and try to do just that. But when you take up your pen, you can seldom write as clearly or as smoothly as you wish. You always end up writing cluttered sentences. All your effort (if you can truly call it that) goes into the clarity of your art.

Yet you know the novel is the least artistic of all the literary genres. The only one that deserves the name of art is poetry. The novel is included in literature only for the sake of the poetry in it. In any other respect, the novel differs little from biography or history. For you, novelists are biographers or historians, relating themselves to the human life of a given age and of a given country. In Japan, the proof of this truth is in the works of the Lady Murasaki and Ihara Saikaku. But the greatest novelists are also always poets, yet always, already impure poets, still obligated to biography, or to history, always, already divided and torn, always, already torn in two; historian and poet, poet and historian.

And so you keep going back, back to the tales, the tales of the past, the tales Aunt Fuki told you, from *Uji Shūi Monogatari*, from *Konjaku Monogatari*, going back to the poetry of *Man'yōshū*, to the language of *Hōjōki*, always going back, back to the past, long, long ago, *mukashi, mukashi* . . .

For suppose you have a particular theme and you want to turn it into a story: in order to express it as powerfully and as artistically as possible, then you need some extraordinary and memorable incident. But the more extraordinary and memorable you imagine it to be, then the harder it is to describe such an incident convincingly if you set it in present-day Japan, for then it seems unnatural, and then the theme is left by the wayside, and then all is lost. But if it is difficult to set an extraordinary incident in contemporary Japan, then the solution is simple: make the incident happen in some remote past (or in the far future), or in a country other than Japan, or both. Then again, if you simply begin with "Once upon a time," and then let the history go at that, then you have failed, too; you have to establish a particular historical time and setting, and then introduce and include some of the social background and conditions of that time, thus making the story seem natural and plausible, thus holding the attention of the reader, the hand of the reader, taking them back, back to the past, making them see the past, making them feel the past, making them live, yes, live the past again, anew . . .

Yes, from your desk, pen in hand, you will resurrect the stories of the past, the tales once told, lifting the veil, you will raise the dead, raise the dead, lifting the veil, tearing the veil, the veil in two . . .

Mukashi, mukashi, you are standing under a gate, the Akamon Gate at the University of Tokyo, standing under the gate, watching the rain fall, the rain falling now, the rain falling then, thinking of another gate, a different gate, in another city, a different city, in another time, a different time: the Rashōmon Gate in Kyoto, the grand city gate which once stood at the southern entrance to Suzaku Avenue; now no trace remains, not even a foundation stone. But you know this gate, you have read of this gate in the *Konjaku Monogatari*, and so you see this gate . . .

Long, long ago, a man came up from Settsu Province to the capital in order to steal. Since it was still daylight when he arrived, he hid out under the Rashōmon Gate . . .

In your mind, you see this gate, this once-great gate, as though you are seeing a painting, a moving, living, breathing painting; the gate abandoned and ruined, beneath a sky thick with crows, cawing and circling, a home for badgers and for foxes, standing in the twilight, the twilight now, the twilight then . . .

At this hour it was still bustling with people, and the man waited patiently under the gate for the city to quieten down. Then the man heard a large group approaching the gate . . .

"Ryūnosuke," says your friend. "I'm sorry to have kept you waiting. But I have good news: we will have the place to ourselves . . ."

Your friend is a student in the Medical School of the University of Tokyo. Now he leads you to the building, he guides you up the stairs, he leads you down a corridor and guides you to the room . . .

To avoid being seen, the man stole up to the gate's top storey, which formed an upstairs room. A dim light was burning in the gloom. Strange! The man peered in through the latticework windows and, stretched before him, he saw the corpse of a young woman . . .

Cardboard tags on fine wires dangle from the big toe of each cadaver, each tag inscribed with a name, an age and a date. Your friend bends over one of the corpses and begins to peel back the skin of its face with his scalpel, gradually exposing an expanse of yellow fat, the hair of the corpse dangling over the edge of the table . . .

The light by her head, an ancient crone was roughly picking out the corpse's hair. For all the frightened thief knew, this old crone could be a demon or a ghost . . .

You are afraid, afraid again. You do not want to look, but you must look, you must; you are writing a story set in the Heian era, a story of corpses. But you have been unable to finish your work, unable to balance the fantastic and the authentic. And so you have asked to be here; you have asked to see a corpse—*"Look, Ryūnosuke!*

Look! You cannot turn your face from horror, you cannot look away from death. You cannot hide, you have to look. So look, Ryūnosuke! Look and see . . ."—And now you look, and yes, you see. See the corpse and see the hair. And now you reach out, reach out to touch the hair, but then you stop, you stop. The smell overpowering, a stench of rotting apricots. You steel yourself, and step closer . . .

The thief opened the door, drew his dagger and charged in with a shout. The terrified crone wrung her hands in a frantic plea for mercy, mercy . . .

"You're lucky," laughs your friend, still working away with his scalpel. "You know, we're actually running out of decent cadavers these days."

"Who are you, what are you doing here," snarled the thief . . .

You reach out again, and now you touch the hair, the hair of the corpse. The hair slips easily into your hand . . .

"My mistress died, sir, and there was no one to do the needful for her, so I brought her up here. You see, sir, her hair is longer than she was tall, and I am picking it out to make a wig. Please, sir, don't kill me!"

Pen in hand, at your desk, under the gate, you are under the gate, in the upstairs room, you are in that room, in that place and in that time. The stench of death, the sound of rain. A flash of lightning, a peal of thunder. You strip the old woman of her robes, you tear the hair from her hands. She clutches at your legs, she clings to your ankles. You kick her, you kick her, violently, violently, sending her sprawling, sprawling back, back among the corpses, back among the dead, then you turn, you turn, turn and descend, down the steep stairs, stair by stair, into the darkness, and into the night . . .

The thief took the corpse's clothes and the old woman's, too, picked up the pile of loose hair, dashed back down the stairs and fled . . .

The old woman lies among the corpses now, naked as if dead, her tiny face ashen, her tiny body lifeless, as though she is already no longer here, always never really there. Then murmuring and muttering, now sighing and groaning, she crawls, she crawls, over the corpses, to the top of the stairs, her hair hanging down, down over her face, she peers down the stairs, staring under the gate, staring out, out, into the dark and empty night . . .

Yes, the upper storey of the Rashōmon Gate used to be filled with human corpses and skeletons. If people couldn't provide a proper funeral, they would sometimes bring the corpse to the upper storey of the gate and leave it there instead. The thief told people about what had happened to him, and thus this story came to be handed down to us today.

At your desk, you stop writing, you look up. For a moment, you do not recognise this place, do not recognise this world. You were in the current and the light that flow through nature and through time, through life and through art, a light more powerful than a thousand shattered stars, a current faster than any river, flowing through your blood, sweeping through your mind, taking the faint spark which glimmers within, turning that spark into a flame, kindling that flame until it burns and burns, brighter and brighter, illuminating your way, forcing you on, moving your hand and moving your pen, word after word, for page after page, absorbing you, consuming you, in letters, in writing. But then, the next moment, it is gone again, gone again. And the instant you lose sight of it, the very moment it is gone, you are overcome by the immense and endless darkness that looms around you now, at your desk, in your study, leaving you lost again, alone again, in the dark and empty night, lost and alone, waiting, just waiting.

*

Once again upon a time, beneath the branches of the red pine, before the blackened gravestone, the child said to the man, No, no. Those are the stories, the narratives you tell yourself, you write yourself, in the mirror in the bathroom, at your desk in your study, you keep telling yourself, will keep writing yourself, these stories, these narratives that do not hold, which will not hold, that break apart, will break apart, in the mirror in the bathroom, at your desk in your study, breaking you apart, tearing you apart, splintering and splattering you, in remembered scenes, on erected screens, until it's all too late, all too late, and all that remains, all that remains are those erected screens, your own hell screens.

Repetition

Westerners say that not to fear death is characteristic of savages.
Well, perhaps I am one of those "savages."
Many times in my childhood, my parents admonished me
that since I was born in the house of a samurai,
I had to be able to perform *seppuku*, to slit my abdomen.
And I remember thinking that there would be physical agony
and that it would have to be endured.
Therefore, perhaps I am one of those so-called savages.
Yet I cannot accept the Westerners' view as right.

Mōsō / Daydreams, Mori Ōgai, 1911

Ryūnosuke hated the summer. The red sun turned to white iron, pouring its light and heat over the thirsty earth, which stared back up into the enormous, cloudless sky with bloodshot eyes. Factory chimneys, walls, houses, rails and pavements; everything on the ground grinned and groaned in anguish. In his study, sweating and bitten, Ryūnosuke felt like a flying fish, lucklessly fallen onto the dusty deck of a dry-docked ship, to die tormented by the screams of cicadas, tortured by the probosces of mosquitoes.

Every year, though, Ryūnosuke did look forward to the summer opening of the Sumida River. He would stand pressed in the crowds along the railings of the Ryōgoku Bridge. He would see the barges and the boats, the hundreds of boats—great square-bottomed boats, fine barges, with their canvas awnings and their red and white hangings, all shimmering with bright-coloured lanterns, thousands of lanterns covering the river as far as his eyes could see—the river illuminated, the banks lit up, the hands of the crowds holding their lanterns aloft, their eyes looking heavenward, transfixed by the Roman candles and the myriad other fireworks fired from the boats into the sky, up to the stars, raining back down to earth, showering the world in millions of tiny, fading, dying sparks. But that year, that day, the *kawabiraki* festival was called off. The Emperor had fallen into a coma.

The temperatures continued to rise, but the city fell under a black blanket of dread silence. Daily notices on police boxes and reports in the newspapers informed the public in explicit detail of the Emperor's suffering, yet "his godly countenance remained in every aspect unchanged." Still, day and night, temples lit sacred fires to exorcize malign spirits, to change the air, to clean the air, while rags muffled the wheels of the trolley buses around the palace moat, where hushed crowds came in their thousands from near and far to kneel in prayer by the Nijūbashi bridge, prostrating themselves in the direction of the Imperial Palace.

Ryūnosuke listened to his sister's tearful account of three young schoolgirls bowing for half an hour before the palace, praying for the recovery of the Emperor, to arrest the twilight, to halt the night. Ryūnosuke now wondered if he himself should go down to the palace gate. But then, after midnight, early on July 30, 1912, as a soft rain began to fall, Ryūnosuke heard the sharp cries of the newspaper boys. Ryūnosuke and his family bought and read the black-boarded extras, all of the black-boarded extras:

THE LAST SCENES AT THE PALACE

PEOPLE LIE PROSTRATE IN PRAYER
AS EMPEROR SLOWLY PASSES

REVELATION OF PEOPLE'S LOVE

PRAYERS GIVE WAY TO SOBS AND LAMENTATION
WHEN THE END IS KNOWN

If an artist had been before the Imperial Palace Monday night with a masterful brush, he could have painted an immortal picture of one of the most impressive and wonderful scenes in Japanese history. That scene, of a divine revelation of the national virtue and supreme sorrow of hearts broken by the lost love, is one that can never be forgotten. The history that will record the numerous and gigantic achievements and works of the late Emperor will not be complete without a series of pictures presenting the scene before the palace, with thousands of people praying for the recovery of their beloved Emperor, and at the end, lamenting over his death.

Midnight had tolled an hour before, but murmuring prayers still floated in the air in an unbroken chorus and with a regular cadence. The multitude that thronged before the palace before dusk remained as if riveted to the ground, while only a few withdrew. With the advance of night, breezes added a chill and seemed to fill the hearts of the ever-increasing mass of humanity with grief and fear.

In front of the iron railing, facing the room in which the Emperor lay dying, hundreds of men, women and children squatted or lay prostrate on the ground in profound prayer. The discomfort of their position was not thought of. Still hoping against hope, they prayed and prayed. In prayers of Buddhist and Shintō words, and in prayers according to the Christian faith, the old could recite all with flawless memory; the young and uneducated followed the words and lines of prayer with difficulty and uncertainty. All united in one great appeal to the mercy of Him who reigns over man and earth. "Oh, canst thou not hear the words of our bleeding hearts? Grant us our prayer!"

Behind those praying on the ground there stood crowds of more excited and less patient persons. They had read in the last official bulletin that the pulse was too weak to be felt, and that the Emperor was rapidly approaching his last moment. They were too agitated and too troubled to be quiet, even in prayer. They restlessly wandered about awaiting the next tidings. The multitude was hushed to silence in a momentary lull of a long-endured suffering. The nerves of the people were strung almost to the snapping point, and the ominous suspense appeared to forbode dreadful news.

And then came the report that His Majesty was dead.

Three minutes later, newspaper reporters were speeding away in *kuruma*; and soon the heart-breaking news was being spread through Tokyo, as fast as the presses could work; and was being flashed under seas to every part of the world. But no pen would be equal to expressing the grief of the sixty million subjects of Japan, in cottages and palaces alike.

The prayers of the throng ceased at once. The people's over-excited nerves gave way, and deep groans and lamentations arose in their despair.

After half an hour of mourning, many went back to their homes to pass the remaining hours of the night in prayer now for the departed soul of the all-beloved ruler of the nation, loved as a Father, revered as a Teacher, relied upon as our Strength, and the greatest of our Emperors.

The pale arc lights in the palace compound shone upon those who remained with a ghastly effect. The city seemed to have collapsed into a trance of sorrow under the heavy pall of black death, as the bell of Ueno Temple tolled in the far distance the knell for the passing of a great soul.

Early the next morning, Ryūnosuke and his family bought black crepe. Ryūnosuke wrapped it around the golden ball at the end of the flag pole by the gate of their house in Shinjuku.

Across the city, across the country, on every building, on every staff, from every lamp post and from every telegraph pole, national flags flew at half mast. Families did not play music, nor even speak aloud. Music halls and theatres called off performances, shops and department stores remained closed. Sales would slump and the stock markets fall. A crowd stoned the house of the Royal Physician.

It was the beginning of Taishō, it was the end of Meiji. One god dies, another is born: Meiji 45, Taishō 1, 1912; cremation time, coronation time, continual time, contradictory times; between the twilight and the dawn.

*

General Maresuke Nogi, the officially acclaimed and popular national folk hero of the Sino- and Russo-Japanese Wars, the internationally lauded military genius who had twice captured Port Arthur, had appeared at the palace to pay his respects one hundred and thirty times in the fifty-six days between the announcement of the Emperor's illness and today, September 13, 1912. General Nogi had waited thirty-five years and forty-five days for this day, the day of the funeral of the Emperor Meiji.

The funeral cortège was to depart from the Imperial Palace at

Nijūbashi at 8 p.m., to the sound of cannon fire, temple bells and then the plaintive drone of the processional dirge. General Nogi was expected to take his place as one of the most esteemed of the mourners in a mammoth funeral train of over twenty thousand persons; the imperial hearse, drawn by five oxen in single file, would be followed by attendants in court dress with bows and halberds, with their fans and staffs, by imperial princes and palace officials, by the *genrō* and government ministers, by high-ranking civil servants and the nobility, many in glittering full-dress uniform, followed by members of the Diet in their black tailcoats, by members of the Tokyo city government, by its chamber of commerce, by prefectural officials and mayors, and by school principals and religious leaders, along with court musicians, military bands and an honour guard of one thousand. Twenty-four thousand more soldiers would be stationed along a route freshly strewn with gravel. Three hundred thousand citizens would line the hushed and silent streets. Across the nation, sixty million people would be bowed in distant worship as the flickering torch-lit procession followed the imperial hearse on its two-hour journey to the specially constructed hall on the parade grounds at Aoyama. Here, seated in the stands, would be foreign diplomats and special envoys from the courts and governments of the world: the princes of England and Germany, the Secretary of State of the United States, representatives of the Japanese Empire of Korea, Taiwan and Sakhalin; ten thousand people gathered to pay their respects as the trumpet sounded at midnight, when the new Emperor, the son of Meiji, dressed in the uniform of a generalissimo, would deliver a brief eulogy, followed then by Prime Minister Saionji. But General Maresuke Nogi, popular national folk hero and military genius, would not take his place in the procession, General Nogi would not stand on the parade ground, Maresuke would not hear the voice of the new Emperor.

Early that morning, General Nogi dressed in the modern Western-style military uniform of an officer in the Imperial Japanese army. His wife Shizuko was dressed in a many-layered *jūnihitoe* kimono of sombre colours.

At eight o'clock, the General and his wife posed separately for formal photographs outside their residence. The photographer, Akio Shinroku, persuaded the General and his wife to have one more photograph taken, inside the house, in the upstairs living room, the General seated at the table, reading the morning newspaper, Shizuko standing to his left by the fireplace, staring into the camera. The couple then left for the Imperial Palace.

On each of the past one hundred and thirty occasions he had visited the palace, the General had usually made the journey on horseback. However, the General had already dismissed the stable boy and the only other male servant for the day. And so that morning, and only that morning, an official car had been sent from the palace for the General and his wife.

After worshipping at the palace, the General and his wife returned to their house on Yūrei Zaka, the Hill of Ghosts, which bordered the Aoyama cemetery in Akasaka-chō, and there ate lunch with Shizuko's elderly sister.

Over lunch, the General and his wife told the sister that they were both feeling unwell. The General telephoned the authorities to say that he was too ill to attend the funeral ceremony for the Emperor Meiji, and so he would be unable to take his place in the procession. His wife informed their staff and servants that the couple would retire to their private quarters, where they were not to be disturbed. The General and his wife then shuttered themselves in their rooms on the second floor for the rest of the day.

A little before eight o'clock that evening, Shizuko came down to the ground floor. She asked for some wine, wine not sake, and then returned with the bottle to their upstairs rooms.

A little while later, in a room downstairs, as the distant boom of the first cannonade signalled the departure of the imperial hearse from the palace, as the temple bells began tolling one hundred and eight times, Shizuko's sister heard a series of strange sounds coming from the second-floor rooms and she called for a maid. The maid ran upstairs to check on her master and mistress. She found the door to their living quarters securely locked, but from within she could hear an incomprehensible, pained voice, and through a crack in the door she could see her mistress lying on the floor.

The elderly sister immediately telephoned the local police station, only to find the line was busy. Nor was she able to reach the neighbourhood doctor, and so she sent the maids to search for help on the street outside. By chance, they found a passing police officer from Nagano who had been seconded to the capital for the funeral, Assistant Inspector Sakamoto.

Sakamoto followed the maids back inside the house. He went upstairs to the second floor and there, with his shoulders, forced open the doors.

In the eight-mat Japanese-style room farthest from the doors, before the framed portraits of the Emperor Meiji, the General's parents, and their two sons who had died in the Russo-Japanese War, the General lay on his side in a pool of blood, his wife on her knees, her forehead touching the floor.

As the imperial carriage bearing the corpse of the Emperor, drawn through the night by oxen, ground past the house, in their shuttered rooms on Yūrei Zaka, Maresuke and Shizuko had turned themselves to ghost.

*

Ryūnosuke bought the newspapers, all of the newspapers, and Ryūnosuke read account after account of the deaths of General Nogi and his wife:

RENOWNED NOGI SUICIDED

GENERAL AND COUNTESS REPORTED COMMITTED OLD-FASHIONED HARAKIRI

FOLLOWED MASTER TO GRAVE JUST BEFORE IMPERIAL FUNERAL PROCESSION STARTED

WHY GENERAL NOGI DIED

LAST TESTAMENT OF GREAT HERO AN EPIC OF DEEPEST PATHOS

TOGO WEEPS, EMPIRE MOURNS, AND THE WORLD LAMENTS LOSS OF THIS SPOTLESS SOUL

The following is the testament left by the late General Count Nogi, the document being written by him on the night of the 12th, the eve of the Imperial Funeral:

"1. I kill myself to follow Him who is gone. I am aware of the gravity of this crime; the offence it involves is not light. But to recall, I was responsible for the loss of the regimental colours in the campaign of Meiji 10, and since then I have searched in vain for a proper opportunity to die. To this day, I have been treated with unmerited kindness, receiving abundant Imperial favours and gracious treatment. Gradually I have become old and weak; my time has disappeared and I can no longer serve my lord. Feeling extremely distressed by his death, I have resolved to end my life.

"2. Since the fall of the two *Sukes* in battle (abbreviation of the names of the General's two sons, who met glorious death at the siege of Port Arthur), my respected seniors and friends have repeatedly urged that I adopt a son. Since ancient times, however, the difficulties of adopted heirs have been discussed, and there are many examples, in addition to the case of my brother. If I still had a child of my own, the honour of having received a noble title would force me to name him my successor, but to avoid leaving behind a possible disgrace I think it is best not to defy heaven's orders by adopting a son. The tombs of my ancestors should be cared for by relatives, as long as they are related by blood. I request that the Shinsaka residence be donated either to the Ward or City.

"3. I have written about the distribution of my property in a separate paper. My wife, Shizuko, will manage all matters I have not mentioned.

"4. As to the distribution of my personal effects, I have left a word of request to Colonel Tsukada that he may use his discretion in giving my watch, range-finder, field-glass, saddleries, swords, and other articles of soldier's use, to my adjutants in my memory. The Colonel did a great deal for me during the late two wars. Shizuko is already informed of this distribution, so please discuss it with her. I leave my other possessions open to negotiation.

"5. The Imperial gifts bearing the Imperial crests should be collected and presented to the Gakushūin Peers School, a word of request being left in this connection to Mr. Matsui and Mr. Igaya to deal with this matter.

"6. Present the Gakushūin those of my books which it can use and give the rest to the Library of Chōfu. Those which are useless may be disposed of in any fashion.

"7. The writings of my father, grandfather, and great-grandfather should be considered part of the history of the Nogi family. They should be scrupulously collected, excluding any truly unimportant works, and preserved for eternity either in the care of the house of Marquis Sasaki or in the Sasaki Shrine.

"8. I bequeath the articles exhibited at the Yūshūkan (the war museum at Kudan) to that institution. This, I believe, is the best way to preserve them in commemoration of the house of Nogi.

"9. As Shizuko gradually enters old age and encounters episodes of illness, the house of Ishibayashi, in addition to being an inconvenient place, will be very depressing. Therefore, this house should be given over to my brother Shūsaku, and Shizuko has agreed that she should live at my residence in Nakano. I leave the house and land in Nakano entirely to Shizuko.

"10. I have left a word of request to Baron Ishiguro as to the treatment of my body, which may be donated to a medical school. Beneath my gravestone, it will be sufficient (and Shizuko consents to this) to place my hair, nails and teeth, including false teeth. I request that my gold watch with the Imperial gift inscription should go to Masayuki Tamaki, my nephew. I forbid him to carry this watch when not wearing uniform.

"As for other matters not mentioned above, they are to be taken care of by Shizuko, and you are requested to consult her. During the lifetime of Shizuko, the name of the house of Count Nogi shall be honoured. But when her life is finished, the goal of extinction of the Nogi line shall be accomplished."

The will is dated the First Year of Taishō, September 12, in the evening, signed "Maresuke" and addressed to Yūji Sadamoto, Countess Nogi's brother, Odate Shūsaku, the General's brother, Masayuki Tamaki, the General's nephew, and Shizuko. It appears evident from the will that the General previously confided his intention of committing suicide to the Countess and that she was to live on.

Day after day, Ryūnosuke kept buying the newspapers, all of the newspapers, and day after day Ryūnosuke kept reading account after account of the deaths of General Nogi and his wife:

HOW AND WHY THE GREAT HERO WISHED TO DIE WITH EMPEROR

DEATH PLANNED FOR YEARS

WONDERFUL FORTITUDE OF THE COUNTESS

Baron Ishiguro, Surgeon-General and a close relative of the late General Count Nogi, gave an interview to the press representatives Monday afternoon. For the benefit of the public, Baron Ishiguro gave a detailed account of General Nogi and his wife.

"General Nogi requested me in his will," said the Baron, "to offer his remains for surgical dissection or for some other use for the benefit of medicine. His body, however, is of but little medical value, as he died by cutting the artery in the neck and not from any other disease. But to carry out the special will of the General, I have offered his body to Dr. Katayama and military surgeons Drs Tsuruda and Haga for medical examination.

"General and Countess Nogi were found in the living room, which was locked within. And the questions are how General Nogi died and which died first, he or his wife. The customary way to commit *seppuku*, as performed by the *bushi*, is to cut the abdomen just deep enough to bleed, and then give a fatal thrust through the throat, because the cutting of the abdomen is not sufficient to put an end to life. General Nogi performed *seppuku* after this customary fashion. It appears that, having cut the abdomen, he readjusted his clothes, and then thrust, piercing it through to the left posterior, the sword in the right side of the neck part. This forceful thrust must have put an end to his life immediately as it completely cut the arteries.

"At first we surmised that the General killed himself after assuring himself of the death of his wife. But that that was not the case is evident in his letter addressed to me, in which he says his wife is perfectly willing to follow him to death. Judging from the character of Countess Nogi, it seems that when he told her of his intention, she must have tried to dissuade him from the deed, but finding his

resolution too firm she decided to follow her husband.

"Countess Nogi was dressed in mourning, with a dull coloured gown and a *hakama* of light orange shade. The weapon she used was a dagger about a foot long. She inflicted four wounds upon herself. One wound was in her hand. First she appears to have thrust the dagger into the middle of her breast, and then into her right side between the ribs; this thrust was about an inch and a half deep. Perhaps still fearing that the wound would not be fatal, she must have given herself the third and last thrust, which went through the heart. By the time she gave herself this last thrust, she had been considerably weakened by the first two wounds. Not having the strength to drive the weapon into her breast, she fell prostrate upon it, thus pushing it almost up to the hilt.

"Personally, I have seen not a few cases of *seppuku*, and know that in performing the act, if one fails to kill himself by the first thrust, he is not able to put sufficient strength into the second thrust to put an end to his life. However, Countess Nogi, woman as she was, gave herself three powerful thrusts, and died in a most noble and decorous way."

General Count and Countess Nogi, having locked the door from within, sat side by side facing the portrait of the late Emperor, and killed themselves in the brave style described above. On a desk in the room were found a heap of letters and other papers, including General Nogi's will. Among those papers, two poems by the General and one by the Countess were also found. General Nogi composed the following two poems just before he killed himself: *"God-like has he now ascended, our great lord, and his august traces, from afar, do we humbly revere"* and *"It is I who go, following the path of the great lord who has departed this transient world."*

Countess Nogi left the following poetical composition: *"I hear there is no Sun to return, as He departed, So sad to face the august procession today."*

Day after day, Ryūnosuke kept reading account after account of the deaths of General Nogi and his wife, kept reading the accounts and kept staring at the photographs, day after day Ryūnosuke kept staring at the photographs of General Nogi and his wife, and day after day Ryūnosuke kept wondering, staring at the photographs and reading the accounts; the initially somewhat contradictory and contested newspaper accounts, accounts filled with the words "suicide," "*harakiri*," "*seppuku*" and then, finally, "*junshi*."

Ryūnosuke had never read the word "*junshi*" in a newspaper before the death of General Nogi; he had only read of it in novels or history books. Ryūnosuke had learnt that the samurai practice of following one's lord in death had been outlawed by the Tokugawa Shōgunate in the third year of the Kanbun era, in 1663. It scarcely seemed believable to Ryūnosuke that one of the most famous figures of Meiji, one of the very architects of Japanese modernity, would perform such an ancient act upon the death of the Emperor.

But the newspapers were all agreed that General Nogi had committed *junshi*, following his lord into death, and then Shizuko had taken her own life, a true samurai wife following her husband into death.

Editorials and opinions, though, did differ as to the meaning and relevance of their deaths. Some judged the incident an international embarrassment for an aspiring modern nation, others that it was an important moral lesson and reminder of traditional values for that same aspiring, modern nation. Mori Ōgai and Natsume Sōseki, the two contemporary Japanese writers Ryūnosuke respected above all others, would be irrevocably affected by the passing of the Emperor, the ending of this era, and by the fact and the manner of the deaths of General Nogi and his wife Shizuko. Ōgai would turn to writing historical fiction, works such as *Okitsu Yagoemon, Abe Ichizoku* and *Sakai Jiken*, works fixated on self-sacrifice, and Sōseki would write *Kokoro*, a work haunted by deaths by suicide.

Ryūnosuke would keep reading all of these accounts, these editorials, opinions and books, and Ryūnosuke would keep staring down at the photographs, the two separate photographs of General Nogi and his wife, the photographs taken on the morning of their deaths, and Ryūnosuke would keep wondering: wondering about the General's modern Western-style military uniform and his wife's many-layered *jūnihitoe* kimono of sombre colours, his body shrunken and lost in his uniform, his face half in humiliation and shadow, her body rigid and noble in her robes, her face full-bold and stark; wondering about the Japanese rooms in their Western mansion; about drinking wine and not sake; the *sakaki* branches arranged on the table, the framed photographs arranged on the table; his obsession with photographs, with reproduction, his desire to disappear, for extinction; *junshi* and *bunmei kaika*, this act of violent tradition in this age of civilised enlightenment, nineteen hundred and twelve, the first year of Taishō.

Photographs of General Nogi, portraits of a Shōgun, were already being displayed in shop windows, adorning the walls of school halls, military academies, factories and offices. Remembered and revered, there was no avoiding them, no escaping him. But Ryūnosuke kept coming back to those photographs, those two separate photographs of General Nogi and his wife, those photographs taken on the morning of their deaths. Ryūnosuke kept staring down at the photographs, and Ryūnosuke kept wondering, would keep staring down at the photographs, and would keep wondering:

Why did he want to have this photograph taken?

And Ryūnosuke refused to mourn.

A pale green moth came and sat upon his shoulder. From outside the window, Ryūnosuke could smell fresh-cut hay, he could hear the oak trees rustling quietly in the evening twilight. In the light of a yellow autumn moon, Ryūnosuke looked up at the clock, at all three clocks.

Ryūnosuke didn't know what time it was.

Jack the Ripper's Bedroom

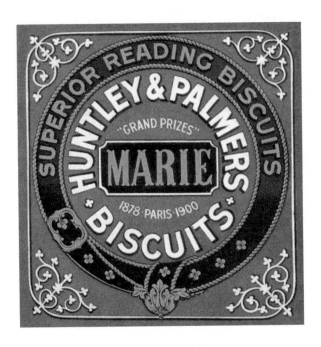

I found your story *The Nose* very interesting.
Your style is well polished, admirably fitting.
The Nose alone may not attract many readers.
Even if it does, they may let it pass quietly.
But without worrying about it, you must go on.
Go on and produce twenty or thirty stories like this one.
You will soon be incomparable in literary circles.
But ignore the crowd—
the best and only way of keeping your integrity.

Natsume Sōseki, letter to Ryūnosuke Akutagawa, February, 1916

"There is a part of me wishes they would wipe the place off the map."

"Was it really such a terrible time, Sensei," asked Ryūnosuke.

Natsume Sōseki closed his eyes, closed his eyes for a long time, and when he opened them, opened them at last, they were red-ringed and damp. "I often wonder if I did not die back then, out there, and all of this . . ."—he waved his hand across the desk, towards the shelves, at the glass doors, the garden outside—"if all of this is not the dream of a dead man . . ."

He paused, eyes closed again, then said, "I know very well the things people say about me, said about my time in London; that I shut myself in my room, that I cried in the dark, that I suffered a nervous breakdown, how I had lost my mind and gone insane."

He paused again, opened his eyes again, sighed and said, "Not that it much matters now, now I have so little time . . ."

Ryūnosuke and Kume protested, "No!"

Sōseki raised his hand, smiled and shook his head, begged their silence. "And your ears, if you will and have the time. For now it no longer much matters, I will tell you what happened. Not to bother you with my personal trials, rather to throw a light on that place, those people, their world and our world. At least, a kind of light . . ."

*

"It was the first month of the first year of their new century and the fourth month of my new life in their country, and already I was in my third set of lodgings, a boarding house in an area called Camberwell, a wretched slum on the south side of the River Thames.

"I've already written of the situation I found myself in: the poverty of the funding I had been given, the economies I was forced to practise, the pitiful place I was renting, bereft of company and society, starved of conversation and stimulation." He paused, he smiled. "Or maybe it was just the weather, maybe just the food, but I hated England and desired only a quick return to Japan as soon as I possibly could . . .

"But, whatever the reason, it was the worst winter of my life," he said, then paused again, then smiled again. "Worse even than this one.

"For then as now, I had problems sleeping, and I was aware my insomnia was only exacerbating my distemper. More than anything, I was tired of myself. So late one afternoon, in that January of 1901, having spent another interminable day reading in my dismal room, I reluctantly decided to venture outside; it was my hope that a long walk would speed me to sleep upon returning to my room. My reluctance, though, was two-fold: I knew almost nothing of the geography of the city, hardly knowing one direction from another, and yet again its buildings and streets were smothered under a bedspread of fog. However, I knew that the Tower of London stood somewhere to the north of my lodgings, on the other side of the river. And so this landmark was the ambition with which I left my room that afternoon.

"Of course, first I had to run the gauntlet of my jailers, my landlady and her younger sister. No matter how soft my tread upon the stair, the door to the gloomy dining room was always open, the sound of their chanting filling the hallway: 'Let us beg and pray Him day by day to reveal Himself to our souls, to quicken our senses, to give us sight and hearing, taste and touch of the world to come . . .'

"That afternoon, I performed my best impression of a silent cat on the tips of my paws down the stairs, paw by paw, down the hallway, paw by paw, towards the front door, but to no avail, no avail—

" 'Mr. Natsume!'

"There they sat, one stout, one slender, dressed in black, their knitting and their needles to one side, their Bibles open, poised in prayer over their tea and toast—toast, toast, it was always toast!— their police-ears ever cocked, their detective-heads now turned—

" 'Mr. Natsume . . .'

"I already had my hand upon the handle of the front door, but I was too late: my landlady had sprung, her hand on the sleeve of my overcoat, and I was caught once again in her missionary grip.

" 'You are going out, Mr. Natsume?'

"I am indeed, Mrs. Nott.

" 'For whatever reason, may I ask? You would be most ill advised, for the weather is most inclement today.'

"I am aware of the weather, Mrs. Nott. However, I have a somewhat pressing appointment, I lied. So if you will excuse me.

" 'You are excused,' she said. 'But as we pray for the health of our Queen, we will also pray for yours and you, Mr. Natsume. Pray you do not catch your death out there.'

"It was true their Queen seemed to be sinking fast, and I had often wondered if their whole island would not be dragged under with her when down she went—

"I am most grateful to you, Mrs. Nott, I replied, then I opened the door, went down the steps and heard the lock turn behind me.

"Outside the house, nothing was visible; the fog tinted yellow, tainted green, green and brown in a muddy beige, it did not drift, it did not shift, but was just there, was always there, a muffled, shuttered world. Yes, this world which greeted me had shrunk to just four frozen, silent yards square, smaller even than the room I had just left behind. However, I knew if I turned and walked left, then I would be set on a northerly course. Thus I proceeded, groped my way, four yards by four yards, another four yards visible as the former yards disappeared into the mists of the past. Indeed, I felt myself drifting, drifting in time, drifting through space. But then

I came to a crossroads, and I stopped on the kerb. The disembodied head of a horse cut through the grey air before my eyes, the people on the top of the bus it pulled presumed lost in the fog. On a better day, a clearer day, I might have been tempted to jump aboard for it was the one mode of transport I had the confidence and purse to use. Carriages were beyond my means, and the trains I detested, both steam and electric, over-ground and under-ground. Particularly the under-ground: the foulness of the air, the swaying of the carriages, from cave to cave, reducing a man to the life of a mole. But I had set myself adrift in this sea of emptiness to walk, and so walk I did. Across one street and up the next. Four yards by four yards, four yards by four yards . . .

"The only measure of time in this void was the muffled tolls of Big Ben, and I counted six as I came upon the river at London Bridge. I crossed over this Styx to the other side, among a horde of shades I could only sense not see, unless a sudden shoulder rubbed or knocked against my own.

"Hard on the other side, I stood before Wren's Monument to the Great Fire. I felt a fresh chill here, two lines by Pope upon my lips: *Where London's column, pointing at the skies, like a tall bully, lifts the head, and lies.* And I too lifted my eyes to look for the gilded urn that tops its fluted column. Of course, its golden head was lost, yet still it casts a shadow across my soul. Quickly, I veered off to the right. Suddenly, a white object flapped fleetingly past my eyes. I strained to see the remains of a gull swallowed up by the dark.

"Yes, the grey world had now turned black on all four sides, blacker than lacquer. Yet still I pressed on, on and on, along the bottom of this pit. My coat damp and heavy, my whole body washed in liquefied peat. The black-stained air started to assail my eyes, my nose and my mouth. I felt my breathing suffocated. I felt I was choking on arrowroot gruel. And, truly, I felt I could not go on. Not another step on. But at just that moment, a yellow light the size of a pea pulsed through the gloom and, heedless of the rocks, I forced my body towards this lighthouse . . .

"It was a public house, its gaslights burning. All brass and glass, all laughter and song. A veritable pantomime! I breathed a sigh of relief. I stepped out of the fog, stepped into the room. And the laughter stopped, and the songs ceased. And the barman said, 'We don't serve Chinamen in 'ere.'

"The stupid thing was, I was surprised! Oh, stupid me! True, I had not been long in London and, for the most part, I had not been abused or insulted before. But, on a couple of occasions, I had found myself the subject of conversation and speculation: a woman remarking 'least-poor Chinese' as she passed me in the street, a couple in a park arguing whether I was 'a Chinaman or a Jap.' So I did not deceive myself; I knew the majority of people simply took no notice of me, did not even see me, their thoughts consumed with making money, with no time to stop and jeer at the likes of a little yellow dog like me. Yet that night, in the bright lights of that public house, I had exposed myself, naked and in plain sight. In the English gaze, to the English hate: 'Are you deaf, are you dumb,' barked the barman. 'Get out of 'ere, you dirty little Chink . . .'

"I turned to leave, to push the door, and as I turned, as I left, the laughter returned, the songs resumed, aroused and louder than before, the dirty little yellow stain removed, all now restored and as it was, as it was before.

"Back outside in the crushing gloom, on the broken paving, I had never felt so alone, so very far from home. Oh, how I dearly, dearly wished to be somehow, somehow lifted up off this street, carried on the wind and dropped safely, softly back in Japan. But one will never find a *sen-nin* even in the Workshop of the World, no matter how hard one wishes. And so I started to walk again, but to walk without a care, hoping only for an early death under the hooves of a runaway horse. Yet the only sounds were the soles of shoes, out of the silence, in the darkness, to the right, approaching then gone again, in the darkness, in the silence, the soles of shoes, to the left now, approaching from behind, approaching, still approaching, closer and closer still—

"A hand on my shoulder, a voice at my side: 'I'm sorry.'

"I jumped in fright and stopped, I turned in fear and saw: a tall man—they were all so tall, I know—yet made taller by his hat, dressed all in black, with a long face and a serious brow, older and more senior than myself, I guessed, standing there in that street, on the border between night and fog, but with a kindness in his eyes, a kindness on his lips: 'I am a stranger here myself, though I've lived here many years. But I was not English-born and so know well how cruel this place, how spiteful these people can sometimes sadly be. Would this world be otherwise, but here we are . . .'

"Yes, I said. Here we are.

"The man smiled, the man said, 'Well then, would you allow one stranger to show a little hospitality to another?'

"Truly, these were the kindest words I had heard since I had first set foot on English soil. I smiled, I said, That would be very kind of you, thank you.

"The man put out his hand. 'Then let us not be strangers any more. My name is Nemo. It's Latin, you know.'

"For 'no man,' I said.

"'Forgive me,' he said, and I did, I did. This land seemed overrun with amateur schoolmasters and mistresses, ever ready to assume the ignorance of the Little Yellow Chap. But apart from my brief and ill-fated visit to Cambridge upon my arrival, and my weekly lessons with Professor Craig, my immediate impression was that here was a rare Man of Culture. I smiled again. I shook his hand and said, A pleasure to meet you, sir. My name is Natsume.

"Nemo gave a little bow: 'How do you do, Natsume-san. It is a pleasure to meet you, too. But may I ask what brings you from the land of the cherry blossoms to these dark, satanic isles?'

"I replied I had been sent by our Ministry of Education, in order to research and study English Literature. But reluctant to discuss my own situation further, I asked if he knew Japan.

"'Sadly, only from books and pictures,' he said. 'The words of the Goncourt brothers first opened my eyes, and then when I saw for myself the prints of Hiroshige and Kunisada, I was enchanted. However, you are the first son of Japan I have had the opportunity and honour to meet.'

"My first impression of a Man of Culture was thus confirmed, and while I hate to be questioned myself, loathing as I do this detective age in which we live, I could not contain my curiosity, and I said, Forgive my impertinence, but may I ask your profession, sir?

"'I am a painter. But not a decorator.'

"Of which school?

"'Ah-ha! Which school indeed? Well, if Monsieur Baudelaire declared Guys to be the Painter of Modern Life, then I declare myself the Painter of Modern Death!'

"Of Modern Death?

"He laughed. 'Whatever does he mean, you wonder, and with good reason. Well, and please in no way feel obliged, but you would be most welcome to visit my humble studio, for I would rather show than tell. A good sketch is worth a long speech, as a little corporal once said.'

"I was intrigued, could not resist, and said, I would be honoured, and delighted, thank you. As Turgenev wrote, the drawing shows at a glance what may take ten pages of prose to write.

"'Splendid,' said Nemo. 'The rooms are nothing much but, for all her faults, my landlady can prepare an adequate if simple supper. That is, if you have the time and would care to join me now?'

"I nodded. I would be delighted, I said. Thank you.

" 'I am to the north of here, but the hour is not yet too late and, if we take the Underground, we shall be there in no time.'

"As I have mentioned, I particularly disliked the Underground, and so I felt the first stirrings of regret now grow within me. But I could hardly now decline an invitation I had only just accepted. So, with a nod and the best smile I could muster, off we set.

"The journey involved a brisk clip to the station—was it called St. Mary's? I cannot now recall—the usual descent in a cage, then two trains through the caves, before our final, thankful ascent. Neither of us spoke in the carriages, less out of custom on my part, more from anxiety: I knew I would have no notion of how to later return to my own lodgings if I did not now concentrate with all my might upon our route.

"Back up on the street, the city and the night were still fog and gloom, with only the odd droplet of dull light here and there, and it seemed we still had some streets to go, invisible streets that reeked of cabbage and urine. My regret was now in full bloom and I could not help but ask my guide where on earth we were.

"With an embarrassed laugh, an apologetic smile, Nemo said, 'Or where on earth is he leading me, you mean? Well, in truth, the fog favours us, for we are far from the districts of gentility or the artistic society of Chelsea, lost in the no-man's-land between Cumberland Market and Regent Street. An insalubrious place, I grant you, yet not without its charms, its peculiarities and its infinite possibilities . . .'

"Infinite possibilities, I asked.

"Nemo grabbed the sleeve of my coat, stopped us both in our tracks, held me in his grip and gaze: 'Its subjects, Mr. Natsume! They may not reveal themselves tonight, but this place fair teems with subjects.'

"I nodded and said, I see.

" 'You will,' said Nemo. 'If not yet, then I hope you will. For we are almost here, almost home . . .'

"We turned a corner, took another few strides, then went down a cobbled passage to a tall and narrow house at the end of the row. Nemo went up its three stone steps, ignored the demon-faced knocker, opened the front door, held it ajar for me and said, 'Welcome.'

"I stepped inside a long and gloomy hallway. It was damp and cold and smelt of sweet and rotting fruit. Nemo closed the door, laughed and said, 'You know, when I was first shown the place, I said to myself, I said, This is the house I shall be murdered in . . .'

"Nemo turned up the lamp. There was a heavy mirror upon the wall, dried flowers in a vase on the chipped sideboard. He smiled and said, 'But I've actually grown to be quite fond of the place. Particularly the rent. However, it's rather cold, I know. I'm sorry. And so please do keep your coat on until we get up to my rooms . . .'

"Suddenly, a hidden voice called out: 'Mr. Sweeney?'

"A dim light appeared from under the steep stairs at the end of the long hall. An old maid wearing black clothes emerged from the jaundiced shaft and came towards us: 'Is that you, Mr. Sweeney?'

"Nemo sighed, then said, 'I've told you, it's not Sweeney. Sweeney doesn't live here any more. It's only me now, Mrs. Bunting.'

" 'But I heard him, heard him walking backwards down the stairs.'

" 'But he's gone, long gone and never coming back.'

" 'Gone? Gone, you say? Well then, what shall I do for the rent? What ever shall I do? He had his faults, I know, his ways. But he was a good boy, he was. Like clockwork. He never missed.'

"The old woman was stood before us now. In her black clothes, with her black hair, her sunken eyes and upturned nose, sharp cheeks and pointed chin, she looked me up and down, then said, 'And who have we here then? Not come about the drains, have you?'

"Nemo sighed again, apologised to me and said to the woman, 'This is Mr. Natsume. He's come from Japan on government business. Here to research and to study all things literary. Now if you would be so kind . . .'

"The old lady squeezed my hand, looked into my face and said, 'Why, you are a handsome Jap, I must say, oh I do say. You know, I'm not from here myself. Not really. She was French, my mother.'

"'Mrs. Bunting, please,' said Nemo. 'It's getting late, we have not yet eaten, and so would you please bring us up a little supper.'

"'I'll do my best,' she said. 'With what we have . . .'

"Nemo took her hand from mine, steered me past her, down the hallway, then up two flights of stairs to a landing with three doors. He opened the door to the left, glanced inside and said, 'Well, at least the woman kept the fire in. After you, Mr. Natsume . . .'

"The abundance of brightly burning coal was a most welcome sight indeed, and the room itself was also a pleasant surprise, with its warm red carpet and white silk curtains. There were two comfortable chairs before the fire, occasional tables here and there, well-stocked bookshelves and a rocking chair by the window. Nemo took my coat and offered me a chair. He changed into a maroon and elegantly embroidered satin dressing gown and then joined me by the fire. He put his hands together, stared into the flames a while, then turned to me and smiled and said, 'Well, here we are.'

"Yes, here we are, I said, but wondered why, why he had invited me, why I had accepted, why I'd come, come not only here, here to this room, this house, but come to this city, this country, leaving my daughter and my wife on the other side of the earth, my pregnant wife, my wife who never answered my letters, if she even received my letters, even read my letters, if she lived, they even lived, not burnt in a fire, not crushed by an earthquake, drowned in a flood, hit by a train, murdered by a fiend or killed by disease, a black-bordered letter in a black-bordered envelope sailing over the seas as I sat here in this house, in this room, before this fire, wondering why, why was I here, why had I accepted, why had he invited me, why, oh why—

"Suddenly, Nemo clapped his hands together, sat forward in his seat and said, 'I do apologise. My mind is sometimes prone to wander, and you must feel me to be a terrible host. But once we have warmed up and had some supper, I'll show you my studio. If you would still care to see it, and the hour is not too late. It's the attic room, just up the steps, but rather cold, I'm afraid. Now where is that woman . . .'

"He got to his feet but, just as he did, there was the sound of footsteps on the stairs and a brief knock upon the door.

"The old woman entered the room with a tray. There were two plates of sandwiches of cold beef—whatever else—a large piece of cheese, some slices of apple and a decanter of red wine and two glasses. She bent forward to set down the tray on one of the tables between our chairs. Then stopped, stopped still. Bent forward over the tray, its handles in her fingers, she crooked her neck, her ear towards the door, and whispered, 'Did you hear, hear that?'

"In fact, I thought I had heard something, some sound from down below. But Nemo said, 'You're hearing things again, Mrs. Bunting.'

"The woman muttered something I could not catch, released the handles of the tray, stood straight again, but then twitched, twitched and looked again towards the door: 'There! There it was again!'

"'Mrs. Bunting, please! It's just the wind under the door.'

"She looked at Nemo and snorted: 'The wind? The wind, my arse. Does the wind turn the key in the door? Does the wind walk backwards up the stairs? Drop its bag upon the floor, run the water in the sink? Stain my towels, stain them red? Messing up my beds, drooling on my pillows. Mafficking in its dreams, screaming in its sleep. That's the wind, is it? The wind, you say? Oh, don't make a stuffed bird laugh!'

"At that very moment, and with a theatrical cue, there was indeed a noise—a brief banging sound, but from the house or the street, I could not tell—and the three of us did now turn our heads towards the door.

"'Well, we all heard that, Mrs. Bunting,' said Nemo. 'And so you win, you take the egg. But before I trouble the local constable or priest, perhaps you would care to check upon your kitchen? From experience, I fear our many mice may be making merry in the pantry. Meanwhile, Mr. Natsume and I will partake of your delicious supper . . .'

"Suddenly, the old woman turned her wide eyes from the door to me and said, 'You're not from here, so you best beware. They don't take to strangers, not round here. They never have, they never will. They ask, What happened to the Romans? I'll tell you what happened to the Romans: the English walked through their villas with their butchers' knives and murdered them. Slaughtered them in their sleep, they did. The whole bloody lot of them. Slit their throats from ear to ear and dumped them in the river, yeah. Oh, they never stopped smiling then!'

"Nemo took the woman by the shoulders and marched her towards the door: 'Really, that is quite enough! You should be ashamed of yourself, Mrs. Bunting, frightening this poor man, our guest, in such a manner . . .'

" 'I'm not frightening him,' she said, 'I'm warning him!'

"Nemo pushed the woman backwards out onto the landing, then shut the door in her face. He turned to me, sighed, then said, 'I really do apologise, Mr. Natsume, whatever must you think?'

"I put him at his ease and said, I do not believe superstitious old crones are native only to the British Isles.

"Nemo smiled and said, 'You're not a superstitious man yourself then, Mr. Natsume? A believer in ghosts, for example? We are often told that Japan is a land overrun with spirits and demons. Of course, one reads so much bunkum these days, one can never know the truth.'

"I smiled, too, and said, Well, as a matter of fact, our ghosts and demons seem rather to have gone out of business since the Restoration of the Emperor. Of course, I do not presume to speak on behalf of the Mrs. Buntings of Japan, of which there are many.

"Nemo laughed, picked up the decanter and poured us each a glass of wine. 'Let us drink then to the Mrs. Buntings of Japan and England. Long may they thrive, for I fear our modern world would be somewhat dull without their sort. And to your own good health, too, of course . . .'

"And to your own health, too, and to your kindness and hospitality, I said, and we raised our glasses, and then began to drink and eat. The bread was stale and the meat tough, the cheese like rock and the fruit without flavour, yet the wine was good and the conversation flowed, too, over books and letters, music and art, politics and history, his country and mine, my travels and his, and so, when the clock chimed ten, I was disappointed our evening was coming to an end.

" 'How time flies in good company,' said Nemo. 'But it's getting late, and you must be anxious to get back across the river. However, fear not! I will accompany you and see you safely home . . .'

"I protested there was no need, but Nemo would not hear of it. We put on our coats, picked up our hats, stepped out onto the landing, and then, it was then I said, But what about the studio?

"In all our talk, and with the wine, as the hours had passed we had forgotten the very purpose, the reason for my invitation, my visit. Yet now, upon the landing, I sensed a reluctance in my host and quickly said, But if not now, then perhaps another time.

"Nemo turned, looked at the steep steps that led up from the landing into the darkness above, and said, 'It had slipped my mind, I had quite forgotten. I'm sorry. But of course, if you insist . . .'

"Forgive me, I said. I do not insist. I am merely curious to see your work. But if it's not convenient and we haven't time . . .

" 'He really should be going,' called up a voice, the voice of the old maid, on the flight below, looking up at us.

"But Nemo just smiled, a thin and brief, sad smile. He put his foot on the first step and said, 'I have the time, and I am grateful for your interest. I only hope you will not be disappointed. But please follow me, and do take care. These stairs can be quite lethal.'

"In fact, the stairs more closely resembled a ladder on a ship, an impression only heightened by a handrail made of rope and to which I clung as I climbed up behind Nemo.

"At the top of the steps, Nemo paused on the narrow ledge before the door. He reached inside his pocket for a key, turned it in the lock, pushed open the door and said, 'Let me first light the lamp . . .'

"I stood before the ledge, on the last of the steps, and waited until the soft light of a lamp fell through the door upon my face and Nemo called out, 'Ready when you are, Mr. Natsume.'

"I stepped through the door into the attic and gasped: even in lamplight and shadow I could sense it was an enormous room, half barn, half church, with a sloping ceiling low on either side but twice the height of a man in the centre and where, at the highest point of its spine, a glass skylight had been installed. The clutter of one hundred junkshops danced before me in the faint and trembling light, but even such a muddle could not diminish my sense of the size of the space.

"Nemo stood some distance in, a lantern in his hand. He waved the light from right to left and said, 'Please forgive the mess, and mind your step, but do come in, come in, come closer please . . .'

"I walked towards him, or rather waded in, the floorboards strewn with a carpet of debris: books and newspapers, boxes and tins, empty bottles and broken crates, remains of furniture and strips of cloth, old clothes and odd shoes, brushes in jars, brushes in vases, a ladder here, an easel there, all covered in dust or caked with paint—

"The artist was before me now. His coat gone, Nemo had put on a cap, pulled it low across one eye and tied a red kerchief about his neck. He set down the lantern on a small deal dining table, pointed to a battered horsehair sofa, smiled and said, 'Do take a pew . . .'

"I sat down, yes, though even then I could not have told you why I did, what made me stay, not turn and leave. For he had changed, and more than his clothes I knew, I knew; within that space, within that moment, I knew he'd changed, knew all had changed, including me, especially me, the me who stayed, the me who said, who said, who said, And the paintings? I do not see any paintings . . .

"Nemo picked up a biscuit tin from the table, sat down beside me on the sofa and said, 'You really are a most persistent chap, I have to say, and I should be flattered you are so keen. But the light it fails us both, so I'm afraid these sad sketches must suffice—'

"I accepted the proffered biscuit tin from his hands and placed it in my lap. I took the lid off the tin, set it to one side, then turned back to look inside. A broken pencil lay in two halves upon a loose sheaf of irregular papers. I took out the sheaf of papers, the parts of the pencil falling with a clink and a clank into the bottom of the tin, and then, one by one, sheet after sheet, sketch after sketch, I went through those pages, those seventeen scraps, until the last, until the end.

"I had come to this country, this city to learn. The biggest, greatest city on the earth, the centre, the capital of the world. To drink from its cups of knowledge, to taste the wisdom of its harvests, then to return to Japan laden with the fruits of my learning, to share my studies, to teach what I myself had been taught. But here I sat, in this city, in this house, in this attic, on this sofa, parched and starved and close to death, the sum total of my account an unreadable report.

"Yes, I had come to the end, the ends of the earth. I steadied my hand, straightened the papers and put them back inside the biscuit tin. I replaced the lid, steadied my voice and said, You see such things, I'm sorry.

"Beside me on the sofa, his knee against my own, Nemo took the tin from my lap and quietly said, 'And you do not?'

"I stared straight ahead, past the lantern on the table, my eyes too inured to the shadows now, a wardrobe looming up over an iron bedstead, its bedding torn, its mattress split, a grim pillow at its head, an easel standing before the scene, a canvas waiting in its place. I closed my eyes, closed my eyes and whispered, No.

" 'No, of course you don't,' said Nemo, his voice a sigh but close, so much closer now. I felt him push my leg, felt him grip my thigh, heard him say, 'You were most fortunate then, for it is a sickness.'

"He released my thigh from his grip. I heard him get to his feet. I opened my eyes. He was standing by the table. He dropped the biscuit tin with a clang and, in one sweep of his arm, he picked up the lantern and turned, span on his heel, moving towards the bedstead, but turning, still spinning, round and around, the light circling, conjuring apparitions from the darkness, illuminating the cavern walls in a primitive, savage glow, revealing canvas upon canvas, the beam ever more brutal, more feral until, until he collapsed, half upon the bed, half upon the floor, his face to the ceiling, the lantern dangling in his hand, its rays still swinging, swaying back and forth . . .

"I stood up, but too late again; I had awoken from my own nightmare into the nightmare of another man, another country—

"He was sat up on the edge of the bed. He grabbed the pillow from the mattress, held it to his nose, closed his eyes, then sighed and said, 'Yes, oh yes, this will help you see . . .'

"He opened his eyes. He stood up, the pillow in his hands. He walked towards me, the pillow outstretched, the yellow cast of its cloth, its leakages of spittle, all brown and stained, coming closer, ever closer, ever closer: 'If you could but see what I have seen, if you could but dream the dreams that he once dreamed . . .'

"I picked up the biscuit tin, gripped it tight, held it up before my face, before this man, his hands, the pillow, that pillow, that pillow in his hands, forcing me backwards, pushing me down, down—

" 'Inhale,' he said. 'Inhale and see!'

"Down, down, the tin against my chest, the pillow pressed into my face, the smell, the stench of oil, of sweat, struggling but falling, falling backwards, falling but struggling, his weight upon me, body crushing me, smothering me, suffocating me, in English dreams, their imperial lusts, I was struggling, still struggling, struggling and falling, falling away and falling apart, I was falling apart, I was falling apart, bells tolling one, two, three, four, pealing five, six, seven, eight, ringing nine, ten, eleven, twelve, striking thirteen, thirteen, thirteen—

" 'Mr. Sweeney, please,' came the voice in the dark, in the light, the silhouette in the doorway. 'Her Majesty has breathed Her last.' "

*

Sōseki had ceased speaking, his cheek resting on his hand.

Ryūnosuke and Kume did not move, they did not speak. Nightingales were singing in fragments in the garden, a breeze through the leaves of the orchard.

"Now Zeppelins rain down bombs upon the place, while their war persists and rages on, on and on without end, without end . . ."

His words, his voice trailed off.

Sōseki stood up behind his desk, unsteady on his feet. He waited, caught his breath. He turned, walked over to the bookcases on the far wall. He knelt down, took out a parcel wrapped in a black cloth from the bottom shelf. He stood up, carried the parcel to his desk. He set it down upon the top, untied the cloth. He picked up a red tin, decorated in yellow, white and black. He handed the tin to Ryūnosuke and said, "Here. You keep it now."

Ryūnosuke stared down at the tin in his hands, the words on its lid: *Huntley & Palmers Biscuits—Superior Reading Biscuits.*

A Twice-Told Tale

Alone now, Yasukichi lit a cigarette and began roaming the office.
True, he taught English, but that was not his real profession.
Not to his mind, at least.
His life's work was the creation of literature.

"The Writer's Craft," Ryūnosuke Akutagawa, 1924

It was the Age of Winter, the autumn after the death of Sensei, and the ninth of the month. Ryūnosuke had finished teaching at the Academy early that day, had caught the train from Yokosuka to Tokyo, crossed the city, bought flowers and come to the northern entrance to the Zōshigaya cemetery. From the dawn, the clouds had threatened rain and Ryūnosuke was wearing a raincoat over the Western clothes in which he taught, carrying a Western umbrella along with the flowers. He entered the cemetery and walked down an avenue lined on each side with Maple and Zelkova trees, their leaves yet to turn. There was nobody else in the cemetery, nobody living. Ryūnosuke turned off the thoroughfare, went down the paths, between the stones, the paths to the dead, the stones for the dead, over roots and moss already damp in anticipation of night and rain, the branches of the trees bowing listlessly, welcoming the approach of twilight, the coming of Ryūnosuke to the grave.

Ryūnosuke leant his umbrella against the low hedge fence which enclosed the plot, stepped inside and stood before the grave. It was a temporary grave, the name of Sensei descending in black characters down the pale wood of a tall *sotoba*, towering beside the smaller marker to his daughter. Ryūnosuke knelt down before the rough mound of earth at the feet of the two markers. There were two vases and narrow incense holders standing in the dirt. Ryūnosuke removed the withered flowers from the vases, laid them to one side. He divided the fresh flowers he had brought into two. He placed them in the two vases. He took a box of incense sticks and his matches from the pocket of his raincoat. He removed nine sticks of incense, put the box back inside his coat, struck a match, lit the sticks and stood them in one of the holders in the mound. He stood up, he bowed his head before the grave of Natsume Sōseki and he closed his eyes . . .

"*Are you working hard? Are you writing something? I am watching your future. I want you to be great. But don't get too impatient. I want you to go forward boldly like an ox; we have got to be oxen. So often we try to be horses, but it's very hard indeed to be thoroughly oxen. So please don't be impatient; don't wrack your brain. March forward untiringly. The world knows how to bow to perseverance, but seldom remembers momentary flares. Push right on to the death. That alone matters. Don't seek out rivals and try to beat them. Then there will be no end to your rivals; they will keep coming one after another and annoying you. Oxen do push on and on, always aloof. If you ask me what to push, I will say: push the man within, but not the artist.*"

Ryūnosuke put his palms together. He bowed once more, then opened his eyes. He bent down, picked up the old flowers from the ground and stepped back from the grave. He smiled and said goodbye to Sensei, then turned and walked away from the grave, back down the paths, between the stones, onto the wider avenue.

Two crows were nosily tracing a circle across the thoroughfare, swooping ever lower and lower, arguing *ka-ah, ka-ah*. Ryūnosuke smiled up at them as he walked, naming them Kanzan and Jittoku, watching them disappear into the leaves of a great *Hinoki* cypress tree up ahead. Under its branches, Ryūnosuke could see the dim figure of a man. The face and features of the figure were hidden in shadow and twilight, but he seemed to be dressed almost identically in a raincoat, holding a Western umbrella. Ryūnosuke sighed, looked down at the dead flowers in his hand, shook his head and turned back towards the grave; he had forgotten his umbrella. But when Ryūnosuke had retraced his steps to the low hedge which surrounded the grave, he found his umbrella was gone.

Ryūnosuke quickly turned and headed back towards the *Hinoki* tree. Perhaps somehow—though Ryūnosuke could not think how—

that man under the tree had picked up his umbrella and had been waiting to return it to him. But now, as he approached the tree, Ryūnosuke could see the man was gone, too. Only Kanzan and Jittoku remained, hopping back and forth under the branches, laughing at his misfortune—*A-hō! A-hō!*—knowing full well what was coming next for Ryūnosuke—

A hard, cold rain on the man without an umbrella.

*

Monday morning, Yasukichi Horikawa opened the door to the teachers' lounge. He was not in the best of tempers; he had had a most unpleasant and unproductive weekend, full of cold, sleeping fitfully, unable to finish the story he had foolishly promised an editor. Typically, the only other teacher in the room was his elder colleague K, the German instructor who had seemingly taken a dislike to Yasukichi on first sight. As always, K was standing with his back to the fire, stealing the heat from the room.

"Good morning," said Yasukichi, as cheerfully as he could, taking out the notes for his first class from his briefcase.

K raised an eyebrow and said, "Well, if it isn't the fashionable young writer who says good morning but not good evening."

"Excuse me," said Yasukichi. "If I have offended you, I'm sorry."

"Not offended me, nor even surprised me, just amused me," said K. "Obviously you do not care to introduce your teaching colleagues to your literary acquaintances, particularly if your 'acquaintance' should happen to be an attractive older lady."

"Really," said Yasukichi. "I have no idea what you could mean."

K snorted, winked and said, "On Saturday? At the cinema?"

"This past Saturday," asked Yasukichi. "I was not at the cinema."

"Really," laughed K, approaching Yasukichi. "Then that is most strange indeed. And then quite a coincidence, too."

"How can it be a coincidence?"

"Well, on Saturday evening, I could have sworn I saw you there—at the Denki-kan in Asakusa—in the company of an older lady. I was so convinced that I called out to you as we were leaving, but you just stared blankly through me and walked past without a word."

"But I wasn't there," said Yasukichi. "It wasn't me, so please don't say 'you,' or that it was a coincidence."

"But it really is a coincidence," said K. "Because the film was the revival of *Der Student von Prag*. You know the film . . . ?"

"Yes," snapped Yasukichi. "I know the film, of course."

"Of course," smiled K. "So then of course you now understand why I say it is quite a coincidence, me watching a film about a doppelgänger, me then seeing you, but it not being you, and so we then can only conclude that I must have seen your doppelgänger."

"Or that you were too easily influenced by the film."

K was now at the table, very close to Yasukichi. He stared at Yasukichi, smiled again and said, "Or maybe you were simply embarrassed to be seen in the company of a woman who was very obviously not your fiancée."

Yasukichi regretted having let his irritation get the better of him. As calmly as he could, he said, "I'm sorry. I wasn't there, it wasn't me. Now if you'll excuse me, I'm going to be late for class."

K looked down at the notes in Yasukichi's hand, and then smiled again: "Well, well, well, if it isn't Edgar Allan Poe today."

"Now that is a coincidence," said Yasukichi with a smile.

"Perhaps," said K. "Then again, we all know they seem to let you teach whatever you want. But only you, of course."

*

In his room in the lodging house in Shioiri, Yokosuka, Ryūnosuke threw down his pen and cursed. He had planned to write a story in a single sitting that night; "planned" because he had no choice if he was to meet the deadline. But it was already gone midnight and all he had scribbled was a dismal, ramshackle chain of words with neither beauty nor point. He lit another cigarette. His mind wandered, searching for targets to blame for his inability to write the story; if only he did not have to teach in the morning, then he could write through the night. But not only had he lessons to teach, there were always so many other demands and requests between the classes: a funeral oration for some captain or other, a revision of a lecture in English for a colleague, a translation of an article from a foreign newspaper, and how could he forget the textbook he was supposed to be putting together. There was also an ever-rising pile of letters from friends and editors which he needed to answer. And then there was his wedding; the endless appointments, discussions and formalities! He cursed again. Then cursed himself; blaming others would solve nothing. He put out his cigarette. He picked up his pen, tried to get it moving again. But still he could not write a single line of worth. He put down his pen again. He needed help, he needed inspiration. And not another cigarette. He picked up a book from the desk. He got up from the desk. He walked over to the bedding already laid out on the floor. He stretched out on the futon to read the book. The book was a collection of stories by Edgar Allan Poe. He began to reread one of the stories, attentive more than ever to the inspiration behind the work, the way in which Poe had adapted his original source. This particular story was based on a brief article by Washington Irving. Ryūnosuke was familiar with that article. He recalled the protagonist was a young man who finds himself followed and thwarted at every turn by a masked figure. Finally, the young man stabs the figure with his sword. But when the young man looks behind the mask, he finds only "his own image—the spectre of himself." Ryūnosuke had even copied out that line by Irving into one of his own notebooks, along with so many other lines and passages from Poe. But now as he reread Poe's retelling, he began to feel ill. In all of Poe's tales, Ryūnosuke felt the fragility of the mind, so easily, easily fragmented and torn, shattered and ripped into so many, many pieces. And yet Poe wrote with such craftsmanship, with such clarity and with such realism, yet with such lyricism; the alchemy of his analytical intellect and his poetic temperament, harnessing and sculpting the truth, the verisimilitude of his dreams, his dreams within dreams, real and yet unreal, in words, in writing, in poetry and prose, tales and stories, so beautiful and so terrifying, and so much greater, so much, much greater than Ryūnosuke could ever, ever hope to even, even attempt. He hurled the book into the corner of the room—

"You have conquered, and I yield!"

Ryūnosuke collapsed back onto the bedding. He stared up at the ceiling, his Night Thoughts reading patterns and signs in the shadows and the stains. And he closed his eyes—

Ryūnosuke was sitting in a box seat at the theatre, a woman by his side, a woman he did not recognise. In the darkness, she was squeezing his arm, resting her cheek on his shoulder. On the screen, an old man in a top hat tore up a sheet of paper, scattered the pieces over the body of a young man lying dead on the floor. The scene then changed, the double of the young man sitting on his grave under a willow tree. Beside Ryūnosuke, the woman was squeezing his arm tighter and tighter, the warmth of her blood burning through her clothes and into his, her mouth to his ear whispering, "Where you go, I'll always be, even to the last of your days. Look, look . . ."

Now Ryūnosuke saw himself up on the screen, in a garden. A garden which looked like the garden of his family home in Tabata. Ryūnosuke was sitting on the steps to the veranda. He was wearing a large-brimmed sunhat, smoking a cigarette, blowing smoke directly into the camera. He seemed much older, his face gaunt, his hair long beneath the hat. Two children, two boys were playing around him in the garden. They seemed to be his children, his sons. Suddenly, this Ryūnosuke sprang up and started to climb the large crepe myrtle tree beside the veranda. Higher and higher he climbed, his underwear visible, swinging from branch to branch until he reached the eaves of the house. He climbed out onto a limb and perched there, staring out at the audience. A caption flashed up on the screen: "Quack, quack! Pleased to meet you. I am a Kappa. My name is Tock."

The children ran screaming into the house, this house which looked like his family house. Ryūnosuke followed them inside the house. The children disappeared down a corridor. Ryūnosuke followed after them, but lost them. Still searching for them, he turned into a room. A man in a Chinese-patterned *yukata* was lying on a futon on the floor. His eyes closed, a Holy Bible open on his chest, the man looked like Ryūnosuke, his exact double. Now the eldest child came into the room. He shook the man, he woke the man. The man sat up, and the man said, "I have been having such an odd dream. I dreamt we were playing in the garden. But you and your brother ran into the house. I followed you, but I lost you. And when I came into this room, I saw myself lying senseless, lifeless on the floor, like an old discarded raincoat."

Ryūnosuke could not contain himself. He cried out to the man on the bed, "I came searching for you, and here you are!"

The man rose from the futon, came towards Ryūnosuke and embraced him. "So you are Ryūnosuke, too. It was not a dream . . ."

"No," cried Ryūnosuke. "It was more true than truth itself."

But hardly had Ryūnosuke finished speaking when the younger child came to the door, looked inside, then turned and ran, crying, "Ma-ma, Ma-ma! Please come to Ryū-chan's room at once . . ."

Now the man rushed from the room as Ryūnosuke called after him, "Please don't go, Ryūnosuke! Please don't leave me . . ."

The older boy looked at Ryūnosuke, stared at him and laughed. "Where is this Ryūnosuke you are calling to, Ryū-chan?"

Ryūnosuke pointed at the door. "He has just gone out."

"Why, you are still dreaming," said the boy. "Don't you know who you are talking to? It is your own reflection in the mirror."

Suddenly, the film jumped, appeared to snap in two. The lights in the theatre went up. The woman beside Ryūnosuke dug her nails into his arm, bit his ear and said, "So that is how it ends."

*

Yasukichi Horikawa was in the Paulista café in Ginza, chatting with the editor of another literary magazine to which he sometimes contributed articles and stories. No sooner had he met one deadline for one story for one editor than Yasukichi would agree to another deadline for another story for another editor. This editor was eating a second baked apple and talking about the works of Edgar Allan Poe. Yasukichi interrupted him: "Actually, I feel I am becoming trapped inside a tale by Poe. Just the other day, at an end-of-year party, I bumped into that one-legged German translator. He said he had seen me in a tobacco shop near here and was offended when I ignored him. But I was in Yokosuka at the time, teaching as usual. But when he described what had occurred, I realised this 'second-self' of mine had been wearing exactly what I had been wearing that day: a raincoat. And this is the second time this has happened to me recently."

"So you are a believer in what the Germans call a doppelgänger," asked the editor. "They do say we live in the Age of the Double."

Yasukichi sighed. He squeezed the bridge of his nose between two of his fingers and said, "I don't know. But if it's not my so-called 'second-self,' then what if someone is deliberately impersonating me, and with some ill intention? I am afraid neither explanation is very welcome."

"Then you also believe the doppelgänger to be a harbinger of bad luck," asked the editor. "Even death?"

Yasukichi sighed again. "I don't know. But either way, I do feel as though I am being stalked by something or somebody."

"If that is what you truly believe," said the editor, "then you should see someone. Someone who might be able to help you."

Yasukichi smiled and said, "Like who? A doctor?"

"A private detective," said the editor.

Yasukichi shook his head. "I detest detectives, I hate detectives. Detectives cannot even pass for human beings. They are machines."

"But detectives and writers surely have much in common," said the editor, smiling. "In different ways, both search for the truth . . ."

Yasukichi snorted. "Nonsense. It is extremely rude to compare a writer and a detective. Theirs is a profession whose essence is to search for the truth in the most vulgar of senses. And if there are writers who only profess truth and do not care what happens to other ideals such as beauty and morality, then such writers must be people with a defect. Perhaps not as individuals, but certainly as writers. And I would say they are unhealthy. Akin to pickpockets and thieves."

"On what unfortunate personal experience are you basing such a rant," laughed the editor. "Have you had trouble with a detective?"

Yasukichi shook his head and said, "No. Luckily, I have never had the misfortune to ever meet a detective."

"So these are simply your observations, then?"

Yasukichi smiled and said, "Not simply my observations, no. Simply my observations would make me no better than a detective, too. These are my opinions; my opinions based on my knowledge, my knowledge formed by my observations."

"But you have had no personal experience with detectives," said the editor. "You have never even met one."

Yasukichi shook his head again. "As far as I know. But more than likely, I have been tailed. In fact, I am certain I have been followed by a detective. And that probably explains my feeling of being stalked. As have you, no doubt. Such is modern life in the modern city."

"But then perhaps you should meet a detective," said the editor with a grin. He took out his wallet, then a name-card from the wallet. He placed the name-card on the table before Yasukichi—

"Know-your-enemy, so-to-speak," he laughed.

Yasukichi looked down at the name-card on the table, then back up at the room. The mirrors set in the café walls reflected him in endless doubles. Coldly, menacingly mocking him.

"At the very least, you'll surely get a story out of it," said the editor.

Yasukichi sighed. "You mean, you will."

*

Ryūnosuke put down his pen again. He picked up the packet of Golden Bat cigarettes. He put them straight back down on the desk. He picked up the packet of Shikishima instead. He took out a cigarette. He put it to his lips. He picked up the box of matches, shook it twice, then took out a match and lit his cigarette. He looked down at the manuscript paper and sighed, blowing smoke across the desk. He reached for the pile of envelopes. He flicked through them, turning them over one by one, reading the name and address of the sender on the back. He came to an envelope with no name or address on the back. He put the cigarette in the ashtray. He picked up the letter knife. He opened the envelope. He took out the letter and he read:

Dear Sir,

You are being watched.

Your behaviour at the Mikado restaurant in Manseibashi the other evening was unpardonable. The woman is married with a young son, and you yourself are engaged. If you do not immediately break off relations with the woman in question, then I will inform her husband and your fiancée.

Please do not doubt my resolve or sincerity.

Remember, you are being watched.

Ryūnosuke let the letter fall from his hand onto the desk. He stared down at the letter, the letter lying on top of the manuscript paper. He reached for the cigarette, but it was now just a fallen column of ash. He picked up the packet of Shikishima, put it straight back down again. He picked up the packet of Golden Bat instead, lit one and smoked it. Then he smoked a Shikishima, then another Golden Bat, then another Shikishima, another Golden Bat, alternating the brands, staring down at the letter lying on the blank sheet of manuscript paper.

*

Thick layers of cloud and smoke hung over the Sumida River. Yasukichi watched the Mukōjima bank drawing closer. The trunks of the cherry trees looked like burnt corpses standing in a row.

Yasukichi disembarked from the small steamer. It was now twilight, it was still raining. Yasukichi began to walk towards the Tamanoi district. He could smell his own rubberised coat. An overhead trolley line was sending purple sparks up into the air. Yasukichi followed the cable and its sparks until he came to a junction. To his left was the river with its banks of trees, to his right was Tamanoi with its houses of lights.

Yasukichi walked straight on, into the darkness. And here, just as his editor had described, among numerous old graves, standing in the middle of a bamboo grove, Yasukichi found a small, Western-style house. And there, on its narrow porch, with its peeling paint, was a porcelain nameplate—

A, Detective.

Yasukichi rang the bell below the nameplate and waited. Presently, the door opened and a little old woman appeared.

"Is Mr. A home?"

"He is, sir. And he is expecting you."

The old woman led Yasukichi into a room directly opposite the front door. The room was only partially illuminated by the weak light from the hallway, and when the woman closed the door behind her, momentarily Yasukichi was left in complete and utter darkness until, gradually, the flame of an oil lamp began to grow, to reveal the stark, white face of a man—

"Well, here you are," said the man. The man was standing in the centre of the room, holding the oil lamp in one hand, gesturing at a chair with the other. "Please, sit down, sit down—"

Yasukichi sat down in one of the two chairs at a table in the middle of the room. Yasukichi looked around the gloomy room. In the shadows, there were piles of books and papers. On the walls, crucifixes and paintings. A large desk in front of a small window. All the furniture worn and shabby. And even the gaudy tablecloth, with its woven border of red flowers, was threadbare and looked as if it might disintegrate at any moment.

The man placed the oil lamp on the table. He looked across the cloth at Yasukichi. He smiled but said nothing, and Yasukichi found himself listening to the sound of the rain falling in the bamboo grove outside. The wind in the trees and the waves on the river.

Presently, the old woman returned with the tea things. She set them down on the table and then retreated again. The man opened a box of cigarettes on the cloth. He turned the box towards Yasukichi, smiled again and said, "Please. Will you have one?"

"Thank you," said Yasukichi.

The man leant forward across the table. He held out a flame

towards Yasukichi. Yasukichi bent forward to light the cigarette from the flame. He felt the man's eyes upon him. Yasukichi looked up from the flame at the man and now, for the first time, he could clearly see the face of the man. He appeared to be of a similar age to Yasukichi. Possibly slightly older, maybe even thirty. But the man was completely bald. Or perhaps his head had been shaved, like a priest. It was hard to tell in the dimly lit room. Yasukichi looked away, staring down at his cigarette.

"You are a bundle of nerves," said the man. "Your whole being is wrapped in an aura of darkness and shadow."

Yasukichi looked up from his cigarette and said, "Everywhere I look, behind me or before me, I see only shadows. Only darkness."

"But wherever there is darkness," said the man, "then light will surely follow. If you are not impatient . . ."

Yasukichi smiled sadly, and then said, "But there is such a thing as darkness without light."

"Momentarily, yes," said the man. "But light always follows darkness. Just as day always follows night. Miraculously."

Yasukichi shook his head. "I do not believe in miracles."

The man smiled. He raised his hand. He held it over the oil lamp. Then he placed his hand on the table. And he plucked one of the red flowers from the pattern woven into the border of the cloth. The man held the red flower out towards Yasukichi. His eyes blinking, his hands shaking, Yasukichi took the flower from the man. Yasukichi brought the flower up to his face. He felt its petals against his skin, he smelt its scent. His eyes still blinking, his hands still shaking, Yasukichi dropped the flower onto the table. Immediately, the flower resumed its place in the woven border of the tablecloth. And try as he might, Yasukichi could not pick it up again. He shook his head again. "I do not understand . . ."

"It is not a question of understanding," said the man. "It is a matter of believing. You stopped believing and so the flower died."

Yasukichi looked across the table at the man. And Yasukichi said, "Can you help me? Can you save me?"

"Only if you want to be helped," said the man. "Only if you want to be saved."

*

A new year, a new start. A new life, married life. After the ceremony, the portraits and the parties. A new house, a married house. In Kamakura, by the sea, by the sea, by the sea. The wind in the pines, the sand in your shoes. A large house, with a garden. A lotus pond and bashō *plants. The rain on the pond, the drops on the leaves. On the pond and on the leaves. A quiet life, a quiet life. It's what you want, that's what you say: a quiet life for you, the quiet life for me. By the sea, by the sea. To become another man, a new and better man. What you want, so you say. To live quietly, composing haiku. The rain on the pond, the drops on the leaves. The wind in the pines, the sand in your shoes. In your socks, between your toes. The grains which rub, the grains that cut. In the bathroom, at the sink. The blood on your feet and the blood on the floor. The wind round your house, the waves at your door. The world lapping at your feet, the world banging at your door. The price of rice, the cost of living. The riots in the streets, the smoke in the sky. A world at war, always at war. Turning fields into trenches, trenches into graves, making soldiers of us all, corpses of us all. The blood on your hands, the blood in your sink. In the bathroom, in the mirror. You stare at your face, your skin and your skull. You stick out your tongue, you pull down your lower eyelids. Turning on the light, turning off the light. Here and then gone, gone and then here. The man you were, the man you are. Off and then on, on and then off. The man you want to be, will never be. Gone and then here, here and then gone. Want to be, don't want to be; will and won't be, can and can't be, can never be, never be. How many men, how many men. In the bathroom, in the mirror. No quiet life for*

*you, no quiet life for me. For me, for you; for us, for us, for all of us. The
quiet life, a half-life. Torn in half, torn in two.*

*

Monday morning, in the classroom, before the board, behind his
desk, Ryūnosuke opened his briefcase and took out the notes for
his lecture: Poe again. Ryūnosuke opened the book. He glanced
up at the class, the rows of students at their desks in their Naval
Academy uniforms, bored before he'd even begun. They were not
the only ones. Ryūnosuke sighed to himself, then began to read
aloud: "The Premature Burial . . . There are certain themes of which
the interest is all-absorbing, but which are too entirely horrible for
the purposes of legitimate fiction. These the mere romanticist must
eschew, if he does not wish to offend, or to disgust. They are with
propriety handled only when the severity and majesty of truth
sanctify and sustain them. We thrill, for example, with the most
intense 'pleasurable pain' over the accounts of the Passage of the
Beresina, of the Earthquake of Lisbon, of the Plague of London,
of the Massacre of Saint Bartholomew, or of the stifling of the
hundred and twenty-three prisoners in the Black Hole at Calcutta.
But, in these accounts, it is the fact—it is the reality—it is the
history which excites. As inventions, we should regard them with
simple abhorrence . . ."

Ryūnosuke paused, glanced up from the text to the class and
froze, petrified: the students in their uniforms were still sat at their
desks, but they were not the only ones; behind each of them stood
their exact double, like the bleached trunks of winter trees, each
double dressed in white hospital robes and a military cap, some
wearing dark glasses, some leaning on crutches, with bandaged
heads, with bandaged limbs, some without arms, some without legs,
some with no faces, no faces at all, row upon row, the sitting and

the standing, an army of doubles, a *Doppelgänger Korps*, the students and their doubles, all staring at Ryūnosuke, Ryūnosuke trembling now, Ryūnosuke shaking now, the students giggling now, giggling at Ryūnosuke, their doubles laughing now, laughing at Ryūnosuke, Ryūnosuke dropping the book, forgetting his briefcase, Ryūnosuke fleeing from the classroom, tearing down the corridor.

*

In his study in the new house in Kamakura, Yasukichi Horikawa threw down his pen, cursed and lit another cigarette. He had hoped to finish the latest instalment of his story, which was being serialised in the *Osaka Mainichi*; some days he felt it was the best work he had ever written, the story of an artist and his devotion, his obsession to his work; other times, times like tonight, he felt it was as flawed as all his other work, flawed by his own lack of devotion to his craft, his own lack of obsession to his own writing, his mind often distracted, consumed by thoughts of money and of time; never enough money, never enough time. Somehow he had managed to reduce his teaching hours while increasing his salary, much to the annoyance, even contempt, of some of his colleagues at the Academy. Yet still he needed more money, so still he accepted more commissions, so still there was not enough time, so this story for the *Mainichi*, this story which was so close to being his best work to date, this story was just one of the many he had agreed to write. If only he could give up teaching at the Naval Academy, if only he could find a position at a university, with a better salary, better hours, more hours to write. If only, if only. He cursed again. Then cursed himself; if only he could stop thinking about money and time, if only he could think solely about writing, his writing, not even thinking about writing, just writing, actually writing! He put out his cigarette. He picked up his pen, tried to get it moving again.

But it was gone, gone; the moment lost, lost again. He put down his pen again. He got up from the desk, from his work. He went to the bathroom, then to the bedroom.

Yasukichi lay down beside his sleeping wife. He picked up a book from the floor and began to read in bed. The book was *The Night-Side of Nature, or, Ghosts and Ghost-Seers* by the English novelist Catherine Crowe, first published in 1848. Yasukichi had found the book one afternoon in Jimbōchō; he knew Baudelaire admired the book, but he had also heard that in the process of researching and writing the book, Catherine Crowe had lost her mind; believing spirits could render her invisible, she was found naked one winter night in an Edinburgh street. Yasukichi had bought the book without a second thought, and had read it twice at least. Now he turned again to the chapter on doppelgängers, yet soon his eyes began to fall, to close, to open and fall again, to open then fall again, fall again and close—

A vaudeville performance; on the stage, a hanging screen, a magic lantern show, scenes from the Sino-Japanese War, scenes from the Russo-Japanese War, the large crowd about him cheering the Japanese flag, screaming at the top of their lungs, "Banzai! Banzai! Banzai!" A hand grabbing his sleeve, the hand gripping his arm, squeezing it tighter and tighter, a woman, a woman he recognised but could not place, laughing now, laughing and pointing, pointing and saying, "It's you, it's you, it's always you . . ."

On the stage, before the screen, Yasukichi saw his double, his exact double, saw him standing on the stage, beside a box, in a tuxedo, in a top hat, calling out to the crowd, calling for a volunteer, the woman, that woman pointing at Yasukichi, pushing him forward, the crowd grabbing Yasukichi, pushing him forward, towards the stage, onto the stage, his double, in his tuxedo, in his top hat, opening the box, the world growing charnel, grim Darkness overspreading the earth, the woman, that woman on the stage, too, before the box, kissing

Yasukichi on his lips, pushing Yasukichi into the box, into the box, the lid falling, the lid closing, the lid shut—

It was dark—all dark; complete and utter darkness. Yasukichi tried to speak, tried to shout, to scream, but his lips, his tongue were parched and silent, his lungs, his heart gasping, palpitating, his arms, his wrists striking the sides of the box, his feet, his face but inches from its wood, the wood, the box now trembling, now shaking, shaking and screaming, screaming with the sound of a saw, a saw and her teeth, her teeth—

How canst thou tranquilly sleep . . . ?

Half-light, grey-light, daylight on a hillside. That woman walking towards the gates of his house, his family house in Tabata, his wife darning some cloth at the *kotatsu*, the woman pausing by a stone lantern in the garden, his wife singing to their son, the woman sliding open the doors to his house, his wife kneeling before her in the *genkan*, the woman holding out her newborn baby towards his wife, his own son crying, the baby screaming, his wife crying, the woman screaming, his wife turning to look for him, on the futon, in a Chinese-patterned robe, on his chest a Bible open, his wife shaking him, shouting at him, pleading with him, "Wake up, wake up . . ."

*

Ryūnosuke, an editor and an older colleague, Jun'ichirō Tanizaki, were sat at a café table in Jimbōchō, puffing on one cigarette after another, listening to the music from a gramophone on the other side of the room, gossiping about politicians, joking about other writers. But Ryūnosuke said very little; in truth, he felt in awe of the older writer, not only the strength of his work, but also the sheer power of his personality, his vitality, his utter vitality. Even the black suit and red necktie he was wearing today loudly announced the confidence and magnetism of the man, attracting the attention of the rest of the room, all eyes and ears turned his way, glued to their table—

"I spent half the day riding around in an automobile."

"Was there some research you needed to do," asked the editor.

His cheek resting on his hand, the older colleague replied with complete abandon, "No, I just felt like riding around the city."

Ryūnosuke envied the older man's freedom, and his eyes must have betrayed his jealousy because now the other man asked, "Are you busy working on something at the moment?"

Ryūnosuke sighed. "Even though I feel as though I am prostituting myself, I have promised to write a detective story for *Chūō kōron* . . ."

"Me, too," exclaimed the older man. "How funny! And I must say, I am relishing the challenge. What is your story about?"

Ryūnosuke sighed again. "Well, I have barely begun, but I plan to write something around the notion of doubles . . ."

"Me, too," exclaimed the older man again. "How funny! Mine is almost finished and is the tale of two artists, Ōkawa and Aono. They are bitter rivals. But Ōkawa comes to see Aono as his doppelgänger and he even cites the famous story by Edgar Allan Poe . . ."

"What a brilliant idea," said the editor. "And how wonderful it will be for readers to be able to compare how you both choose to address the same theme; the two brightest stars of the literary firmament, side by side, in direct competition, so to speak . . ."

Ryūnosuke felt ill. He excused himself and got up from the table. Quickly, he walked towards the bathroom door, locked himself inside, crouched down and vomited into the toilet. Again and again.

Ryūnosuke stood back up. He turned to the sink. He ran the water, washed his face, washed his hands, dried his face, dried his hands, and then stared at his reflection in the mirror: *what have you done* . . .

On the way back to the table, Ryūnosuke stopped by the gramophone. The music had ended. He leant over the gramophone to read the label on the record: *Schwanengesang—Schubert.*

Ryūnosuke felt afraid. He looked across the room for his older friend and the editor. But his friend and the editor were not there. And at their table was only one coffee cup. His own coffee cup. Ryūnosuke put down a silver coin on the counter and started out of the café—

"That will be twenty sen, sir."

The coin Ryūnosuke had thrown down was copper, not silver.

*

Yasukichi Horikawa put down his pen again. He picked up the packet of Golden Bat cigarettes. He put them straight back down on the desk. He picked up the packet of Shikishima instead. He took out a cigarette. He put it to his lips. He picked up the box of matches, shook it twice, then took out a match and lit his cigarette. He looked down at the manuscript paper and sighed, blowing smoke across the desk. He reached for the pile of envelopes. He flicked through them, turning them over one by one, reading the name and address of the sender on the back. He came to an envelope with no name or address on the back. He felt the blood in his veins freeze over, the air sucked from his lungs. He dropped the cigarette in the ashtray. He picked up the letter knife. He opened the envelope. He took out the letter and read:

Sir,

You are being watched.

I warned you, but you did not listen. You doubted my resolve and sincerity. But you will not doubt me now:

You were seen together on the Ginza, among the crowds, all the people, brash and brazen, casually strolling along as though you had never known the existence of sin, under the electric lamps, before the store windows, pausing before a Western tailor shop, laughing at the mannequins, entering a bookstore, browsing through the titles. Yes, your face may well burn with embarrassment as you read, yet still you cling to the notion that this letter is but a lucky guess, an elaborate prank, do you not? Well, in the bookstore, on its second floor, with the woman at your side, that woman on your arm, you came to the collected works of Dostoevsky, and you took down one volume, and you turned to its title page: the novella Dvoynik.

You bought the book, you left the store, and together you walked on, on and on, until you came to a second-hand shop. In the window was a stuffed swan, its neck erect, its wings yellow and moth-eaten. Here, before this stuffed swan, in plain sight, you embraced, kissed and parted. She headed south, you headed north.

You stood in a queue, you boarded a trolley. Between the red lettering of the advertisements hanging from the ceiling, before the ashen flecks of the dirt staining the windows. You sat among the passengers. The carriage moving out of the lights, the trolley heading into the darkness. You got up from your seat, you alighted from the trolley. The crowds now absent, only shadows now present. You walked up a slope. You turned right, you turned left. You pushed open a gate in the wall around a house. And the gate swung shut behind you. In the night and in the rain. Among the stone lanterns, behind the tall trees. Despite the hour, despite its lateness. There was a light in the house, children's voices from a bedroom. Then the light was gone, now the children were silent. You climbed the steep ladder, you walked along the passage. You entered your study. The study was lined with books, the floor covered in papers. On a table were pots, in the pots were brushes. You took off your raincoat. You hung up the coat. Then you took off your skin. You hung up your skin. And the thing that remained stood in the centre of the room. Smaller than a man, maybe just over three feet. Lighter than a man, perhaps but thirty pounds. Its pallor green, its sheen reptilian. The thing had webbed hands, the thing had webbed feet. And an oval-shaped saucer on top of its head, beneath short, coarse brown hair. Now the thing picked out a fine brush. Then the thing walked over to the skin. The entire pelt of a human body hanging from a peg. And the thing began to touch up the skin with its brush. A dab here, a spot there. Now the thing stepped back from the skin on its peg. Then the thing put back the brush in its pot. The thing walked back to the skin on the peg. The thing lifted up the skin from the peg. Now the thing shook the skin out like a cloak. Then the thing wrapped the skin around itself. And now the thing was a man again, the thing was you again. And then you turned to the window. And in the night, and in the rain. You smiled at me, without shame, without shame, then laughed and said, "Quack, quack! Pleased to meet you. My name is Tock."

Your true-self has been seen. Now you will be exposed.

No more warnings, no more chances.

Yasukichi let the letter fall from his hand onto the desk. He stared down at the letter, the letter lying on top of the blank sheet of manuscript paper, lying beside his copy of *Dvoynik*.

*

Ryūnosuke could hear the sound of the rain falling in the bamboo grove outside. The wind in the trees and the waves on the river. Ryūnosuke looked down at the cigarette he was holding between his fingers. It was still lit, it was still long. Ryūnosuke shook his head and said, "I do not understand . . ."

"It is not a question of understanding," said the man. "It is a matter of believing. Simply believing . . ."

Ryūnosuke looked across the table at the man again. And Ryūnosuke said, "So you cannot help me?"

The man rose from the table. He walked over to one of the piles of books and papers. He picked up a book from the pile. He sat back down at the table. And he handed Ryūnosuke a Bible—

"Only the man who governs his passions can attain peace and sainthood. But the man who fails to control his passions, that man is condemned to live in Hell as a demon."

*

It was the Age of Winter, still the Age of Winter, around the second anniversary of the death of Sensei. Yasukichi Horikawa had caught the train from Kamakura to Tokyo, crossed the city, bought flowers and come to the northern entrance to the Zōshigaya cemetery. He was wearing a raincoat, carrying the flowers. He entered the cemetery and walked down an avenue lined on each side with Maple and Zelkova trees, their leaves fallen. There was nobody else in the cemetery, nobody living, only two crows, noisily flying over him, swooping ever lower and lower, their wings overshadowing him as he walked. Yasukichi looked up at the two crows, naming them Han-shan and Shih-te, but Han-shan and Shih-te seemed now to be laughing at him—*A-hō! A-hō!*—mocking and taunting him. Yasukichi walked on, turned at the junction onto the central avenue, down its broad path, then took the second turning on the left and finally came to the grave of Sensei.

This was the permanent grave, a tall, grey tombstone, made of granite, completed for the first anniversary of the passing of Sensei, grand and imposing, a monument to the man. But somehow, in some way, Yasukichi felt the design of the grave was out of character with the man, the writer he had been honoured, privileged to have known. Still, Yasukichi divided the flowers into two. He placed them in the two metal vases on the low altar shelf before the tomb. He took a box of incense sticks and his matches from the pocket of his raincoat. He removed nine sticks of incense, put the box back inside his coat, struck a match, lit the sticks and laid them in the granite tray between the two metal vases of flowers. He stepped back, he bowed his head before the grave and he closed his eyes . . .

"Approach everything rationally, and you become harsh. Pole along in the stream of emotions, and you will be swept away by the current. Give free rein to your desires, and you become uncomfortably confined. It is not a very agreeable place to live, this world of ours . . ."

Yasukichi put his palms together. He bowed once more, then opened his eyes. He said goodbye to Sensei, then turned to walk away from the grave—

A man was standing in his way, blocking his path, the man his exact, ink-stained double.

"How in the world," said Yasukichi, "did you follow me?"

"Ce grand malheur," said the man, *"de ne pouvoir être seul."*

"Is that all you have to say for yourself," asked Yasukichi. "After all this time? Your only words are still but borrowed words?"

"No," said the man. "I have come to say goodbye. And to give you one last chance: leave me alone, leave my world! Be gone, be gone! Take refuge somewhere else, with someone else . . ."

"How dare you! How dare you say such things to me," said Yasukichi. "It's *you* who should leave me alone, leave my world! You who should become a new and better man. For I have seen you, seen you as you really are, as you are now and as you will be. And a great disaster is on its way."

And with these words Yasukichi left Ryūnosuke standing before the grave, *in the green grove, at the dark frontier,* in his raincoat, his Western umbrella propped up against the granite fence which enclosed the grave of Natsume Sōseki, Kanzan and Jittoku cawing and fighting with each other, screaming over his head, the tenant of the grave whispering to him—

"How can we escape, except through faith, madness or death . . ."

*

A new year, a new start. A new life, the writer's life. You have resigned from the Naval Academy, you have signed an exclusive contract with the Osaka Mainichi *newspaper. You will move back with your wife to live in Tabata with your adoptive parents and Aunt Fuki, and leave this house behind. In Kamakura, by the sea, with its lotus pond, with its* bashō *plants. The rain on the pond, the drops on the leaves. On the pond and on the leaves. The quiet life, that quiet life. No more, no more. In the bathroom, in the mirror. You stare at your face, your skin and your skull. You stick out your tongue, you pull down your lower eyelid. Turning on the light, turning off the light. Here and then gone, gone and then here. You are the magician, you are the sorcerer. In your tuxedo, in your top hat. On the stage, before the box. The lights in your face, the saw in your hand. You flex the blade, you test its teeth. You set about your work, the saw through the wood. You saw and you saw, you saw and you saw. You drop the saw, you part the box. The box in half, the man in half, the man inside, sawn in two. On the edge of their seats, the audience gasp. You push the box back together again, and you stare down at the wound in the wood. The drum roll, the audience waiting. Rolling again, still waiting. On the stage, before the box. You stare down at the wound, you search for the spells. To make the box whole, to make the man whole. On the stage, before the box. The man sawn in two, the man in two halves. The man you are, this man is you. The man who smokes Golden Bat, the man who smokes Shikishima, the man who abstains, the man who drinks, the man who is faithful, the man who cheats, the man who is a good father, the man who is a bad father, the man who is a good son, the man who is a bad son, the man from the East, the man of the West, the man who believes, the man who does not, the man who lies, the man who lies; this man, these men, these men are you, these men are me, these men are us. But we lack the spells, for we lack the will. So we cannot put ourselves together again, you can never put me together again.*

The Yellow Christ

About ten years ago, for the sake of art,
I was in love with Christianity—above all, I loved Catholicism.
Even today, in my memory, I have a vivid image—
of the Japanese Temple of the Holy Mother in Nagasaki.
But I was nothing but a crow,
pecking through seeds already sown,
by Hakushū Kitahara and Mokutarō Kinoshita.

"Man of the West," Ryūnosuke Akutagawa, 1927

In nineteen hundred and nineteen, in the eighth year of Taishō, I am waiting; waiting for the morning with open eyes, for the house to wake and rise, waiting for the smell of miso soup, for the taste of oatmeal, milk and boiled eggs, waiting for the touch of newsprint, to read the news of the price of rice, always the price of rice, the price of rice and . . .

JAPAN'S LAST EFFORT ON RACIAL DISCRIMINATION
Will Ask Powers to Make Declaration Separate from Covenant,
Recognising Principle of Equality

ADOPT DRASTIC STEPS IN KOREA
Situation Grows Worse—Tokyo Decides on Stern Measures

THE DEVASTATION IN YOKOHAMA
3,700 Buildings Burnt, 20,000 Are Homeless, 50,000,000 Yen Loss

EARTHQUAKE IN TOKYO
An earthquake was felt in Tokyo at 9:53 o'clock yesterday, lasting about two minutes. The centre was off the coast of Kinkazan, 120 miles from Tokyo.

PERSONAL AND LOCAL
Mr. Ryūnosuke Akutagawa, 27, and Mr. Kan Kikuchi, 31, the esteemed men of letters, will leave Tokyo this morning, Sunday 4th May, for Nagasaki and are expected to return later this month.

. . . waiting to shave, to wash and to dress, to put on my coat and pick up my hat, to stand in the genkan, *to put on my shoes and pick up my cases, to say goodbye to my family and wife, and leave this*

house, to leave my house, the taxi waiting, to cross the city, to get to the station, to stand on the platform, to wait on the platform, to wait for Kikuchi, to meet Kikuchi, to board the train, the Super Express, to leave this city, this city behind, for Tokyo to fade, to fade and to vanish, to speed and to speed, through this land, to watch the cities come and go, their factories and chimneys to pass us by—Yokohama, Nagoya, Kyoto, Osaka, Kobe, Okayama, Hiroshima, Ogōri, on to Shimonoseki, to cross the Tsushima Strait by ferry to Mojikō, then on through Kokura on to Hakata—station to station through station to station, I'm waiting, I am waiting; waiting to see the sun on the bay, the rhombus kites soar in the sky, swallows dart over roofs, ducks sail under bridges, bananas and mikans *piled up by the roads, the Holy Mother Temple high on the hill, so high on the hill, so tall in the sky, waiting to climb, to climb that hill, to follow in the steps, the steps of the masters, of Mokutarō and Hakushū, those steps of the masters in the steps of the Master, and the songs they sang, O the songs they sang, waiting to hear, to hear those songs, waiting to sing, to sing those songs, to hear and to sing those songs, myself . . .*

I believe in the heretical teachings of a degenerate age,
    the witchcraft of the Christian God,
The captains of the black ships, the marvellous land of the Red
    Hairs,
The scarlet glass, the sharp-scented carnation,
The calico, arrack and *vinho tinto* of the Southern Barbarians:

The blue-eyed Dominicans chanting the liturgy who tell me
    even in dreams
Of the God of the forbidden faith, or of the blood-stained Cross,
The cunning device that makes a mustard seed as big as an apple,
The strange collapsible spyglass that looks even at Paradise.

They build their houses of stone, the white blood of marble
Overflows in crystal bowls; when night falls, they say,
　　it bursts into flame.
That beautiful electric dream is mixed with the incense of velvet
Reflecting the bird and beasts of the world of the moon.

I have heard their cosmetics are squeezed from the flowers
　　of poisonous plants,
And the images of Mary are painted with oil from rotted stones;
The blue letters ranged sideways in Latin or Portuguese
Are filled with a beautiful sad music of Heaven.

Oh, vouchsafe unto us, sainted padres of delusion,
Though our hundred years be shortened to an instant,
　　though we die on the bloody cross,
It will not matter; we beg for the Secret, that strange dream of
　　crimson: Jesus, we pray this day,
　　bodies and souls caught in the incense of longing.

. . . *"Jashūmon Hikyoku," the "Secret Song of the Heretics"; to hear it
myself, to sing it myself and believe it myself, to believe it myself, a man
of the East at this gate to the West, this tapestry of East and West, this
"Little Rome," my "Little Rome," my Nagasaki; for my Nagasaki, I am
waiting* . . .

*

Tokutarō Nagami was waiting in the *genkan* of his family's large
house in Nagasaki. He was anxious and he was nervous, and he
had been waiting a long time. His guests were supposed to have left
Tokyo on April 30th, arriving on the first of May. However, they
had been delayed and had not left Tokyo until yesterday, May 4th.

Furthermore, adding to his anxiety, adding to his nerves, he had never met his guests before. Their visit had been arranged through an elder mutual acquaintance, Kōichirō Kondō, and so he knew his guests only by reputation, and by their works.

In the *genkan*, Tokutarō Nagami sighed and looked at his watch again: it was almost six o'clock. He knew he should have gone to the station, he knew he should have met their train. However, Mr. Akutagawa had been so apologetic for the delay, for the inconvenience they were causing, so determined not to put him to any further trouble, and insistent that they would take a taxi from the station to his house. Yet still there was no sign of them. He knew he should have met their train, he knew . . .

Now Nagami heard the sound of an automobile, its brakes and its doors. He called for the servants, he opened the doors to the *genkan* and he went down the garden path to the gate of the house.

Ryūnosuke Akutagawa was standing in the street, a suitcase in his hand, another at his feet, a coat over his arm and a hat in his hand. He was wearing a fashionable Western suit, with a white shirt and a dark tie, and traditional *geta* on his feet. His hair brushed back and long, his face was tired but smiling, an apologetic smile—

"I am so very, very sorry to have kept you waiting," said Akutagawa, bowing deeply, "and for all the inconvenience I have caused you. But thank you for your kindness and for your hospitality. I am Ryūnosuke Akutagawa, and I am very pleased to meet you."

"I am Tokutarō Nagami," said Nagami, bowing, "and I am very pleased to meet you, too. Welcome to Nagasaki, and welcome to my house."

Akutagawa bowed again and said, "Thank you."

"But may I ask," said Nagami, glancing up and down the empty street outside his home, "what has happened to Mr. Kikuchi?"

Akutagawa smiled again, his apologetic smile, and said, "I am afraid, soon after we passed through Kobe, Kikuchi began to complain of a severe headache. He was concerned he had not yet fully recovered from the attack of Spanish flu he had only recently suffered, and worried he would infect me again, for I have already been stricken twice, and feared he might bring the epidemic to your own house. And so he alighted the train at Okayama, intending to head to Sanuki, which is the place he was born."

"How terrible," exclaimed Nagami.

"Really," said Akutagawa. "I have heard it is quite charming."

"No," said Nagami. "I mean, how terrible that Mr. Kikuchi is so ill. I only hope he managed to make it to Sanuki . . ."

"Indeed," said Akutagawa. "There is a beautiful symmetry, is there not, in returning to the place of your birth in order to die?"

"Well, I sincerely hope and pray it does not come to that," said Nagami, staring at the cold and blasé man of letters before him.

Akutagawa smiled, then said, "I am sorry, sincerely. I should not make such jokes when we have not met before. I have worried you unnecessarily. For all his talents, Kikuchi is a worse hypochondriac than even me. I suspected all along his headache was the result of too much conversation, and too many cigarettes, in the confines of our carriage. And when I reached Mojikō, my suspicions were confirmed. A telegram at the terminal informed me that our Lazarus has risen from the dead, and is once more making his way to Nagasaki, though he plans to spend tonight in Onomichi."

"Oh, what a relief," exclaimed Nagami.

Akutagawa smiled again, his apologetic smile again, and said, "Sincerely, I am sorry to have alarmed you so, Mr. Nagami. Please forgive me . . ."

"Not at all," said Nagami. "In fact, I must apologise to you, making you stand out here in the street, answering my questions, after you have travelled the length of the country to be here. Let us get you inside, Sensei . . ."

Nagami led his guest through the gate and through the garden, into the house and into the room he had had prepared. "I hope this room will be both comfortable and interesting for you. During the early years of Meiji, this room was used for meetings between the magistrates of Nagasaki and the trade ministers of England. I only hope it will be adequate."

"It is more than adequate," said Akutagawa. "Thank you."

Nagami smiled, relieved, and said, "You are most welcome. And a bath has already been prepared for you. And though I know you must be exhausted by your journey, I hope the bath will refresh you, and you will join me then for dinner. I hope it will be to your liking and taste, but I have arranged a Nagasaki *shippoku* dinner to welcome you . . ."

"I am sorry to have put you to so much trouble," said Akutagawa. "But thank you. I very much look forward to such a dinner."

"You are too kind," said Nagami. "The food will be nothing much, but I look forward to seeing you in an hour so . . ."

Now Nagami left his guest to the maids, and went back to his study to pace and to prepare, rehearsing his conversation, practising his lines, hoping not to bore his visitor from the capital, picking up the celebrated works of this famous author, rereading a passage here, a passage there . . .

"It is an honour to welcome you to my home," said Nagami, seating his guest before one of the red round tables on the tatami mats in the main dining room, the red round table filled with dishes of Chinese origin, dishes of Portuguese origin, Dutch and Japanese. "This is our *shippoku* dinner, and you may eat from these dishes in the order you prefer. But our custom is to first begin with an *ohire* soup and a short speech from the host . . .

"And so please, let us begin with the soup . . ."

"Thank you," said Akutagawa.

After the soup, after his short speech, having introduced each of the dishes to his guest, and while they ate, Nagami then said, "I must say, I greatly admired your recent *Life of Saint Christopher*. It is a stylistic tour de force, so impressive in the way in which you use the language of the Japanese translation of *Aesop's Fables* by the sixteenth-century Jesuits."

"Thank you," said Akutagawa. "It is the only work in which I myself have any confidence and, in truth, I am finding it hard to move on from. But I feel the same way about this pork, it really is quite delicious . . ."

Nagami smiled. "Thank you. If you are so taken with the *tōbani*, I must ensure you taste one of the *dōngpōròu* buns in our Shinchi Chinatown. But going back to your *Life of Saint Christopher*, I feel it is at least the equal of Monsieur Flaubert's *The Temptation of Saint Anthony* . . ."

"Thank you," said Akutagawa again. "You are too generous, though I believe *La Légende de Saint-Julien* to be the better work and a story that has been a greater influence. I fear, though, the quality of your local sashimi will be a bad influence, deterring me from ever eating the fish of Tokyo again!"

Nagami laughed. "Now you are being too generous, Sensei, thank you. But you have written a great number of stories on a Christian theme, so many wonderful stories, and so may I ask from where your interest stems? Were you yourself raised in a Christian household, Sensei?"

"No," said Akutagawa. "No, not even a particularly religious house in any sense. However, it was and is a superstitious house, and I am told, though of course I do not recall, that I was abandoned as a baby on the steps of a Christian church in Tsukiji, to be found by a certain Bishop Williams, who handed me over to one of the managers of the dairy shops owned by my father, and who then returned me to my parents as a foundling . . ."

"How fascinating," said Nagami.

"You may say so, it may sound so, but the whole charade was an attempt to protect me from the ill omens of my parents' age at my birth. And, I have to say, it was an attempt which seems to have been wholly futile."

"I am sorry," said Nagami. "And forgive me then for being so insistent, but do you think that is from where your interest in Christianity comes?"

"Perhaps," said Akutagawa, a melancholy smile upon his lips. "Perhaps the bishop did baptise me before returning me. Perhaps that would explain why then I have always felt drawn to the Bible and its tales . . ."

"Yet this is your first time in Nagasaki, is it not?"

"It is," said Akutagawa. "Yes."

"And yet," said Nagami, "in a story such as your *Death of a Martyr*, you write so convincingly, so realistically of this place and its history."

"Thank you," said Akutagawa.

"I must confess, the references to ancient local sources at the end of the story had me foolishly scouring the Prefectural Library, until I realised these texts had been but a part of your fiction, a most believable deception."

"Then I must apologise," said Akutagawa. "It was not my intention to make a fool of my reader. Only to entrance them with the tale."

"Well," said Nagami, now rising from his low red round table, "you succeeded, and admirably so, I must say. But now, if you are not too tired, before retiring for the night, may I trouble you to visit my own library, to show you some of the trifles I have collected, bits of local colour . . . ?"

"I would be delighted," said Akutagawa. "Thank you."

Nagami led Akutagawa from the dining room, down a corridor, to his library and study, the lamps already lit and waiting. And there, one by one, Nagami showed Akutagawa various pictures, books and objects: Hasami porcelain and *vidro* glass from his collection of Nagasaki *objets*; a painting of a Dutch house at Hirado, a plate depicting a Dutch ship anchored in the bay, old books illustrated with scenes of life in Dejima.

Akutagawa was very taken with the glassware, but naturally seemed most interested in the relics from the city's Christian past, particularly a white porcelain statue of the Bodhisattva Kannon, about a foot in height, which had been worshipped in secret as the Virgin Mary by Japanese Hidden Christians during their long, long years of persecution.

"How rare are such statues," asked Akutagawa, turning the figure over in his hands, examining it intently. "Are they hard to come by?"

Nagami shook his head. "White statues such as this are relatively common. More scarce are the ones carved in black ebony."

"Really," said Akutagawa, looking up from the figure. "There were black robed Marys?"

Nagami nodded. "Oh, yes. In fact, I have seen one, but only once. It belongs to the family of a friend of mine from university. It was quite beautiful, about the same height as this one, the body carved from black ivory but with a face of white ivory and a touch of red coral on the lips. And the necklace which hung around its neck was styled after a Christian rosary with a cross, and the cross itself was inlaid with gold and blue shells."

"Incredible," exclaimed Akutagawa. "It sounds most exquisite."

"Exquisite indeed," said Nagami. "Yet, according to my friend, there was a strange legend associated with this particular black robed Mary."

"How fascinating," said Akutagawa. "In what way strange?"

Nagami lit his pipe, then said, "Well, according to my friend, and he is not a man prone to telling supernatural tales, the power of this particular black robed Mary worked in reverse, changing good fortune to bad."

"So it was cursed," said Akutagawa, putting down the white porcelain Mary and picking up a cigarette. "Please do tell . . ."

Nagami smiled, then said, "Well, I am no raconteur, and would feel somewhat embarrassed before a storyteller such as yourself . . ."

"Please," said Akutagawa. "You have already whetted my interest."

"Well then," said Nagami, "and if it will not bore you, according to my friend, before the black robed Mary came into the possession of his family, it had belonged to a wealthy family called Inugami who lived in Tochigi.

"For the Inugami family, the black robed Mary was no mere collector's piece; they worshipped her as a protective deity. But one autumn—in fact, the autumn following the summer in which the Black Ships of Commodore Perry had first appeared at Uraga, and so it must have been the autumn of the sixth year of Kaei, 1853—the youngest of the family, who was but eight years old, and its only son, and who was named Mosaku, contracted a severe case of measles. Having lost both their parents in a smallpox epidemic a few years earlier, this boy and his elder sister Oei had been raised by their grandmother, who was already over seventy years old. Naturally, the grandmother was most distressed by the boy's condition, which did not improve at all, despite the best efforts of the family doctor. And within a week, the boy's condition had become so critical that it seemed he might not survive for many more days and would surely pass away.

"Late one night, when Oei was asleep, her grandmother suddenly came to her room, and woke and dressed her. Still half asleep, Oei was taken by her grandmother down the hallway and out of the house. They walked to a dark earthen storehouse in the garden. In the storehouse was a small shrine made of white wood. The old woman opened the shrine door with a key. Inside the shrine, reflected in dim candlelight, Oei saw the black image of a Maria Kannon standing behind a heavy brocade veil. Overwhelmed by the ominous atmosphere of the dark and silent earthen room, Oei clutched the sleeve of her grandmother and began to sob. But the old woman ignored her tears, knelt before the image of the black robed Mary, crossed her forehead and her chest, and began to pray intently in words unknown to Oei.

"After a while, the old woman stopped her prayers. She picked up Oei, soothed her and had her kneel beside her, then began to make a vow to the black image in a language Oei understood: 'Our Holy Virgin Mary, please listen to my prayers. This girl and her younger brother, Mosaku, are the only ones upon whom I can rely in this transient life. My granddaughter, Oei, is still too young to take a husband to look after my family. If something happens to my grandson, my family, the Inugami, will have no male heir. Please protect the life of Mosaku so that no misfortune will fall on him. But if my faith is not strong enough for such a wish, then at least let him live until my own life ends. As I am old, it won't be long before I give up my soul to the Heavenly Lord. But may Oei have become old enough to marry by then. So please render us your mercy, please stay the sword of the Angel of Death, let it not touch my grandson before my eyes are closed forever.'

"Thus, her head bowed, the old woman earnestly prayed. And as her grandmother finished the last words of her prayer, Oei timidly looked up at the black image and now felt it smiling slightly. With a small cry, Oei again clutched at the sleeves of her grandmother in fear. But the old woman seemed quite satisfied, and stroked Oei's back and said, 'Let us go now. I am sure Our Holy Virgin Mary has heard this wretched woman's prayer.'

"The following day, as if the vow of the old woman had been fulfilled, the boy's condition improved; his fever went down and he finally awoke from his coma. Seeing this, the grandmother was filled with an indescribable joy; Oei would never forget her tearful, joyous face that day.

"Now, as her grandson calmly slept, the exhausted old woman lay down herself in the next room and finally closed her eyes to rest.

Beside her, Oei quietly played with marbles, occasionally glancing up at her peaceful grandmother. But then, about an hour later, the old maid who was attending to the boy quietly opened the sliding door and asked, 'Miss Oei, will you please wake your grandmother for a moment now?'

"Oei went over to her grandmother and gently shook her shoulders a few times, calling to her, 'Wake up, Grandma, wake up.' But the old woman did not move, would not be stirred from her sleep. Concerned, the maid returned to the room, looked at the grandmother, and in a shocked and tearful voice cried, 'Oh, Madam Inugami, Madam Inugami!'

"But the old woman remained still, slight purple shadows beneath her closed eyes. Now Oei heard another maid hastily open the door and, as she looked down at the old woman, in a trembling voice the maid said, 'Madam, your grandson . . .'

"Oei knew something terrible must be happening to her little brother. But her grandmother's eyes were still closed, would not open, the two maids tearfully crying by her pillow, wailing now.

"And sure enough, a few moments later, Oei's young brother took his last breath; it seemed the black robed Mary had fulfilled the prayer of the grandmother by preventing the grandson from dying, as long as she lived."

Nagami stopped speaking now, struck a match and relit his pipe, then looked across the table at his guest.

Akutagawa was staring intently at the white porcelain Maria Kannon on the table before him. Now he turned away to look up at Nagami. "And what became of the granddaughter, Oei?"

"She was adopted into the family of a distant relative," said Nagami. "And so according to my friend, her branch of the Inugami family was thus ended. Furthermore, it is said that the only son of the adopted family, and to whom Oei was betrothed, later died in the Battle of Utsunomiya Castle."

"And so how, then, did the family of your friend come upon the black robed Mary," asked Akutagawa, "and hear its legend?"

"That was my question, too," said Nagami. "Tashiro-kun, my friend, told me that his father, who was a noted collector of antiques and relics, bought the statue from a curiosity shop close to the Futarayama Shrine while on business in Utsunomiya. However, the proprietor of the shop would only sell the statue to him after first ascertaining that Tashiro's father was not a follower of the 'Mary Faith,' as the shopkeeper said, while warning him of its curse and the story associated with this particular black robed Mary."

"It is a most fascinating, mysterious and sad tale," said Akutagawa. "Thank you for sharing it with me. And I confess, I am most envious you saw the statue for yourself, held it in your hand and looked upon its face."

"I did indeed," said Nagami. "And I must say, beautiful though she was, this Mary wore a most disdainful, almost scornful smile."

Akutagawa nodded. "I can imagine."

"Her expression certainly added to the veracity of the tale," said Nagami. "At least to my mind. And I am also reminded now of one final detail which might be of interest to you: on the base of the stand on which this black robed Mary stood, there was an inscription in Latin which I still recall—

"*DESINE FATA DEUM FLECTI SPERARE PRECANDO.*"

There was a tearful look upon the face of Akutagawa now as he whispered, "Do not expect your prayer will change what God has already ordained."

*

How long wilt thou forget me, O LORD? For ever? How long wilt thou hide thy face from me?

How long shall I take counsel in my soul, having sorrow in my heart daily? How long shalt mine enemy be exalted over me?

Consider and hear me, O LORD my God: lighten my eyes, lest I sleep the sleep of death;

Lest mine enemy say, I have prevailed against him; and those that trouble me rejoice when I am moved.

But I have trusted in thy mercy; my heart shall rejoice in thy salvation.

I will sing unto the LORD, because he hath dealt bountifully with me.

*

At his desk in his study, upstairs in the wood-framed "Latin Seminary," in the grounds of the Ōura Catholic Church, Father Léon Gracy opened his eyes and stared out of the window at the sky above, then the bay below, and he sighed. He did not like this place like he used to like this place, did not love this place like he used to love this place. He knew it was still God's place, on God's earth still; he knew he had been sent here to do God's work, had come here to spread God's word. To bring education, to give instruction; to train Japanese priests to spread God's word. His words of love, His words of peace, His words of mercy, His words of forgiveness. He had joined the Société des Missions Étrangères de Paris to spread those words, His words; he had prayed to be sent here to do this work, His work. And God had heard his prayers, and God had answered his prayers. More than twenty years ago now, he first arrived in Japan. He had studied Japanese in Kagoshima, he had ministered in Ōita, then he had come here to Nagasaki, to this church and its seminary, and later become the headmaster of this seminary. Doing God's work, spreading God's word—His words of love and words of peace, His words of mercy and of forgiveness—in God's places, on God's earth.

But all God's places across God's earth had changed, they had fallen; fallen so very, very far. It was said—but by whom and to whom, who knew—that there were more believers at the end of the war than at its beginning, both in and out of uniform. Thanks to *Dieu et patrie*, thanks to *la foi patriotique*: if not a Holy War, if not a Holy Crusade, then a Just War, a Just Crusade, they said, fighting to halt the age-old Teutonic barbarism, fighting to end all wars, so they said. But for three years, those three years he had been conscripted, those three years he had served, he had seen only Catastrophe, only the suicide of civilised Europe; Catholic killing Catholic, Christian killing Christian, believer killing believer, man killing man, over and over, again and again, killing and killing; all the horror he had seen, all the horror he had witnessed, he could not forget, he could not forgive.

At his desk in his study, Father Léon Gracy turned again to stare again, as he always turned to stare again, at the framed portrait of Father Bernard-Thadée Petitjean, a man he had never met, but a man he felt he had once known, the man who had been his inspiration as a child, the man who had been his motivation in joining the Société des Missions Étrangères. In different times, in a different world. Now Father Léon Gracy turned to stare at the other portrait on his desk: a man in a different uniform, a man he had met, a man he had known, a man he had loved; a young man who had been cut down in that uniform, slaughtered and killed in the blood and the mud of Verdun, a brother priest Philippe, but just one brother of so many, many brothers, so many, many dead; cut down, slaughtered and killed, forever lost, while he lived and breathed here, here in this place, God's place on God's earth; God's earth that had eaten, had swallowed and taken so many—

How long wilt thou forget me, O LORD? For ever?

With tears in his eyes, with sorrow in his heart, Father Léon Gracy looked up at the wall, at the cross on the wall—

How long wilt thou hide thy face from me?

Our Lord, Father Philippe and Father Petitjean: every day, every hour, this trinity watched over him, smiled down at him, but every day, every hour, he knew he failed them, every day, every hour, he failed and betrayed them; unable to forget, unable to forgive, his eyes dark, he slept—

The sleep of death; in the sleep of death . . .

Unable to forgive, unable to love.

With his eyes red, his shoulders low, Father Léon Gracy rose from his desk and left his study, and with a melancholy gait, his robes trailing in the dust, he walked from the seminary out to the church and up its steps.

Inside, the building was as dark and as empty as ever, the glass and the cross dull and hidden. Only for Masses on Sundays or on holy days was the building ever lit and full, but most of the parishioners and attendees were Europeans or Americans, prominent businessmen or government officials; the only Japanese who ever came were the wives of these men.

Father Léon Gracy walked down the aisle towards the altar and the cross, and there, sat in a pew on the right, before the tomb of Father Petitjean and the statue of the Holy Mother and Child, he saw a young Japanese man, dressed in a Western suit, seemingly lost in thought.

"*Konnichi-wa*," said Father Léon Gracy.

The young man turned to Father Gracy, bowed his head slightly, smiled and said, "Good afternoon, Father."

"Good afternoon," said Father Gracy. "I do not wish to disturb you, however if there is anything I can help you with, I will be here."

"Thank you," replied the young man. "Actually, and please forgive my ignorance as I am a visitor from Tokyo, but is this the place where the hidden, underground Christians first revealed themselves to Father Petitjean?"

"Yes," said Father Gracy. "According to the letter he wrote the next day, Father Petitjean came across a group of twelve or fifteen

Japanese men, women and children standing outside the church—this was very soon after it had been erected in 1865—and when he opened the door to the church, they followed him inside. He came to this spot, or one very near, and then, when he began to pray the Our Father, an elderly lady named Isaberina Yuri Sugimoto, placing her hand upon her heart, said to Father Petitjean in a whisper, The heart of all those present is the same as yours . . ."

"The Miracle of Ōura," said the young man.

"Indeed," said Father Gracy. "After some two hundred and fifty years of isolation, it truly was a miracle."

"But forgive me," said the young man again, "for in this miracle were not the seeds of a tragedy already sown? When one reads of the persecutions and deaths that followed, what we call the *kuzure*, or the Fourth Collapse? Sincerely, Father, should these Christians not have stayed hidden?"

Father Gracy stared down upon this young Japanese man in his Western suit, seated in the pew, and smiled and said, "May I sit with you a while?"

"Of course," said the young man. "Please . . ."

Father Gracy sat down beside the young man, before the tomb of Father Petitjean and the statue of the Holy Mother and Child, and said, "Indeed, what you say is true. The *Urakami Yonban Kuzure* was most severe. Many of the once hidden Christians were tortured, and almost three and a half thousand were sent into exile and forced labour, and it is said at least six hundred of them died. Indeed, it was a tragedy. But that very tragedy, those persecutions and exiles, so shocked the world that the Meiji government was forced to repeal the ban on religious freedom, a ban that had stood for over two and a half centuries. May I ask, have you been to Urakami?"

"Not yet," said the young man. "I hope to go tomorrow."

Father Gracy smiled again. "That's good, that's good. For when you visit the magnificent new church at Urakami, one of the grandest churches in the whole of East Asia, I hope you will see, I hope you will feel the persecution the Urakami Christians endured, the suffering they bore, was not in vain."

"I'm sure," said the young man, his eyes fixed upon the statue of the Holy Mother and Child, and then started to say, "But . . ."

"Please," said Father Gracy. "Please, do go on . . ."

"Well," said the young man, "I have read that some of the so-called Hidden Christians are still not yet reconciled to the Church; that the beliefs and practices they had followed during their long time underground had become heretical, that they had veered from the doctrine of the established Church in Rome, and they are still now reluctant to renounce these beliefs."

"For some," said Father Gracy, "there has been a schism, yes."

"I am very interested in the history and stories of the Christian faith in my country," said the young man. "And I have read and collected many such stories and tales. But then I am often left feeling that the entire history of the Christian faith in Japan is one of a series of misunderstandings . . ."

"Misunderstandings," asked Father Gracy. "In what way?"

"A misunderstanding of God, the very meaning of God."

Father Gracy glanced at the young man beside him in the pew, then turned his face back, back towards the tomb of Father Petitjean, as he asked, "Which particular stories and tales are you thinking of . . . ?"

"Well," said the young man, "and only if you have the time, there is one story which might serve to illustrate my point."

"I have the time," said Father Gracy. "And I, too, am interested in the stories of our faith in Japan, and have read and am familiar with a great many of them. Which story do you have in mind?"

"The Faith of Genta," said the young man.

Father Gracy, his eyes still fixed upon the tomb of Father Petitjean, shook his head and said, "I don't know this story. Please . . ."

"Well, this happened in a time of persecution," began the young man. "And happened near to here. One day, on the banks of the Urakami River, close to its mouth by the bay and the sea, an old woman found a baby boy, abandoned in a bamboo basket, hidden in the tall reeds. The old woman was a servant in the house of the head of the village of Urakami, a man named Saburōji, and she took the baby in its basket back to her master's house. Her master and his wife had many children of their own, and so had no need for an extra mouth to feed, an extra mouth whose hands could not yet work for its food. Yet the old woman had been a good and faithful servant, tending to the master since he was himself a child, then welcoming his wife, helping to raise their children as though they were her own, for the old woman had never married, and so had no children of her own. And so, seeing the old woman taking pity on this baby in its basket, the master and his wife took pity on their servant, letting the woman keep the baby boy to care for as her own. With tears of joy, the old woman thanked the master and his wife, named the baby boy Genta, and she raised the baby into boyhood . . .

"But when Genta was but seven years old, the old woman passed away. The master and his wife consoled the child, let him continue to live in their house, in the room he had shared with his adopted mother, allowing him to become one of their servants, with chores and with duties. The work and life of Genta was hard and tough, in truth not much more than that of a cow or a horse. But Genta never complained, never shirked, ever attentive to his chores, ever diligent in his duties, a light in his eyes and a smile on his lips. And on the rare occasions when he was allowed time off from his chores and his duties, Genta would first tend to the grave of his adopted mother, bringing her flowers and watering her stone, then wander along the banks of the river, down among the reeds, down to the mouth, to stare at the sea and watch the waves, with a light in his eyes and a smile on his lips.

"But one such day, when Genta was in his fifteenth year, and had tended to the grave of his adopted mother and had gone to wander down by the sea, a great and sudden typhoon struck the region and the village, lifting the roofs from the houses, flattening the crops in the field, bursting the sides of the river, drowning the reeds on its banks. And after the storm had passed, after the floods had subsided, and after the master had had the servants search and search, there was no trace of Genta. It was assumed he had been washed out to sea, believed drowned under its waves.

"But then, after forty days and forty nights, Genta returned to the house of his master. His clothes were but rags, his hair matted with dirt, and on his forehead was a mark in mud, a Christian cross. Genta was brought before his master and asked to account for his disappearance and reappearance. And with that familiar light in his eyes, that same smile upon his lips, but with a voice much changed from his voice of old, now calm and dignified, he said, When I wandered along the banks, through the reeds, down to the beach and the sea, I came upon a red-haired stranger. He told me many things about this world and about the next; he took away my old name, he gave me a new name. Then he led me down to the water's edge and held me down beneath the waves, as the storm raged up above and the waters rose about me. And then I was released, and when I came back up above the waves and felt the air flowing through my lungs, I knew I felt the breath of God Himself.

"The master had been sad when he believed the boy had drowned and happy when Genta had returned alive to his house. He had listened in silence to the tale the boy told, but now he stared at the mark in mud upon his forehead and asked, What new name did this red-haired stranger give you?

"And the boy said, Yaso."

In the dark and empty church, its cross dull and hidden, Father Gracy turned abruptly to the young man telling him this tale and said, "Yaso?"

"Yes," said the young man. "Yaso, our old word for Jesus."

Father Gracy nodded and said, "I know. Please go on . . ."

"As I have said," continued the young man, "this happened during a time of persecution, the Christian faith forbidden and severely punished. And so the master was most afraid. He had the servants confine the boy to the stables while he thought what best to do, for he was confused and torn. True, the boy was but a servant, yet a good and faithful servant. Perhaps he had been driven mad by fear in the storm, then plagued by lack of food and water. Now he had returned, and with food and with water he might yet be restored, returned to his old self, the good and loyal servant boy named Genta. And so the master decided to wait a while, but he strictly admonished the servants of his house to say nothing of the boy's return or of the tale he had told.

"But people talk, and the servants talked, and so word soon spread of the boy and the tale he had told. And one day the word reached a village, a village where the folk still secretly followed the Christian faith. Despite the danger, despite the risk, the elders of the village decided they had to see this boy for themselves, to hear his tale for themselves. And so one night, under cover of its darkness, they sent three of their number down to the house of Saburōji, to sneak into the stables. There they found the boy, there they heard his tale, heard him say his name, a light in his eyes, a smile on his lips, Yaso.

"These hidden Christians were shocked, these secret Christians confused, and they asked the boy, How can you be Yaso?

"I am the son of God, I am the child of Mary, said the boy. For we are all the sons of God, we are all the children of Mary.

"But these Christians were appalled, these Christians were angry, and they said, This is blasphemy, this is heresy. You are no son of God, you are no child of Mary. You are a blasphemer, you are a heretic. And these Christians left the boy in the stable, and these Christians journeyed on to Nagasaki. There they sought out the magistrate, there they spoke to the magistrate, never mentioning their own beliefs, never revealing their own faith, speaking only of the boy, telling only of his tale.

"Immediately, the magistrate dispatched his officers to the house of Saburōji in Urakami. The magistrate had his officers arrest the entire household and bring them to the prison in Nagasaki.

"Now Saburōji had been on good terms with the magistrate for many years. He had always paid his taxes on time, he had never protested whenever they were raised. And so when Saburōji told his story, the magistrate was inclined to believe him, and when Saburōji and his household all trampled and spat upon the face of Christ, the magistrate released them.

"But there still remained the matter of the boy who said his name was Yaso, a matter that was not so easy to resolve.

"The boy was brought before the magistrate, and the boy repeated his tale to the magistrate. He did not change his story, he did not deny his name. And the magistrate listened in silence, then the magistrate thought for a while. For the magistrate was a learned man, and not an impulsive man. He was not from Nagasaki; he had been born in Edo. There he had been schooled in the Law, and there he had studied the Christian heresy. And the Law was very clear: all heretics were to be put to death by crucifixion. That was the Law.

"Now the magistrate asked the boy, After you had been given your new name, and after you had come back up above the waves, what then became of this red-haired stranger of whom you speak?

"With that familiar light in his eyes, with that same smile upon his lips, the boy said, He walked upon the waters, out across the sea.

"And so you have not seen this stranger since, asked the magistrate.

"No, said the boy. But he told me he will return.

"Really, said the magistrate, and did he tell you when?

"Yes, said the boy. He will return at the end.

"At the end, repeated the magistrate. Well, unless you renounce your heretical beliefs, unless you trample upon the face of Christ, then your own end is close at hand, you realise that, do you not?

"With the light in his eyes, with the smile on his lips, the boy said, I do.

"And you are prepared then to accept your fate, your death?

"Yes, said the boy. I am."

Beside the young man in the pew, in the dark and empty church, Father Gracy felt his shoulders sag and his eyes moisten as he stared through the dark at the cross hidden in the shadows by the altar.

"Now as I have already said," continued the young man, "the magistrate was a learned man, a man who had studied the Christian heresy. And though the Law clearly stated that all heretics had to die by crucifixion, the magistrate now decided upon a different fate for the boy who called himself Yaso: there would be no repetition, there would be no crucifixion.

"Late that afternoon at low tide, while the people of Nagasaki and Urakami gathered to watch from the shore, the magistrate and his officers led the boy down onto the beach, close to the mouth of the Urakami River. There the officers began to dig a hole in the sand, to plant a tree trunk in the hole, to tie the boy to the trunk. But the boy stopped them, saying, There is no need for you to toil. For I will stand here and wait upon the beach, and wait for Him to come again, for Him to return again for me.

"The officers looked at the magistrate. The magistrate stared at the boy. The boy smiled, and the magistrate nodded, So be it.

"And the magistrate and his officers left the boy standing on the beach, the water already lapping at his feet, his hands clasped together, his face turned to the sky, a light in his eyes and a smile on his lips.

"In the deepening dusk, the magistrate took his seat before the people of Nagasaki and Urakami, his eyes fixed upon the boy on the beach as wave by wave the tide came in, the wind in the reeds, the wind on the water.

"One *sun*, one *shaku*, the tide came in, the water came in, over the beach and over the boy, his ankles then his shins, his knees then his thighs, over his waist and up to his chest, the boy never moving, his face never turning, turned to the sky, the darkening sky, the rising waters and the endless waves, up to his neck and over his chin, into his mouth and through his hair, over his hair and over his head, the boy now under the water, the boy now under the waves, the boy drowned, the boy dead.

"Early the next morning at low tide, the officers of the magistrate found the body of the boy washed up among the tall reeds, his hands still clasped together, his eyes still open, a smile upon his lips. But, it is said, when they moved his body, when they raised it from the reeds, a delicate fragrance filled the air and his mouth fell open. And in the mouth of the boy, a lily bloomed. So ends the story of the Faith of Genta, the Yaso of Nagasaki."

For a long, long time, in the dark and empty church, Father Gracy did not speak. Then with the trails of tears still wet upon his face, he turned to the young man sat beside him in the pew. There were tears in the eyes of the young man, too, as Father Gracy said, "*Merci*. Thank you."

"You are welcome," said the young man. "Of all the tales of martyrs in Japan, this one, this life of this Holy Fool, is my favourite story."

Father Gracy nodded, then asked, "And why is that?"

"I was born in these modern times," replied the young man, hesitantly. "But I feel I can do no work of any lasting worth. Day and night, I just live a desultory and decadent life, standing on the beach, yet then running from the waves, always wanting to believe, yet never having faith . . ."

Father Léon Gracy nodded again, then smiled sadly and said, "Well, and though it can be of little comfort, you are not alone. For maybe in all our mistakes and in all our misunderstandings, we are all just running from the waves, all then just hiding and hidden, yet still wanting to believe, still waiting to have faith. And so in the end, perhaps the wanting and the waiting, perhaps that is belief, that is faith. Just wanting, just waiting—

"The most we can hope for, the very most we deserve."

*

Arrived Nagasaki, hosted by Mr. Nagami, who is showing us around. Already quite impressed by what a good place Nagasaki is. Very good mixture of Chinese and Western tastes. There are a lot of foreigners and Chinese. Mostly, it is stone-paved, with stone bridges in the Chinese style. There are three Roman Catholic Temples. All of them are quite grand. Yesterday, I visited one of them and talked with a French priest for almost the entire afternoon. On the way back, I strolled around the town and found a surprisingly good bargain which I will send to you.

Postcard from Akutagawa to his wife Fumi,
in Tabata, Tokyo, dated May 7, 1919

*

At his desk in his office at the Nagasaki Prefectural Hospital, Mokichi Saitō, chief of the psychiatric division, chairman of the Department of Psychiatry at the Nagasaki School of Medicine, counselling physician to the Nagasaki First Aid Station, and renowned tanka poet, closed his eyes. He was exhausted and he was depressed; exhausted by his workload, depressed by this place. And now he was trapped here, trapped here because of Ishida.

Noburo Ishida had graduated from Tokyo Imperial University Medical School three years ahead of Mokichi. The most brilliant psychiatrist of their generation, Ishida had published the standard textbook on psychiatric disorders. Not only that, Ishida had also translated *Don Quixote* and, under the pen name of Hamatorō Ojima, written short stories and novels of his own. In January 1918, Ishida had left for the United States to study the treatment of schizophrenia with Adolf Meyer at the Johns Hopkins Hospital in Baltimore. For the duration of Ishida's studies in America, Mokichi had agreed to temporarily cover for him in Nagasaki. However, things had not gone as planned; in fact, things had gone most awry.

In Baltimore, Ishida had developed schizophrenic symptoms himself, suffering from delusions and auditory hallucinations. He believed he had fallen in love with the head nurse, but then believed he was caught in a "love triangle" with the nurse and a German doctor named Wolf. Early on the morning of the twenty-first of December last year, Ishida hunted down and shot and killed Dr. George V. Wolf. The Baltimore police caught and arrested Ishida, but there were then conflicting opinions as to his sanity. Now Ishida was incarcerated in a Baltimore prison, and now Mokichi was trapped in a prison of his own, here in Nagasaki.

There was a knock on his door. Mokichi opened his eyes, rubbed his face, looked at his watch and sighed; he had forgotten, forgotten he had agreed to this visit from Mr. Nagami and his two celebrated guests from Tokyo.

There was a second knock now. Mokichi stood up behind his desk and called out, "Yes. Please come in."

Nagami opened the door, leading in his two guests, bowing and excusing the interruption, thanking Mokichi for his time, introducing his guests—

"This is Mr. Kan Kikuchi, or Hiroshi Kikuchi, as he prefers, and Mr. Ryūnosuke Akutagawa," said Nagami, as the two young men from Tokyo bowed, apologising for the intrusion, but simply honoured to meet Mokichi.

Mokichi came out from behind his desk, dismissed their apologies and any honour they felt, and offered the three of them seats. Mokichi then left his visitors sitting silently in his office, walked across the corridor and asked one of his staff to bring in tea. Mokichi then walked back into his office, sat back down behind his desk, looked across his piles of work at Nagami and his two celebrated guests from Tokyo, both in their fashionable Western suits, one rather plump and bespectacled, the other rather gaunt and foppish, and Mokichi wondered what on earth to say to these two Literary Young Turks.

The embarrassed silence lasted until the plump Kikuchi said again, "It really is the greatest of privileges to meet you, Sensei."

"It truly is," agreed the gaunt Akutagawa.

"Surely," said Mokichi, but with a sigh he somehow could not suppress, "surely any man should be grateful and impressed to be able to welcome two men such as yourselves, two of our brightest young literary stars."

"Well," said Nagami, "since arriving here in Nagasaki, they have talked of little else but the prospect of meeting you, Sensei."

Mokichi smiled a somewhat sardonic and sceptical smile, and said, "You flatter me. I am sure I am the very least this place has to offer. And so, gentlemen, I trust your host has been giving you a full and thorough tour."

"He has indeed," said Kikuchi. "Why, only today we have visited so many stimulating places. Actually, we began our day in the Nagasaki Prefectural Library, where, by chance, sheer chance, we met Mr. Kunio Yanagita."

"Ah, yes," said Mokichi. "My wife mentioned he was here."

"How is your wife," asked Nagami. "I trust she is well."

"I presume so," said Mokichi. "She left for Tokyo this morning."

There was another silence in the office now, a silence only broken by the arrival of the tea and Mokichi finally asking, "How was the esteemed folklorist?"

"Most charming," said Akutagawa, "and very friendly."

Mokichi looked across his desk at this gaunt and foppish young star, smiled, raised an eyebrow, then turned to Kikuchi and asked, "And where then?"

"Where have we not visited," laughed Kikuchi. "The temples of Sōfukuji, Daionji and Kōfukuji, the churches of Urakami and Nakamichi . . ."

"Mr. Akutagawa is most interested in and taken with the Christian history of the city and its legacy, Sensei," said Nagami.

"I am not surprised," said Mokichi, but with deliberate disdain.

Akutagawa now sat forward in his seat, looked across the desk piled high with papers and with work, and stared at Mokichi as he said, sincerely said, "Sensei, I will never forget the night I first read the opening of *Shakkō*, the first three tanka of your sequence—*running and running, along this dark road, and my unbearable remorse, dark, dark, running too / that faint firefly glow, of itself, out of itself, I crush on my dark road / nothing, nothing to be done, the light's gone out, and in my palm this crushed firefly*—I was living in Shinjuku; it was the year after the death of the Emperor, the suicides of General Nogi and his wife, and I was blind, I was but a blind youth. But when I read *Shakkō*, when I read your tanka, I was no longer blind, no longer but a blind youth, for I could see, I could see the light of poetry."

There was silence again; silence while Mokichi bowed his head, silence until Mokichi said, "Thank you, sincerely, Akutagawa-sensei. Forgive me; I am in a wretched mood, I know. In truth, I have not found this city as conducive as I had hoped, either for my research or for my poetry. Maybe you've all heard that Hakushū-sensei has declared he will retire from writing tanka. And though his declaration fills me with great regret, at least I know he can continue to display his power in other forms of poetry or prose. Sadly, that is not the case with me. But I do not need to publicly declare an end to my tanka; as any reader can sense, my tanka is dying by itself, like a demented person who dies quietly and leaves no will."

133

"No," protested Kikuchi. "You cannot say that, please do not say that, Sensei! Why, only on the train from Tokyo, Akutagawa and I were quoting your last lines from *Aratama*, your tanka on first arriving here in Nagasaki: *At daybreak the great steam horn sounds from the ship, its echo lingering: the mountains arrayed* . . . Such poignancy, such . . ."

"Such a long time ago now, it seems," said Mokichi. "Yet it's not even been two years. I fear I have been too long in this place."

And now there was silence again, another silence, a silence, long and strained, until Kikuchi said, "We were all so very shocked by the news of Dr. Ishida, the incident, the murder, a tragedy . . ."

"Yes," said Mokichi. "Indeed."

"It almost defies belief . . ."

"Yes," said Mokichi again.

"Is there any news from America," asked Nagami. "Any further developments?"

Mokichi sighed, shook his head, then said, "As you may already know, the Japanese Psychiatric Association are seeking to have Ishida extradited, so that he can be cared for and treated here. However, even if we are successful, I fear it will be a long, drawn-out affair. And so, for now, Ishida remains in a prison in Baltimore."

Akutagawa now sighed, too, then said, "Perhaps it is something about the place, something about Baltimore. After all, it is the place where Edgar Poe lost his mind and went insane."

"Indeed," said Mokichi.

"Strangely, I was already reminded of the last hours of Poe," continued Akutagawa, "when I first read the textbook by Ishida-sensei, in which he writes of how the diseases of the mind reduce a man to but a lump of flesh, plagued by delusions, and the doctor concludes it is surely better to die than to stay alive in such a state of madness and insanity. It is reported that when Mr. Poe was taken into the Washington University Hospital in Baltimore and asked about his friends, he replied, My best friend would be the man who gave me a pistol that I might blow my brains out . . ."

Again, Mokichi looked across his desk at this gaunt, intense and haunted man, and asked, "So you are a student of psychiatry then, Mr. Akutagawa?"

"Not a student," said Akutagawa, with a smile and a shake of his head. "But I am interested and do try to read the latest papers . . ."

"Is there a particular reason for your interest?"

"My mother," said Akutagawa. "She went insane."

"I see," said Mokichi. "I am sorry."

"And so, of course, I am interested in the hereditary nature of insanity, and naturally fearful. But," said Akutagawa now, and with a smile again, but a different smile, lonesome and resigned, "whether one is the child of a madwoman or not, as Sōseki-sensei wrote in *Kōjin*, how can any one of us escape this world of ours, except through faith, madness or death . . . ?"

"Indeed," said Mokichi, abruptly arising from his chair and desk, turning to the window, staring through the glass, the big crane of the Mitsubishi shipyard visible through the trees, the steam horn of the Shanghai liner sounding in the port. And then, his back to his visitors still, Mokichi sighed and said, "It seems no matter where one goes, no matter where one hides, whether in the West or East, America or Japan, Nagasaki or Tokyo, it seems that trinity of choices remain our only exits . . ."

In the Nagasaki Prefectural Hospital, in the heavy silence of this office, within this last and final silence, almost in a whisper now, Akutagawa said, "In the end, as Poe said, at the very end, *Lord, help my soul.*"

*

In nineteen hundred and nineteen, in the eighth year of Taishō, I am waiting; waiting at the station in Nagasaki, for the train back to Tokyo, waiting on the train back to Tokyo, at the station back in Tokyo, waiting in the taxi back to Tabata, in the genkan *of my house, waiting in the hallway, in the bathroom, in the bedroom, in the study, waiting at my desk, among my books, among my papers, I'm waiting, I am waiting; waiting to hear the wind through the reeds, waiting for the tide and waiting for the waves, waiting, just waiting, still waiting, always waiting, I'm waiting, I am waiting; waiting and longing, longing to feel the breath of God Himself . . .*

After the War, Before the War

"Master Peachling," called a pheasant, "Where are you going?"
"I'm going to the Land of the Demons," said Momotarō,
"to carry off all their treasures . . ."

Momotarō, the Peach Boy, a Japanese folk tale

1

The tide was high, the time was now, and with long strides, up the gangway, Ryūnosuke boarded the *Chikugo-maru* at Mojikō . . .

"I have no courage to go to China," Kume had declared at the Ueno Seiyoken to their gathered friends, at the farewell party, the big send-off—

The *Chikugo-maru* began moving, her engines turning, as Ryūnosuke marched out onto the upper deck and sat down in a wicker chair . . .

"But Mr. Akutagawa here, he has the courage. And he will be resolute and he will be strong. For he is great; he is the best of us!"

On the deck, in his chair, with a cigar in his hand and the wind through his hair, Ryūnosuke stared out across the ocean at the horizon . . .

"The Chinese were great in the past," Ton Satomi had told him. "It is unthinkable that these great people suddenly became so weak now. So when you visit China, don't look solely at China's greatness in the past; look for China's greatness today. Old China exerts itself like an old tree, but new China is striving to come up like young grass, like wild grass . . ."

"And forget about the uninformed Japanese guides," Jun'ichirō Tanizaki had added. "In my experience, the local Chinese are quite gentle, and I never saw any of them behaving badly. Only the soldiers present a threat; in the tumult of the Revolution, there are a great many in the cities, especially in Nanjing. And so find someone reliable and Chinese . . ."

In his chair, with his cigar, Ryūnosuke watched the white-capped waters off the coast now turn into the waves of the open sea . . .

How he had envied Tanizaki-sensei all his Chinese adventures; how he had begrudged Haruo Satō his Chinese trip; how he had begged the *Osaka Mainichi* to let him follow in their footsteps please, beseeching his editor to let him, too, walk on Chinese soil, please; a Japanese man with Chinese dreams, a Japanese child of Chinese books; raised by *Saiyūki*, schooled by *Suikoden*. With greedy eyes, in dim light. Nights not sleeping, nights spent reading. At his desk, in the toilet. On a train, in a street. Night after night, day after day. Dreaming and imagining, fierce warrior beauties and brave wild monks. The monstrous tiger of the Jinyang Pass, the battle flag proclaiming: "We Act on Heaven's Behalf." Battling with this imaginary cast, armed with his wooden sword. From then until now, reading, still reading; over and over, laughing and crying. Over and over, changing him, transforming him. Those Chinese books, his Chinese dreams. Then and still now, changing him, transforming him, then a toy sword, now a trembling pen: his own words, his own stories, inspired by China, in love with China—

His first inspiration, his first true love . . .

"Please just be sure to take good care of yourself," his wife had said, had pleaded at the station, on the platform, through the steam and through her tears. "Be careful what you eat, and what you drink. And be sure to rest, and not to worry about us, please . . ."

Bubbling now, churning now, the waves of the open sea were now hills of grey, smacking the sides of the ship, spraying the chairs on the deck, the hills of grey now mountains of black, drenching his jacket, dousing his cigar, he turned up his collar and sucked on a mint, churning and tossing, his stomach unstable, his head unhinged, his hands in his pockets, his back against the chair, tables tilting, men slipping, his back rigid, his eyes fixed, on the horizon, the rolling horizon, a little boat, a small tugboat, thin wisps of smoke, a trail of bravery, soon swallowed up, now lost at sea, his sea legs lost, his legs at sea, lurching this way, pitching that way, Ryūnosuke admitted defeat and went below, to his berth, on his bunk, the cabin still rolling, his stomach still turning, he glanced at the porthole, out of the porthole, the horizon now falling, the horizon now rising, rolling and turning, he looked away from the porthole, he looked down at his hands, with another roll, with another turn, books fell from the bunk, papers slid from the desk, a bigger roll and a bigger turn, the crash of porcelain dishes from the kitchen, the fall of wicker chairs up on the deck, he got up from his bunk, he clung to the wall, bile in his mouth, bile in the sink, he collapsed back on the bunk, another roll, another turn, he got back up from the bunk, half on his feet, back at the sink, more heaving, more bile, reaching for the wall, struggling to the bunk, with a final roll, with a final turn, all that he had dreamed of, all that he had longed for, falling and rising, the country he had dreamed of, the land he longed for, rolling and turning, falling and rising, mountains into hills, tossing and churning, hills into waves, churning now bubbling . . .

Out on the fresh deck, back in his damp chair. A crumpled cigarette in his hand, calm waters before his eyes; the sea with no memory, land on the horizon: the country he had dreamed of, this land he had longed for. Ryūnosuke lit the cigarette and Ryūnosuke waved to the land. It was the afternoon of March 30, 1921—

This is what you want, what you want.

2

Off the sea, up the river. Past the warehouses, the endless warehouses. The piles of lumber, the piles of metal. The docks and the foundries. The cotton mills and the shipyards. On stilts, the billboards. Promising curatives, touting cigarettes. Round the bend, towards the harbour. A line of warships, in grey and white. Cruisers and destroyers. Watchdogs at anchor, horses in their stalls. All the coloured flags, all the great powers. Their freighters and their mail steamers. Floating by, swimming along. Local *lorchas*, native junks. With bat-winged sails, with bright-painted eyes. Watching and waiting, waiting and waving; Ryūnosuke waving again, waving at the wharf, at his two old friends: Murata of the *Osaka Mainichi Shinbun* and Jones of United Press International, waving to Ryūnosuke, waiting for Ryūnosuke—

His first steps on Chinese soil. Engulfed by rickshaw pullers, overwhelmed by their stench as they screamed in the frightened faces of the disembarking passengers, grabbing onto Ryūnosuke by the sleeves of his coat. Now Jones barged between the pullers and their prey, and shouted over their din, "Stay close to us, Ryūnosuke, and walk quickly . . ."

Through the crowds and coolies, to a waiting line of horse-drawn carriages. But aboard their carriage, at the first crossroads, their horse careered into a brick wall, sending its cargo out of their seats and onto their knees. The driver beating and whipping the horse, its stubborn nose smack against the brick wall, its hind legs spastically dancing and violently kicking, rocking the carriage this way and that, worse than any waves at sea. But Jones simply smiled and said, "Welcome to Shanghai, Ryūnosuke."

Beaten into submission, or simply exhausted, the horse now backed away from the wall, and soon they were trotting along beside a river. So many barges, so many sampans, side by side, bow to bow and stern to stern, Ryūnosuke could not see the water. To their left, a railroad bridge carried luminous green trains. To their right, red brick buildings, three or four storeys tall. Beneath these buildings, Chinese and Westerners were walking briskly along the large, wide asphalt street, but yielding to their carriage at the signal from an Indian policeman in a red turban. First appalled by the ferocity of the rickshaw pullers and the violence of the horse-drawn carriage, now Ryūnosuke marvelled at this sudden order in a sea of chaos.

The carriage pulled up in front of a hotel. The driver already had his hand outstretched. Murata dropped a few cents into the open palm. However, the driver did not withdraw his hand. Spittle flew from the corners of his mouth as he yelled something over and over into all of their faces. Murata and Jones ignored the man, marching briskly through the hotel doors. Ryūnosuke glanced back, only to see the driver already back in his seat, coins in pocket and whip in hand. Ryūnosuke felt somehow cheated by the man's performance: *If he had not really cared, why make such a fuss?*

Inside the Dong-Ya Yangxing Hotel, Ryūnosuke had fresh worries. The deserted reception room was gloomy, yet gaudy.

Jones smiled again and said, "You know this was the very place where Kim Ok-kyun was assassinated? Shot through the window of his room . . ."

"I do not doubt it," began Ryūnosuke, but was interrupted by the sound of slippers loudly slapping on the floor and the sight of the Japanese proprietor, grandly dressed in Western clothes, exclaiming, "Welcome, gentlemen. Welcome, welcome . . ."

"I believe my colleague Sawamura has made a reservation for Mr. Akutagawa here," said Murata.

"Ah, yes," said the proprietor, bowing deeply. "It is a great honour to welcome the esteemed author, Akutagawa-sensei. Our very best room, reserved only for our most important guests, awaits you, sir. This way, please . . ."

Quickly, the proprietor ushered Ryūnosuke into a room just off the entranceway. A room of two beds and no chairs, the walls covered in soot, the drapes eaten by moths; Ryūnosuke knew this was the very room in which Kim Ok-kyun had opened a window for the very last time—

"I don't suppose you have any other rooms?"

The proprietor shook his head. "No, sir. We do not. This is our best room, and our only available one."

After initial apologies and excuses, then un-pleasantries and threats, the party of three found themselves back out on the street—

Jones smiled and said, "To the Banzaikan . . ."

. . . An hour later, Jones was waiting for Ryūnosuke in the lobby of the Banzaikan. "Chop-chop! The Shanghai night awaits . . ."

In Shepherd's restaurant, the waiters were Chinese, the patrons all foreign, Ryūnosuke the only customer with a yellow face. But the curry was much better than he had expected, the room most pleasant, and Jones as talkative as ever, if still as melancholic as he always was. "China is my hobby, but Japan is my passion."

"You must miss Japan then," said Ryūnosuke.

"Soon after I arrived," said Jones, "I was sitting in a café where one of the waitresses was Japanese. She was alone, in a chair, staring into space. I asked her, in Japanese, When did you come to Shanghai? She said, I just arrived yesterday. I said, You must miss Japan then? And I thought she was going to break down in tears as she said, Of course. I want to go home. I knew how she felt then, and that is still how I feel now. Awfully sentimental, I know . . ."

"Perhaps," said Ryūnosuke.

Jones laughed. "Come on, *sa-ikō* . . ."

Along a busy four-lane road, on the northern border of the French Concession, to the Café Parisien. Its dance hall was large and Western, blue and red lights flickering on and off in time to the music from the orchestra, just like in the dance halls of Asakusa. However, the music and the orchestra were far superior to Tokyo.

In a corner, at a table, Jones and Ryūnosuke ordered two cups of anisette. A Filipino girl dressed in bright red danced with a group of young Americans in fashionable suits. All happy, all laughing. An old British couple, both rather stout, came dancing their way.

Ryūnosuke smiled. "I believe it was Whitman who said the young are beautiful, but the beauty of the old is much more precious . . ."

"What utter rot," shouted Jones. "The old should not dance. And the lines by Whitman you should be quoting are: '*Through the laughter, dancing, dining, supping, of people / Inside of dresses and ornaments, inside of those wash'd and trimm'd faces / Behold a secret silent loathing and despair . . .*'"

"Ah yes, 'Song of the Open Road'?"

"Indeed," said Jones, and now he laughed again. "*Sa-ikō . . .*"

Outside the Café Parisien, the wide avenue was deserted now except for the rickshaw pullers. Ryūnosuke looked at his watch and asked, "Isn't there anywhere else we could get a drink round here?"

"Yes, yes," said Jones. "Just up here . . ."

Only the sound of their shoes echoing in the street of three- and four-storey buildings, looking up at the stars in the sky, then down at the occasional lights of the shops—a pawnshop with white walls, a placard for a doctor, a worn stucco wall covered with advertisements for Nanyang cigarettes—as Ryūnosuke said, "I'm awfully thirsty . . ."

"Patience," said Jones. "It's just up here . . ."

The café was far more low-class than the Parisien. Near the glass doorway, an old Chinese woman sold roses. In the middle of the room, three or four British sailors danced suggestively with heavily made-up women of the world. At the back, before a pink wall, a Chinese boy with his hair parted down the middle was banging away on a huge piano. In another corner, at another table, Jones and Ryūnosuke ordered two cold sodas—

"I feel as though I am looking at a newspaper with illustrations," declared Ryūnosuke. "And there is no doubt 'Shanghai' could be the only possible title for that illustration . . ."

Drunkenly, a group of six more sailors fell through the door, knocking the basket of roses out of the arms of the old Chinese woman and onto the floor, rushing into the middle of the room, frantically dancing with their shipmates and their women, crushing the flowers under their feet, stepping on the fingers of the old Chinese woman—

Jones stood up. "Let's go . . ."

"Yes," said Ryūnosuke.

Jones threw a coin in the old woman's basket as he said, "Let me tell you about life, Ryūnosuke . . ."

"Go on then," said Ryūnosuke. "What is life?"

Jones held open the door for Ryūnosuke, declaring, "Life . . . life is but an open road strewn with roses . . ."

Outside, rickshaw pullers descended on them from all four directions. Ryūnosuke felt a hand on his sleeve, pulling him back towards the café. The old flower woman was gripping his arm, her other hand stuck out like a beggar, spittle on her lips, shouting something over and over into his face.

"Madam, I feel truly sorry for your beautiful roses," Ryūnosuke told her. "Being trampled on by those drunken sailors, yes, but also being sold by such a greedy person as yourself . . ."

But Jones just laughed and, for the second time that day, said, "Welcome to Shanghai, Ryūnosuke. Welcome to China . . ."

"Thank you," said Ryūnosuke. "But I refuse to believe Shanghai is China."

"Perhaps not yet," said Jones. And then, suddenly, he sneezed.

3

Feeding charcoal to the fire, we speak of the foetus . . .

In the Banzaikan, in his room, in his bed, Ryūnosuke awoke suddenly from a terrible dream. A twisting knife under his ribcage, a stabbing pain in the side and lower part of his chest. Ryūnosuke sat up in bed and coughed. But the pain was real, the pain intense.

Spreading from his abdomen, crawling along his shoulders, tightening around his neck. Again Ryūnosuke coughed, again the pain. Shooting through his chest, digging into his shoulders. He was shivering, he was burning. Ryūnosuke collapsed back onto his pillow. It was cold, it was damp. Ryūnosuke lay sweating on his bed. He cursed his ill luck, he waited for the maid. And then the doctor. The diagnosis was dry pleurisy. Ryūnosuke would need to rest in the Satomi Hospital, on Miller Street, for two weeks, maybe longer. Dr. Satomi would personally administer a shot to him every other day.

Helpless and in despair, Ryūnosuke feared he would have to cancel his trip. He dictated a telegram to Osaka. The reply came quickly: *Get well soon, but take your time. Then continue as planned. We await your reports and travelogue as soon as you are fit again.*

On his back, in his bed. In the room, on the ward. Jones or Murata visited every day. From time to time, baskets of fruit and bunches of flowers from unknown admirers also arrived. After a while, in a row, by his head, there were so many cans of biscuits that Ryūnosuke did not know how he would ever dispose of them. Luckily, Jones always brought a voracious appetite with him. Thankfully, he also brought books: the stories of Friedrich de la Motte Fouqué, the essays of Herbert Giles and the poems of Eunice Tietjens.

Ryūnosuke was grateful for any distraction. His fever did not easily subside, his mind constantly stricken. In the daylight, he was certain sudden death was just around the corner. In the twilight, he took Calmotin to spare him the terrors of the night. But Ryūnosuke was always awake before the dawn, repeating the line from the poem by Wang Cihui: "Imbibing medicine with no effect, leads only to the recurrence of strange dreams . . ."

A vaudeville performance back in Tokyo; on the stage, a hanging screen, a magic lantern show, scenes from the Sino-Japanese War: the Battle of Weihaiwei, the sinking of the *Dingyuan*, Captain Higuchi directing his troops with one arm, protecting a Chinese baby in his other; all around him, a large crowd was cheering the Japanese flag, screaming at the tops of their lungs, "Banzai! Banzai! Banzai!" A hand grabbing his sleeve, the hand gripping his arm, squeezing it tighter and tighter, the hand of a woman, a woman he recognised; a woman he once lusted after, a woman he now loathed, the woman laughing now, the woman saying now, "*Sa-ikō . . .*"

Above his head, a Chinese lantern, through the window, a Chinese balustrade; in a courtyard, a locust tree, through the gates, a city burning; at a station, on the platform, a baby charred, its mother dead, its arms outstretched, its mouth open in a scream, a silent scream; that woman now, that same woman, smiling now. "See for yourself, Ryūnosuke. That's all that's left now. Nothing but a wilderness now . . ."

Half-light, grey-light, daylight on a hillside. That woman, that same woman, walking towards the gates of his house, his family house in Tabata, his wife darning some cloth at the *kotatsu*, the woman pausing by the stone lantern in the garden, his wife singing to their son, the woman sliding open the doors to his house, his wife kneeling before her in the *genkan*, the woman holding out her newborn baby towards his wife, his own son crying, the baby screaming, his wife crying, the woman screaming, his wife turning to look for him, on the futon, in a Chinese-patterned robe, on his chest a Bible open, his wife shaking him, his wife shouting at him, pleading with him, screaming at him, "Wake up, wake up . . ."

Feeding charcoal to the fire, we speak of the foetus . . .

For twenty-two nights, for twenty-three days. On his back, in his bed. In the room, on the ward. In the hospital, on Miller Street. Mongolian winds banging on his window, yellow dust blocking out the sun. The sun fighting back, the spring now arriving. His fever finally subsiding, the pain now relenting.

Dr. Satomi smiled and said, "Good news, Sensei. You are recovered. You are well enough to leave . . ."

4

Down a busy street, sitting in a carriage, driven at great speed. With Mr. Yosoki, the distinguished poet, as his guide. Ryūnosuke had no more time left to lose. The afternoon rainy and already dark. Through the showers, through the gloom, the passing shops—

Dark red roasted birds, hanging side by side, catching the lamplights, illuminating and reflecting, shop after shop, silverware and fruit, piles of bananas, piles of mangoes, hanging fish bladders and their bloody torsos, skinned pigs' carcasses, suspended hooves-down, on butchers' hooks, flesh-coloured grottos with vague dark recesses, sudden white clock faces, their hands all stopped, a shabby old wine shop with a worn old sign, written in the style of the poet Li Taibai.

A wider avenue now, then around another corner, and another, into another alleyway—

The heart of the Old City, the heart of the Real Shanghai, once encircled by walls, walls built to repel Japanese pirates, the Dwarf Bandits from across the sea, the walls now gone, the heart of the Old City now open, open and beating, beating and welcoming, welcoming him—

Out of their carriage, into a second alley. The pathway precarious, the cobblestones crumbling. Stores selling mah-jong sets, stores selling sandalwood goods, sign after sign, one on top of another, ordinary Chinese in long-sleeved black robes, bumping and banging into each other, but with no words of apology, yet no words of anger, no words at all.

At the end of the alleyway, the entrance to the Yu Gardens, and a large ornamental lake. The lake covered with thick green algae, carp hidden in its waters, crossed by the Bridge of Nine Turnings, lightning flashes zigzagging this way and that, built to confuse evil spirits, devils unable to turn corners, and in its centre the Huxinting Teahouse. Dilapidated, forlorn. A ruined stone wall around the lake, before the wall a Chinese man. In blue cotton clothes, his hair in a queue. Pissing into the lake, oblivious to the world; Chen Shufan could raise his rebellious banner in the wind, the Anglo-Japanese Alliance could come up for renewal again, nothing would disturb his nonchalant manner as the serene arc of his urine poured into the algae-choked lake before this famous old pavilion and its bridge. A scene beyond melancholia, a bitter symbol of this grand old country—

"Please observe," chuckled Yosoki. "What runs over these stones is Chinese piss and only Chinese piss . . ."

One whiff of the overpowering stench of urine in the late-afternoon air, and all spells were broken—

The Huxinting Teahouse was nothing more than the Huxinting Teahouse. And piss was only piss. One should not indulge in careless admiration, thought Ryūnosuke, on his tiptoes, tottering after Yosoki, past a blind old beggar sat on the ground; so many beggars, beggars everywhere. Dilettante beggars and hermit beggars, professional beggars and genuine beggars. Dressed in layers of old newspapers, licking their own rotting knees. On the cobblestones, before this beggar. His whole miserable life, written out in chalk, in calligraphy better than Ryūnosuke's own: *Aching, longing for something you can never, never truly, truly know. That must be Romanticism . . .*

"Come on," called Yosoki. "Come on. No time to be daydreaming with the beggars of Shanghai, Sensei . . ."

Back in another alleyway, lined with antique shops. Their Chinese proprietors, water pipes in mouths, among clutters of copper incense burners, clay horse figurines, *cloisonné* planters, dragon-head vases, jade paperweights, cabinets inlaid with mother-of-pearl, marble single-leaf screens, stuffed pheasants and frightful paintings by Chou

Ying. But at the end of this alleyway, there stood the Temple of the City God. The old focal point of the town, a venue for entertainers and a site for fairs. And here dwelled the City God—

The Lord of Old Shanghai.

Many years ago now, Ryūnosuke had bought a postcard of this legendary temple. He had used it as a bookmark, often preferring the picture to the words he was reading, dreaming of the day he would stand here before the City God—

Amidst the smoke and the noise, thousands of people, coming and going, paying their respects, offering up incense, burning paper money, bills of gold and silver, hanging from the ceiling, the beams and the pillars, covered in dirt and grease, the judges in Hell seated on both sides—pictures and statues evoking illustrations from *Strange Stories from a Chinese Studio* or *The New Jester of Qi*; magistrates from Hell who killed thieves who terrorised towns, clerks from the netherworld who broke elbows and chopped off heads—the red-faced City God himself towering, rising into the evening sky, before Ryūnosuke, Ryūnosuke entranced, Ryūnosuke overwhelmed, loath to leave here, reluctant to follow Yosoki—

Back out among the stalls; sugar-cane stock and buttons of shells, handkerchiefs and peanuts. Here among the crowds, a man in a bright suit with an amethyst necktie pin, an old woman in shoes only two inches long. All around him, Ryūnosuke could see characters from *The Plum in the Golden Vase* or *The Precious Mirror of Ranking Courtesans*. But Ryūnosuke could see no Du Fu, Yue Fei or Wang Yangming; the new China was not the old China of poetry and essays; rather, it was the cruel, greedy and obscene China of fiction . . .

Back along the lake, into the deserted teahouse, deafened by the sudden screeching of an invisible shower of birds, birdcages hanging from the beams of the ceiling. So many cages, so much shrieking, their eardrums bursting as they fled from this horrible teahouse of screaming birds, their hands still over their ears in the street, yet more birdcages hanging in every shop, as Yosoki shouted, "Please wait while I buy a bird for my children . . ."

Down a quiet side street, before a shop window, Ryūnosuke was looking at a picture of the famous opera singer Mei Lanfang, but thinking of Yosoki's children waiting for him to return home, and of his own son, waiting in their house, back in Tabata, back in Tokyo.

"Come on," said Yosoki again, a bird in a cage in his hand. "As the locals say, the sun sets on the old city and rises on the Concessions . . ."

5

Mr. Sawamura had arranged for Ryūnosuke to meet and interview a number of important Chinese intellectuals. Mr. Nishimoto, the editor of the weekly magazine *Shanhai*, had kindly agreed to accompany and interpret for Ryūnosuke. In a study in the French Concession, their first appointment was with Zhang Binglin. A philosopher and a scholar, a leading political figure during the various revolutions and recent upheavals, Zhang Binglin had been imprisoned, then had spent time in Japan. Now the man welcomed Ryūnosuke into his study; a tiled room, a cold room, with no stove, with no rugs, only books. In a thin serge suit, on a cushion-less wooden chair, Ryūnosuke stared at a large stuffed crocodile mounted flat against a wall. The skin of the crocodile offered no comfort, the cold of the room piercing his own skin. Ryūnosuke was certain he would catch his death of cold.

In a long grey official gown and a black half-length riding jacket with a thick fur lining, on a fur-draped wicker chair, with his legs outstretched, Zhang Binglin seemed oblivious to the cold. His skin almost yellow, his moustache very thin, his red eyes smiled coolly behind elegant frameless glasses as he spoke. "I am sad to say that contemporary China is politically depraved. You might say that since the last years of the Qing dynasty, the spread of injustice has reached immense proportions. In scholarship and the arts there has been an unusual stagnation. The Chinese people, however, do not by nature run to extremes. Insofar as they possess this quality, communism in China is impossible. Of course, one segment of the students welcomes Soviet principles, but the students are not the populace. Even if the people were to become communist, at some point would come a time when they would dispense with this belief. The reason is that our national character—love for the Golden Mean—is stronger than any momentary passing enthusiasm for fireworks . . ."

On his hard chair, Ryūnosuke desperately wanted to smoke, but just nodded along, Zhang waving long fingernails as on he went—

"So, what would be the best way to revive China? The resolution of this problem, no matter how concrete, cannot emerge from some theory concocted at the desk. The ancients declared that those who understood the requirements of the times were great men. They did not deductively reason from some opinion of their own, but inductively reasoned on the basis of countless facts. This is what it means to know the needs of the times. After one has ascertained what those needs are, then and only then can plans be made. This is ultimately the meaning of the dictum of governing well according to the times of the years . . ."

Ryūnosuke nodding along, his eyes wandering to the crocodile again. The rays of the spring sun, the warmth of the summer water, the fragrance of the lotus blossoms: once you knew them all, but now how lucky you are to be stuffed. Have pity on me!

"The Japanese character I detest the most," declared Zhang abruptly, "is the Momotarō of your favourite fairy tale, who conquered the Land of the Demons, and which you tell to all your children. I cannot suppress a feeling of antipathy for the Japanese who love this Momotarō."

Ryūnosuke had heard many foreigners talk about Japan, holding up Prince Yamagata to ridicule or praising Hokusai to the skies. But until now, Ryūnosuke had never heard any of those so-called Japanese experts utter one word of criticism of Momotarō, the boy who was born from a peach. Zhang's words contained more truth than all the eloquence of those experts.

Now Ryūnosuke looked at Zhang Binglin; now Ryūnosuke knew he was in the presence of a true sage.

6

In the Public Garden that was not public. No Chinese allowed, only foreigners here. The nannies and their charges, the sycamore trees with their budding leaves. It was all very pretty, but it was not China. It was the West. Not because it was advanced; it was no more advanced than the parks of Tokyo. It was simply more Western. And just because something was Western did not necessarily mean it was advanced. It was the same in the French Concession. The doves cooing quietly, the willows already budding. The smell of peach blossoms in the air. It was all very pleasant. But Ryūnosuke did not care for the Western houses. Not because they were Western, just because they seemed somewhat unrefined. Like the Japanese who insisted on wearing only Western clothes, putting on their thick socks and tight shoes, stumbling up and down the Ginza or the Bund—

"Hypocrite," laughed Jones. "You yourself actually prefer Western suits to Japanese clothes. You also prefer to live in a bungalow rather than a traditional house. You always order macaroni instead of udon. And you prefer Brazilian coffee to Japanese tea . . ."

Ryūnosuke shook his head and said, "No, no. For example, I admit that the Westerners' cemetery on Temple Street isn't so bad . . ."

"It's nice enough," said Jones. "But, personally, I would prefer to be buried under a Buddhist swastika than a Christian crucifix. I don't want angels and whatnot leering over me in my grave, grimacing and proselytising. You just mean you are disappointed by Shanghai and are not interested in the Western things here . . ."

"On the contrary, I'm very interested. But as you said, in one sense Shanghai is the West. And so, for better or for worse, it's fun to be able to see the West. Particularly because I've never laid eyes on the 'real' West. I'm just saying, even to my ignorant eyes, the West seems out of place here."

"Really," said Jones, feigning disbelief. "I actually think it's a match made in Heaven. Or should I say Hell . . . ?"

This City of Evil, this Demon City Shanghai. Ryūnosuke had heard the horror stories of rickshaw pullers turning bandit by night, slicing off women's ears for their earrings—

"The worst are the Chaibai Gang," whispered Jones. "Luring women into automobiles, stealing their diamond rings, and then strangling them, inspired by the movies. Those cloak-and-dagger ones that are all the rage here . . ."

At sunset, outside the Green Lotus teahouse, the Wild Pheasants flocked. Surrounding both Ryūnosuke and Jones, speaking both Japanese and English. Other girls hanging around in rickshaws, waiting for fresh crumbs, all wearing dark round glasses—

"All the rage," said Jones, again.

Inside a building, an opium den. In the stark white light of a bare electric bulb, a bleached, lone prostitute lay puffing "Western Medicine" on a long pipe with a foreign customer.

Ryūnosuke had seen so many strange foreigners in Shanghai, male and female, many of whom seemed to have migrated from Siberia. Even in the Public Garden, a Russian beggar had kept haranguing Ryūnosuke and Jones. "It's not so bad really," Jones had said. "The Municipal Council is actually very strict these days. Such shady cafés as the El Dorado and the Palermo have disappeared from the Western parts of the town. Now you have to go out to the suburbs, to places like the Del Monte . . ."

In the opium den, under the harsh light. Ryūnosuke shook his head again and said again, "But this is Shanghai—

"Not China, Young China . . ."

7

Ryūnosuke and Murata were on their way to meet Li Renjie. Li was twenty-eight years old, a representative of "Young China" and a socialist. Through the windows of the trolley, the avenues of verdant trees, summer was on its way. But Ryūnosuke and Murata were not talking about the foliage or the seasons. In low voices, they were discussing Chinese public opinion concerning Japan and the formation of the new foreign consortium. A strange thing had happened to Ryūnosuke: he had succumbed to a weird fever in which all he ever thought and talked about was politics, and never art. Ryūnosuke blamed Shanghai: the peculiar atmosphere of this peculiar city which had nurtured twenty years of problems to think and talk about.

A servant led Ryūnosuke and Murata into a drawing room of several Western-style chairs before a rectangular table with a bowl of porcelain fruit. These humble imitations of apples, grapes and pears were the only decorations in the room, a pleasing simplicity filling the empty room. In the furthest corner, a ladder came down from above, a pair of Chinese shoes now coming down the rungs of the ladder—

A rather small man, in a grey full-length gown, with long hair and a slim face, intelligent-looking eyes, very quick nerves and an extremely serious disposition, Li Renjie made a good first impression. He sat down across the table from Ryūnosuke.

Li had studied at a university in Tokyo, his Japanese fluent, and Ryūnosuke was further impressed by his detailed reasoning:

"What shall we do with contemporary China? The resolution of the problem lies not in a republic or a monarchical restoration. Political revolutions have been useless in improving China. This has been proven in the past and is now being proven again in the present. Thus, what we are trying to bring about is a 'social revolution' . . .

"And so if we are to bring about such a revolution, we have to rely on propaganda. Therefore, we write things. Enlightened Chinese scholars are not indifferent to new learning. In fact, we are starving for knowledge. But what shall we do about our lack of books and magazines to satiate our hunger? At this moment, our immediate duty is to write."

Ryūnosuke nodded and said, "I have become disappointed in the Chinese arts. Neither the novels nor the paintings I have seen so far are worthy of discussion. Nonetheless, judging from the present situation in China, to expect a revival of the arts—or, perhaps I should say, to expect the revival of anything—might be a mistake . . ."

"I have a seed in my hand," said Li. "But I am afraid the land is only wilderness for ten thousand miles. Nothing but a wilderness. And there is nothing we can do about it. That is the reason I have no choice but to be depressed about whether or not our body is strong enough to endure . . ."

Ryūnosuke nodded again and said, "But other than as a means of propaganda, can you afford to even worry about the arts?"

"Virtually not at all," said Li. "What we must really pay attention to now is the power of Chinese banks. It is not a question of the power behind them, rather it is their tendency to influence the government in Beijing. But we need not be sad about this; we know our enemies—the targets of our guns—and they are only a group of banks, after all . . ."

Back outside the house, Murata said, "That guy is very smart."

"Very impressive, indeed," agreed Ryūnosuke.

Murata smiled and said, "And you know, when he was a student in Japan, Li was an avid reader and admirer of your own work?"

"Every man has his flaws," sighed Ryūnosuke.

8

On his last night, in another café, in another corner, at another table, under a Chinese lantern, Ryūnosuke and Jones were drinking whisky and sodas, watching crowds of Americans and Russians swarming around the room, women leaning against the tables, listening to the Indian musicians of the orchestra. One particular woman, wearing a gown of celadon green, fluttered from one man to the next, her face beautiful, yet with something porcelain, almost morbid about her: *Green satin, and a dance, white wine / and gleaming laughter, with two nodding earrings—these are Lotus . . .*

"Who is she," asked Ryūnosuke, "the girl in the green dress?"

Jones shrugged and said, "Her? French, I think. An actress."

"Do you know her? Her story . . . ?"

Jones shrugged again. "People call her Ninny. But just look at him, that old guy over there. Now there is a man with a story . . ."

Ryūnosuke glanced at the man at the next table. He was holding a glass of red wine in both hands, warming the glass, rocking the wine, moving his head in time to the music of the band.

Jones whispered, "He's Jewish, you know. He's lived here for almost thirty years. But he's never said what brought him here, or what makes him stay. I often wonder about him . . ."

"What do you care," said Ryūnosuke.

Jones said, "I just wonder. I'm already fed up with China."

"Not with China," said Ryūnosuke. "With Shanghai."

Jones nodded. "With China. I lived in Beijing for a while, too."

"Because China is gradually becoming too Western?"

Jones seemed about to answer, but then stopped.

"Then if not China," asked Ryūnosuke, "then where would you live? How about Japan again? You could return to Tokyo . . ."

Jones shook his head and said, "You should never go back to the places you've lived. You can't really . . ."

"So where then?"

Jones smiled and said, "Russia, under the Soviets."

"Then you should go! You can go anywhere you want . . ."

Jones closed his eyes, was silent for a while, a long while, and then, in Japanese, quoted lines from the *Man'yōshū*, lines Ryūnosuke had long forgotten: "*The world is full of pain / And the shame of poverty / But I am not a bird / I cannot fly away . . .*"

Ryūnosuke smiled.

Jones opened his eyes, looked again around the room and said, "I don't know about that old Jewish guy, but even Ninny seems happier than me . . ."

"Ah-ha," laughed Ryūnosuke, "I knew you must know her!"

Jones shrugged and said, "I am not a straightforward person, Ryūnosuke. Poet, painter, critic, journalist and more. Son, brother, bachelor and Irishman. And on top of all that, a romantic in my mind, a realist in my life and a communist in my politics . . ."

"And a lover of Ninny," laughed Ryūnosuke.

Now Jones laughed, too. "Yeah, yeah. And an atheist in religion and a materialist in philosophy. Now, come on. *Sa-ikō . . .*"

Outside, the city was lost in a strange yellow fog. Its false fronts, buried for now. Ryūnosuke followed Jones along the streets, towards the sound of the water, the sound of the waves . . .

By the water, they stopped. A customs-house spire dimly visible through the fog. A black sail, torn and tilted, creaking along, adrift and alone. The river swelled and flowed backwards. The black legs of a wharf bound in chains. Mountains of off-loaded cargo. Coolies on barrels stacked on the embankment in the damp air . . .

"It's too late," said Jones, "to change anything."

"Then that means you've wasted your life."

A group of exhausted Russian prostitutes sitting on a bench. The blue lamp of a sampan moving against the current, rotating ceaselessly, hypnotically before their silent, wasted eyes . . .

"Not only me," said Jones, "but all the people of the world."

The dull clank of copper coins, Chinamen gambling on top of barrels. The gaslights in striped patterns, through the yellow fog and the wet trees. The boats tied to the quay rocking in the waves, floating up and down in the flicker of the lamplight.

"Hey, look at that," said Jones, pointing into the dark water—

At their feet, on the tide, the pale corpse of a small dog kissed the stones of the quay. A wreath around its neck—

Rising and falling, on the tide.

Ryūnosuke turned his back, lit a cigarette and watched the prostitutes stand and saunter away along an iron railing. A young woman at the end of the procession glanced back furtively with her pallid eyes, and Ryūnosuke felt overwhelmed by the sudden, crushing sadness of a dream: when that woman Shigeko had told him that her second child was his, then turned and walked away, she had glanced back at him in that very same way. Now the young woman stepped over the ropes that moored the boats, then disappeared among the barrels with the others. All they left behind was a banana peel, stepped on and splattered. Ryūnosuke stared back out across the water. Day and night, coins and goods flowed in and out from the port, and all along the river the warships of the world spread out their batteries of guns.

"I wonder why we do that," said Jones, quietly, still watching the dead dog bobbing up and down on the black water.

"Do what," asked Ryūnosuke.

"Make a wreath," said Jones. "For the dead."

Ryūnosuke stared back down at the corpse, then shook his head and said, "I don't know. But I'm glad we do. Or some of us do."

"Maybe it was Ninny," said Jones.

Ryūnosuke looked back up at Jones, remembering again lines from that poem by Eunice Tietjens: *You too perhaps were stranded here, like these poor / homesick boys, in this great catch-all where the / white race ends, this grim Shanghai that like a / sieve hangs over filth and loneliness . . .*

Ryūnosuke flicked his cigarette out into the night and the water and said, "For hope and all young wings are drowned in you . . ."

"Awfully sentimental," said Jones.

Ryūnosuke nodded. "I'll be sorry to leave you, but not Shanghai."

"The rest of China is no better," said Jones. "You still have too many illusions, you always do. So I'm afraid you'll be very disappointed."

"Then I hope when we meet again it will be in Japan and in happier times, and you'll be much happier, too."

Jones was staring up the river at the shadows of the warships. In the night, with their guns. Silent and waiting. Now Jones turned to Ryūnosuke and said, "I'm sorry, old friend. But I very much doubt it."

Ryūnosuke said nothing. There on that quay, here in this night, he was remembering their first meeting. A fire burning brightly in a fireplace, its flames reflecting in the mahogany tables and chairs. They had talked all night, of literature and of Ireland, until Ryūnosuke had been overcome with drowsiness. It had not been so very long ago, not even ten years, but it felt like a memory from another life, another world. The flames of that fire no longer seemed comforting and warm, but threatening and portentous, filling Ryūnosuke with a vague feeling of anxiety and dread.

On the quay, in the night, Ryūnosuke shivered in the damp air and said, "Do you still detest George Bernard Shaw?"

"More than ever," laughed Jones.

"And the words of Christ?"

"Awfully sentimental."

Ryūnosuke stared into the water again, the dog and its wreath not moving now, just floating. The face of Jesus on the water. There were tears in his eyes, on his cheeks and now his collar, as he said, "It's surely better to believe in at least the possibility of forgiveness, and of redemption . . ."

"You should return your ticket," said Jones. "The East and the West cannot be reconciled. They will tear you apart, Ryūnosuke."

And now, suddenly, Jones sneezed again.

9

After the goodbyes, in the night. Ryūnosuke walked out onto the deck of the *Hōyō-maru* and lit a cigarette. On the pier, no souls abroad. Lights shone downstream, along the Bund. All a forged facade, all a grotesque parody. And in the night, out on the deck, Ryūnosuke closed his eyes . . .

Long, long ago, there was a giant peach tree, its roots in the underworld, its branches above the clouds. One fine morning, Yatagarasu, a mythical crow, landed upon one of the branches of the tree. Yatagarasu pecked off one of the fruits of the tree. The fruit fell through the clouds into a stream far down below. A childless old woman saw the peach in the stream. Inside the peach was a boy. The old woman took the boy home. And the old woman and her husband called this boy Momotarō.

Now Momotarō had the idea to conquer the Demon Island, because he hated working in the fields, the mountains and the rivers like the old man and woman who had adopted and raised him. The elderly couple, exhausted by this naughty foundling, prepared a banner, a sword and some dumplings, and off he set.

Soon Momotarō was joined by a starving dog, a cowardly monkey and a dignified pheasant on his quest to the Demon Island.

But despite its name, the Demon Island was actually a beautiful natural paradise. And the demons themselves were a placid, pleasure-seeking race. They played harps, sang songs and danced dances. Their grandparents, though, would often tell cautionary tales of the horrible humans across the water: "If you are naughty, we'll send you to the land of the humans. Their men and women tell lies. They are greedy, jealous and vain. They set fires, they steal things, and even kill their friends for pleasure or profit."

With the banner of the peach in one hand, waving his sun-emblem fan, Momotarō brought terror to the demons, ordering the dog, the monkey and the pheasant: "Forward! Forward! Kill the demons, leave none alive!"

The dog killed one young demon with just one bite. The monkey ravaged and then throttled the demon girls. The pheasant pecked countless demon children to death. And soon a forest of corpses littered the Demon Island. And the demon chieftain surrendered to Momotarō—

"Now in my great mercy," declared Momotarō, "I will spare your life. But in return, you will bring me all your treasure and you will give me all your children as hostages . . ."

The demon chieftain had no choice but to agree. And in triumph, with his treasure and his hostages, Momotarō returned victorious to Japan. However, Momotarō did not live happily ever after. The demon children grew up to be most ungrateful adults. Endlessly trying to kill Momotarō, ceaselessly trying to escape from Japan, to return back home, back to the Demon Island—

Endlessly, ceaselessly . . .

Her engines turning, the *Hōyō-maru* began to move now. Ryūnosuke opened his eyes, threw his cigarette butt into the water and reached back into his pocket. But instead of the yellow box of Egyptians, Ryūnosuke felt something else in his fingers—

"Roses, red roses . . ."

The petals already withered, the fragrance already gone, already spent now, but a dream now—

A nightmare . . .

The sudden crack of shotgun fire, the shrill whistle of a gunboat. Firefly larvae feeding on a paralysed snail. New flesh, fresh meat. Devils turning corners, evil reading maps. A great noise, all around him, grinding and screaming. Through valleys of darkness, through vales of tears—

"Awfully sentimental . . ."

In the night, on the deck. Ryūnosuke tossed the wilted red rose into the churning dark waters. Then his fingers in his ears, now his fingers in his eyes, Ryūnosuke cursed Momotarō, Ryūnosuke cursed Yatagarasu. And then he cursed himself. And now Ryūnosuke prayed, his ticket in his hand; Ryūnosuke prayed and he prayed no birds would ever disturb the branches of that tree again. No babies ever be born of peaches again.

What you want, you should not want.

The Exorcists

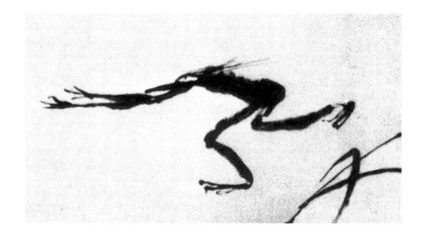

From on the bridge
as I throw away the cucumber,
the water sounds and thus I see,
a bobbed head.

—for Owaka-san, by drunken-Gaki

Tanka on a folded screen, painted with a Kappa,
Ryūnosuke Akutagawa, Nagasaki, May, 1922

A man is standing in my way, blocking my path and shouting in my face, "An angel will bring down his sword against this city in judgement! For this is a sinful nation, a people laden with iniquity, a bed of evildoers! Look at the Diet and the city council. Look at the theatres and the department stores and the frivolous men and women who frequent them. Look at the intellectuals and literati they worship, and the magazines and newspapers who encourage them. They do not fear slandering the sacred, they do not fear slandering God! They are apostates, they are heretics! This is not Tokyo, this is not Japan; this is Sodom and Gomorrah! And soon you will feel the wrath of Heaven, for soon you will know the punishment of Heaven!"

I push past the madman, into Tokyo station, through the ticket gates, up the stairs, onto the platform, onto my train, and away . . .

*

Kyō Tsunetō, his oldest and dearest friend, and the reason he had stopped off in Kyoto, had just started in his new position in the Faculty of Economics at Kyoto Imperial University, and so, during the days, Ryūnosuke wandered across the city, meandered through its streets, dreaming and imagining the streets as they were before, the city of old. Under its blue skies, under its cherry blossoms; the gaze of its skies, the madness of its blossoms.

That particular day in early May, in his serge kimono and his *geta* sandals, with his notebook in his satchel, his cigarettes and his fan, Ryūnosuke left Tsunetō's lodgings overlooking the Shimogamo Shrine in Morimoto-chō, first heading south to the fork in the river, then turning onto Imadegawa-dōri and walking west, west all the way past the top of the park of the Imperial Palace and the lower edges of the campus of Dōshisha University, west and further west, west all the way past the Kitano Tenmangū Shrine, west until he turned south again down Nishiōji-dōri, then west again when he came to Myōshinji-dōri, west again until he reached the southern entrance to the walled enclave of the Myōshinji Temple itself.

Here, Ryūnosuke crossed over the stone bridge, went under the wooden gate and entered this other world, this other city, a city within a city—with its forty or more sub-temples, with its avenues of pine and fir trees, its narrow stone paths and raked-gravel lawns, its temples of red and temples of wood—through this labyrinth of low white stone walls with their grey *kawara*-tiled roofs, Ryūnosuke meandered and wandered, weaving his way towards his aim, his aim for the day; he could have stopped to see the rock garden, the *karesansui* of the Taizōin Temple, he could have stopped to stare up at the *Unryūzu* painting by Kanō Tanyū, "the dragon glaring in eight directions" in the hall of the Myōshinji Temple, but Ryūnosuke had only one aim, one thing in mind today.

Between a small bush of blooming peony and a weeping tree of cherry blossom, Ryūnosuke crossed over another tiny stone bridge, went under another small wooden gate, and entered yet another world, another world within another world: the grounds of the Shunkōin Temple.

Here, Ryūnosuke was greeted by a monk. Ryūnosuke introduced himself, apologised for calling without an appointment, but asked if it might be possible to see what he had come, come so very far to see. The monk smiled and led Ryūnosuke into the main building. And here, at last, Ryūnosuke saw for himself the Bell of Nanbanji.

Nanbanji had been the great Christian Temple of Kyoto, founded by the Jesuit Father Gnecchi-Soldo Organtino in 1576, with the blessing and support of Oda Nobunaga. The Great Bell had been cast in Portugal and arrived at Nanbanji in 1577. But ten years later, the Nanbanji Temple was destroyed under the orders of Toyotomi Hideyoshi, during the first great persecution of Christians. Still now, no one could be sure where the Nanbanji Temple had once stood. During the destruction and the persecution, the bell had been lost, too. But early in the nineteenth century, the bell had been found and then brought here, here to the Shunkōin Temple; now all that remained of the great Christian Temple of Nanbanji was its bell, this bell.

Ryūnosuke stood before the bell, staring at the bell, transfixed by the bell. On its surface, there were engraved three Jesuit seals. The three seals contained the Christogram *IHS*, of which there were three possible readings and interpretations: the first three letters of the Greek name of Jesus; the initials of the Latin phrase *Iesus Hominum Salvatore*, Jesus, Saviour of Man; or the Latin phrase *In hoc signo vinces*, in this sign I shall conquer. Above the Christogram was the cross and under the Christogram were three nails, and engraved on the side of the bell was the year 1577.

Ryūnosuke reached out across the centuries, over the ocean of history, and touched the surface of the bell, his fingers warm and its metal cold, but in his ears and in his mind, Ryūnosuke could hear the ringing of the bell, sounding across the grounds of the Christian Temple of Nanbanji, calling the faithful to prayer, across the old capital of Kyoto, in his ears and in his mind, and in his heart, echoing in his heart, the chambers of his heart.

"The Bell of Nanbanji is not the only Christian relic housed here," said the monk. "In the garden there stands a *kirishitan-dōrō*, a stone lantern, its leg in the shape of a cross and in which has been chiselled an image of their Holy Mother, the Virgin Mary . . ."

Ryūnosuke followed the monk along polished dark corridors, past painted gold screens, and out into the main garden of the Shunkōin Temple, the Garden of Boulders, the *Sazareishi-no-niwa* . . .

Here at its edge, here in the shade, here Ryūnosuke stood before the stone lantern, staring again, transfixed again . . .

"No one knows for sure," said the monk, "how this stone lantern, this Hidden Icon, came to be here . . ."

Again, Ryūnosuke reached out across the centuries, over the ocean of history, and touched the surface of the lantern, then bending down, squatting down, he ran his fingers gently over the stone image of the Holy Mother, Her arms raised, folded and crossed before Her breasts and over Her heart, his fingers warm and the stone warm, warm to his touch, warm from Her touch, Her touch in his heart, in the chambers of his heart.

"If you would like," said the monk, "please do rest in the shade of the room which looks out upon our garden."

Ryūnosuke thanked the monk, and for all his kindness in showing him the Great Bell of Nanbanji and the Stone Lantern of the Holy Mother, and then the monk left Ryūnosuke sitting on the polished dark wooden steps in the shade of the veranda, staring out at the Garden of Boulders . . .

On the steps, in the shade and in the silence, his eyes closing then opening again, how long he stayed sat there he did not know, nor could he tell what time of day it was, what day or even year it was. But in the shade and in the silence, now Ryūnosuke sensed a shadow over him, falling behind him now, a shadow in the shade, a shade within a shade, and Ryūnosuke turned, and Ryūnosuke saw—

A Western man, well-built and tall, sockless and barefoot in a three-piece suit, his long hair oiled and slicked back, nose large and face puffed, he smiled down at Ryūnosuke and said in accented English, "I must say, I do say, I rather like this garden, this Garden of Boulders. And you . . . ?"

Ryūnosuke looked up at the man, this Western man, and with a brief nod of his head then said, "I agree, it is very attractive."

"Attractive," echoed the man, "because, quintessentially, Japanese."

Ryūnosuke smiled slightly. "Perhaps, but there must be many attractive gardens in the West that are not Japanese."

"Sadly, that is no longer true," said the man. "It is already closing time in the Gardens of the West, their grounds overgrown and their gates locked. And I'm afraid if you do not take care, soon here, too, your gardens will close . . ."

"Really," said Ryūnosuke, looking from the man back out at the garden, not knowing what else he could or would like to say.

Now, with the palm of his hand, the man gently touched Ryūnosuke on his back as he sat down beside him on the dark polished steps of the veranda and softly said, "But I'm sorry to paint such a gloomy picture and to disturb you, as you sit here before such a beautiful sight."

"Not at all," said Ryūnosuke. "In fact, your enthusiasm for this garden only refreshes my tired eyes and their gaze."

"And so what do you see," asked the man, "with your fresh eyes?"

Ryūnosuke now regretted his last remark, surveying the scene before him, struggling to think of anything astute to say, anything but "Harmony."

"Exactly," said the man. "Harmony, and forgive me if you are already aware of its design and history, but the theme of this Buddhist temple garden is the Ise Shrine, Ise Jingū in Mie Prefecture, which, as you know, is the chief shrine of all the Shintō shrines in Japan. Yet this Buddhist garden has a forest to Amaterasu-ōmikami, the sun goddess, and a tiny shrine to Toyouke-no-ōmikami, the goddess of agriculture. You know, it was once common to see Buddhist and Shintō objects enshrined at the same place because, until your Meiji Restoration—or revolution, whichever you prefer—it was a popular belief in Japan that the native Shintō deities were actually various forms of the Buddha that existed to help and save people. Hence, you sense the harmony of this garden, for we feel the attraction of its syncretism."

Looking out over the main garden of the Shunkōin Temple, over the Garden of Boulders, Ryūnosuke said, "I didn't know that."

"And yet you felt it still," said the Western man. "In your heart, your Japanese heart."

Ryūnosuke smiled, then said, "Well, in truth, this Japanese heart came here in search of just one thing: the Bell of Nanbanji."

"I am not surprised," said the man—an echo of the words Mokichi Saitō had said to Ryūnosuke that afternoon, three years ago, in his office at the Nagasaki Prefectural Hospital—but this Western man, he said these words with sadness not disdain, and now went on, "Ah, yes, yes, Nanbanji . . .

"What a place it was—on this side of the Kamo River, on its western bank, between Sanjō and Shijō, close to where the Rokkaku-dō still stands—an enormous place, enclosed by walls of wood, with two gates to the south, the main temple was laid out in the shape of the cross, and its bell tower with its cross on its roof could be seen for miles and miles, and the ringing of the Great Bell, sounding the hours, calling the faithful, could be heard all across the old capital of Kyoto, in all our ears and in all our hearts, echoing in our hearts, in the chambers of our hearts. Listen . . . Listen, Ryūnosuke . . ."

In the shade, on the steps, Ryūnosuke abruptly turned to look at this man, this stranger who had just said his name, who knew his name, who was looking at him, was smiling at him, a finger to his lips, another to his ear, and now to his eye as he whispered, "Listen, Ryūnosuke, and look . . ."

The finger of the man now moved from his eye, pointing out towards the garden, Ryūnosuke following the path of the finger of the man out over the Garden of Boulders, watching it lifting, his finger lifting, lifting a veil—

"Look and see, all these exotic Western plants—rose and olive, laurel and cinnamon—growing here among the native pine and cypress trees, and see and smell the mysterious aromas, the sweet perfumes, the faint scent of the roses just beginning to bloom, for we are in the springtime still, the springtime now and the springtime then, yet somehow no longer Japan, yet somehow still in Japan; do you know where we are, Ryūnosuke? Do you recognise this place? The ringing of that bell, sounding and echoing . . ."

His eyes wide, his mouth agape, Ryūnosuke could smell the scents of the roses, could hear the ringing of the bell as he whispered, "Nanbanji . . ."

"Exactly," said the man. "This is the garden of the Great Temple of the Southern Barbarians, and now—look, look!—who do we see here, we find here?"

And now he looked and now he saw the silhouette of a man, walking with a melancholy gait down a path of red sand, the dark skirts of his long robe trailing in the pink dust, and Ryūnosuke said, "Padre Organtino!"

"Exactly," said the man again, taking Ryūnosuke by his elbow and his arm, lifting Ryūnosuke up from the steps, saying, "Come on . . ."

Arm in arm, the man led Ryūnosuke briskly down the red path, over its pink sand, quietly following the figure of Padre Organtino, step by step, closer and closer, until they could hear the priest mumbling, hear the priest muttering—how much he missed Rome, how he longed for Lisbon, the taste of almonds, the music of the *rabeca* lute, the heavenly voices of the *Magnificat*—then again and again, now over and over, chanting and reciting the name of Deus, Deus, Deus, his eyes on his feet, his eyes on the path, then on the dark moss beside the path, now on the pale petals upon the moss, the petals stopping him dead in his tracks, seemingly blocking his path and filling him with fear, the priest startled, looking up at the trees of the garden, and there, among the gloomy shadows of the dwarf palms, there Organtino saw a single weeping cherry tree, its branches hanging bowed and low, its ghostly, spectral blossoms spread and splayed, haunting the garden—

"God save me! Lord protect me," cried the priest, falling to his knees, crossing himself again and again, calling over and over to "Deus . . ."

On the path, beside him, Ryūnosuke's Western companion had one hand over his mouth, quelling his laughter, his other hand holding his ribs, his shoulders shaking, his whole being consumed by mirth at the sight of this foreign priest on his knees beneath the falling blossoms of the weeping cherry, making the sign of the cross, crying out at Christ—

"How long wilt thou forget me, O Lord . . ."

Suddenly, the man stopped laughing. He looked at Ryūnosuke, shook his head, rolled his eyes and hissed, "Jesuits! They want the world, but when the world doesn't want them, they fall to their knees in tears and blame Christ! Incredible, would you not agree? They blame the one who should not be blamed; the only man—and believe me, Ryūnosuke, I have met many—the only one among the many who was truly blameless . . ."

Beneath the blossoms, on his knees, Organtino must have heard the laughter and the whispers in the shadows behind him, for now the priest spun round, rising to his feet, pointing into the dark at the man and Ryūnosuke, wagging his finger and shouting, "You! You again!"

The man looked at Ryūnosuke, shrugged his shoulders, and then, with the most innocent smile one can imagine, asked, "Does he mean me?"

"Who else would I mean," spat Organtino, coming closer to the man. "Of course I mean you! How on earth did you find me?"

"Find you," laughed the man. "I rather think you found me. As I told you before, many times before, you will find me in the garden, if you want me."

"I do *not* want you," yelled the priest. "Get away! Get ye hence!"

The man turned to Ryūnosuke again, shook his head again and said, "You see what I mean? Jesuits! Telling me to go away, to go hence, when it is they, it is you . . ."—the man turning to Organtino now, turning on Organtino now—"it is *you*, you who are the uninvited, unwelcome guest here, Padre . . ."

"God save me, Lord protect me," whispered Organtino again, crossing himself again, then looking back into the dark, to the shadows and the man, saying, "This is God's place on God's earth, and I have been sent here to do God's work, I have come here to spread God's word . . ."

"Yeah, yeah, yeah," said the man, walking around behind the priest, turning back to whisper in his ear, "I've heard it all before, many times before, so save your breath, Padre, and save your time and go back to your palaces in Rome, back to your burnings in Lisbon or wherever, because this time, in this place, you will be defeated, and you will lose."

Padre Organtino clutched the cross around his neck, shook his head and said, "The Lord God is omnipotent and so there is no one, no place or no thing that can triumph over Him, so the Lord God will be victorious . . ."

"Well," said the man, glancing up from the ear of the priest, winking at Ryūnosuke, "naturally, I would beg to disagree. And once again, and as always, reality, history, fact—all would seem to agree with me . . .

"And so listen carefully, Padre, and you might even learn something for once, because you and your God are far from the first to come to this land. Greater men than you, bringing wiser words than you, have come from far away to here and yet floundered in this place: Confucius and Mencius, to name but two. Yet is this now China, or still yet Japan?

"And the Chinese, they did not come empty-handed, no! They brought silk from the state of Wu, they brought jewels from the state of Ch'in. And they also brought their wonderful written words, their exquisite Chinese characters. You talk, as you always talk, about 'spreading God's word,' Padre, so then here's a telling tale for you . . .

"As I say, the Chinese visitors arrived with their written characters, and the native Japanese smiled, bowed politely and took their written characters. Thank you very much, they said, we will use your written characters, but—and here's the rub, the rub for you, Padre, and the genius of the people, the people of this land—they took the Chinese written characters, but they retained their own native sound. For example, when the Japanese historians write that the big-nosed, red-haired Southern Barbarians arrived here by boat, they use the Chinese character *shū* for boat, but when they read their work aloud, they still say '*fune*,' the original sound of their native word. Ingenious, is it not?"

Twilight was now engulfing the garden of Nanbanji, and Padre Organtino now again fell to his knees, kneeling down on the red path, clutching the cross of his rosary, mumbling and muttering, "O God, thou art my God; early will I seek thee: my soul thirsteth for thee, my flesh longeth for thee in a dry and thirsty land, where no water is . . ."

The man in the shadows ignored the words of the priest kneeling in the pink sand, simply, gently placing a hand on his shoulder, leaning into his ear and saying, "You are probably ignorant and unaware of them, never heard of them, but one only has to look to the magnificent works of Kūkai, Dōfū, Sari and Kōsei, the great calligraphers of this land who first imitated the Chinese style but then created and developed their own style, their kana style . . ."

"To see thy power and thy glory, so as I have seen thee in the sanctuary. Because thy loving kindness is better than life, my lips shall praise thee . . ."

"Of course," went on the man at the ear of Organtino, "it is true not only of characters and writing, but also ideas and thought. Think about the harsh Tao of Lao-tze, how it was softened on these shores, and then, of course, there is the telling fate of that sorry little Prince Siddhartha . . ."

"Thus will I bless thee while I live," said Organtino, his voice rising now, his grip on the cross of his rosary tightening now, "I will lift up my hands in thy name. My soul shall be satisfied as with marrow and fatness; and my mouth shall praise thee with joyful lips: when I remember thee upon my bed, and meditate on thee in the night watches . . ."

The man glanced up again at Ryūnosuke, shook his head again, sighed and then, back in the ear of Organtino, said, "You are not listening to me, I know; it's not in your nature, I know. Still, you would do well to heed my words, Padre, to listen and to save if not yourself, then save those poor natives who will die because of you— your ignorance, your persistence and delusions—die because of you, and die in vain, believing not in your God, but mistaking your God for theirs . . ."

"Because thou hast been my help, therefore in the shadow of thy wings will I rejoice," called out Organtino. "My soul followeth hard after thee: thy right hand upholdeth me . . ."

"Yes, yes, babble on, Padre, babble on. But do you not think for one moment that the reason the natives of this land are so happy to worship the Great Sun Buddha is only because they believe that God to be simply their own Great Sun Goddess, Ōhirume? You know, Padre, I have walked in many gardens; I have walked under the flowers of the Sara tree with the great priests of this land, with Shinran and Nichiren, and I can tell you, Padre, when I looked into their hearts, when I gazed upon the image they worshipped there, I found no dark-skinned *gaijin*-Buddha there, no! No, I found only the pale and gentle, noble image of their own Prince Shōtoku shining there, in their hearts, in the chambers of their hearts . . ."

"But those that seek my soul to destroy it," shouted Organtino, closing his eyes, "they shall go into the lowest parts of the earth . . ."

"Fool," sighed the man, "always talking of destroying, of destruction if not conversion, crusading and conquering, with all your trials and your burnings, clutching the poor, poor figure of Jesus on his cross, the Blameless One, the only Blameless One, donning your regal robes in the name of a man who would never be a king—even though he could have been, oh yes, he could have been, believe me, Padre—building palaces in the name of a pauper who shunned possessions—that old Jew Karl will come closer to the truth than thee, Padre—for you are blind to the wonders of the lands you come to uninvited, deaf to the wisdom of the natives you would seek to subjugate . . ."

"THEY SHALL FALL BY THE SWORD," screamed Organtino, "THEY SHALL BE A PORTION FOR FOXES . . ."

"There you go again," sighed the man, a sad smile playing on his lips, "with your swords and your portions for foxes. But if you would only open your eyes, if you would only get off your knees, Padre, and walk about you, look about you, looking and listening, then you would see and hear and know that the history and tradition of this land, of this place is one of learning and adapting, of recreating and transforming . . ."

"But the king shall rejoice in God," said Organtino now, opening his eyes now, getting off his knees now, getting to his feet now, holding the cross of his rosary out into the dark, out towards the man, out towards Ryūnosuke. "Everyone that sweareth by him shall glory . . ."

The man smiled sadly at Ryūnosuke, slowly shook his head again and said, "Never listens, so never learns. I don't know why I bother, I really don't know why . . ."

But in the twilight, now on the path, Padre Organtino was before them now, his cross in the face of Ryūnosuke now, as the priest thundered, "BUT THE MOUTH OF THEM THAT SPEAK LIES SHALL BE STOPPED!"

And then the cross was gone, and now the path was gone, and only the twilight remained, but now the twilight of the Garden of Boulders of the Shunkōin Temple, Ryūnosuke sitting on the polished dark steps of the veranda, Ryūnosuke sitting beside the Western man—

Looking out over the garden, the man made a spyglass of his hands, then the man raised the glass to his eye and said, "Farewell to Nanbanji—for the wind passeth over it, and it is gone; and the place thereof shall know it no more—goodbye to Organtino; the good Padre prefers to stroll along the shore, under a broad umbrella carried by a negro boy, plotting and talking with the captains and the traders, waiting for the Black Ships and their cannons, the Silver Birds and their bombs, waiting to have his revenge, the revenge of the big-nosed, red-haired Southern Barbarians, making burnt-out prairies of this land, leaving nothing, nothing but shadows, shadows on the stones . . ."

"Who are you," asked Ryūnosuke.

"I am Nemo," said the man, with a wink. "That's Latin, you know . . ."

"For 'no man,'" said Ryūnosuke. "I know."

"Yes," said the man, with a smile, "you know many things, you've read many things. But have you read this story, I wonder, do you know this tale, one last little story for you, a Zen tale, seeing as we are sitting in this temple here, the story of Nanquan Puyuan and the cat? Once, Nanquan—or Nansen Fūgan, if you prefer—saw the monks of the eastern and western halls arguing over a cat—Does the cat have the nature of the Buddha or not? In the future, will the cat become a Buddha?—endlessly fighting over this cat. And so Nansen seized the cat by the scruff of its neck, held it up before the squabbling monks and said, If any one of you can say one true word about this cat, then you can save the cat. Of course, none of the monks could say a thing, and so Nansen cut the cat in two and threw it at their feet. Later that evening, Jōshū returns to the temple, and Nansen tells him what happened. Jōshū listens, then takes off his sandals, puts them on his head, and walks away, as Nansen says, If you'd been there, you could have saved the cat."

"I know the story," said Ryūnosuke.

"Of course," said the man, with a smile again. "But now I think it's time you, too, walked away, for you really should be going. Your friend has just finished his classes for the day, and will soon be awaiting you in Kane-yo. You have a long journey in a short time, and so don't be late again . . ."

"But . . ." Ryūnosuke started to say. "How . . ."

"Fear not," said the man, "for we will meet again, Ryūnosuke. As I said, you will always find me in the garden . . ."

Ryūnosuke turned away from the Garden of Boulders, stood up, then looked down at the Western man and said, "I pray not."

"Pray all you want," laughed the man, "but always remember, Ryūnosuke: *desine fata deum flecti sperare precando . . .*"

*

The fool hath said in his heart, There is no God. They are corrupt, they have done abominable works, there is none that doeth good.

The LORD looked down from heaven upon the children of men, to see if there were any that did understand, and seek God.

They are all gone aside, they are all together become filthy: there is none that doeth good, no, not one.

Have all the workers of iniquity no knowledge? who eat up my people as they eat bread, and call not upon the LORD.

There were they in great fear: for God is in the generation of the righteous.

Ye have shamed the counsel of the poor, because the LORD is his refuge.

Oh that the salvation of Israel were come *out of Zion! when the LORD bringeth back the captivity of his people, Jacob shall rejoice,* and *Israel shall be glad.*

*

It had rained and rained since Ryūnosuke arrived in Nagasaki, so he had stayed in his room at the Hana-ya Ryokan in Gotō-machi, trying to write, but failing to write, trying then to read, but failing even to read; as the rain fell, the stench of the toilets rose and filled the second floor of the ryokan, engulfing his room in a greasy, stinking cloud of urine and excrement. Now he regretted not staying someplace more refined, somewhere such as the Midori-ya or Ueno-ya. But then, on the third day, the clouds rolled away and the sun shone again, Ryūnosuke released again, at last . . .

There were merchants out selling *biwa* fruit on the streets, a taste of summer on its way, azalea blooming red in gardens glimpsed, a scent of summer already here, even Nagasaki fighting kites practising their battles across the warm, blue skies as Ryūnosuke wandered through the streets of Manzai-machi, meandering across Tokiwa Bridge, over the Nakashima River, making his way to Sōfukuji Temple again, through the Ryūgumon Gate, the gate of the Dragon Palace, and into the grounds of the temple, this temple he loved most, loved most of all the temples in Nagasaki, with its elegant, faded vermilion walls and upturned roofs in the Chinese style.

Here in the courtyard of the Sōfukuji Temple, high above the city, Ryūnosuke sat to rest a while, the *bashō* plants full, but the place deserted; Ryūnosuke was grateful for the tranquillity, savouring the calm and the silence, yet feeling mournful and somehow sad such a beautiful, tasteful place could be so deserted, only hoping it could survive, not fall into neglect and ruin while Shintō shrines such as Yasaka, the former Gion-jinja, prospered, always bustling and crowded with parties of schoolchildren and soldiers.

From here, Ryūnosuke wandered and meandered on, down the steps and up the slopes, morning into the afternoon, through the temples of Daikōji and Daionji, making his way towards the Kōfukuji Temple in Teramachi . . .

Along the streets of Teramachi were cluttered antique and junk shops, and Ryūnosuke struggled to tell the treasures from the rubbish, for it seemed the flotsam of the world had washed up here, piled up in these little stores. But now Ryūnosuke paused before one particular shop; its windows were half shuttered, so it was a challenge to see inside, and this, along with the name of the shop—*Shōhin*, or Small Pieces—aroused his curiosity. Tentatively, Ryūnosuke pushed open the door and stepped into the dark interior.

Inside the little shop, the only light came from the street, falling through the half-open shutters and door in long-fingered shadows, dancing across the tall cabinets lined up along the walls and the one large table standing in the middle of the room. Ryūnosuke kept the door ajar, both for light and for breeze, for the air in the shop felt close and humid, and glanced quickly around the room, at the antiques and curios displayed in the cabinets and laid out on the table, looking for a counter, searching for the owner. But Ryūnosuke could see no shopkeeper, nor even a cash register, and he began to feel uncomfortable, as though intruding into a private room, and suffocated by its clawing warmth and lack of fresh air. The sound of the shawm of a street vendor was echoing down the street outside, and he turned to leave, back to the door, when he thought he heard, suddenly heard a whisper—

Why the long face, such a very sad face? Are you feeling unwell . . . ?

Ryūnosuke turned back, looking around the empty shop—

It's nothing, I'm fine. Maybe just a headache from the heat . . .

Still the shop was deserted, yet still he heard voices—

Well, it is unusually close today for the time of year . . .

It's no headache! He's lovesick, he's lovesick . . .

Ryūnosuke walked towards the sound of the voices, the sound of the voices coming from the large table, the objects on the table—

Be quiet! Be silent! I'm not lovesick at all . . .

His eyes wide, Ryūnosuke stared down at a sketch of a Dutchman in Dejima, drawn in the style of Shiba Kōkan, angrily gesticulating at a stuffed parrot perched among flowers made of leather and cloth, while inked on an old teacup a trader from the Dutch East India Company laughed—

Go on then, if he's lovesick, then who has he fallen for?

He's lovesick for her, he's lovesick for her . . .

The parrot was squawking away, its head and its beak pointing towards a painted plate on which Ryūnosuke could see a woman holding a fan—

Not her, really? She's as conceited as she is beautiful . . .

The Dutchman now turned to glare at the trader—

How dare you be so insulting and rude!

The parrot was squawking and laughing now—

If you love her so much, then marry her! Marry her! Marry her!

Marry him? Impossible! Frankly, I detest my fellow Dutch!

The woman on the plate now raised her fan, glanced furtively up at Ryūnosuke, smiled and then haughtily turned her head away as the Dutchman in the sketch began to cry, holding his heart, before pointing at a long, antique *Tanegashima* Japanese matchlock lying on the table—

Hopeless, I know. I may as well shoot myself in the heart . . .

No, no! Please don't commit such a rash act! No!

On the table, before the gun, a small metal *Bateren* priest, engraved in the *Koftgari* fashion and inlaid with gold, was beseeching the Dutchman—

For the gates of Paradise are forever locked to suicides . . .

Then what on earth am I to do, asked the Dutchman. *You forbid me to die, yet I'm driven insane with unrequited love; what then should I do, Padre?*

Pray, my son! Pray to our Holy Mother for her succour . . .

Forlorn, the Dutchman looked around the landscape of his sketch, this little island of Dejima, that little island prison, and shook his head—

This is Japan, Padre; Mary will not hear me here . . .

And then, in that small, dark and curious shop on Teramachi, Ryūnosuke heard the tiniest, the most beautiful and haunting voice he had ever heard say—

I hear you, my child. For I am here, and here for you . . .

As though in a dream, a dream within a dream, Ryūnosuke walked towards one of the cabinets along the wall and stared through its glass doors at a worn, white statue of the Buddhist deity Kannon, the Goddess of Mercy, about a foot in height and carved from ivory, her folds all blackened by dirt, a child in her hands on her lap, the head of the child long lost, the stump of its shoulders stained with dust, with a cross around her own neck, the cross of a Catholic rosary, her eyes staring up at him, smiling—

I am here, Ryūnosuke, I am here for you . . .

Slowly, Ryūnosuke opened the glass double doors, reached inside, picked up the Maria Kannon and lifted her out of the cabinet, into the cradle of his arms, her eyes staring up at him, smiling up at him—

Thank you, Ryūnosuke, my love . . .

Quickly, Ryūnosuke glanced around the shop again, looking for the owner, the proprietor of the place, walking towards the back of the store, searching for a counter or a door to the back or the upstairs of the building; Ryūnosuke could find nothing, could see no one, but, pinned on the back wall of the shop, there was a handwritten notice: *Once these small pieces were lost, now these small pieces are found—*

Ryūnosuke wrapped the flaps of his jacket around the statue and walked out of the shop, through the door, onto the street, again the sound of the shawm of a vendor, calling and echoing through the twilight of Teramachi as he turned to close the door behind him with one last, quick peek back inside the little *shōhin* shop—

From within the shadows at the back of the store, a small old woman was staring out at him, puffing on a long, thin pipe, her hair held up in a bun by a comb, watching him. Now she took the mouth of the pipe from her lips, tapped its black barrel on the edge of the table, looked back up at him, smiled and said, "Conk!"

Half in the doorway, half out on the street, Ryūnosuke looked away from the woman and stared down at the Maria Kannon— Mary staring up at him, Mary smiling up at him—and on the base of the stand on which she stood Ryūnosuke now read the inscription carved in Latin at her feet—

DESINE FATA DEUM FLECTI SPERARE PRECANDO.

*

Under a full May moon, on the Bridge of Hesitation, I am breaking apart a Castella cake from Fukusaya, stuffing great chunks of Castella into my mouth, longing and yearning, under this full May moon, on this Bridge of Hesitation, longing for a path to follow, a different path, yearning for wings, oh had I the wings, under the moon, on the bridge, the tranquil breezes from up the hill, the golden fruits there on the hill, longing and yearning, under the moon but off the bridge, beneath the willows, the weeping willows, through the lights of Maruyama-chō, her veiled lanterns shining red, longing and yearning, the currents raging, the torrents rising, taking me up the hill, walking me up the hill, to the horror of my soul, the horror of my soul, longing and yearning, without courage, without faith, no hand from the gods or a God, going up the hill again, walking up the hill again, longing and yearning, carrying me up the hill, walking me up the hill, on a promise of wonder, from longing by yearning, up the hill, to wonderland.

*

High up on the hill, up above Maruyama-chō, above the lanterns, above the rooftops, through the gate, past the well, through the garden, past the chestnut tree, in the grounds of the former residence of the mistress of Takashima Shūhan, at a geisha house named Tatsumi, in the second-floor room named Useirō, the Tower of the Voice of the Rain, sat on a cushion in the window, his notebook in his lap, Ryūnosuke had been doodling and sketching, doodles of thin, black, reptilian figures, sketches of the mythical Kappa; now he looked up and out of the window, watching the lights from the house fall through the night, over the barley and the bamboo of the garden, listening as sudden drops of an early summer rain fell on the pantile roof, on the stones of the path and the leaves of the plants below, imagining this house and its garden as they once must have been, the place now lost, the time now gone, the sound of the raindrops now gone, too, lost in the noise from the rest of his party; gathered around the large table on the mats in the centre of the room, Kanbara, Nagami and Watanabe chatting and drinking with the geisha of the house, Dateyakko, Kikuchiyo and Terugiku, everyone joking and laughing, the faces of the men shining red, their cheeks ruddy with drink, playing and singing, standing to dance, then falling to sleep . . .

Now Terugiku, the geisha of this house to whom Ryūnosuke had grown quite close, very close, in fact—indeed, his only reason to come back here tonight, on this night, his last night in Nagasaki— now Terugiku sat down beside Ryūnosuke, stared down at the doodles and the sketches he had drawn, looked back up, then asked, "Are you bored of this place, Ah-san?"

"Not any more," said Ryūnosuke, looking back at Terugiku—

Her kimono of a *chijimi* weave and her obi of a *hatan* weave were very different from the geisha of Tokyo, and though her hair was drawn up into a ginkgo-leaf bun and her make-up pale, the features of her face were also uncommonly strong for her trade, her brows and her nose pronounced, and her dark eyes and downturned lips gave her a melancholy air, even when she smiled, even as she asked, "Do you believe Kappa really exist, Ah-san?"

"Do you believe we really exist," he replied, "you and me?"

Terugiku gently squeezed his arm, smiled and said, "Of course . . ."

"Then, of course, I believe Kappa exist, too."

She touched his arm again and said, "You've touched a Kappa?"

"No," laughed Ryūnosuke, "they are much too quick for me. But you know, there are so many tales of Kappa, from down the ages, from all over Japan, so one must conclude these tales are based on truth . . ."

Terugiku gently squeezed his arm again, smiled again, and said, "Well, I suppose, by the nature of your trade, you must believe the words you read."

"No," laughed Ryūnosuke again, "not at all. Though I suppose, by the nature of your trade, you must doubt every word you hear . . ."

Her arm still on his arm, Terugiku looked up at Ryūnosuke, slightly shook her head and quietly said, "Not every word, Ah-san."

Ryūnosuke glanced away from Terugiku, glanced back at the room, saw his muddy-faced companions passed out on the cushions on the mats, their glasses now empty, the geisha now gone, saw the peeling flakes on the gold-plate screens of the room, again filling him with a sad nostalgia for the place as it must have been once, the place now lost, the time now gone, just the dusty face of an old clock staring back at him across the silent room—

"It can't be only eleven," he said. "It must be much later?"

"Yes," said Terugiku, "it's much, much later now. But the hands of that clock always stop at exactly two minutes past eleven, no matter how many times we wind it, no matter who comes to repair it, that stubborn old clock always sticks and stops at two minutes past eleven, no matter what."

"One plus one plus two equals four," said Ryūnosuke.

Terugiku gently touched her hand to his cheek as she softly said, "Not everything in this world is an ill omen, Ah-san . . ."

"I know," said Ryūnosuke, holding her hand to his cheek with his own. "But I also know I really should be going now."

"Now," asked Terugiku, "really . . . ?"

Ryūnosuke took her hand from his cheek, squeezed it gently, then placed it in her lap and nodded.

"But what about your friends," asked Terugiku. "Should I wake them, so you can say goodbye?"

Ryūnosuke shook his head and said, "I don't like goodbyes."

"Then why are we saying goodbye," asked Terugiku, leaning over to look up into his face, smile up into his eyes. "Is this goodbye?"

Ryūnosuke looked away, turned away, to his notebook, to tear out a page, to hand her a page, a page on which he'd written—

Kanzōmo saitabatten wakarekana . . .

"The summer lily just bloomed, but now we say goodbye," read Terugiku, and then, her eyes downcast, she said, "So this is goodbye."

Ryūnosuke stood up and walked towards the doors, Terugiku standing up and following him. Ryūnosuke opened the sliding doors, then turned back to Terugiku and said, "I hope not . . ."

"Thank you," said Terugiku, kneeling down on the floor before him, placing one hand on the other on the mats. Then, bowing her head, she said, "My name is Waka Sugimoto. Next time we meet, please call me Waka."

Ryūnosuke turned and walked out of the room, he did not turn or look back, he walked out of the house, through the garden, the rain now stopped, the rain now gone, a figure in the garden, the figure of a man, a Western man, his hands a spyglass, but Ryūnosuke did not stop, he did not look back, he walked through the gates and back down the hill, through Maruyama-chō, its lanterns no longer lit but its willows still weeping, under the willows and over the bridge, over the Matsugae Bridge he walked, looking never back, looking only up, the stars still in the sky, up through the Triangle of Prayers, up towards the Ōura Tenshudō, the stained windows of the Temple of the Holy Mother, the Passion of the Christ illuminated in the darkness, shining through the coming dawn, calling to Ryūnosuke, summoning Ryūnosuke, calling him to prayer, summoning him to his knees, in a pew, among the faithful, his hands together, his lips moving, "Lead us not into temptation . . ."

After the Mass, his prayers said, Ryūnosuke stayed in the pew, stayed in his seat, before the tomb of Father Petitjean and the statue of the Holy Mother and Child, his eyes moistening as he stared up at the cross on the altar.

And then with a deep intake of breath, now rubbing his face with both hands, Ryūnosuke got up from his seat, left the pew, and walked down the aisle, past the baptismal font, to a table standing before the doors, piles of prayer books and crosses on rosaries for sale on the table by the doors—

Ryūnosuke held up a rosary to a priest by the table. "How much?"

The priest took the rosary from Ryūnosuke, the cross from his hands, and said, "I'm sorry, sir. This is only for Christians, not for tourists . . ."

Ryūnosuke looked at the priest, this foreign priest on native soil, and said, "Excuse me, my mistake; I mistook you for a salesman, this place for a museum."

The priest started to reply, but Ryūnosuke was walking through the doors of the Ōura Tenshudō, down its steps and down the hill, teardrops in his eyes, falling on his cheek, echoing in his heart, the chambers of his heart . . .

On the bridge again, standing on the bridge, on the Shianbashi bridge again, the Bridge of Hesitation, Ryūnosuke heard a sound from the water under the bridge, he looked down over the edge of the bridge into the water, and in the water he saw a face, a face staring back up at him, a face reflected in the water, the face of a Kappa staring back up at him, the face of a Kappa reflected in the water, reflected and staring back, smiling now, saying now, "Quack, quack! Pleased to meet you. I'm a Kappa; the name is Tock."

*

I alight from the train onto the platform, go down the stairs, through the ticket gates, out of Tokyo station and into the path and the screams of a madman: "Humanity has become too proud, people become too arrogant! They laugh in the face of nature; they no longer respect the Heavens. But beware, and keep your pride in check. For do you think your duty to the gods is merely to wear beautiful kimonos, eat rich foods and live in gaudy palaces? Something dreadful will come of it, something terrible is on its way. This city will be destroyed in less than the span of a single day. And all will be ruin, and all will be corpses. For when the world is touched by Heaven's anger, then the world will be turned upside down."

After the Disaster, Before the Disaster

In an emergency such as this earthquake,
art is useless, to say the least.
Our recent experience only helped to expose
the ultimate futility of all artistic endeavours.

Ruminations on the Earthquake, Kan Kikuchi, 1923

After the disaster, Ryūnosuke would live for four more years.

Before the disaster, during that summer, Ryūnosuke and the artist Ryūichi Oana had been staying in Kamakura. They had returned to Tokyo on August 25, the heat in the capital still extreme, but then, just four days later, at twilight, Ryūnosuke had started to shiver, his temperature rising to 38.6. Dr. Shimojima diagnosed influenza; Ryūnosuke's mother, aunt, wife and children had all caught colds, too, to varying degrees.

Before the disaster, the day before, Ryūnosuke had gradually begun to feel better, reading *Shibue Chūsai* by the late Mori Ōgai in bed.

Before the disaster, during that morning, there had been brief showers and a strong wind. Ryūnosuke had finished reading the last chapter of *Shibue Chūsai* and had then flicked through the various newspaper reports on the formation of a new cabinet under Count Yamamoto, ignoring yet more articles on the love-suicide of Takeo Arishima and Akiko Hatano: the degenerate decadence and moral bankruptcy of the literati.

Before the disaster, just before noon, Ryūnosuke had had a piece of bread and a glass of milk, and was just about to drink some tea and smoke a cigarette when he felt a slight vibration. Moments later, the house was shaking to an extraordinary degree and he could hear tiles falling from the roof above him, his family screaming from the rooms about him. And the shaking did not subside, as was usual, the motion only becoming more intense, so Ryūnosuke led his mother out of the house and into the garden, while his wife rushed upstairs to rescue their second son, Takashi, who was sleeping on the second floor, his aunt gripping the feet of the steep ladder, trying to stay on her own feet, continuously calling their names. But then, after a short while, his aunt and wife emerged from the house holding Takashi, joining Ryūnosuke and his mother in the garden as the ground continued to tilt and to roll. Yet there was still no sign of his father or his first son, Hiroshi; their maid, Shizu, rushed back inside the house, then came back out with Hiroshi in her arms. And soon his father, too, appeared in the garden, and now the whole family stood together, holding and clinging and clutching each other as, monotonously, Ryūnosuke repeated, "It's okay. It's okay," while thinking, *It's not okay. It's not okay.* For still now the ground continued to rumble, continued to sway, heaving and tossing, the air filled with the thickening fog of a smothering dust, the choking stench of turning soil and the deafening screams of grinding timbers: *Gii-ko, gii-ko, gii-ko, gii-ko . . .*

After the disaster, the official record would state that the Great Kantō Earthquake had started at 11:58 a.m. on September 1, 1923, and had stopped after four minutes.

After those four minutes had passed, the biggest shakes seemed to stop, the waves of shocks seemed to lessen, and his wife, his aunt and their maids immediately began to bring essential provisions and the family's most valued possessions from out of the house. They lined them up in the garden. His wife suggested Ryūnosuke should do the same with his most treasured books. Ryūnosuke went back inside the house to his study on the second floor. Many things had fallen or moved since he had last sat at his desk. He righted piles of books, he straightened sheets of paper. Then, for some time, Ryūnosuke stared around the room at his library, wondering which books to save and which to forsake: Baudelaire or Strindberg? Flaubert or Dostoevsky? But Ryūnosuke did not want to read poetry. He did not want to read drama. He did not want to read short stories or novels. Ryūnosuke picked up a volume by Voltaire. He put it back down.

He picked up a volume by Rousseau. He put it back down. Finally, he chose the Bible and *The Communist Manifesto*. Then Ryūnosuke wrapped up the calligraphy by Sōseki-sensei in a *furoshiki*, picked up the statue of the Maria Kannon he had acquired in Nagasaki, and took them all down the ladder, out into the garden. He pulled leaves off a *bashō* plant. He put the leaves on the dirt of the ground. Then he put the books, the *furoshiki* and the Maria Kannon on the green of the leaves. His wife and his aunt looked at him with contempt. Ryūnosuke could not tell if their disdain was directed at his choice of books, the Maria Kannon or his treatment of the plant. Or maybe it was not contempt, maybe it was fear—

"Look! Look," shouted his eldest son, Hiroshi, pointing at the sky.

From the gate of their house on the hill in Tabata, Ryūnosuke and his family could see thick black clouds of smoke rising from the fires that were now raging across the lower parts of the city, and Ryūnosuke and his family knew they had been spared the worst of the quake and, so far, the ravages of the flames; a few loose tiles had slid off their roof and smashed on the ground; the stone lantern near the gate had toppled over and broken into pieces. Ryūnosuke gathered up the fragments of the tiles. He stacked them neatly in a pile. But then the ground shook again and the pile collapsed. Ryūnosuke stared at the fragments of the roof tiles and then at the four pieces of the stone lantern. He tried to right the base of the lantern, but it was too heavy to lift. He left the fragments and the pieces lying where they had fallen.

That afternoon, their neighbour, Kurasuke Watanabe, a student, came to check on Ryūnosuke and his family. Even though he still felt rather weak, Ryūnosuke agreed to accompany Kurasuke on a tour of their neighbourhood.

People had escaped into the streets, yet were chatting amiably with a newfound cordiality, offering each other cigarettes and slices of *nashi* pears, and looking after each other's children in a scene of unprecedented kindness. But further on, on the slopes of Shinmei-chō, there were houses that had been destroyed, and when Ryūnosuke and Kurasuke stood on the bridge of Tsukimi, for as far as they could see the sky over Tokyo had turned to mud, towers of flame and columns of smoke flashing and rising up.

Kurasuke decided to continue his tour, to find out what news he could, while Ryūnosuke would return to the house and his family. But when he arrived back home, Ryūnosuke discovered the lights and the gas no longer worked, and his family fretting about shortages of food.

And so off Ryūnosuke set again, back around the neighbourhood, buying candles and rice, canned goods and vegetables. But back on the Tsukimi Bridge at twilight, staring back out over Tokyo, Ryūnosuke felt as though he was looking into the blast of a furnace, the sky so very, very red, the fires getting only stronger, not weaker, a never-ending river of people now flooding through Tabata and Nippori, the streets all lined and blocked with chairs and mats, no one sleeping indoors tonight.

That evening, Kurasuke called back in on Ryūnosuke and his family with the reports from his tour, with the news he had heard—*Honjo-ku, all burnt; Hongō-ku, all burnt; Shitaya-ku, all burnt; Kōjimachi-ku, the palace and the block south of Hibiya Park safe; the Imperial Hotel and the district south, safe; Koishikawa-ku, the River Edo side, burnt; Kyōbashi-ku, all burnt; Shiba-ku, mostly burnt; Azabu-ku, partly burnt; Ushigome-ku, safe; Yotsuya-ku, mostly safe; Asakusa-ku, all burnt; Nihonbashi-ku, all burnt; Akasaka-ku, the half towards the city centre, burnt; Fukagawa-ku, all burnt; Yokohama and the Shōnan areas all lost, too*—and Ryūnosuke feared the houses of his sister and half-brother in Shiba and Honjo must have been completely burnt out, worried how they and their families could possibly have survived. Before moving to Tabata, Ryūnosuke and his family had lived in Honjo. *Had we not moved*, thought Ryūnosuke, *then surely we would all be dead by now.* And Ryūnosuke feared for his friends who had stayed on in Kamakura, too, only praying they had somehow, somehow survived.

A little later, Dr. Shimojima also called on them, to check on their health, offering them medicine if needed. For luckily his supplies had been saved by his wife. During the quake, she had gone back into their dispensary and held all the cabinets, shelves and drawers of medicines in place, all by herself, so they had had no need to worry about any sudden fires inside. *How brave she was,* thought Ryūnosuke. He knew he could never have done what she did; surely she was the reincarnation of Shibue Chūsai's wife!

But the ground continued to shake, their nerves continued to fray, smoke still filling the air, ash falling from the skies on the house and garden, and more visitors continued to call, now to borrow their money, to eat their food, to drink their water, now to share their reports of destruction and fire, their rumours of insurrection and invasion, their accusations of arson and looting, their whispers of rape and murder, their words of death and words of fear.

Finally that evening, the head of the Neighbourhood Association also called on Ryūnosuke and his family; the head of the Neighbourhood Association asked Ryūnosuke if he and his family were all healthy and well, their house habitable and safe; then the head of the Neighbourhood Association told Ryūnosuke that martial law had been proclaimed, that all troops in Tokyo had been mobilised, and that anyone refusing to comply with requisition orders would be subject to three years' imprisonment or a three-thousand-yen fine. Now the head of the Neighbourhood Association asked Ryūnosuke if he, as a Good Citizen, would join their newly formed local Committee of Vigilance, so he, as a Good Citizen, could help safeguard their neighbourhood during this period of uncertainty and upheaval. Ryūnosuke, as a Good Citizen, nodded. Now the head of the Neighbourhood Association handed

Ryūnosuke a helmet. And Ryūnosuke, as a Good Citizen, put it on.

After the head of the Neighbourhood Association had left, Ryūnosuke dashed round to see Kurasuke; he explained his fever had returned and he had a headache, a headache so terrible he could barely stand, so would Kurasuke kindly take his turn on watch for the Committee of Vigilance that night? Kurasuke readily agreed, laying out a small dagger, putting on a wooden sword and looking every inch the Good and Vigilant Citizen.

That night, back home, Ryūnosuke lay on the futon between his wife and two sons. He tried to read the Bible. But he could not concentrate. He tried to read *The Communist Manifesto*. But, again, he could not concentrate. For under the ground he could feel the earth continue to grind and scream, a gigantic mechanical worm burrowing through caverns and tunnels, pushing the ground up, then pulling it back down in its wake. Ryūnosuke imagined the turning gears and spinning cogwheels deep within the metallic body of the beast. And he could hear again and again those accusations and whispers, of rape and murder, of death and fear. He put his fingers in his ears, he put his fingers in his eyes, and Ryūnosuke waited for the dawn.

*

I am a Good Citizen. But in my opinion, Kan Kikuchi is lacking in this respect.

After martial law was imposed, I was conversing with Kan Kikuchi, a cigarette dangling from my mouth. Though I say conversing, we spoke of nothing but the earthquake. As we were talking, I said that I had heard the cause of the fires was XXXXXXXXX. Upon hearing this, Kikuchi raised his eyebrows and exclaimed, "What a lie!" When put to me this way, I could do nothing but agree, "Hmm, so it's not true." But I still said again that it seemed that the XXXX were the fingers of the Bolsheviks. Kikuchi again raised his eyebrows and scolded, "It's not true, you know, what they say." Again I said, "Oh, so that's not true either," and immediately withdrew my explanation.

Nevertheless, in my opinion, a good citizen believes in the existence of conspiracies between Bolsheviks and XXXX. If, by chance, one could not believe, one should at least put on a show of believing. But that barbaric Kan Kikuchi didn't even make a show of believing, let alone actually believe. This should be seen as a complete renunciation of the qualifications of being a good citizen. I—the good citizen and courageous member of a self-protection group that I am—could not help but feel pity for Kikuchi.

But then, becoming a good citizen requires a lot of hard work.

*

After the disaster, the next morning, Ryūnosuke was overcome with worry for his friend Yasunari. Yasunari lived in Asakusa and, throughout the long night, all the rumours and whispers Ryūnosuke had heard filled him with dread for the fate of his young friend; he saw the delicate, refined face of Yasunari broken and crushed beneath the weight of a building, pale and bloodless, or his thin, hollow frame burnt and charred on a mountain of corpses, black and anonymous. And so with a great sense of foreboding and some degree of duplicity, for fear of worrying his wife and family, Ryūnosuke left the relative calm and safety of Tabata—his little *bunshi mura*, this "village of the literati" on the outskirts—and set off for the Asakusa area.

The journey from Tabata was not an easy one for there were no streetcars and the roads were clogged with survivors, children strapped to their backs, shouldering enormous bundles or pushing handcarts piled high with their belongings, all heading out of Tokyo, in the opposite direction to Ryūnosuke. A military law had already been passed that allowed people to leave Tokyo but forbade others from entering, and so there were soldiers and police on every corner. There were Committees of Vigilance, too, formed by Good and Upright Citizens, all carrying clubs or pipes, sticks or swords, and often wearing helmets similar to the one Ryūnosuke now sported. And as he walked towards Asakusa, Ryūnosuke watched as these committees dragged men from the columns of survivors to accuse them of being non-Japanese, either in blood or spirit, and up to no good. Without fail, these accusations were punctuated by blows from the clubs or pipes, sticks or swords of the Committees of Vigilance. Ryūnosuke was certain that had he not been wearing his new helmet, then he, too, would have been subjected to such accusations and blows. Or worse, much worse.

Finally, Ryūnosuke reached Asakusa. Or the place where Asakusa once had stood. For here the destruction was total; mile after mile of completely charred and still-smoking ruin, from the river in the east in every direction, and everywhere corpses: charred-black corpses, half-burnt corpses, corpses sprawling in gutters, corpses floating in rivers, corpses piled up on bridges, corpses blocking off whole streets at intersections. Every manner of death possible to a human being was on display. And everywhere, the stench of death; an odour of rotting apricots which, even through the handkerchief Ryūnosuke pressed against his face, burnt his nose and scalded his eyes with horror and with grief. For now, at last, tears came, tears flowed as Ryūnosuke remembered the people and the place Asakusa once had been, the little pleasure stalls, all now cinders, the pots of morning glories, all now withered, all now harrowed—

All now dead.

And Ryūnosuke despaired for Yasunari. But then, at that very moment, he heard the very voice of his friend and Ryūnosuke turned; he blinked; he blinked again; he rubbed his eyes with his handkerchief and blinked again. *But yes! Yes! It was true!* Here, here among all this destruction, here among all this death, here was Yasunari, alive and unhurt, walking towards him across the rubble, coming towards him through the smoke, in animated conversation with Tōkō Kon, another of their friends—

"Kawabata-kun," exclaimed Ryūnosuke, "I was certain you must be dead! Sure you must be a ghost . . ."

"Everyone is a ghost now," laughed Yasunari. "Or an orphan."

Yasunari and Tōkō Kon were walking up to the Yoshiwara to see what had become of the old pleasure quarter, and they urged Ryūnosuke to join them. And as they picked their way through the wasteland, Yasunari never stopped jotting down his impressions in his notebook, or recounting his recent adventures and observations—

"In the moments after the first great shock, before the fire consumed my lodgings, I was able to salvage some bedding. And so, last night, I slept on that in the park. I even managed to construct a mosquito net. And then who should crawl under the net beside me, but my landlord's wife and her child."

But when the three friends came upon the Yoshiwara quarter, even Yasunari fell silent in the face of what they saw there.

The Benten Pond was now a cauldron of five hundred corpses, bodies piled upon bodies, some burnt and some boiled. Muddy red cloth was strewn up and down the banks of the pond, for most of the dead were courtesans.

Ryūnosuke stood among the smouldering incense, his handkerchief pressed to his face, his eyes fixed upon the corpse of a child of twelve or thirteen years. Ryūnosuke looked away, up at the sky, his eyes smarting with the smoke and the sun. He wanted to cry out, to scream at the gods:

"Why? Why? Why was this child ever born, to die like this?"

And again, as he had many times before, Ryūnosuke saw the image of Christ on the cross, and again he heard the words that haunted him:

"My God, my God, why hast thou forsaken me?"

Beside Ryūnosuke stood a young boy of a similar age to the corpse. The boy was staring at the body, too. He stifled a sob, he looked away. But his older brother grabbed his arm, gripped his face and scolded him, "Look carefully, Akira. If you shut your eyes to a frightening sight, you end up being frightened for ever. But if you look everything straight on, then there is nothing to be afraid of . . ."

Suddenly, Ryūnosuke felt the eyes of the young boy upon him. Ryūnosuke turned to smile at the child. But when their eyes met, the boy hid his face in the folds of his older brother's clothes. Ryūnosuke turned on his heel and marched off, thinking, *It would have been better had we all died.*

*

Viscount Shibusawa has said that we should think of this earthquake as a heavenly punishment. There is surely no one who remains unscathed by this disaster, but looking back upon the deaths of his own wife and child, and then to others whose houses remain undamaged, who would not be surprised at the injustice of such heavenly punishment? It is better to forgo belief in heavenly punishment altogether than to believe in a partial heavenly punishment, and to recognise nature's cruel indifference to us as humans . . .

Before the disaster, during the summer, when Oana and I were staying in a cottage at the Hirano-ya Bessō in Kamakura, over the eaves of our room were trails of wisteria, and between the leaves we could see some purple flowers here and there; to see wisteria blooming in August seemed like something from a chronicle. But not only this, looking out at the garden from the window in the bathroom there were Japanese roses blooming, too. Moreover, and stranger still, in the pond of the garden of Komachien, their irises and lotuses were all in full bloom, too . . .

Thinking of the wisteria, the roses and the irises all blooming in

*August, I came to believe nature must have gone mad. And every time
I saw someone, I spoke of a cataclysmic convulsion of nature occurring
now, changing the heavens and moving the earth . . .*

*Yet no one took me seriously; Masao Kume just smirked at me, mocked
me, and said, "You are just making Kan Kikuchi even more nervous."*

*Oana and I arrived back in Tokyo on August 25, and the Great
Earthquake happened eight days later; now Kume greatly respects my
prediction: "Before, I'd simply wanted to argue against you as a pose.
But, in fact, your prediction has come true."*

*Yet if I'm honest, I must confess I did not believe my own prediction.
Nature is cruelly indifferent towards humanity. The earthquake did
not differentiate between proletarian and bourgeoisie, the good and the
bad; it's just as Turgenev wrote in his poems—*

In the eyes of nature, humans are no different from insects . . .

*

After the disaster, on the way back to Tabata, passing through Iriya,
under a tangle of scorched electric lines, beside streetcars burnt in
their tracks, Ryūnosuke suddenly heard the voice of a child by the
side of the road, the child playing in the rubble, the child singing,
My Old Kentucky Home . . .

In a trice, the song of this child overcame the spirit of negation
which had gripped and overwhelmed Ryūnosuke: *Yes,* thought
Ryūnosuke, *there will always be those who say that art is excess and
surplus to our existence. And it is true, when your head is on fire, you
do not think how best to represent the flames. Just as when you take a
piss or have a shit, you maybe don't think of Rembrandt or Goethe. Yet
surely what makes humans human is always this excess and this surplus
we create, which gives us our dignity, which helps us to transcend and
to sing a song no quake or fire can ever destroy . . .*

But then, approaching Nippori, Ryūnosuke fell in step with a policeman. As the two men walked, Ryūnosuke questioned the policeman at length about the earthquake, about the fires and about the various rumours of crimes and insurrection that seemed to still fall from every passing mouth, hanging in the air with the smoke and the odour of death, that stench of rotting apricots.

The policeman, impressed perhaps by Ryūnosuke's helmet, was talkative but confessed that while he knew many had been accused of malicious or revolutionary acts, he himself had seen no evidence of any such deeds.

Just outside Nippori station, Ryūnosuke and the policeman came across the body of a man tied to a pole, his head beaten in, his body horribly mutilated, with a sign around his neck which declared he was both a Korean and an arsonist. The man must have died by inches, and even now, perhaps hours after his slow death, as Ryūnosuke and the policeman stood before him, another passer-by approached to whack the corpse with a rolled-up parasol. This passer-by now turned to Ryūnosuke and the policeman; he thanked them for their good work, bowed and then sauntered off, swinging his now-bloody parasol as he went. The policeman shook his head; he urged Ryūnosuke to take care, bade him farewell, and then walked on.

After the disaster, in the twilight, Ryūnosuke remained transfixed before the body of the Korean, the ground beneath him still rising and falling. And as Ryūnosuke stared at the body of the Korean, at all the bodies of the dead, as he stared across this city of rubble, across this city of smoke, everywhere he saw gears and wheels, translucent against the earth, luminous against the sky, turning and spinning, grinding and screaming.

Now four crows landed on two adjacent tilted, twisted poles. They stared first at the corpse, then at Ryūnosuke—

Ryūnosuke took off his helmet, Ryūnosuke bowed his head. The biggest crow lifted its bloody beak heavenwards and cawed once, twice, a third time, and then a fourth.

After the disaster, the official record stated that the Great Kantō Earthquake had had a magnitude of 7.9 on the Richter scale, that it had started at 11:58 a.m. on September 1, 1923, and had stopped after four minutes.

Ryūnosuke did not believe the official record. Ryūnosuke believed the earthquake had not stopped, would never stop. Ryūnosuke knew the disaster was still-to-come.

*

All who bear the name of socialist, whether a Bolshevik or not, appear to be considered a threat. Especially at the time of the recent Great Earthquake, many seem to have been cursed this way. But, if we are speaking of socialists, Charlie Chaplin is a socialist, too. If we are to persecute socialists, shouldn't we persecute Charlie Chaplin as well, then? Imagine that Chaplin was killed by a military police lieutenant. Imagine that, while doing his duck-walk, all of a sudden he was stabbed to death. No one who has gazed at his figure on the screen could possibly not feel indignant. If we were to project this indignation to the present situation . . . Anyway, the only thing that is sure is that you, dear reader, are on the blacklist, too . . .

"Saint Kappa"

If you want to live a comparatively peaceful life,
it is best not to be a novelist.

"Ten Rules for Writing a Novel,"
Ryūnosuke Akutagawa, May, 1926

Late in the morning of July 15, 1927, the second year of Shōwa, I received a telegram from Ryūnosuke Akutagawa asking me to come as soon as I could to his house in Tabata, Tokyo. I was surprised, to say the least.

I had seen very little of Akutagawa since his last visit to Nagasaki, which was over five years ago now. Remembering that visit, that time, was as though viewing scenes from someone else's life. My rubber business in Malaysia had gone bankrupt, and I had lost everything. Last year, I had moved to Tokyo, the remote and cheaper outskirts of the city, hoping to make some kind of living through writing and publishing, hoping then to turn my financial loss into a personal gain, if nothing else, fulfilling my long-held literary ambitions. And though my wife and I were far from comfortable, I had managed to publish two books on the art and history of Nagasaki. Yet even here, on the outskirts of the capital and its literary circles, I had not seen much of Akutagawa. From what I had heard, he himself had not had the best of times either, and these rumours were confirmed on one of the rare and last occasions I had seen him, four or five months ago.

Earlier this year, towards the end of winter, Kaizōsha had thrown a party at the Kabukiza to celebrate the success of their *Enbon* series of one-yen books and, between the performances, I was in the corridor smoking when, suddenly, Akutagawa came rushing up to me, gripped my shoulders in both hands, pushed me up against the wall and said, "I can't bear it!"

"What," I said, shocked at his words, his actions and his appearance; he looked so frail, almost emaciated, his cheeks hollow and his nose even more pronounced, his face a pale blue and his lips a sickly red, with his hair long and falling over his forehead. In truth, he appeared the replica of one of those caricatures he had often drawn of himself as a Kappa in Nagasaki.

"When I caught the train from Kugenuma today," he said, opening his eyes as wide as they would go, as though about to share the strangest story in the world, "the landscape along the tracks was burning red!"

"Really," I asked. "Was somewhere on fire?"

But Akutagawa didn't answer, his eyes downcast now, yet smiling to himself, suddenly looking up again, then back down again, then up at me, until at last he said, "You know my brother-in-law committed suicide?"

"I know," I said, and nodded. "I heard."

"It really is unbearable . . . I still haven't been able to settle the matter. There are so many things to sort out . . . I can't stand it any more . . ."

There, in that dim, narrow corridor of the Kabukiza, his shoulders, his whole body seemed weighed down with the burden, his face so exhausted, so isolated and so pained, yet almost childlike in his agony and despair.

I put a hand on his shoulder, gently patting him, and said, "Yes, we seem to have reached the age when such things fall on us, caring for our older relatives, yet still supporting the younger ones . . ."

"Well," he sighed, "I just can't bear it."

"But what choice do we have," I said, less as a question and more as a fact, thinking of my own financial problems, knowing the mental burdens were enormous, and I continued, as much to myself as to Akutagawa, "But if we constantly think of our situation as a burden, then it really does become unbearable. It's surely better just to accept it all as part of the natural order of things as we age, and that now our turn has come around . . ."

Again, Akutagawa didn't answer; again, his eyes downcast, still smiling to himself, leaning against the wall of the corridor, smoking cigarette after cigarette; I couldn't even be sure he had heard what I'd said and, as the bell rang for the next performance, as people began to go back inside the auditorium, as I said goodbye, once again urging him to do his best to endure the situation, as he looked up at me with his wide but beautiful eyes, I remember thinking, wondering what on earth they saw, those beautiful eyes, when he looked at this world, burning red along the tracks . . .

And that winter night was the last contact I had had with him, until his sudden telegram that summer day, and so, as I made my way from the western outskirts to Tabata, it was with some degree of trepidation.

Uncomfortable and weary from the heat and the journey, I arrived at the Akutagawa house late that afternoon to find one of the maids showing out Dr. Shimojima. Dr. Shimojima was widely known and respected in haiku circles, but he was also the family doctor for the Akutagawa household, and so I was naturally concerned to see him. However, the doctor's call had been a purely social one and he proudly showed me the signed copy of Akutagawa's latest book, *The Folding Fan of Hunan*, which he had just been given. Feeling somewhat relieved, I was then shown up to the second floor and into Chōkōdō, the name Akutagawa had given to his study, and which could be read as either "Clear River House" or "Sumida River House."

Inside Chōkōdō, Akutagawa was seated on the floor at his writing desk, drawing those thin, black, reptilian figures with one hand and chain-smoking with the other, his hair long over his face, his eyes on the paper.

I coughed and said, "Good afternoon, Sensei."

Akutagawa looked up at me blankly, trying to place me, then nodded, then smiled and said, "Ah, Nagami-san, you came. And on such a very hot day, in such unbearable heat. Thank you . . ."

"Thank you for inviting me, Sensei."

Akutagawa stood up. His *yukata* was loose, his underwear clearly visible and very grey, and his body beneath seemed even more emaciated. He walked over to one of his many piles of books and papers. He picked up an envelope, then handed it to me and said, "If it's not a great burden and inconvenience for you, I'd like to entrust this manuscript to you."

Of course, I gratefully received the envelope and started to open it.

"I'm sorry to be so abrupt and demanding," said Akutagawa, "but if you are inclined to read the shabby story contained inside that envelope, I'd be most grateful if you would do so later."

"Of course," I replied, "and thank you. I am honoured, Sensei."

"The honour is mine," said Akutagawa. "And if I could beg one last honour, would you stroll with me a while, allow me to treat you to some tea and sweets?"

And so that summer day, the two of us strolled through the twilight until late in the evening, spending some hours in one particular sweet parlour. Sadly, I cannot now recall all our conversations, all Akutagawa said that night. However, I do remember one moment, as we were both indulging in a second bowl of sweet-bean soup, when Akutagawa stifled a yawn and then suddenly said, "I'm having such terrible trouble sleeping, you know."

"Yes, it happens to me, too, from time to time," I said. "But usually after too much caffeine and tobacco."

Akutagawa looked forlorn as he said, "Would that were true for me, too. In my case, I am being haunted by a horrible dream. But forgive me, it's such a bore to have to suffer the dreams of others . . ."

"Not at all," I said. "If in any way it may help you to share such a horrible dream, then by all means please do."

"Thank you," said Akutagawa. "Well then, in this dream, in a deserted, ruined and wasted garden, there is an iron castle with iron grilles on its narrow windows. Inside the iron castle, there is only one room. In the room, there is only one desk. At that desk, a creature who looks like me is writing in letters I cannot read a long poem about a creature who in another room is writing a poem about another creature who in another room is writing a poem, and so on, and so on, and so on . . ."

"And you've had this dream more than once?"

"Every night," sighed Akutagawa. "The dream recurs, it never ends, but I can never read the poem. That is the most terrifying aspect; eternally, I will never be able to read the poem . . ."

I did not know what to say, nor can I now recall if in fact I did say anything. But I do remember thinking, that explained why Akutagawa was so keen to stay out so late, so reluctant to return home that night to sleep.

It was well past midnight when I returned to my own home. However, my curiosity outweighed my tiredness, so I opened up the envelope, took out the manuscript, and I began to read, to read and to read . . .

Kappa: A Postscript

Late one morning, I received a telegram from Tock asking me to come as soon as I possibly could to his house.

Early on, after I had first found myself in the land of the Kappa, I had been befriended by a student called Lap. In turn, Lap had introduced me to Tock; Tock was a poet, and I often went to visit him as a way of passing time. I would always find him smoking and writing at his desk in his study, among his books and his papers, Kappa texts and Human texts—Jonathan Swift and William Morris, Hirata Atsutane and Kunio Yanagita, Oscar Wilde and Anatole France—so many texts, so many more, Tock surrounded by pots of alpine plants, a female Kappa sat in a corner of the room, silently knitting or sewing. Tock seemed not to have a care in the world, always greeting and welcoming me with a big warm smile, and we would sit for hours, talking about the life and art of the Kappa. Tock had very strong opinions and views on art, insisting art should be unfettered by any rules of life, art being purely for art's sake and therefore the true artist should first and foremost be a Super-Kappa, existing beyond good and evil. Tock was not alone in holding such views, and he would occasionally take me to the Super-Kappa Club. In this salon, under bright electric lights, I found all sorts of other Super-Kappa: poets, novelists, dramatists, critics, painters, musicians and sculptors, both professional and amateur. Long into the night, they would smoke and drink and talk and shout and argue and fight about life and art, the meaning and worth of the one and the other. More-often-than-not, at the end of such an evening, Tock and I would stagger off arm in arm, slowly making our way home, occasionally even singing a song or two. As I say, Tock always seemed the most carefree Kappa I knew, and I could not imagine what had prompted his telegram, and so I hurried as fast as I could to his house.

On arriving, I was shown up to the second floor and entered Gakikutsu, the name Tock had given to his study, and which meant something like "Demon's Cave" or "Demon's Lair," after Gaki or "Demon Self," a nom de plume he sometimes adopted. As usual, Tock was seated on the floor at his writing desk, among his books and plants, but today he was drawing thin, black, avian figures with one hand and chain-smoking with the other, his hair hanging long over his face, his eyes staring down at the paper.

I coughed and said, "Good afternoon, Tock."

Tock looked up at me with a start, trying to place me, and then said, "Ah, ah, A-san, you came at last. Thank you . . ."

Tock stood up. His body seemed almost emaciated as he walked over to one of his many piles of books and papers. He picked up an envelope, then handed it to me, saying, "If it's not a great burden and inconvenience for you, I'd like to entrust this manuscript to you."

Of course, I gratefully received the envelope and started to open it.

"I'm sorry to be abrupt and demanding," said Tock. "But if you are inclined to read the shabby story contained inside that envelope, I'd be very grateful if you would do so later, at your leisure."

"Of course," I replied, "but thank you. I'm honoured."

"The honour is mine," said Tock. "And if I could beg one last honour, would you stroll with me a while and allow me to treat you to some tea and sweets?"

And so that day, the two of us strolled through the twilight until very late in the evening, spending some hours in one particular sweet parlour. Sadly, I cannot now recall all our conversations, all Tock said that night. However, I do remember one moment, as we were both indulging in a second bowl of sweet-bean soup, when Tock stifled a yawn and then suddenly said, "I'm having such terrible trouble sleeping, you know."

"Yes, it happens to me, too, from time to time," I said. "But usually after too much caffeine and tobacco."

Tock looked forlorn as he said, "Would that were true for me, too! In my case, I'm being haunted by a horrible dream. But forgive me, it's such a bore to have to suffer the dreams of others . . ."

"Not at all," I said. "If in any way it may help you to share such a horrible dream, then by all means please do."

"Thank you," said Tock. "Well then, in this dream, in a deserted, ruined and wasted garden, there is an iron castle with iron grilles on its narrow windows. Inside the iron castle, there is only one room. In the room, there is only one desk. At that desk, a creature who looks like me is writing in letters I cannot read a long poem about a creature who in another room is writing a poem about another creature who in another room is writing a poem, and so on, and so on, and so on . . ."

"And you've had this dream more than once?"

"Every night," sighed Tock. "The dream recurs, it never ends, but I can never read the poem! That is the most terrifying aspect; eternally, I will never be able to read the poem . . ."

I did not know what to say, nor can I now recall if in fact I did say anything. But I do remember thinking, that explained why Tock was so keen to stay out so late, so reluctant to return home that night to sleep.

It was well past midnight when I returned to my own home. However, my curiosity outweighed my tiredness, so I opened up the envelope, took out the manuscript, and I began to read, to read and to read . . .

The Book of Tock: A Postscript

In the land of the Humans, in the country of Japan, at the heart of their capital in Tokyo, lies Jimbōchō, an area which is home to hundreds of bookstores, some large and selling new books, but mostly small and dealing in old or rare texts. Recently, on one of my nocturnal excursions to this land downriver, sneaking into Tamura Shoten for the night, I came across a compendium entitled *Taishō Monogatari*. Among the many interesting stories in this diverse collection was one by a certain Yasukichi Horikawa. I had not heard of Yasukichi Horikawa and, despite extensive enquiries on my part, I have been unable to find any record of the author, other than his story . . .

La Mort d'un Auteur

. . . and which Horikawa introduces with the following note:

This poor excuse for a story is based upon Tu Tze-ch'un, *a T'ang era tale, and the more recent popular retelling by my esteemed contemporary Mr. Ryūnosuke Akutagawa. And so I make no claims for the originality of the following words, and can only beg any reader's forgiveness for the liberties I have taken with the two preceding and vastly superior masterpieces upon which I have based my own shabby, sorry story . . .*

And then it begins . . .

1

In the Age of Winter, at the death of Taishō, under a black and starless sky, north of Asakusa and south of Senju, on the banks of the Sumida River, Y was cold and hungry. Once Y had been a celebrated and successful author, well praised and widely read. But Y had succumbed to the temptations and vices of the Literary Life in the Big City, with all its pleasures of the flesh, its distractions of the mind, and Y had squandered first his talent and then his means. And so Y had lost all he had been given: his readers, his publishers, his friends, fake and real, his lovers, professional and amateur, and finally even his family. And now Y found himself here, in the winter night, on the riverbank, with nowhere to stay, with nothing to eat, not a coin to his name, not a soul to count on. And Y looked up at the black sky, and Y looked down at the black river, looked down and then stared out, across the dark water, over its polluted depths, his eyes smarting in the wind, his voice cracking in the night. "There is nothing else for it . . ."

Slowly, Y got to his feet. Methodically, Y began to search the riverbank for stones. And one by one, Y picked up the stones he found, and one by one, Y put them in the pockets of his thin and tattered overcoat, until the coat hung heavy upon his shoulders.

Slowly, Y walked down to the river's edge and, with a certain sad but resigned smile upon his lips, stepping into the river, wading into the water, he began to hum the tune of the popular "Boatman's Song," with its refrain, "*I am dead grass on the riverbank. You are dead grass on the bank as well / I am dead grass on the riverbank . . .*"

"Stop! Wait," shouted a voice. "What are you doing?"

Waist-high in the water, weighed down by the stones, Y turned his face back to the bank. And there, at the water's edge, stood an old man, his arms outstretched, his palms open, beckoning and beseeching him: "Stop! Stop! Come back, come here . . ."

But over the sound of the waves, the call of the current, Y shouted, "No! No, I do not deserve to live. I am resolved to die."

"Then I will come to you," said the old man, stepping into the river, wading through the water, out towards Y, "and join you."

The wind was rising now, the river moving faster now, the old man already unsteady in his footing, the old man quickly slipping under the water. And Y shook his head, and Y cursed his luck; he could not even die in peace. And Y turned back in the river, and Y waded back through the current, pulling the old man back above the water, dragging the old man back to the bank, until they reached the river's edge and fell upon its bank—

Now side by side, Y and the old man lay upon the land, their faces turned towards the sky, gasping for air and panting for breath, soaked through their skins, soaked to their bones—

"Thank you," said the old man. "You saved me."

Y laughed, Y snorted and said, "You left me no choice."

"No," said the old man. "There is always a choice."

Y laughed again. "Yes. Hobson's choice."

"It's still a choice," said the old man. "To take it or leave it, to act or not."

Y sighed. "Well, I had made my choice. And I had decided to act. But thanks to you, here I am again, on the riverbank, having failed even to die. So thank you, for nothing."

"Don't despair," laughed the old man. "You may yet die of hypothermia. But assuming you don't, I still owe you a debt of thanks for saving my own life. And so if you should survive this night, when you first sense the light of the morning sun, then you will wake to find your reward. Use it or don't, take it or leave it; that choice will be yours."

His teeth chattering, his limbs trembling, Y closed his eyes and laughed. "If you're gone, that will be reward enough for me . . ."

2

The winter sun strangely warm upon his face, its piercing rays dancing on his lids, the sound of boats upon the river, the scent of *fukujusō* on the breeze, yet with an aching pain in his back and in his neck, Y now opened his eyes. The sky above him was a brilliant bright December blue, with not one single cloud or wisp of smoke from a factory yet. Even the ground on which Y lay seemed no longer hard, his clothes no longer sodden, yet still this dull crick, in his back and in his neck. Rubbing his face, massaging his neck, Y now sat up and looked around him: he had been resting his head upon a pillow, the pillow a large *furoshiki*, the cloth a pattern of red and white waves, enfolding a giant bundle, held together in its knot.

Uncertain if he was dreaming, Y slowly undid the knot, Y slowly opened up the cloth, and then he froze, froze until Y blinked, and blinked again, and rubbed his eyes, and rubbed his eyes again. Now Y looked away, now Y looked around: the empty bank, the busy river; all here, all real. Y rubbed his eyes, and looked again. Certain now he was not dreaming, Y slowly reached out and touched the contents of the *furoshiki*: piles and piles of banknotes, all crisp and new, all neatly bound, more than he had ever seen, could ever have imagined. And there, lying on top of the piles of banknotes, was a sheaf of manuscript paper and a fountain pen. Y picked up the pen and the manuscript and quickly began leafing through the papers; all were blank but for the first page, on which was written: *A Postscript.*

Swiftly now, glancing about him, Y put the papers and the pen back on top of the piles of banknotes. Swifter still, Y retied the knot, picked up the *furoshiki* and began to hurry away, as fast as he could carry the bundle, to stumble away, back to the city—under the blue sky now bleaching white, to the shrill chords of factory whistles— back to the city, back to its lights, and back to the life, the life he'd thought lost . . .

In the course of one night, Y had become richer than he had ever dreamed possible, and Y wasted no time in purchasing both a house in Hongō and a villa in Kamakura. But Y knew he had been given a second chance, a second chance he had not deserved, and so he was determined to cherish this chance, this gift he had been given. And so Y began to write again, with the paper and the pen he had been left, soon completing a short *shishōsetsu* novel that, naturally enough, he called—

A Postscript.

Immediately upon publication, the book was hailed as a masterpiece, embraced by readers of all ages, and welcomed as an antidote to these ever-darkening times of naked self-interest and spiritual bankruptcy.

But lauded and loved as he was, Y struggled to write another work, succumbing once again to the temptations and vices of the Literary Life in the Big City, its pleasures of the flesh, its distractions of the mind. For Y was not short of pleasures and distractions now: friends old and new, all fake now, lovers old and new, all professional now, flocked again to gather around Y as his time passed in nights of oblivion and days of regret, while the papers and pen lay abandoned and forgotten, the nights and days turning to months and years, until first the villa in Kamakura and then the house in Hongō were lost, and Y found himself once again under a black and starless sky, on the banks of the Sumida River, with nowhere to stay, with nothing to eat, not a coin to his name, not a soul to count on, watching the waves, staring at the stones, knowing, knowing there was nothing else for it now. . .

"I am dead grass on the riverbank. You are dead grass on the bank as well / I am dead grass . . ."

"Well, well, well," said a familiar old voice in the cold, dark night. "Fancy meeting you here again."

Shocked, Y turned to see the old man sitting beside him on the riverbank.

"What luck," said the old man, "that our paths should cross again." Y shook his head and said, "It's hardly luck, is it? You've been following me, stalking and spying on me, no doubt. Who are you? What do you want?"

"I am simply a man with a debt," said the old man. "A grateful man, wishing to thank the person who saved my life. Nothing more . . ."

Y shook his head again and said, "Well, if that is truly the case, then you more than repaid me. So forget any sense of debt; you owe me nothing."

"No! How can you say that," asked the old man. "The gift of life is the most precious gift there is. It can never be repaid in full. And so lay your head upon these stones, upon this riverbank, and when you first sense the light of the morning sun, then you will wake again to find your reward. Please lay down your head, please now close your eyes . . ."

Shocked again, Y felt himself caught in a sudden tempest of emotions and sensations: the promise of blank sheets of paper, the urgency of a flowing pen and its words upon those sheets, the applause of his critics, the adulation of his readers, the scent of alcohol, the taste of women, pride and greed, gluttony and lust, oblivion and regret, bankruptcy and despair, a black and starless sky, the riverbank, the stones and the water . . .

"No," said Y. "No, thank you. I return your gift, I refuse your gift. For I am not worthy to receive it. Please give it to someone else. For I would only squander it again. And so I do not want it."

"Then tell me," asked the old man, "what do you want?"

And now, for the first time, Y saw the old man, saw the old man as he truly was: far from being the eccentric philanthropist Y had once imagined, the old man sat beside him now was dressed in threadbare, stinking rags, his hair long and matted, his skin ingrained with dirt, ancient and weather-beaten. And Y reached out and took the old man's hand, squeezed it in his own and said, "I want to live as you live, I want to be as you are. Please take me as your disciple. Please, I beg you. Please teach me . . ."

For a long while, the old man was silent, staring down at his own hand pressed tightly between Y's hands. Then slowly, the old man raised his face and stared into Y's eyes and said, "What you are asking is far from easy. What you are asking involves great pain and suffering. So please look into your heart, please ask yourself, Is this truly what I want?"

His grip tightening, Y nodded and said, "It is, it is. Believe me, please."

"Then if you're truly certain," said the old man, "I will do as you ask."

Elated, Y shouted with joy, "Thank you! Thank you!"

"No," whispered the old man. "For this you do not need to thank me, and for this you will not thank me. Just remember: you asked for this, and remain certain in your heart, be certain in your heart . . ."

Y nodded and said, "I will, I will . . ."

"Then please now close your eyes . . ."

And Y closed his eyes.

"And only open them again on the count of three," said the old man. "One, two . . .

"3"

The air thin, the wind biting and his footing precarious, Y opened his eyes; the world had vanished, leaving only the clouds around him and the ground beneath him. Y tried to steady himself, timidly shifting from foot to foot. Y tried to get his bearings, nervously straining to even glimpse his feet: Y seemed to be standing on a flowing heaping of tumbled fragments, rolling and turning under his feet, empty shells bursting beneath him, clattering and crashing down, down, down with soft, hollow echoings as faint, cold fires lighted and died at every breaking far down, down, down below him. Dizzy and nauseous with fear and vertigo, Y closed his eyes, and Y cried out, "Where am I? Where am I? What is this place?"

Now Y felt a hand upon his arm, steady and sure, and Y opened his eyes again; the clouds had parted and the old man was stood beside him, dressed in a coat of shining white feathers, his head clean and shaved, his skin translucent and newborn.

Y reached for the old man's hand, gripping and squeezing it in his own, tighter and tighter, asking, "Where am I? Tell me, what is this place?"

"Look," said the old man. "Just look, and then you'll see."

And now, for the first time, Y saw this place, saw this place for what and where it truly was: not ground, not ground beneath him, not ground above nor ground about him, but naked steeps, steeps of heapings, yes, but endless heapings, heapings of fragments, yes, but measureless and monstrous, of skulls, of skulls and fragments of skulls, and of teeth and bone, of bone and dust of bone, all strewn, all drifting in the wrack of some eternal tide.

"This is the Mountain of Skulls," said the old man. "And I must leave you here, to face what you and only you must face. But no matter what you face, no matter what you see, do not speak, do not make a single sound. For if you speak, if you make one sound, then you cannot live as I live, you cannot be as I am; your wish will be denied. So no matter what, you must not speak, you must not utter one single sound. But then I will return."

Slowly, Y let go of the old man's hand, and said, "I understand."

The old man nodded, and then the old man began to walk away, away, and down, down the mountain, soon but a distant speck, now out, out of sight.

Alone on the mountain, balanced on its shifting tide, his stomach turning with the sudden swells and his constant dread, Y waited and Y waited, his heart pounding and his thoughts racing, sometimes whispering, sometimes deafening, his body and soul churning . . .

"Who are you," whispered a voice, a voice from behind him, closer now, in his ear, closer still, its breath fragrant with delicious food, expensive wine, again it whispered, "Who are you?"

But Y did not answer, Y did not speak, his mouth tight and eyes, too, not opening, not speaking.

"Of course," laughed the voice, "the old man told you not to speak. But it matters not, for we know who you are: you are Yasukichi Horikawa, celebrated and successful author, once lauded by critics and loved by readers, but now suffering something of a slump, a little case of writer's block, just a temporary crisis of confidence. And so here you are, draped in self-doubt, swathed in self-pity; how comforting for you, how easy for you. How pathetic! How pointless! Just say your name, just admit who you are, and all will be returned to you, all will be restored to you; your acclaim and your sales, your admirers and lovers, they are all still here for you, they are all just waiting for you, in your villa in Kamakura, in your house in Hongō. Just open your eyes, then open your mouth, and admit, admit: I am Yasukichi Horikawa, the celebrated and successful author!"

Still Y did not answer, still Y did not speak, his mouth and eyes shut, not opening, not speaking.

"How predictable you are," sighed the voice, "how very vain the writer. Relishing your so-called pain, welcoming your so-called suffering. Well, let's see how you'll relish real pain, see if you'll welcome true suffering . . ."

Suddenly, Y felt a rope tightening around his neck, suddenly Y felt a razor cutting into his wrists, suddenly his veins coursing with poison, suddenly his lungs filling with water . . .

"Speak!" screamed the voice. "Speak! For this is your last and only chance; say your name, admit who you are: I am Yasukichi Horikawa, the celebrated and successful author! Then all will be returned to you, all will be restored for you. But if you do not speak, if you do not admit who you are, then you will die, and die the death of the suicide, damned eternally, damned forevermore, to die, to die, and die again, over and over, a thousand deaths eternally, a thousand deaths forevermore, over and over, without end. So speak! Speak now! Speak now!"

But Y would not speak, still Y did not speak, did not speak . . .

"Last chance," whispered the voice, "last chance . . ."

The rope tightening tighter, the razor cutting deeper . . .

"For Yasukichi Horikawa . . ."

His veins coursing and his lungs filling . . .

"Celebrated and successful author . . ."

But Y did not speak . . .

"Last chance . . ."

Y did not speak . . .

"Then here is death, now here is hell . . ."

Not speaking, not speaking, his neck broken, his blood drained, poisoned and drowned, Y fell back, back and down, down and into—

死

Here, death and hell, endless death and endless hell, here his neck endlessly breaking, here his blood endlessly draining, endlessly poisoned and endlessly drowning, here without end, here in the river, the River of Sins, bloody and boiling, here at the foot of the Mountain of Skulls, here Y was dying over and over, one moment pulled under, one moment pushed up, then under and up again, in the River of Sins, bloody and boiling, dying over and over, pulled under and pushed up again, under and up again, each time glimpsing, glimpsing, glimpsing a figure sat on a throne on the Mountain of Skulls, in a crow-black robe with a snow-white face, beneath a pale crown of broken mirrors, savagely reflecting all he surveyed, now staring at Y, glaring at Y, yet smiling at Y, laughing at Y: Satan-Yama, Lord of Hell!

"No doubt," said Satan-Yama, "you are in pain and you are suffering. But no doubt you believe you deserve this fate, so no doubt you will endure your martyrdom eternally. But look! Look about you, and see who suffers with you, see who suffers because of you, because of you . . ."

Dying over and over, pulled under and pushed up, Y now saw he was not alone in the bloody and boiling River of Sins: dying over and over, a thousand other deaths, pulled under and pushed up, in the bloody and boiling River of Sins, dying over and over, a thousand other souls; various friends and former lovers, and no! His wife, his children! No! Even his father and mother, dying over and over, pulled under and pushed up, endlessly—

"One word from you," said Satan-Yama, "just one single word from you, and their suffering will cease, and they will be released. Just say one word, just speak, just speak one word . . ."

Dying over and over, Y watched his mother and his father, his

children and his wife, one moment pulled under, one moment
pushed up, each time their mouths filling with blood, each time
their eyes filling with tears, pleading with Y, beseeching Y—

"Just say one word. . ."

Dying over and over, his heart flayed and soul skinned, amidst
the pitiful, wrenching stares of friends and lovers, of his wife and
children, his father and mother, Y pulled under, Y pushed up, now Y
saw another face, a face he struggled to recall, her eyes not pleading,
her eyes downcast, but which now caught his own, and now Y
remembered a night he thought forgotten, wished forgotten, in a
dim and dirty Nanking room, a brass crucifix upon a wall, a bottle
spilt upon the floor, an upturned chair, the coins across the bed,
between her forced, reluctant thighs, his weeping, puss-filled cock,
infecting her, condemning her, her eyes upon the cross, her name
upon his lips, her name he had not known he knew, her name, her
name Y cries, "Xin!"

The air thin, the wind biting and his footing precarious again, Y
opened his eyes; the River of Sins, bloody and boiling, filled with
his friends and former lovers, his wife and children, his father and
mother, dying over and over, was gone, were gone, all gone, leaving
Y alone again on the Mountain of Skulls, standing on the flowing
heaping of tumbled fragments, rolling and turning under his feet,
empty shells bursting beneath him, tears streaming down his face,
knowing, knowing he had failed—

"Yes," said the old man, again beside him now, dressed in his
coat of shining white feathers, his head clean and shaved, his skin
translucent and newborn. "You failed. But you had already failed,
and you would have only failed again if you had not spoken."

"But I could have chosen not to speak," said Y. "The choice was
mine. For I know I had a choice."

"Yes," smiled the old man. "There is always a choice."

Y nodded, staring at the naked steeps of endless heapings of skulls and fragments of skulls, and Y said, "And I have chosen the Mountain of Skulls."

"Yes," said the old man, bending down to the eternal tide of skulls and bones, picking up one skull, now holding up the skull. "But you were already here, you have always been here. For this skull and each of these skulls is your own skull; each skull is you! And only you. The nest of your dreams, all your delusions and desires. Always you, already you, you and only you . . ."

"I know," said Y, "I know."

And Y closed his eyes, but now, now, now Y felt the sun strangely warm upon his face, its piercing rays dancing on his lids, the sound of boats upon the river, the scent of *fukujusō* on the breeze, and slowly, slowly, slowly Y opened his eyes again. The sky above him was a brilliant bright December blue, with not one single cloud or wisp of smoke from a factory yet, a dull crick again, in his back and in his neck, and now Y sat up and looked around him: he had been resting his head upon a pillow again, again the pillow a large *furoshiki*, the cloth a pattern of red and white waves, enfolding a giant bundle, held together in its knot. But this time Y did not undo the knot, Y did not open up the cloth. This time Y got to his feet, and Y began to walk away, to walk away, away from the bundle, away from the city—

Some men go mad, some men go missing, some men do both.

*

The morning after our evening together, and the long night I had spent reading Tock's manuscript, most concerned and keen to discuss Tock's state of mind, I set out to call upon his friend Mag, the philosopher.

Mag was a very hospitable Kappa who loved nothing more than to open up his home to guests and, that grey day, there was already quite a congregation: Judge Pep, Dr. Chack and Gael, the president of a glass corporation. They were all smoking heavily, a thick haze of tobacco smoke hanging in the room under the dim light of a glass lantern of seven colours.

Already, they seemed very much engaged in a conversation about rising crime rates and the penal code, and so, as I took my seat and lit a cigarette, and putting to one side for now my worries about Tock, I joined in, asking, "Do the Kappa have capital punishment?"

"Yes," replied Judge Pep. "However, we prefer not to hang people as you humans do. I do admit, though, electric devices are occasionally used, but only in the very rarest of cases. Usually, we simply just announce the name of the criminal and the crime that has been committed."

"And that is enough to kill a Kappa?"

"Of course," said Mag. "We Kappa have much more delicate and more sensitive nerves than you humans."

"But," interjected Gael, "this is also how some murders are committed. Why, only the other day a bloody socialist called me a thief! I almost had a heart attack. I thought I was going to die!"

Mag nodded and said, "It seems to me such types of murder are becoming increasingly common. I know a lawyer who was killed that very way."

"Really," I asked. "But how?"

Mag smiled and said, "One day he was called a frog. And, as you know, there is no greater insult to a Kappa than to call him a frog. Who can possibly bear to be branded such a cold-blooded brute!"

"And he dropped dead on the spot?"

"Not instantly, no," said Judge Pep. "But day by day, he kept asking and arguing with himself, Am I really a frog? I can't be a frog! I must be a frog, and so on. And so eventually he pined away and died."

"Is that not suicide," I asked.

"No! Not at all," said Mag. "The evil fiend who called the poor lawyer a frog did so knowing damn well it would kill him. It was intentional, premeditated murder!"

"Still sounds like suicide to me," I insisted. "And talking of which, I am most concerned for the well-being of our friend Tock . . ."

"Me, too," exclaimed Mag. "Why, only the other day, I chanced to run into the poet in the street. He was far from his usual cheerful, carefree self, continuously wiping his forehead with his handkerchief, constantly glancing about. And then, just as we were saying goodbye to each other, Tock suddenly cried out and clutched my arm. Whatever is the matter with you, I asked him. And do you know what he said? He'd seen a giant black bird driving the motor car which had just sped past us, laughing . . ."

"What utter rot," snorted Gael. "That Kappa is nothing but an attention-seeker, as self-obsessed as all artists are . . ."

"I'm not so sure," said Judge Pep quietly, staring at the end of one of his gold-tipped cigarettes. "I saw him, too, the other night. He was standing with his arms folded in front of a small house, staring in through the window at a family of Kappa at dinner: a husband, a wife and their three children. Of course, I asked him what on earth he was doing, peeping in on this family. But Tock sighed and then, shaking his head, said something about envying such scenes of family life, and how a good plate of scrambled eggs is much more wholesome than any love affair or work of art . . ."

"Tock might have a point there," I said. "But I really do think we should encourage him to seek some help."

"I've already tried," said Mag. "I suggested he consult our good friend Dr. Chack here, but Tock simply would not listen to me, muttering something about not being an anarchist, how I should always remember that, and how he would never have anything to do with doctors anyway, even with our good Dr. Chack here . . ."

The doctor adjusted his pince-nez on his beak, then declared, "There is no such thing as a lost cause."

"You're all wasting your breath," said Gael. "That Kappa is too narcissistic and self-absorbed to ever contemplate suicide, trust me . . ."

But at that very moment, the sharp report of a revolver rang out, echoing and reverberating, shaking the walls and the air, outside and in—

"Tock," shouted Mag. "That came from Tock's house, I'm certain, quite certain. Quick, quick, to Tock's house!"

We all sprang to our feet and rushed round to Tock's house, running up the stairs into Gakikutsu—

There in his study, amidst the piles of books and papers, sprawled among the pots of alpine plants, Tock lay face up on the mats, a revolver in his right hand, blood still pouring, streaming and spurting from the concave saucer on the top of his head, and by his side, on her knees, her face buried in his breast, a female Kappa was wailing and weeping loudly.

Gently, fighting my instinctive aversion to touching the slimy skin of a Kappa, I lifted her to her feet and asked, "What on earth happened?"

"I don't know," she cried. "I don't know. He was just writing something, when, before I knew it, he'd picked up the revolver, stuck it to his head and pulled the trigger. Oh, what shall I do? Whatever shall I do?"

"How thoughtless, self-centred and selfish Tock truly was," said Gael to Judge Pep. "Never thinking of others, always wanting his own way . . ."

Judge Pep lit another of his gold-tipped cigarettes and said nothing, silently watching Dr. Chack at work.

The doctor was kneeling over Tock, examining the wound. Now he stood up, adjusted his pince-nez and announced, "There is nothing to be done. Tock is dead. I know he was suffering from chronic dyspepsia, and that alone would be enough to give someone of his disposition the excuse he needed."

"His woman said he was writing something," murmured Mag to himself, picking up a piece of paper from the desk. And as the others craned their necks, I looked down over Mag's shoulder to read—

Now I shall up and go
to the valley which divides this secular world.
The rock-face is steep,
the mountain-spring clear,
this valley scented with flowering herbs.

Mag put down the piece of paper and, with a tart smile, he said, "Those words are by Goethe, from his poem 'Mignon.' So even Tock's last testament, even his suicide note, his very last words are cribbed from the work of somebody else. No wonder Tock blew out his brains! Our poet knew he was completely, totally and utterly burnt out."

Of course, as they were all reading and discussing Tock's last words, I was thinking of the postscript to *The Book of Tock*, the manuscript sitting on my desk back in my own study, wondering whether or not I should say anything. But motor cars were arriving now, crowds gathering outside, the room filling up; Craback the musician was already here, and Lap the student, too. And all the while, the female Kappa was still weeping bitterly, and the sight of one so lost and suffering so touched and tugged on my heart.

Softly, I put my arm around her shoulders and led her towards a sofa in the corner of the room where a very young Kappa, no more than two years old, was innocently still smiling. I began to play with the child, hoping to distract it and so ease its poor mother's burden, until I felt the tears in my own eyes welling up, too; I confess, throughout my whole time in the land of the Kappa, this was the only moment I ever shed tears.

"What a pitiful misfortune," Gael was saying, "what a sorry lot, to find oneself a member of the family of such a selfish, self-centred and self-obsessed Kappa as Tock, don't we all agree?"

"Quite so," replied Judge Pep, lighting another gold-tipped cigarette. "Tock gave no thought whatsoever to his family, his poor offspring, and made no provision whatsoever for their future."

"Capital!" cried Craback the musician to the surprise of us all, the draft of Tock's last poem still clutched in his hand. "I've just thought of an absolutely splendid funeral march. I've not a moment to lose. Farewell . . ."

With a bright spark in his narrow eyes, Craback shook Mag's hand and dashed for the door. But by now, the whole neighbourhood had amassed outside Tock's house, all loudly trying to push or peep their way in. Undeterred, Craback forced his way through the crowd, sending Kappa this way and that, then jumped in his motor car and swiftly made his exit, to the sound of his engine backfiring.

"Will you stop gawping! Have some respect," shouted Judge Pep, slamming the door in the faces of the crowd of Kappa outside, the room now becoming suddenly quiet, suddenly still. Even the female Kappa on the sofa next to me had stopped her wailing, her shoulders still heaving and her body still shaking, her tears still falling, but silently now as her child stared down at the open palms of his tiny hands, the stench of Tock's blood and the scent of the flowers of the alpine plants mingling, engulfing us all in this sudden quietness, this sudden stillness.

I got to my feet and walked over to Mag, who was standing, staring down at Tock's dead body. I tapped him on the shoulder and said, "I'm sorry, but I'm going to leave now."

Mag did not reply, did not take his eyes off the corpse of the poet sprawled at his feet.

I tapped him on the shoulder again. "Mag, I'm going now . . ."

"Sorry," said Mag, turning to face me. "I was just thinking . . ."

His voice trailed off, so I asked, "Thinking what?"

"Well," he said in an embarrassed, hesitant whisper, "you know, just thinking about this life of the Kappa . . ."

"What about it, Mag?"

His eyes left mine, drifting back to the body before us, and then, barely audibly, he said, "Well, when all is said and done, at the end of the day . . . We Kappa, whatever we may say . . . If we want to fulfil our Kappa lives . . . Well, it seems to me, I have to say . . . We need to believe in a power other than Kappa . . . Above and beyond us . . . Some 'thing' more than ourselves."

"Yes," I said, "but not only you Kappa."

*

Ten days after our evening together, and the long night I had spent reading his manuscript, Akutagawa ascended into Paradise.

Now over twenty years have passed since that night, and I am sitting again in a sweet parlour as I write these words. I have ordered two bowls of sweet-bean soup, and I give one to your soul, Sensei—

For Saint Kappa, in Paradise,
a bowl of *shiruko*, I offer.

*

Another author's note:

After the war, Tokutarō Nagami went missing in Atami, a city by the sea on the Izu Peninsula. He was never seen again, his body never found. When his wife passed away, her grave was made for two, sharing its stone and the date of her death with her husband: October 23, 1950 / Shōwa 25—

Some men go mad, some men go missing, some men do both.

The Spectres of Christ

I am living now in the most unimaginable unhappy happiness—
yet strangely, without regret.
I just feel sorry for those who had me as
a bad husband, father and son.
And so goodbye—
I have tried—at least, *consciously*—not to justify myself here;
. . . and so please, go ahead and laugh—
at the fool in this manuscript.

"To My Friend, Masao Kume,"
Ryūnosuke Akutagawa, June 20, 1927

1. "Black & White"

In the summer, this endless summer, in the cottage at Kugenuma, this cottage by the sea, in its study, at my desk, I gather up my Bible and my books, the sheaf of manuscript papers and my pens, put them in my bag and stand up, I stand up . . .

Unsteady on my feet, I come out of the house and get into the waiting taxi. I tell the driver to take me to the station on the Tōkaidō line. The driver sets off, but we are not likely to make the Tokyo-bound train for we are going so slowly. Thick pine woods line both sides of the road. The old driver says, "You know, so many strange things have been happening around here these days. I hear people have been seeing a ghost, even in the daytime . . ."

"Really? Even in the daytime," I reply in a half-hearted manner, staring into the passing pine woods, searching for a trace of sunlight.

"What I heard," says the driver. "But only when it rains."

"Maybe the ghost likes to get wet," I say.

"That's funny," says the driver. "But I hear he wears a raincoat."

We pull up outside the station just as the Tokyo train pulls out. I get out of the cab and go into the waiting room. There is only one other person sat inside: a man of about my age, blankly staring into space, wearing a raincoat. I realise I am wearing a raincoat, too, and wonder if that was why the taxi driver had said what he said. I look across at the other man again and I decide to wait for the next train in the café opposite the station.

I sit down in a corner at a table covered in white oilcloth with a border of red flowers, the coating worn away in places, revealing a grubby canvas. I order a cup of cocoa, but it smells of fish, and a layer of grease floats on the surface. I push it away, light a cigarette and stare down at the flowers in the border.

A pack of cigarettes later, I board the train for Tokyo. I usually ride in second class, but I decide to sit in third class. The carriage is crowded with a group of elementary-school girls and their teachers, on their way back from some outing. They talk without a break as I smoke.

Unfortunately, at one of the last stations before Tokyo, a woman I know boards the train with a young child. The woman has a reputation as a tanka poet and is married to a well-known cartoonist. Fortunately, she does not see me until we are about to pull into Shimbashi, but then, when I stand up to get off at this station, she exclaims to the whole carriage, "Akutagawa-sensei! I didn't realise it was you, can hardly recognise you . . . you've lost so much weight, look so pale . . . I thought you must be . . ."

"A ghost! A ghost," shouts the child at her side, pointing up at me.

I feign a smile and, as she quietens the child, I make my apologies and quickly get off the train, escaping from the woman and the child.

Bag in hand, I walk from the station to the Imperial Hotel. Tall buildings line both sides of the street, as dark and as thick as the pine woods this morning. But now, as I look at the passing buildings, I realise my vision is strange again; I am seeing sets of translucent, spinning, turning gears and wheels. This is not the first time this has happened, and it is always the same: the number of gears and wheels gradually increases until they block out half my field of vision. It only lasts a few moments but, when they disappear, the gears and wheels are replaced by an excruciating, searing headache. My eye doctor blamed cigarettes, or the amount I smoke, but I didn't believe him. All I can do now is to use only my left eye, which is thankfully always fine. But as I stumble towards the hotel with one eye closed, I can still see the gears and wheels behind the lid of my right eye.

By the time I enter the Imperial, the gears and wheels are gone, but the headache is here now. I check in as quickly as I can and head upstairs to the room. I walk down a deserted corridor and go into my room. I sit down at the desk in the window and close both eyes now, massaging my temples. Immediately, I start to feel a little better, but then there is a banging on the door, and a bellboy brings in my bag with my hat and coat. He hangs the hat and coat from a hook on the wall and then leaves. I glance up at the hat and the coat hanging on the wall; they look like my own standing figure. Worse, I remember my brother-in-law had been wearing a raincoat when he threw himself in front of the train. I jump up from the desk, throw the hat and the coat into a corner of the room, and go into the bathroom to splash cold water on my face. I catch my reflection in the mirror above the sink and recoil; I can see only the bones of my skull. I step back from the mirror, out of the bathroom, out of the room, and into the corridor. The corridor is still deserted but looks like that of a prison. I walk down the corridor to the landing at the top of the stairs. In a corner stands a tall lamp, its green shade reflecting in the glass fittings. The light gives me a peaceful sensation, at last, and I sit down in one of the chairs on the landing. I take out a cigarette from my pocket and am about to light it when I notice something dangling over the back of the nearby sofa: a raincoat. Quickly, I get up from the chair and go back down the corridor to the door of my room. I steel myself, I open the door, I step inside, avoid the bathroom and its mirror, and sit down at the desk in the window. The seat is an armchair done in a reptilian green Moroccan leather. But at least my headache seems to be subsiding, so I open my bag, take out the sheaf of manuscript paper, dip my pen in the ink and try to get it moving, to work on the story I have been writing. But the pen will hardly move at all and, if and when it does, it just keeps writing the same word over and over again: "Ghost . . . Ghost . . . Ghost . . . Ghost . . ."

I can't bear it, can't bear anything, especially myself, myself in this room. I am sure I can hear the scratching of rats in the walls, hear the beating of wings in other rooms. I need some fresh air. I get up from the desk, pick up my hat and coat from the corner, put them on and leave

*the room. The corridor is still as depressing as a prison. I walk down
the stairs to the lobby. A man in a raincoat is arguing with a bellboy. I
ignore them and go out through the hotel doors to the street and start to
walk. All the branches and leaves of the park trees along the street have
a blackish look again, just like the pine woods by the coast this morning.
But each tree has a front and a back, just as we human beings do; I
remember the souls in Dante's* Inferno *who had been turned into trees
and I decide to walk on the other side of the road, across the streetcar
line, away from the park, where only buildings edge the street, heading
as fast as I can towards the Ginza.*

*When I reach the Ginza, the sun is already beginning to set, but the
shops lining both sides of the streets and the dizzying flow of people only
make me more depressed; all the people casually strolling along as if they
have never known the existence of sin. I walk on northwards, through
the confusion of the day's fading brightness and the light of the electric
lamps. I pass mannequin after mannequin in the windows of the
Western tailor shops. A bookstore piled high with magazines and such
catches my eye and I cannot resist. I walk in and let my eyes wander
upwards over several shelves of books. I pick out one volume from the
collected works of Dostoevsky to browse through. But the page I chance
to open almost knocks me over: it's the title page of the novella* Dvoynik.
*In horror, I put it straight back on the shelf, grabbing another book, any
book to break the spell. But when I look down at the yellow cover in
my hands, I see this is a volume of Greek myths, apparently aimed at
children. And once again, the page I chance to open, the line I chance to
read, nearly knocks me over—*

"Even the greatest of the gods, Zeus himself, was no match for
those goddesses of vengeance, the Furies."

*I drop the book, flee the bookstore and plunge back into the crowd.
But as I walk along, I feel a relentless gaze on my back, on my raincoat
back, the relentless gaze of the Furies—*

When did this start?

But still I walk on, on and on through the twilight, until I come to Nihonbashi. Out of habit, I suppose, I enter Maruzen and go up to the second floor. Again out of habit, I skim through Strindberg's Legender *a few pages at a time; it describes an experience not much different from my own. Not only that, this edition has a yellow cover. I put it back on the shelf and then, at random, I pull down another thick volume and flick through its pages. This, too, has something for me: one of its illustrations shows rows of gears and wheels with human eyes and noses; I turn to the title page and find it is a German compilation of drawings by mental patients. I feel consumed by a sudden spirit of defiance and, with the reckless abandon and desperation of a compulsive gambler, I start to pull book after book from the shelves, opening page after page, and every page, every single page, conceals some kind of needle to stab me, whether it be a sentence or an illustration. Every single one, you ask? Well, even in* Madame Bovary *I can see and sense myself as the bourgeois Monsieur Bovary.*

It is almost closing time now, and I seem to be the very last customer. I turn my back on the big bookcases and stride into the small display room. The first thing I see is a poster of St. George running his sword through a winged dragon, and the caption is written with the same "Dragon" character I use in my own name. To make matters worse, the grimacing face of the saint half hidden beneath his knight's helmet resembles the face of one of my many enemies. I have had enough; I can't bear it any more. I leave the exhibition, go down the broad stairway and out of the store.

Night has now fallen in Nihonbashi and, as I walk down the dark street, I think again and again about this story I am trying to write; I'd hoped to make it more autobiographical, but it has not come as easily as I'd imagined. I know this is because of my own pride and scepticism, and I despise these traits in myself. At the same time, I cannot help feeling that when we "remove a layer of skin, everybody is the same." I am planning to call the story "Night of Sodom," or maybe "Night of

Tokyo," or perhaps simply "Night"; as always, these days, I just can't decide. Equally, I do believe that Goethe's title Aus meinem Leben: Dichtung und Wahrheit *would suit anybody's autobiography. But now more than ever, I also know not everyone is moved by literature and that, in particular, my own works are unlikely to appeal to anyone who is not like me, has luckily not lived a life like this—*

I come to a second-hand shop and stop. In the window is a stuffed swan. It stands with its neck erect, but its wings are yellowed and moth-eaten. Both laughter and tears well up inside me; all that lies before me is either madness or suicide. I turn away from the stuffed swan and the shop window. I look up at the sky, thinking how small the earth truly is—how much, much smaller then am I—among the light of limitless, numberless stars. But the sky, which has been so clear all day, has clouded over now and, all of a sudden, I feel as though "something" is determined to get me, and I decide to seek refuge in a basement restaurant across the streetcar tracks.

At the bar, I order a glass of whisky.

"All we have is Black & White, sir."

I pour the whisky into soda water, take a sip, light a cigarette and look around the room. To my left, I notice a portrait of Napoleon hanging on the wall and I feel anxious, uneasy again. When he was still a student, on the last page of his geography notebook, Napoleon had written: "Saint Helena, a small island." Most people would say it was pure coincidence, but it must have surely filled Napoleon with sheer terror in his last days. And staring at the portrait of Napoleon, thinking back on my own works, certain phrases drift up to haunt me: "Life is more hellish than Hell itself," I had written in Words of a Dwarf; *there was the fate of the artist Yoshihide, the protagonist of my* Hell Screen; *and then poor Yasukichi . . .*

I take another sip of whisky, light another cigarette, and then glance to my right, trying to escape my own thoughts and words. But sat at the bar next to me there are two men in their late twenties or early thirties.

They seem to be newspaper reporters, conversing in low voices, and in French, for some reason. I keep my back turned to them but I can still feel them looking me over, up and down, from head to toe, actually feel their gazes through my raincoat, onto my flesh, and they know my name, seem to be talking about me: "Bien . . . très mauvais . . . pourquoi?"

"Pourquoi? Le diable est mort!"

"Oui, oui . . . d'enfer . . ."

I throw my last silver coin down on the bar and flee from this underground chamber, back up onto the street, into the night and its wind. But the electric-lit streets are still full of people. I cannot bear the thought of running into any acquaintances by chance, so I choose only the darkest streets, slinking along like a thief or a murderer, thinking of Raskolnikov, imagining I am Raskolnikov, desperately wanting to confess all I have done. But I know my confessions would only bring tragedy for others, besides even my immediate family. And I'm far from certain my desire to confess is even genuine. If only my nerves could be as steady as those of ordinary people.

I walk down another dark street, this one alongside a canal, and I'm reminded of my adoptive parents' home in the suburbs, the two of them waiting there each day for my return. My children, too, perhaps. But I dread the power that would naturally bind me if I go home to them all. I pass a barge moored at the embankment, upon the choppy waters of the canal, a dim glow seeping from within. Even in a place like this, families are living, men and women hating each other in order to love each other . . .

Perhaps buoyed by the whisky, I decide to go back to the hotel, to try to write, to salvage something from this day, this life . . .

In the hotel room, I light a cigarette and stare down at the blank sheaf of manuscript paper. I turn to my bag and take out a pile of books. On the top is The Collected Letters of Prosper Mérimée; *letters which give me the strength to go on living. But as I read, I learn the author had become a Protestant at the end of his life and, for the first time, I see the face behind the mask: he, too, was one of us, condemned to walk through the darkness—*

As Sainte-Beuve said, "Mérimée does not believe that God exists, but he is not altogether sure that the Devil does not . . ."

In the middle of the night, there should be no one in the corridor outside my room. Yet I can still sometimes hear the sound of wings outside my door; who could be keeping birds in their room?

Unable to stand anything more, especially the blank pages of manuscript paper, I go over to the bed. I lie down and open up A Dark Night's Passing *again; everything about the protagonist's spiritual struggle is painfully familiar to me. Yet compared to him, I feel such an idiot. Tears well in my eyes and I let them fall, sobbing on the bed, feeling at peace at last. But not for long, never for long; again I begin to see those translucent, spinning, turning gears and wheels in my right eye, and again they gradually increase until they occupy and blind half my field of vision. I know the headache is not far behind. And now I can hear the rats in the walls again, maybe even closer, maybe in the bathroom, maybe in the wardrobe, maybe under the bed, and the beating of wings, too, the beating of wings becoming louder and louder, the gears and the wheels spinning, turning, faster and faster. Enough is enough; I throw the book to one side, go over to my bag and take eight-tenths of a gram of Veronal, just wanting to knock myself out . . .*

In my dream, that dream again, in a deserted, ruined and wasted garden, there is an iron castle with iron grilles on its narrow windows. Inside the iron castle, there is only one room. In the room, there is only one desk. At that desk, a creature who looks like me is writing in letters I cannot read a long poem about a creature who in another room is writing a poem about another creature who in another room is writing a poem. Yet still I try to read the words the creature is writing, but now it turns to look at me and shrieks, "Quack! Quack . . ."

I open my eyes, the room flooded with a bright early-morning, early-summer light. I leap from the bed, go to the desk and begin to write, my pen sailing over the paper with a speed that startles even me, just writing and writing with a savage joy, then smoking and smoking, getting up from the desk to pace the room, on top of the world, then back to the desk and back to my pen, writing and writing, no parents, no wife, no children, just the life that flows from my pen across these papers, these pages; two pages, four pages, seven pages, ten pages more, more and more: under my pen, before my eyes, the manuscript grows and grows, just keeps on growing, as I write and I write with a frantic intensity, filling the decaying world of this supernatural story with horrific beasts, one of whom is my own self-portrait—

The telephone by the bed rings.

I stand up, go over to the bed, pick up the phone and say, "Who is it?"

"Quack, quack," whispers a voice. "I'm the ghost of Tock . . ."

"What? What," I scream. "What, what did you say?"

"Are you ready to go yet, ready to go now . . . ?"

"What? Who are you, who is it?"

"It's Uno's wife," says the voice now. "I'm sorry to disturb you . . ."

"What is it," I ask. "Has something happened to Uno?"

"I called your house," she says, "and your aunt said you were here, and I hate to disturb you, but Uno's condition is really deteriorating . . ."

"Don't worry," I tell her, "I'll come as soon as I can . . ."

"Thank you," she says, then cuts the connection.

I put the receiver back in its cradle. I go back to the desk, stuff my books and the manuscript into my bag, pick up my hat and my coat from the corner and leave the room. The corridor is as depressing as an asylum now. I walk down the stairs to the lobby. A man in a raincoat is arguing with a bellboy again. I check out at the front desk, then go out through the hotel doors to get a taxi. I walk towards the young cab dispatcher in his green uniform, but, before I can say anything, he asks, "You are Mr. A, are you not?"

"I am," I say, not knowing what else to say.

"I thought so," he says. "I knew it. I'm your most devoted reader, Sensei.

I've read everything you've written. It is an honour to meet you, Sensei."

I touch the tip of my hat, bow and thank him, but feel sick inside; I have committed every sin known to man, yet still I receive such praise and respect, as though someone or something was mocking me. I don't even have a conscience any more; all I have is nerves.

"Would you like a cab, Sensei?"

I nod, then say, "But a green one, please. Only a green one."

The young cab dispatcher smiles. "Of course, Sensei."

I thank him again and get into the back of the lucky green cab; for some reason, every time I take a yellow one I'm always involved in an accident. I tell the driver the address, then slump back in the seat and stare out at the buildings, feeling anything and everything is a lie. Politics, business, science, art; it's all just a mottled layer of enamel covering over this life in all its horror. I begin to feel as if I am suffocating in the back of this cab. I open the window as wide as possible, but the constriction around my heart will not give way, just tightening, tightening, tighter and tighter . . .

Eventually, we reach the main intersection at Jingūmae. We should be able to turn down a side street here, but today, for some reason, I cannot find it. I have the taxi go back and forth along the streetcar line, but finally I can't stand it any longer; I give up and get out of the cab.

Somehow I have ended up at the Aoyama Funeral Hall; I've never even passed the front gate of this building in the ten long years since the memorial service for Sōseki-sensei. I had not been happy back then, either, but at least I had been at peace. I peer in at the gravelled courtyard and, recalling the delicate bashō plants at the Sōseki Retreat, I cannot help feeling my own life has now come to an end. Yet I also feel "something" must have drawn me back to this crematorium today, after all these years; a shiver runs down my spine, shaking my whole body, shaking the place where my soul should be.

I turn and walk away, heading towards the mental hospital, unable to suppress the prayer now rising on my lips—

"Oh Lord, oh Lord, oh Lord, rebuke me not in thy wrath: neither chasten me in thy hot displeasure. For thine arrows stick fast in me, and thy hand presseth me sore, sore, sore . . ."
How can any of us escape, except through faith, madness or death?

2. The Houses of the Mad

At his desk in his office at the Aoyama Mental Hospital in Akasaka-ku, Mokichi Saitō, head of the hospital, and renowned tanka poet, closed his eyes again. He was exhausted and he was depressed: exhausted by his workload, the responsibilities and burdens of his position; depressed by this place, not only the asylum, the hospital, but the city, the country, Tokyo and Japan.

Once, Mokichi had escaped; escaped from Nagasaki, escaped from Japan, and gone to Europe, first to Vienna, appointed by the Ministry of Education as a researcher abroad. He had studied at the Neurologischen Institut of Vienna University under Heinrich Obersteiner, had submitted his research as his doctoral thesis in Vienna, and it had been accepted and published. This work had also earned Mokichi a doctorate in medicine from Tokyo Imperial University. But Mokichi had refused to return home to Japan; Mokichi had left Vienna and gone on to study under Emil Kraepelin at his institute in Munich. Nothing would make Mokichi return to Japan, not the inflation and privations of post-war Austria and Germany, not the death of his own father, not even the news of the Great Kantō Earthquake; nothing had made him return until that telegram on the last day of 1924.

Ironically, the Aoyama Mental Hospital had survived the earthquake and fires of 1923, only to be destroyed by a fire on New Year's Eve, 1924. The fire had apparently begun in the kitchen during the preparation of *mochi* for the New Year, and then rapidly spread through the main building. Twenty-three patients, a doctor and a staff member had perished. The fire also claimed the many books Mokichi had been sending home from Europe. The situation had been further complicated because his father-in-law and mentor, Kiichi, had neglected to renew the fire insurance. The hospital had been the life's work of Kiichi Saitō, the culmination of his long medical career, and its destruction had devastated the old man.

On his reluctant return to Japan, the burden of the lack of insurance and the resulting financial problems, the opposition of the authorities and neighbours to reconstruction on the original site in Akasaka-ku, the raising of funds and the search for a new site, all had fallen entirely on Mokichi. The process of rebuilding the Aoyama Hospital as an annexe, along with the construction of a larger new main hospital out at Matsuzawa, had been slow and painful. Two and a half years later, the smoke of that fire enshrouded him still; once again, Mokichi was trapped and imprisoned—

"Beyond the boundaries / of bitter shock / and deep grieving / words failed me / before the bright sun . . ."

There was a knock on the door. Mokichi opened his eyes, rubbed his face, looked at his watch and sighed; he had forgotten, forgotten he had agreed to a request from Ryūnosuke Akutagawa to visit the writer Kōji Uno.

There was a second knock on the door now. Mokichi stood up behind his desk and called out, "Yes, yes. Please come in . . ."

Akutagawa opened the door, bowing and excusing the interruption, thanking Mokichi for his time and for agreeing to visit Uno—

"Since the spring, Uno's been displaying the symptoms of an increasingly severe nervous breakdown," began Akutagawa, at speed, "one minute up, one minute down, high and then low, manic then moribund. But his wife says Uno's been out on the streets this morning, bellowing and shouting wildly at passers-by, stopping the traffic. The woman's at her wits' end, desperate for help, so I promised to call you . . ."

"Let's go then," said Mokichi, coming out from behind his desk, picking up his bag, but conscious Akutagawa himself did not seem so well.

Since their first meeting in Nagasaki, almost ten years ago now, and then more frequently following his return from Europe, Mokichi had met Akutagawa quite often, had come to like him, but be concerned for him, too. Akutagawa had always been thin, but now he was painfully gaunt, his skin grey, his hair and nails both long and dirty, and today, perhaps stimulated by the condition of his friend Uno, he seemed manic, almost possessed—

"It's so shocking, so frightening. Terrifying . . . Any one of us, at any moment, could end up like Uno . . . I feel as though what's happening to him is happening to me," ranted Akutagawa, yet grinning broadly, opening his eyes wider, and then shivering in mock fear.

Mokichi knew Akutagawa feared he had inherited his mother's insanity, that he was also plagued by insomnia, and so, for the last year or so, Mokichi had been prescribing draughts to help him sleep. But as he led him out of the office, past the temporary buildings, towards the waiting car, Mokichi wondered if Akutagawa was sleeping, had slept at all.

Suddenly, Akutagawa veered off from Mokichi, over to a patch of grass, close to the burnt-out ruins of the old hospital, and standing there, staring at the treetops of the Aoyama Cemetery, he smiled and said, "I hadn't noticed, but it's actually a nice day, this breeze most refreshing . . ."

"It is," said Mokichi. "Let's go to see Uno . . ."

In the car from Aoyama to Ueno Sakuragichō, Akutagawa was again most animated, speaking as though delivering a lecture on insanity, citing statistics on the rapid rise in the numbers of people being institutionalised, quoting the popular phrases of the day, such as "civilisation disease," "city disease," "modern disease," "the sickness of our age" and even "American disease," while constantly saying, over and over, again and again, "It's all so shocking, it's all so frightening; it could happen to any one of us at any moment, happen to me, especially me," then shivering in mock fear again. Yet had he not known of their long friendship, and his own maladies and fears, Mokichi might have thought Akutagawa was even being flippant, almost relishing and enjoying the adventure of Uno's breakdown.

Fortunately, when they finally arrived at the house, Uno seemed much calmer than he had been earlier, sitting quietly in the dim room under the staircase with the light from the shabby passageway falling on the right side of his body, not even the least bit suspicious of Mokichi, a stranger.

"You seem to be suffering from a slight nervous breakdown," Akutagawa told Uno in a calmer tone now. "So I thought Dr. Saitō here should check your condition."

Uno smiled, gently nodded, and then cheerfully, almost proudly announced to Mokichi, "I have never, ever had such clarity of thought as I've had these past few days. Two hours' sleep a night is more than enough."

"That's very good," said Mokichi, opening up his doctor's bag. He took out a brush, asked Uno to open up his *yukata*, and then, while lightly stroking his skinny chest, he softly said, "That tickles, doesn't it?"

"Yes," giggled Uno, squirming, "it tickles."

Mokichi poked out his tongue in jest, smiled and said, "Well, it seems your nerves are just a little bit too stimulated, and so it might be better to take a tranquilliser for now, don't you think?"

Uno giggled again and nodded.

"And you should rest and sleep as much as you can, shouldn't you? You'll feel much better then, won't you? And so let's take a tranquilliser now, shall we? Then I'll leave you some more for later, if you would like?"

"Actually, I have a very good tranquilliser with me," said Akutagawa suddenly, putting his hand inside his pocket and taking out a package.

"It's okay, thank you. I'll give him mine instead," said Mokichi, taking out a sachet from his bag, dividing the powder into two. He then reached back inside his bag, took out a needle and syringe, and said, "And just as a precaution, I think we should take a little blood. Just to check . . ."

Uno still remained very calm, smiling and agreeing to the blood test, still smiling and giggling as Mokichi gently took the blood, then smiling and nodding, swallowing the tranquilliser, washing it down, still smiling and promising to rest and sleep as much as he could, then cheerfully saying goodbye to Mokichi and Akutagawa, happily showing them out, hoping they would call again soon, urging them to take care on their way home—

"For who knows when and who disaster will strike down next . . ."

Outside on the street, Akutagawa was relieved the visit had gone so well, most grateful to Mokichi for his help and for his time. "The day is almost done, and so if you're not too busy now, and it's not an inconvenient place, will you join me for dinner at Jishōken, so I can thank you properly?"

"You really don't need to thank me," said Mokichi. "However, as always, I would be delighted to dine with you, so thank *you*."

Mokichi had been to Jishōken with Akutagawa a few times before; the restaurant seemed to be Akutagawa's favourite, his regular choice, very close to his house in Tabata. Mokichi had hoped the prospect of dining at a familiar place, one so close to home, together with the apparent success of their afternoon visit, might have helped to soothe Akutagawa, but, in the back of the taxicab, the writer still appeared most anxious and agitated—

"Uno's breakdown has spooked our fellow writers. People are terrified they will be next. Just the other evening, Murō Saisei told me if the same thing were to befall him, then he would surely turn into a nymphomaniac! He made me promise to be sure he always kept his trousers on and his belt fastened . . . But you don't think that by going there so often, Uno's family feel I am interfering and meddling? And then what about Seiji? You don't think I am making Seiji look bad . . . ?"

Seiji Tanizaki, the translator of Poe and younger brother of Jun'ichirō, was one of Uno's oldest and closest friends. Yet he'd called just once.

"I'm sure you don't need to worry about Seiji," said Mokichi. "He's so highly strung and weak, it's probably more upsetting for Uno if he does visit . . ."

"But I'm such a very weak person, too," said Akutagawa.

"But you've been very helpful to Uno and his wife."

"You really think so? You really do . . . ?"

"Yes, I do."

"You're certain," asked Akutagawa again. "I'm sure Seiji must resent me calling on Uno, intruding every day . . ."

"I'm sure Seiji is very grateful to you, given his own reluctance to visit. It really does seem to be beyond him . . ."

"You're right," said Akutagawa. "The one time he did call, Seiji simply sat there in tears. That night, he told me he couldn't sleep for thinking about Uno's situation, despairing for his future. He was distraught, claimed if he were to visit again, then he feared he, too, would become infected by Uno's disease . . . But in that case, I must also be at risk . . ."

"No," said Mokichi, calmly but firmly. "Insanity itself is not infectious. However, you do need to take care. Your anxiety and concern for your friend and his condition are taking their toll on you, affecting your own health."

In the back of the cab, Akutagawa nodded. "You're right."

Mokichi gently put his hand on Akutagawa's arm and asked, "How have *you* been sleeping these days? *Are* you sleeping?"

"Not much," said Akutagawa, "and only with the Veronal you prescribed. Calmotin no longer has any effect at all."

"It's still much better to use Veronal than not to sleep at all."

"You're right," said Akutagawa again. "It's terrible if I can't sleep, simply unbearable, too unbearable. But even with Veronal, even then it never lasts more than thirty minutes or so, an hour at most. But it's so dangerous not to sleep, almost an act of violence, I'd say. An act of violence . . ."

In the back of the cab, Mokichi nodded and said, "I'll have someone deliver you another ounce of Veronal, but Veronal imported from Germany; it's much better than the Japanese-made product. I'll also send you some Numal, because if you can alternate Veronal and Numal, then I think you can avoid addiction. And please don't worry about the cost; although the Japanese drugs are cheaper, the imported ones are still less than a taxi home. It's important not to worry about the price, so please don't."

"Thank you," said Akutagawa. "I'm still having to contend with all the debts my brother-in-law left my sister; the interest alone is thirty per cent! Sincerely, I appreciate your kindness, thank you."

"You don't need to thank me," said Mokichi. "It's nothing."

"It's not nothing," said Akutagawa, in a low and sad voice, turning to stare out of the cab window, out into the twilight.

The taxi had come down through Yanaka into Nezu, then gone along Shinobazu-dōri onto Dōzaka, and now stopped.

Mokichi and Akutagawa got out of the cab, walked up an unlit, narrow side road, passed through the gate and the garden and entered Jishōken, warmly greeted by the owner, led down the wooden corridor and shown to their usual table overlooking the garden, the only customers.

The clear day had become a clouded night, the lanterns and stones in the garden of the restaurant already draped in shadows.

Mokichi turned from the window, looked across the table at Akutagawa, smiled and then said, "As I wrote in my last letter, I was so greatly impressed by *Kappa*, and so I hope, despite all you are having to contend with, you are still managing to write, and the writing is bringing you some respite?"

"Thank you," said Akutagawa, "but you are too generous and kind in your praise. And to be honest, if I had had more time, and if I had taken more care, I could have written more of *Kappa*. Now I regret finishing it so prematurely, but I wanted to go on to *Mirage* . . ."

"An exceptional work," said Mokichi.

"Thank you," said Akutagawa again. "It might be the only work of which I feel confident. But even this is so far from what I had hoped to achieve. I just feel I am getting more and more tired . . ."

"But at least you are still writing," said Mokichi.

"Continuously," said Akutagawa, "but it no longer brings me the sense of peace I used to feel. In the next life, if there is such a punishment, I wish to be reborn as sand."

The waitresses knelt before their table now, exchanging pleasantries with them, placing two large lacquer trays before Mokichi and Akutagawa.

"I know how much you enjoy *unagi* and *takuan*," said Akutagawa, "and so I had asked the restaurant if they could prepare your favourite dishes."

"Thank you. That was most kind of you, and very good of them," said Mokichi, marvelling again at the care and consideration Akutagawa always showed to his friends, no matter what trials he himself was enduring.

"It is the very least I can do," said Akutagawa. "Your help, your kindness and your poetry, too, they all sustain me in these difficult times."

"Thank you," said Mokichi again, smiling now, "and I am sure this tasty-looking eel will help sustain us both, in all our work . . ."

"Yes," said Akutagawa, nodding and smiling, too. "Let's eat . . ."

But Akutagawa hardly ate at all, just picking at the various dishes, just toying with the food, then setting down his chopsticks—

"I think it was Ikkyū who said he had spent thirty years in an obscure blur. But I've spent thirty years doing nothing worthwhile, and so, over and over, I say to myself, Kill yourself, kill yourself . . ."

"You're not alone in that," said Mokichi, but with a little laugh, trying to lighten the mood of his companion. "I very often feel much the same . . ."

"Yes, but in your poetry, in your tanka, you create or you find such beauty in all that afflicts you, in all that you suffer . . . I never can, I always fail . . . You know, I recently read the prison diary of Kyūtarō Wada . . . I mean, even an anarchist can wrest beauty from suffering, in his descriptions of the hardships of prison life, when he writes: 'It's all so quiet, all I hear is a flea jumping . . .' or 'The number of insects in the barley rice is rising, there is a cloud in the summertime . . .' But the best is surely, 'This malady of piles, Jack Frost is piercing me.' I can truly feel how he must feel, can truly imagine the hardship of suffering from piles in prison, but I'm so impressed, so envious an anarchist can write such poetry . . ."

"For his try, life for Kyū-san," said Mokichi in a sing-song voice, echoing a popular jingle of the day, "for his killing, ten years for Ama-san."

"How dark these times truly are," said Akutagawa. "But amidst all the horror he must endure, a man like Wada never lets the darkness overwhelm him. And in your own poetry, too, you light a lamp and walk on, Sensei."

"What other choice do we have," said Mokichi, gently.

"I never can, I always fail," said Akutagawa again, and then, softly, he began to quote Mokichi's own words, from his recent work:

"When I shut myself away / I am resigned to / almost anything / and sit here with legs crossed / while the night is wearing on—"

Mokichi could hear drops of rain falling on the stones in the garden now as he sighed and said, "There does seem to be a sense of doom and death around us all these days. Like me, you seem to have been engulfed in bad luck, too. Yet we have to keep writing, what other choice do we have?"

"Perhaps I should end this half of my life in your new hospital," said Akutagawa, quietly, staring out into the garden, staring out into the night and its rain, "and then spend the rest of my life out there . . ."

Mokichi closed his eyes; he could not count the number of times he had discovered patients who had hung themselves or cut their own throats, the number of times he had been obliged to notify their families, the numberless feelings of failure he had experienced, the feeling of failure he always felt. Mokichi opened his eyes again; he looked across the table at the man sat staring out into the night, his body gaunt and skin grey, his hair and nails both long and dirty, and solemnly, and sternly, Mokichi said, "First you need to rest, and so you have to sleep; then when you are rested, when you are stronger, then you can think about the future, only then should you search for the light again . . ."

"You are right," said Akutagawa. "For when I look to the future, when I search for the light, I see only darkness, I feel only dread . . ."

After the dinner at Jishōken, at the gate of the restaurant, the door to the taxi, under borrowed umbrellas, Mokichi thanked Akutagawa, Akutagawa thanked Mokichi, and then Mokichi said, "You remember the first time we met, in my office in Nagasaki? Well, I was in a wretched mood because I had just sent my wife packing to Tokyo after a terrible quarrel. I hated Nagasaki, felt trapped and imprisoned there for ever. And we talked about Ishida, and you spoke about Poe, and of Sōseki-sensei and *Kōjin*, the only escape from this world being through faith, madness or death?"

"It seems so long ago now," said Akutagawa. "A different time, a different world; a better time, a better world. But, of course, I remember . . ."

"Well, of those three exits," continued Mokichi, "more than ever I have come to accept and to believe in faith as our only hope, our only possibility. But I do not mean faith in gods or a God, I mean faith in our work, faith in our writing; the power of words, of salvation through art . . ."

Under his borrowed umbrella, Akutagawa nodded.

"And so please, Sensei," said Mokichi, "please have faith in your work, have faith in your words . . ."

"Thank you," said Akutagawa. "I feel better, thanks to you, Sensei."

Mokichi raised his umbrella, looking up towards the hill on which Akutagawa lived, and said, "It's good you are so close to your home tonight, and so I hope you will be able to sleep soon, and to sleep well."

"Thank you," said Akutagawa again. "I do plan to write a little first, but then to take a draught and sleep, all thanks to you, Sensei."

In the dark, narrow road, by the open door to the taxi, Mokichi smiled, patted Akutagawa on his shoulder and said, "As long as one can both write and sleep, then one can endure all fate throws our way."

"Thank you," said Akutagawa again, one last and final time, and then, in the night and in the rain, as Mokichi got into the back of the cab, in the last and final silence, almost in a whisper now, "In the end, as Poe said, at the very end, *Lord, help my soul* . . . help all our souls . . ."

In the back of the taxi, as the cab made its way down the dark side road towards the bright lights of Dōzaka, Mokichi turned to look for Akutagawa, to wave goodbye to Akutagawa, but Akutagawa was not there; Akutagawa was already gone.

3. A Psalm, Again

O LORD GOD of my salvation, I have cried day and night before thee:

Let my prayer come before thee: incline thine ear unto my cry;

For my soul is full of troubles: and my life draweth nigh unto the grave.

I am counted with them that go down into the pit: I am as a man that hath no strength:

Free among the dead, like the slain that lie in the grave, whom thou rememberest no more: and they are cut off from thy hand.

Thou hast laid me in the lowest pit, in darkness, in the deeps.

Thy wrath lieth hard upon me, and thou hast afflicted me with all thy waves. Sê-läh.

Thou hast put away mine acquaintance far from me; thou hast made me an abomination unto them: I am shut up, and I cannot come forth.

Mine eye mourneth by reason of affliction: LORD, I have called daily upon thee, I have stretched out my hands unto thee.

Wilt thou shew wonders to the dead? Shall the dead arise and praise thee? Sê-läh.

Shall thy loving kindness be declared in the grave? Or thy faithfulness in destruction?

Shall thy wonders be known in the dark? And thy righteousness in the land of forgetfulness?

But unto thee have I cried, O LORD; and in the morning shall my prayers prevent thee.

Lord, why castest thou off my soul? Why hidest thou thy face from me?

I am afflicted and ready to die from my youth up: while I suffer thy terrors I am distracted.

Thy fierce wrath goeth over me; thy terrors have cut me off.

They came round about me daily like water; they compassed me about together.

Lover and friend hast thou put far from me, and mine acquaintances into darkness.

4. An Attic of Faith

Beneath the crucifix on the wall of the attic, Fumitake Muroga smiled at Ryūnosuke and asked, "How have you been recently?

Fumitake Muroga worked as a caretaker-cum-handyman for the American Bible Society on the Ginza, living alone in the attic room of the religious publishing house, devoting his time to reading and prayer. Many years ago now, he had worked for Ryūnosuke's father Toshizō Niihara as a dairy deliveryman, and so Muroga had known Ryūnosuke since childhood.

"A nervous wreck, as usual," said Ryūnosuke, with that familiar sad, resigned smile Muroga had come to expect. "When I wonder if I can take another summer like this, another month of this, I feel wretched beyond belief . . . My head feels so strange . . . Even the most futile matters cause me to sink into a state of utter despair . . . Day after day, night after night, I just seem to subsist on opium extracts, strychnine, laxatives and Veronal . . ."

Muroga offered Ryūnosuke an apple and said, "You have to accept that drugs and medicines won't cure or help you. But if you accept Jesus Christ, if you believe in Him, then you can be helped, then you can be saved."

"If only He could," said Ryūnosuke, looking from the wooden crucifix on the wall down to the yellow apple in his hand. "If only I could."

"If thou canst believe," quoted Muroga from the Gospel According to Mark, "all things *are* possible to him that believeth . . ."

"Help thou mine unbelief," sighed Ryūnosuke.

"But it's not difficult, it's not hard. If you would just believe in

God, believe in Jesus Christ and accept Him as the Son of God, and believe in His miracles, believe in His power . . ."

"I can believe in the devil and his power," said Ryūnosuke.

"Then why do you refuse to believe in God? If you believe in the darkness, then surely you have to believe in the light, too?"

"There is such a thing as darkness without light."

"Momentarily, yes," said Muroga. "But light always follows darkness. Just as day always follows night. Miraculously."

"I don't believe in miracles," said Ryūnosuke. "Miracles of the devil, these days maybe, but even then I'm not so sure . . ."

"Why do you only ever speak of the devil?"

Ryūnosuke fell silent for a while, staring up again at the crucifix on the wall, and then said, "Actually, I've just gone through the Sermon on the Mount again, and though I've read it many times before, I was struck with many new meanings which had hitherto escaped me, and it has inspired me to begin working on a new text of my own, on the Life of Christ . . ."

Muroga stood up, walked over to his ancient bookcase, took down a copy of the Holy Bible, handed it to Ryūnosuke and said, "Please take it."

"Thank you," said Ryūnosuke, "but I already have two copies."

The old man smiled at Ryūnosuke and said, "You can never have too many copies of the Bible, you can never read the Bible enough. This is the *Shin'yaku Seisho* edition. It's all in there, all very simple . . ."

"Thank you," said Ryūnosuke again, this time accepting the Bible from Muroga, "and I promise you, I will read it again."

"Then please begin with the Gospel According to Mark."

"Why Mark," asked Ryūnosuke.

"It is short, powerful, and contains all you need to believe."

"I will read it," said Ryūnosuke again.

Muroga reached over, holding Ryūnosuke's hands and the Bible in them, and looking up into his eyes—his hands cold, his eyes empty, as one dead—he said, he pleaded and he begged, "But then please read it with your heart, Ryūnosuke, and then believe it in your soul . . ."

5. The Exit Wounds

In the house, in my study, I read the Bible, I read the Bible, over and over, again and again, I read the Bible, I read the Bible, then in my house, then in my study, I write, I write, over and over, again and again, I write and I write, in my house, in my study, until it stops, and when it stops, then I stop, I stop . . .

In the twilight, always the twilight, in the summer, always the summer, I come out of my house, my house in Tabata, and I start to walk, I start to walk, with a bag in my hand, always the bag in my hand, I walk and I walk, with a Bible in my bag, always the Bible in my bag, I walk and I walk . . .

In my dark kimono and old geta, *with my bag and umbrella, I come to Ueno, into the park, the scent of the green leaves of the cherry trees intense, the evening air heavy and humid, close upon the city, close upon my skin, as I walk and I walk, through the clinging, clawing night and its shadows, my own shadow now, now and evermore the image of a Kappa, that one particular Kappa, the one I've been drawing all these years and years, writing about these past months and months; he is clinging to me, he is clawing at me, he refuses to go, just won't let go, walking alongside me, always beside me, a soul in exile, begging to return, to return, return, return . . .*

At last, at last, I come out of the park, out under the bright lights of Hirokōji, more melancholy than ever, more fraught than ever; I can't bear it, I can't stand it. I want to have fun, to have fun and forget. Forget the world, forget myself. I go across the tramlines; I go into a café.

I order a whisky, a bottle of whisky: "Preferably Black & White . . ."

"You don't drink alcohol," says my companion.

"I can't drink alcohol at all," I laugh, "but recently I take the occasional glass of whisky. Preferably Black & White . . ."

"But then why Black & White?"

"I like the picture of the two terriers on the label," I tell him, sipping my drink and then, for his amusement, I shudder in mock horror at its strength and declare, "Why, I feel completely drunk already . . ."

It feels such a long time since we've shared a joke and the release which laughter brings. But now I look up at him, and now I see him, see the wound still weeping through his hair, the wound from the bullet bleeding onto the table, in drops, in drops it pools, it pools, and my jovial mood is gone, my comedic turn finished; I lean towards him and say, "I've made a mistake. I should change brands . . ."

"But it's your favourite . . ."

"But the two dogs, it's one dog," I whisper to him. "Its two colours, their two natures, they're the two sides of our soul, our own duality . . ."

I've turned a sudden, dark corner, back again on the mental ward of the asylum with Uno, my fears for him, his family, and for me, for myself, my own family—

"You know, when his mother finally found him in the restaurant, Uno was eating the roses from the vase on the table, saying over and over, I'm so hungry, I'm so hungry . . . But I would say, it's actually fortunate for the life of an artist . . . Yes, in spite of all that's happened to him, I think it's excellent for Uno! Insanity and madness are no shame for an artist. One might even say Uno has attained a higher level, reached a higher plane . . ."

My companion seems not to agree with me, shaking his bleeding head, even somewhat irritated. "You might say that, but what on earth will become of Uno's family if he cannot be cured quickly, or if he then cannot write, or if his madness leads even to his death; how then will they survive?"

"But as artists, we cannot avoid such things," I say, shrugging my shoulders. "It is the age we are cursed to live in. As Uno himself told me, just the other day, we are possessed by the demon of the fin de siècle . . ."

"Do you really believe that? In such things?"

"Yes, I do," I say, "I do."

"Well, personally, I now regret all my romantic notions of the suffering artist dying young. Those who loved me, those I left behind, they were all much weaker than me, all relied upon me. I wish now I'd lived longer . . ."

"Enough Gogol! Enough Strindberg," I shout, leaping up from the table, startling not only my companion but the entire café, pointing with my umbrella at the door, exclaiming, "We want to have fun! And so fun we shall have. Quack! Quack! To Kameido, to Kameido!"

In the back of the taxi, I tell him: "You know, the eastern bank of the Sumida, that was my playground as a child: Honjo, Ryōgoku and Kameido. In those days, before the flood, the garyūbai in the garden at Kiyogaoen really did resemble reclining dragons, so long and sinuous were their branches. I was enchanted, yet petrified . . ."

"We once saw the famous wisteria at the Tenjin Shrine," he says, "but whenever I hear mention of Kameido now, I can only think of the earthquake and its aftermath, the horrific murders of Keishichi Hirasawa and Uhachi Nakatsuji, Sakae Ōsugi and Noe Itō, and all the others. And from all I've heard, Kameido is still a most desperate place, more likely to crush our souls than fill them with cheer . . ."

"Exactly," I say, as the taxi speeds across Kototoi Bridge, down through Koume, south towards Kameido. "But at night, when all is darkness, you cannot see the factories. And then to walk that ground, to inhale the stench of its drains, that is reality, is it not? For two 'hommes des lettres' such as we, it should be life-affirming, returning us to our homes and our work, to our words and our art with a renewed sense of vigour and vitality!"

I know he is not convinced, but it's too late; the taxi stops somewhere to the north of the shrine. I pay the fare and get out of the cab onto a street beside a canal. It's true, the stench from the canal is considerable, few other people about, and certainly no hint of "fun." But then I spy a group of youths up ahead, poke my companion in his skinny ribs and laugh and say, "They look like they know where they're going, let's follow them . . ."

And before he can moan and protest as he usually does, I grab him by his damp, thin arm and off we set, down the street, past rundown houses on a lower level than the road, past dirty boards advertising fortune-tellers and medicines, until we come to a crossing, turn left and then find ourselves at the edge of a warren of narrow alleyways of clapboard housing. The rows of lattice doors on both sides of every alley are all illuminated, one panel in each door made of transparent glass, solitary men walking up and down the passageways, stopping to peer through the panels into the houses.

"Now we're here," I say, "we may as well take a look . . ."

And we join the flow of silent, serious men, ambling up the first of the alleyways, crisscrossing from one side to the other, stopping to peer in through the peepholes, occasionally glimpsing the full face of the woman inside but mostly seeing only their eyes, trying so hard to shine and to smile, to welcome and invite, and every now and again, I stop and turn back to him, with a wink and a smile of my own. But we do not dally for long, soon coming to the end of the passageway, out onto a wider street lined with kiosks and a Western restaurant, and with taxis here, too. I know my companion is not in the mood, feels he has seen enough. Still, I point to the next alleyway and say, "It would be a shame not to complete our tour, no?"

And I lead the way again, down the next alley, then back up another, house after house, peephole after peephole, until each pair of eyes inside becomes but one single pair of sad and desperate eyes, and we find ourselves back where we'd begun, where we'd come in—

"Let's go home," says my companion.

"Yes, we could just go home," I tell him. "But seeing as we've come so far, and might never have the chance again, how about one last turn?"

He doesn't say yes, he doesn't say no; he just follows me up and down the alleyways again, peeping in here and peering in there, quicker the second time around, until we're back at our original spot.

The humidity has grown ever more oppressive, the stench of drains ever more overpowering, and now big fat drops of rain are falling like leeches from the heavy, low night sky on the tops of our heads—

"Is that really all there is to this place," I say, feigning outrage. "Well, I must say, I do say, it's really rather disappointing!"

"Not only disappointing," he says. "Depressing and exhausting."

"Indeed," I agree, bending down to rub my thighs and my knees. "I'm completely shattered. I don't think I can take another step . . ."

Now the rain is starting to fall heavily, as he says, "Well, if you can just make it back to the main road, we'll be able to get a taxi . . ."

"I really do want to go home," I tell him. "Honestly, I do. But I'd also really like to rest for a while first. Just a little while . . ."

"But where," he says, looking around.

"You don't think one of those places might offer us tea," I say. "After all, we're going to have to walk back up the alleyways anyway."

He shakes his little head. "I very much doubt it."

"But we can at least try," I insist, standing up straight again now, squaring my shoulders. "I'm sure we can find a willing place, if we negotiate. But don't worry, leave the negotiating to me!"

And so for the third time, we go back up the alleyway—me purposefully striding up to one of the first lattice doors, him reluctantly following behind—and as I bend my neck to look in through the peephole, I beckon him over, and looking through the glass, we can see a slightly plump woman in her middle-twenties, with a gentle, pretty face, sitting all on her own inside the house, and I whisper to him, "Shall I try?"

"If you want, if you must . . ."

"Excuse me," I say, speaking through the door, still looking through the glass. "My friend and I are a little tired and would like to rest a little while, and so we wondered if you could kindly offer us a little tea?"

Perhaps our pale faces and intense stares through the glass alarm her, for the woman nervously says, "There's nobody here."

Undeterred, I immediately cross to a house diagonal to the last, peeping in and asking, "Could we possibly have some tea?"

"Please, do come in," calls the voice of a woman from inside the house; we can see her silhouette rising now, moving towards the door, but then, still leaning forward, still staring through the small glass window, I can see her, see her clearly, clearly as she is, and what she really is, and I spring back, I cry out, scream out, "Oh! Oh! Oh, no . . ."

"What is it," he asks me. "What?"

"It's too frightening," I whisper, spinning round and running quickly off, off up the alleyway as fast as I can go—

"What is it? What happened," he calls after me, but I do not stop, cannot stop, just keep on running, until I come to the corner, to the end of the alleyway, hiding round the corner, my hands over my face, my whole body trembling, mumbling over and over, "Did you see? Did you see? Did you see? Did you . . ."

"See what," he asks. "See what?"

I grip him by his slimy, bony shoulders, stare into his red and tiny eyes and ask, "Really? Didn't you see? See what I saw . . . ?"

"See what," he asks again. "What did you see?"

"That woman," I shout. "That woman!"

"I only caught a glimpse of her face, but I didn't feel there was anything particularly strange about her . . ."

"It was a ghost!"

"Who?"

"Her," I tell him, shuddering again. "I saw her full face, her whole body when she stood up . . ."

But he just shakes his stupid wounded head and tries hard not to laugh. Yet I know what he's thinking: if anyone in this hellhole resembles *a ghost, it's me and only me; a miracle the poor woman did not scream out in terror at the horror of my face, my own face—*

"Let's just go home," he says.

In the taxicab, the rain running down the windows, neither of us speak until he asks the driver to pull up beside the Shinobazu Pond in Ueno. He gets out with a sigh, but then, just as he's about to turn to say goodnight, I reach across to grab his cold and scaly arm and ask, "Please tell me honestly, you really didn't see anything strange at all back there?"

"Nothing at all," he says, "I'm sorry."

"I wish you'd gone back to look."

He smiles. "I'm glad I didn't."

The lights from the street and the rain on the glass throw strange black characters across us both as I smile back and say, "I'm sorry."

"I'll see you soon, back in the valley," says Tock, closing the cab door, the taxi driving off as I turn to look for him, to wave goodbye to him, to see him standing by the pond, one hand still trying to stem and stop the blood streaming and spurting from the concave saucer on the top of his head, the other hand waving goodbye, goodbye, goodbye, goodbye . . .

6. The House of Sleep

"Hello," said Hyakken Uchida, "hello . . . hello . . . hello?"

But Akutagawa did not move, he did not stir; his chin on his chest, his hair over his face, his body sunk in the rattan chair, in front of the *tokonoma*, in his upstairs study, in his house in Tabata.

It was almost evening, twilight now, in the middle of July, the hottest July on record. Even here in this dimly lit study, the heat was unbearable. Hyakken wiped his face again, he wiped his neck again, sitting on a cushion among the papers and the books, three different editions of the Bible open among the boxes of Golden Bat cigarettes scattered here and there, Hyakken just staring up at his friend; even in this heat, even in such a state, Akutagawa looked so elegant, he looked so refined, occasionally opening his eyes, raising his face towards Hyakken, half smiling as he said, "I'm sorry."

"What's wrong with you," asked Hyakken.

"My stomach has been hurting," said Akutagawa, his tongue struggling to move in his mouth, his words slurred. "I've not been able to sleep, so I had to take something, and then I got up before I was really awake . . ."

"You shouldn't take so much medicine, you know."

His heavy lids had closed again, his thin body slack in the chair again, yet still Akutagawa mumbled, "And you shouldn't drink so much, you know . . ."

Hyakken had no idea what to say to him, what to do for him, just sitting there, watching him drifting in and out of sleep, his own eyes closing in the gloom now, opening then closing again, his neck hanging in the heat . . .

"About the money," said Akutagawa, suddenly.

Hyakken sat up and said, "Yes, I'm sorry . . ."

Akutagawa stood up slowly, unsteady on his feet, tottering towards the doors. His eyes still half closed, he reached up to a picture hanging above the door. He put his hand behind the frame. He took out a crisp new two-hundred-yen banknote. He handed it to Hyakken and said, "Here you are, and I can arrange to give you more . . ."

"Thank you," said Hyakken, embarrassed. "But this is more than enough. I'm just sorry to be such a burden . . ."

"Excuse me," said Akutagawa, slumping back into the chair.

Hyakken felt he should go, let his friend rest. But now he realised he didn't even have change for the train. Hyakken cursed himself; he'd meant to make sure he had some prepared . . .

"Don't worry," said Akutagawa, standing up again, again looking so dizzy. "Just wait a moment, please . . ."

Akutagawa stumbled through the door, down the corridor

towards the steep ladder staircase. Hyakken followed him out into the corridor, worried he might fall down the stairs. He felt dizzy himself, but Akutagawa seemed to manage, disappearing down the steps, and so Hyakken just stood there, waiting for him to return, staring out at the garden, quivering in the heat.

From the moment they had first met, Akutagawa had always been so kind to him, and even now, still now, Hyakken could not imagine why. They had first become properly acquainted when Akutagawa had started to visit Sōseki-sensei, and joined the Mokuyō-kai. But even after the death of Sōseki-sensei, even when so many others had already begun to shun Hyakken, Akutagawa had always remained a good and loyal friend; when Hyakken had been complaining about his low salary from the Imperial Military Academy in Ichigaya, how his paltry wage and big family meant he could not cover his monthly expenditures, Akutagawa had recommended him for a second job at the Naval Engineers Academy in Yokosuka, even though they hardly knew each other. And when Hyakken had asked him why, Akutagawa had simply smiled and said, "Because our grandmother will be pleased."

Akutagawa seemed to have been gone for an age but, just as he was wondering whether he should have followed him down the stairs, Hyakken heard him coming up the other ladder, at the opposite end of the corridor, Akutagawa swaying as he walked towards him now, the hem of his summer kimono ridden up on his leg, with his hands cupped together.

Akutagawa stopped in front of Hyakken, just standing there, still swaying from side to side, his whole body shaking and trembling, and yet smiling proudly, raising his hands before Hyakken, holding them up to his face, offering him a huge handful of nickel and silver coins.

"Why did you bring so much," asked Hyakken.

"I kept trying to pick out your fare from my purse, but I couldn't.

In the end, I just emptied everything out into my hand. Please just take it all . . ."

Hyakken picked out a ten-sen coin from his palm and said, "Thank you, and I'll go now, goodbye."

Akutagawa took one step back into his study and parted his palms, showering his rosewood desk with the coins, the noise ringing through the house, following Hyakken down the steep ladder, his wife calling up the stairs, "Are you okay? Are you okay? Did you fall . . ."

7. "Are You Ready to Go Now?"

The first-class battleship Uno *went into dry dock at Yokosuka. Her friend the battleship* A *lay at anchor in the harbour. The* A *was a younger ship than the* Uno. *Now and then they would communicate wordlessly across the broad expanse of water. The* A *felt sorry for the* Uno, *not only because of her age, but also because she had a tendency to steer erratically (the result of an error on the part of the architect). But in order not to upset her, the* A *never referred to this particular problem, and always spoke to the battle-seasoned* Uno *in the most respectful terms . . . But one cloudy afternoon, a fire broke out in the hold of the* Uno, *and suddenly, with a fearful roar, she heeled over in the water. The* A, *who had never been in battle, was naturally shocked, could scarcely believe it . . . Three or four days later, since there was no longer any pressure from the water on her sides, the* Uno's *decks gradually began to crack. When they saw this, the engineers began to hurry along with their repair work even faster. But soon the* Uno *had given up all hope . . . And staring out across Yokosuka harbour, the* A *awaited her own fate now with a growing sense of unease as she began to feel her own decks warping, little by little, the architects of her own design worse even than those of the* Uno, *the racking on her corners ever more intense, the tide coming in, flooding in, the rising waters and the endless waves, up to her neck and over her chin, into her mouth and through her hair, over her hair and over her head—*

I wake in my chair, gasping for air, struggling to breathe, coughing and spluttering, phlegm in my mouth and drool down my chin, the Bible falling from my hands, falling to the floor, as I wipe my chin and dry my eyes; Uno's condition had deteriorated again, the situation becoming unbearable for his wife and family, and so Dr. Saitō had arranged to have Uno hospitalised at the Komine Research Institute in Ōji. When I last visited him, in the asylum, on the ward, strapped to his bed, Uno just stared up at me, shook his head and said again, "You and me, me and you, we're peas in a pod, Ryūnosuke, peas in a pod, possessed by the same demon: the demon of the fin de siècle . . ."

"Shu-shu pop-po, shu-shu pop-po, shu-shu pop-po . . ."

I get up from my chair, pick up the Bible from the floor, put down the Bible on my desk. I light a cigarette and step out of my study, into the corridor. I stand and smoke at the glass windows, watching my two older boys in the sun-drenched garden, playing locomotives—

"Shu-shu pop-po, shu-shu pop-po . . ."

They are not only making the sounds of a locomotive, they are moving their arms, imitating the motion of a locomotive. Not only my children do this, I know, many children do, but I wonder why? Is it because they sense the power of a locomotive, with all its noise and steam and speed, all its violence? Perhaps they want to have the violent life of a locomotive? But then the possession of such a desire is not limited to children; adults are the same, we're all the same, rushing headlong down the tracks, just like a locomotive, but down the tracks to who knows where; the tracks can be many things, anything: fame, women, money, power. But they are always tracks, tracks we cannot leave, and tracks we want to be able to pursue as freely and as selfishly as we can, blind to the fact they are tracks, tracks we cannot leave. And countless generations, in countless societies, have tried to put the brakes on our engines, upon our desires, but they have always failed, and so still we hurtle on, down the tracks—

"Shu-shu pop-po . . ."

I turn from the children in the garden, unsteady on my feet, leave the window in the corridor and return to the desk in my study. I light another cigarette, then stare down at the two manuscripts which lie unfinished; one is my autobiography, which perhaps I should call "The Art of Slaughtering Dragons," the other my attempt to write a biography of Christ, in the meagre, shabby words of a useless, washed-up bourgeoisie hack, an attempt to write "My Christ," and which I've called "Man of the West" . . .

In fact, because I'd come to the day of the deadline, I was forced to abandon this work, and have already submitted it to Kaizō; yet I cannot let it go, let Him go, and so I want to write more . . .

But looking from one incomplete work to the other, lighting another cigarette, I cannot decide which manuscript to work on now; I need to finish them both, and finish them both today. But before I'm able to decide, now I hear the voice of my wife, calling up the stairs, calling me down to lunch.

Despite the heat and their exertions in the garden, the two older boys are still lively, filled with a seemingly boundless vitality; they never stop talking, even while eating, and Takashi keeps kicking the leg of the table. I scold him and, instantly, in that moment, the mood changes; both boys stop speaking, just silently eating their lunch now, and my wife says nothing, too, her eyes downcast and filling with tears; once again, yet again, I have failed, as a father and as a man, as a human being, wracked with guilt and regret, knowing I bring only pain and misery to the ones who have the misfortune, the curse of loving me, knowing they'd be better off, they'd be happier if I disappeared, if I wasn't here, was never here, was gone.

I get up from the dining table, go back up the steep ladder, up to my study and back to the desk. I pick up the autobiography, stuff it into an *old envelope, scrawl "RUBBISH" on its face and put it by the bin to be burnt; I don't have the strength to go on writing it, to go on feeling like this, living on like this—*

Is there no one kind enough to strangle me in my sleep?

I sit back down at the desk and turn back to "Man of the West," this "Man of the West Continued"—

If I can only finish this manuscript today, by the end of this day, then I'll find peace, can die in peace. And so, with a trembling hand, I pick up my pen again, this chipped and narrow sword again, and I start to write again, in these meagre, shabby words of a useless, washed-up literary hack, to write and to write "My Christ"—

". . . who in these last days I have come to love, who is no longer a stranger, but who is yet still a spectre, a spectre on the Cross at which I stare and I stare, though most have tired of looking, though many have tried to bring it down, yet still I stare and I stare at 'My Christ' on his cross . . .

". . . who was born for me in Japan, born to Mary—an ordinary woman we sense in all women, in the burning fire of the hearth, in the abundant harvests of the field, her life lived with a ceaseless patience in 'the vale of tears'—born to Mary and the Holy Ghost—neither a Satan nor an Angel, the Holy Ghost who walks on the other shore, beyond Good and Evil . . .

". . . who eluded Herod, who escaped his machine, the machine that is always necessary for those who wish to avert change, to avoid revolution; this Herod in fear of change, his machine in terror of revolution, slaughtered the children and the thousands of other Christs all mingled among them; yet with his hands of crimson, his face of melancholia, we cannot hate him, cannot despise him, only pity him, dying among the olive and the fig trees, leaving not one line of poetry . . .

". . . who spent time in Egypt, returned to Galilee, and then lived in Nazareth, just as the children of naval officers are transferred to Sasebo, next to Maizuru, then to Yokosuka; perhaps these forced and sudden changes helped to forge the Bohemian Spirit of 'My Christ'?

"*. . . who knew he was not the son of his father Joseph, a superfluous man, who realised he was a child of the Holy Ghost, who in the gloom of this revelation, who after the solitude of his childhood, who then encountered John, a Christ born before him, a Christ come before him, John who in his last lament would ask of him, Was it you who were Christ, or was it me?*

"*. . . who walked alone into the wilderness, who fasted for forty days and forty nights, who entered into a dialogue with Satan, but who refused to succumb, who rejected temptation: materialism, power, all the worldly desires of our hearts, and who vanquished Satan, 'for a season' . . .*

"*. . . who then travelled from village to village, first on his own, then with disciples, who began to speak, who began to talk, in allegories and in parables, an ancient Bohemian and an ancient journalist, who in the genius of his examples, in the passion of his poetry, brought new wood to the old fire, to burn and to illuminate, who in all his masterpieces—the Sermon on the Mount, the Good Samaritan and the Prodigal Son— and in all his words trampled on the conventions of all ages, and turned the world upside down, our world upside down, but who then sowed the seeds of fear, the fear of change, and who then made enemies, so many enemies . . .*

"*. . . and yet who loved and was loved by many, and most by Magdalene, with a poetic love which transcended her profession, with a poetic love which forgave her sins, a love still as fragrant as an iris . . .*

"*. . . who saw the lilies of the field, with whom even Solomon in all his glory could not compare, yet who in such poetry vanquished tomorrow . . .*

"*. . . who performed miracles, though he hated miracles, for they pandered to the people, drained him of his strength, made him question the strength of his words, his words and his self, and left him human, all too human . . .*

"*. . . who could not bear the tears of Martha and Mary, who raised Lazarus from the dead, to stem their tears, too human, all too human . . .*

"... who then rejected his mother and all such love, who chose Jerusalem, chose a known and certain death, to show us what we are searching for, the absence which torments us still, who revealed to us what lies beyond, beyond our world, within our souls: the Kingdom of Heaven, of Heaven on Earth ...

"... who went up the mountain to speak with the Dead, as he shone like the sun, as white as pure light, but who knew today is never yesterday, the Red Sea no longer parted, and who asked then, asks now, How should we live?

"... who then came down from the mountain to settle the accounts of his life, a life he would now soon, soon now leave behind, this life beginning to have its revenge, his life taking its revenge upon him; the star that had announced his birth, the Holy Ghost which had given him life, they would not give him peace, they would not let him be, as he cursed the fig tree ...

"... who entered Jerusalem on an ass, the Cross already on his back, always, already on his back, who said, Render unto Caesar the things which are Caesar's, and unto God the things that are God's, who turned the tables in the temple, cast out monies from the House of God ...

"... who in the Garden of Gethsemane, in the darkest night of his soul, his soul exceedingly sorrowful, even unto death, who fell on his face and then prayed, prayed and prayed for this cup to pass from him ..."

I stop writing, put down my pen. I light a cigarette, get up from my desk and step into the corridor. I stand and smoke at the glass windows, staring down, down and out at the garden of my house, my garden in twilight, my garden in silence: God hears our prayers, but waits.

I turn from the garden, and in the twilight and in the silence, unsteady on my feet again, I return to my desk, my desk and "My Christ"—

"... from whom the cup would not pass, who found his companions sleeping still, and who knew the hour was at hand ...

"... who was betrayed in the night, betrayed by a kiss, from a suicide for a suicide, who was denied at the dawn, denied by those he left behind ...

"... who came before Pilate and then the people, and then as now, who was not chosen, who was rejected, but who spoke not a word ...

"... who felt the thorns of the crown, the spit from their mouths and the smote of the reed, and then the wood of the Cross ...

"... who felt the nails through his hand, felt the nail through his feet, who from the Cross looked down on the world, who then from the Cross looked up to Heaven, and who cried, Eli, Eli, lama sabachthani?"

I stop writing again, put down my pen again. I wipe my neck, wipe my face and dry my eyes; I dry my eyes and turn again to Him—

"... who in his last cry, in those last words, moved closer still to us, then gave up the ghost for us, and died for us, who died for us ...

"... who ... who ... who if not you?

"... a ladder cruelly broken off in the ascent from earth to Heaven, still aslant amidst the downpour from the gloomy, murky sky ..."

I stop again, pen down again, head in my hands, hands to my face, fingers in my eyes, rubbing my eyes, in my eyes, in my mind—

My Christ, my Christ, so many Christs:

My Christ is a mirror, the Universal Mirror; my Christ is a poet, a Bohemian poet; my Christ is a journalist, an ancient journalist; my Christ is a pacifist, a non-resistant Tolstoy, yet softer, softer still; my Christ is a communist, who came for the poor, who loved the poor, and who said, The foxes have holes, and the birds have nests, but the Son of Man hath not where to lay his head ...

In the dread and in the terror of these words, my Christ, he speaks to me, in dread and in terror, he speaks to me, of the misery of his life, the example of his life, speaks to me and to every Child of the Holy Ghost, all the Children of the Holy Ghost; Christianity may one day perish, one day soon no doubt, but the Life of Christ, this Life of Jesus will continue to move us, whether in the West or whether in the East, will always move us, every Child of the Holy Ghost, all the Children of the Holy Ghost, move and speak to us—a ladder sadly broken off in the

*ascent from earth to Heaven, still aslant amidst the downpour from the
gloomy, murky sky—for we are all travellers on the way to Emmaus,
always seeking the Christ who will burn up our hearts.*

*In the horror and the quiet of the house now in night, I take my
fingers from my eyes, take my hands from my face, and I look down
at my desk, the papers on the desk, strewn across the desk, the books
on the desk, open on the desk; I begin to close all the books, to tidy
away all the books, all these Lives of Christ: Strauss, Renan, Farrar and
Papini; closing all the books, tidying away all the books, the books and
the Bibles, my three editions of the Bible: the one from Kyō Tsunetō, the
one from Fumitake Muroga, and the one I will not close, I will not tidy
away; the one I will take down the stairs, the one I will read before I
sleep, I sleep tonight . . .*

*Now I reach across the papers, reach across the desk, I pick up a sachet
of Veronal, open the sachet of Veronal, and I take the Veronal. Then I
straighten up the papers, all the manuscript papers, put them into piles
and put them to one side. And then I pick up my pen again, this chipped
and narrow sword again, and for one last and final time, I write, I
write and I write: a poem for my doctor, letters to my friends, letters I
have practised, letters I've rehearsed, then a letter to my wife, and then,
most difficult of all, most painful of all, then I begin to write the last
letter, a last letter—*

For My Children—

1. Never forget life is a war which leads to death.
2. Accordingly, don't take life for granted, but nurture your
   abilities; let this be your principle.
3. Regard Ryūichi Oana as your father, and so heed his advice.
4. If you lose the battle of life, you should commit suicide like
   your father, in order to avoid causing unhappiness to others.

5. It is difficult to recognise your own destiny in life. But as long as you do not rely on your family, and renounce such a desire, then you may find the way to be at peace with yourself.

6. You should feel pity for your mother, yet this pity should not change your will. In this way, you will make your mother happy later.

7. Inevitably, all three of you will inherit and share my anxiety; you all then should be aware and careful of this fact.

8. Your father loves you; if I didn't love you, if I had deserted you or not cared for you, then I might have found a way to survive.

Ryūnosuke Akutagawa

I put down my pen, put the letters in the envelopes and seal the envelopes. I pick up my pen again, address the envelopes, place the envelopes on the Bible, then put down my pen again, for the last time, I put down my pen.

I wipe my neck, wipe my face and dry my eyes, but my eyes are dry, my eyes are dry. I try to remember if I've taken the Veronal, but I can't remember if I've taken the Veronal, so I reach across the desk, pick up a sachet of Veronal, open the sachet of Veronal, and I take the Veronal.

I wipe my neck again, wipe my face again, then get up from the desk again, for the last time, I get up from the desk. Unsteady on my feet, most unsteady on my feet, I step out of my study, into the corridor. Unsteady on my feet, so unsteady my feet, past the garden in the night, in the night and in its silence, I walk along the corridor, and then I stop, turn and go back, back to my study, back to my desk, and I pick up the poem, the poem for Dr. Shimojima, then I put it back down, back down on my desk. I wipe my neck, wipe my face and try to remember if I've taken the Veronal, but I can't remember if I've taken the Veronal, so I reach down to the desk, pick up a sachet of Veronal, open the sachet of Veronal, and I take the Veronal, then another sachet, open another sachet, and I take the sachet of Veronal. Then I wipe my neck again, wipe my face again, pick up the letters and the Bible, put the letters in the Bible and pick up the poem. Then I step out of my study, for the last time, I step out of my study and walk along the corridor, so unsteady on my feet, very unsteady on my feet, for the last time, I walk along the corridor, and go down the ladder stairs.

I don't know what time it is, I have no idea what time it is, except it is summer, always summer and hot, always so hot, except it is night, always night and silent, always so silent, but I come to a room, the room of my aunt, her light still on, her light always on, and I knock on the door, knock on her door, then enter her room, I enter her room, see her on her bedding, lying on her bedding, and I hold out the poem, the poem and say, "I may still be sleeping when the doctor calls, so would you please give him this, when the doctor calls, saying I'm sleeping, so leave me be, please let me sleep."

I hand her the poem, and she takes the poem, she takes the poem and then she says, she says, she says, don't know what she says, but I smile and I smile, I smile and I say, "Thank you, Auntie, thank you, thank you and goodnight, Auntie, goodnight, I'm going now, Auntie, I'm going now . . ."

I leave her room, leave her room and go to my room, our room, our room where we sleep, my wife, my children and I, my children sleeping, hands to their faces, my wife sleeping, her face to the wall, and I see my yukata, *the* yukata *I bought in China, folded on my futon, lying on my futon, and I put down the Bible, the Bible and the letters, and then I stagger around, taking off my clothes, and then I stumble around, putting on the* yukata—

"Did you take your usual sleeping draught," asks my wife, raising her head, then lying back down, closing her eyes . . .

"Yes," I say, "I did. Don't worry, I did . . ."

And then I take the letters from the Bible, place the letters inside my yukata, *the folds of my* yukata, *then lie down, down on the bedding, lay my head down, down on the pillow, then open the Bible, for one last time, I open the Bible and begin to read, my eyes closing, my eyes opening, for one last time, I begin to read,* and I read, Behold, I stand at the door, and knock: if any man hear my voice, and open the door, I will come in to him . . .

Then in the night, and in the night, now I see Him, and I see Him; not a shadow, not a spectre, but the man I love, the Christ I love . . .

The Yellow Christ on the Cross, on the Waiting Cross, the Patient Cross, my Christ, my Christ, at last, at last, at the very last . . .

As I sink and I sink, once and for all, for all and always, into the grove, into the grove between our lives; in the grove . . .

He is, He is, He just is, He just—

After the Fact, Before the Fact

Snot!
Only at the tip of the nose
Remains
A trace of twilight.

"Self-Mockery," Ryūnosuke Akutagawa, July 23, 1927

It was the Age of Shōwa, the summer after the death of Taishō, still early in the morning. Yasukichi was walking through the pine woods, along the shore at Kugenuma. Beyond the dead-still pines, beyond the low sand dunes, the sea yawned, clouded and grey. On the edge of the pines, among the dunes, Yasukichi came upon the frame of a swing, just its frame, for the seat of the swing was missing, its seat gone. Only two ropes remained, the two ropes dangling down, hanging-still from the frame; a gallows by the sea.

A crow landed on the redundant, topmost pole, then another, and another, then another. The four crows turned to stare at Yasukichi—

Yasukichi took off his panama hat and bowed his head. The biggest crow lifted its enormous beak heavenwards and cawed once, twice, a third time, then a fourth; exactly four times—

Should I take it as a sign, as a warning?

Yasukichi snorted, laughed; he couldn't remember ever feeling this bad, the worst days he'd ever had. He hadn't been able to write or even read for the heat, hadn't slept for the humidity. Even way down here, down by the sea, the heat and the humidity were the worst he'd ever known. Intolerable, unbearable. For days, weeks now. But then this morning, just before the dawn, he'd heard the rain begin to fall, drop by drop, falling upon the cottage and its garden, drop by drop, on the pond and on the stones, with a chill through the house, a shiver down his spine.

Yasukichi stuck out his tongue at the four crows, put his hat back on his head, and then walked on, following the darkened, damp sandbanks of bleached, withered grass, the tops of the short, sparsely growing pines, on and on he walked, beside the banks, along the shore, on and on, the houses and trees of Enoshima island looming up closer, ever closer in the melancholy, morbid gloom of this oppressive, smudged-grey morning.

Yasukichi tried not to look at the sea, not out to sea, to keep his eyes on the beach, on the sand. But a pair of black ruts, tracks made by a cart, cut diagonally across him and again, again *Wheat Field with Crows* came to his mind and again, again he felt bereft, bereft then overwhelmed; once, a long time ago now, he'd been standing outside a bookstore, turning the pages of pictures in a volume on Van Gogh, when suddenly, quite suddenly, he understood what a "painting" was; he knew these were only reproductions, he would never see the originals, but even in these photographs of his paintings, Yasukichi saw something, sensed something: a different way, a new way of looking at the world, of being in the world. He'd felt renewed, had felt restored, looking at the branches of a cherry tree, seeing the curve of a woman's cheek. But as he looked at the black ruts, their two tracks in the sand, he felt, sensed someone had come this way before, with a bandage wrapped around his head, over the place where his ear had been, a long-stemmed pipe in his mouth and a vision in his eyes, on his way to work, to work and to insanity, to insanity then suicide, on his way to death—

"Don't think like that," cried a voice on the air, the coquette, teasing voice of a woman, laughing, "it's a new age, a new era!"

Up ahead, sat on the sand with her back to a dwarf hedge of bamboo, Yasukichi could see a young woman with bobbed hair and an unnecessary parasol talking to a man in an Inverness raincoat and a panama hat—

"Don't tell me what to think," said the man, his figure and voice rising in anger now. "Just listen to yourself! What kind of *animal* are you?"

"What kind of animal am *I*," the young woman cried . . .

Yasukichi didn't stop to listen to the rest of their argument, to watch the rest of their scene, quickly walking away, away from the argument, away from the scene, all arguments and all scenes, over the sand and shells and off the beach, walking as fast as he could, onto the pebbles and pine cones, a crow flitting out of nowhere, casting a shadow across him; Yasukichi glanced up then away, but now tripped, then stumbled and almost fell—

At his feet, Yasukichi saw a wooden tally lying on the path, framed in black pitch. He picked it up, tried to read the inscription on the sea- and weather-worn wood, but all he could read were the dates: *1892–1927*. The tally must have belonged to a foreigner buried at sea, nailed to the sailcloth wrapped around his corpse—

Yasukichi dropped the wood; the dates on the tally meant the man had died at thirty-five, the age Yasukichi was now—

Should I take it as a sign, as a warning?

Yasukichi shuddered; born in Meiji, alive through Taishō, here in Shōwa still, but he felt cursed, he felt jinxed, no longer welcome in the world, as though someone or -thing was out to get him, to get him to leave.

Beside the clouded sea, beneath the muddy sky, uncertain what to do, unsure where to go, Yasukichi just walked, the sea watching him go, the sky following him still as he walked and he walked; walked and walked until he came to a street, a street of shops, a street and shops he knew, but the street was deserted, deserted but for a black and white dog sitting in the road.

The dog turned its face to stare at Yasukichi, and then barked once, twice, a third time, then a fourth; only four times, exactly four times—

Yasukichi had had enough of signs, enough of warnings; he walked towards the one shop which at least seemed to be open, a shop he had known for a long while, that overpowering bright red TOBACCO sign hanging down from its eaves as always. Yasukichi paused under the eaves, before the window of the shop, smiling at the familiar model of the battleship *Mikasa*, its Rising Sun flag hoisted, enclosed in a bottle of Curaçao, displayed among the adverts for condensed milk, then went inside, inside the familiar, welcoming shop; the coloured glass above the shop door cast its customary green light over the stucco walls and myriad goods of the store: the Kamakura hams still dangling from the rafters above, the poster for Kinsen Cider still hanging over the door to the back, just as they had always done; the tins of English cocoa, the boxes of American raisins all neatly arranged on the shelves as usual; the Yamatoni beef, the Scottish whisky, the Manila cigars and the Egyptian cigarettes, all were as they always were, all as it always was, familiar and comforting, welcoming.

Yasukichi picked up a large box of his usual matches; he loved the design of this box so much that he had often been tempted to frame its trademark. But as he looked down at the sailboat on the choppy sea now, he was reminded again of the wooden tally he'd stumbled, almost tripped over, the man buried at sea, lost to the sea, and again he felt inundated, again overwhelmed, drowning on dry land, drowning in this store. His palms sweating, Yasukichi put the box back on the shelf, wiped his palms on his handkerchief, then walked over to the woman sat at the counter.

Yasukichi had known the woman since the first day he had come into the shop, the same day he had started to teach at the Naval Academy, eight years ago now. In fact, if he was honest, with her hair done up in a Western style, with her pale cat-like face, she had been the initial, real reason he had become such a frequent, regular customer. But today, sitting at the counter as she always did, reading a newspaper as she usually did, the woman seemed somehow changed, in some way different, not the same, no longer the same.

"Excuse me," said Yasukichi. "I wonder if you have any other matches, other than Ship, perhaps a box of Swan Vesta?"

The woman did not look up at Yasukichi, appeared not to even hear him, but then she got up from her seat and walked into the back of the store.

How strange, thought Yasukichi, but he stayed where he was, waiting for her to return, glancing at the abacus standing on its end, looking down at the newspaper spread over the counter, its characters all upside down.

A few moments later, the woman returned from the back of the store, holding a box in her hand. But still she did not look at Yasukichi, not even to glance his way. The woman sat back down in her seat, opened up the box, took out a caramel, unwrapped its paper, put the sweet in her mouth, and then picked up the newspaper, now holding up its front page, its photograph and headline staring Yasukichi in the face—

RYŪNOSUKE AKUTAGAWA, RENOWNED AUTHOR, COMMITS SUICIDE AT TABATA HOME

Yasukichi tried to cry out, to protest, "*Mada-dayo!* Not yet—"

The woman looked up from the newspaper, over the counter, down to the floor. She put down the paper, got up from her seat, came out from behind the counter and picked up a box of matches that must have somehow fallen to the floor. The woman put the box back on the shelf, then returned to her seat and the newspaper, and turned the page.

Bare Bones

A Brief Biography of Ryūnosuke Akutagawa

His children did not call him Papa, they called him Ryū-chan. He played locomotives in the garden with them, climbed the trees and impersonated apes for them. He regretted his affairs and much of his writing. He was living then in a large house in Tabata, on the northeastern edges of Tokyo, with his adoptive parents, his aunt, his wife, their three sons and a maid. He provided for them and for his extended family from his study on the second floor. He had named the study Chōkōdō and wrote at a desk made from rosewood. He stared through the large windows at the plants and the trees, the bamboo, plantains, Japanese crepe myrtle, fatsia and chinquapin, and smoked his cigarettes. He favoured Golden Bat and Shikishima, alternating the cigarettes in order to better appreciate their flavours. He shook the matchbox three times before taking a light and smoked two packs of each brand a day. He would retire around midnight, always with a book, and rise around eight, earlier in the summer. He was comfortable in both Japanese dress and Western clothes. He had his hair cut only three or four times a year and shaved himself with a safety razor. He read only the *Asahi* and *Nichi-Nichi* newspapers. If anything was written about him elsewhere, either complimentary or insulting, someone would always let him know. He turned first to the international news and the situation in China, then to the local news and the stock market reports. He read the papers while eating and was punctual in his mealtimes. He took oatmeal, milk and eggs for breakfast. He preferred Japanese food but could eat most Chinese and Western dishes apart from broad beans. He loved bananas and figs, loquat and persimmon. He avoided *mikan* and sour fruits due to his gastric hyper-acidity. He was partial to sweets but particular about the quality of the sugar. He rarely drank alcohol, though he liked the taste of white wine. He drank green tea constantly and always kept a kettle on the brazier beside his desk. He drank coffee and red tea, too, but never in the evening.

He felt constipated and knew he was unpleasant before he began to write. He preferred the mornings yet would often return to his desk in the evenings. Late winter into early spring was the best season for his work. He hated noise or to be interrupted. He wrote in blue-black ink from Maruzen bookstore on blue-lined, half-sheet Matsuya manuscript paper. He frequently discarded his work and if he was stuck at a particular point, he would stop. Yet he always returned to finish the piece. He adopted a modest pose and feigned humility in regard to his work, but he was acutely sensitive to criticism. He remembered slights and he bore grudges. He disliked these traits in himself. He was the most well-read man of his generation, absorbed in a world of literature since childhood, a truly world literature: Japanese, Chinese and Western, ancient and modern, across all forms and genres. He owned three copies of the Holy Bible, one of which he had heavily annotated in red ink, and he had come to love the Christ of the Gospels. He was sympathetic to Socialism and to the ideas of Kropotkin and Tolstoy. He considered himself liberal and urbane, yet he longed for ancient and classical lands, real and imagined. He despaired of modern life, despised the base and animal nature of man. He was appalled and disgusted by his own self, the skull beneath the skin. He was attentive to his friends and set aside Sundays to receive callers. He kept pristine new bills behind the paintings and scrolls in his study. He lent money freely without expectation of repayment. He enjoyed traditional card games, playing late into the night with his friends. He was competitive, another trait he disliked in himself. He believed in ghosts and spirits, the mythical beings and creatures of folklore. He was deeply superstitious and afraid of many things, from wooden *tanuki* to yellow taxis. Most of all he feared he had inherited his mother's mental illness. He was plagued by stomach pains, insomnia and hallucinations. He studied medical and psychological textbooks. He kept a pharmacological dictionary on his desk and enjoyed the company and friendship of doctors.

He was thirty-five years old, the most famous writer of the day, and in the early hours of July 24, 1927, a warm and gentle rain falling on the leaves of the garden, Ryūnosuke Akutagawa was about to take his own life.

*

Ryūnosuke Akutagawa was born Ryūnosuke Niihara on March 1, 1892. He was named Ryūnosuke, "dragon-son," because he was born in the hour of the dragon, in the month of the dragon, in the year of the dragon. The year of the dragon, 1892, was also Meiji 25, the twenty-fifth year of the reign of the Emperor Meiji. These three concurrent calendars and their times—Chinese, Gregorian and Japanese—and his two family names, they matter with Akutagawa; they will define and, ultimately, condemn him.

Twenty-five years before the birth of Ryūnosuke, the Meiji Restoration ended the two hundred and sixty-five years of the Edo period, sweeping away the feudal rule of the Tokugawa shogunate. This so-called restoration of Imperial sovereignty was in fact the culmination of a revolutionary civil war as traumatic and far-reaching in its consequences as the revolutions of England, France and Russia. The victors were the modernizers of the samurai caste, intent not only on opening up Japan to Western ideas, inventions and trade, but on competing with the West and beating the Great Powers at their own Imperial games.

Toshizō Niihara, the father of Ryūnosuke, was one of the

victors. He was born a commoner but joined the Imperial rebel army at seventeen, fighting in the decisive battle of Toba-Fushimi which defeated the Tokugawa army and brought about the final collapse of the shogunate. Toshizō was an aggressive entrepreneur who flourished in the freedoms of post-feudal Japan. By the time Ryūnosuke was born, Toshizō owned five dairies and was living in the Tsukiji area of Tokyo, providing milk and butter to its growing foreign settlement. He had also married above himself.

Fuku Akutagawa, the mother of Ryūnosuke, was one of the vanquished. Before the Restoration, the Akutagawa family had been of minor samurai status but had enjoyed the hereditary position of tea masters to the shogun, guardians of cultural tradition. All their privileges were lost now, and Fuku was forced to marry the parvenu Toshizō Niihara.

The philandering Toshizō was everything the refined Fuku was not and their marriage proved ill-fated. Their eldest daughter died aged just six in 1891 and Fuku blamed herself. Ryūnosuke was born the following year, but less than six months later, his mother developed mental illness. She would live out the remaining ten years of her life in an upstairs room of the Niihara house while Ryūnosuke was sent to live with her elder brother's family in Honjo, a shabby and increasingly industrial ward on the eastern banks of the Sumida River; this would be his childhood home. His uncle and aunt would formally adopt him as Ryūnosuke Akutagawa in 1904 and he rarely, and only reluctantly, ever saw his real parents again. Yet the two families remained inextricably joined, and the tensions of their conflicting backgrounds and personalities would continue to fracture and plague Ryūnosuke for the rest of his life.

His childhood in the Akutagawa household, however, was a happy and cultured one. His uncle Dōshō was a minor government bureaucrat with a relatively low salary, yet he had inherited the family's passion for the traditional arts. From an early age, Ryūnosuke received private tutoring in calligraphy and haiku, as well as in Chinese and English. He was the only child of the house and the centre of its attention, particularly from his mother's unmarried elder sister, Fuki; Ryūnosuke loved her more than anyone else. Their relationship was the most intense and important of both their lives, and they would continue to live together even after his marriage.

Fuki nurtured a love for the ancient stories of Japan in the young Ryūnosuke; these stories led him to the Chinese classics, then to more contemporary Japanese and Western literature. By the age of ten, he was producing literary magazines with his school friends. He excelled academically and entered the elite First Higher School in 1910.

Two years later, the Emperor Meiji died. His reign had seen unprecedented modernization; in less than fifty years, Japan had become an industrial and military power, victorious in wars against China and Russia. The national trauma of such a rapid engagement with the forces of modernity is perhaps best articulated in the novels of Natsume Sōseki (1867–1916), the most famous writer of his day and still Japan's most celebrated author. Sōseki would also come to play a decisive role in the career of Ryūnosuke.

In 1913, the second year of the new Taishō era, Ryūnosuke entered Tokyo Imperial University. He majored in English literature, specialising in the works of William Morris, and founded a literary magazine with his classmates. Ryūnosuke contributed various essays, translations and also a number of original short stories, including "Rashōmon," which drew its inspiration from one of the tales found in the twelfth-century *Konjaku Monogatari* so loved by his aunt Fuki. Yet among his university contemporaries and the literary establishment, his fiction was either ignored or derided for its lack of originality. In 1916, however, Ryūnosuke published "The

Nose," again inspired by a tale from the *Konjaku Monogatari*, and this work drew the attention and praise of Sōseki. The elder writer, now in the final year of his life, took Ryūnosuke into his circle, encouraged and promoted his work, and thus helped to launch Ryūnosuke on his literary career.

The literary life of Ryūnosuke Akutagawa lasted just thirteen years and coincided almost exactly with the reign of the Emperor Taishō. The writing and study of Japanese history is very often determined and defined by the names of the Imperial eras. It is easy and tempting then to view Japanese history as a chronology apart from the Western calendar and to forget, say, that the Taishō era was contemporaneous with the First World War, the Russian Revolution, continual instability in Republican China and a worldwide flu pandemic, but all of these events had profound consequences for Japan. Domestically, however, the Taishō era is often seen as a brief and exciting period of liberalism, coming as it did between the austere, paternalistic Imperial pomp of Meiji and the repressive militarism and tragic nationalism of early Shōwa. It is true that Taishō encompassed certain democratic reforms, burgeoning consumer spending and women's independence among the metropolitan bourgeoisie, the rise of mass entertainments and Western fashions, and a flourishing of avant-garde movements in the arts and philosophy. Yet Taishō was also a time of growing state censorship, rural poverty, rice riots, political assassinations and the devastating earthquake of 1923, which destroyed most of Tokyo and Yokohama and left hundreds of thousands dead. This brief, complex and turbulent time has come to be personified in the figure of Akutagawa, the quintessential Taishō writer.

During his lifetime, however, and despite his success, Akutagawa was most commonly seen as standing apart from the contemporary literary trends of the day. Little of his work owed anything to the popular Naturalist or Proletarian movements and, until the very last year of his life, he resisted the searing autobiographical honesty of Naoya Shiga or Tōson Shimazaki, the overt Modernism and eroticism of Jun'ichirō Tanizaki, or the sustained experimentalism of Riichi Yokomitsu and the young Yasunari Kawabata. Rather, Akutagawa continued to be dogged by charges of unoriginality and dilettantism, called a "mosaicist" who merely cherry-picked from or imitated the works of the past. And yet, if one tears down the borders and confines of country and nationality, Akutagawa's assemblages of the fragments and ruins from the past find their parallels in *Ulysses*, "The Waste Land" and the poetry of Pound, while his love of the fable and the fantastic compares with Kafka, Bulgakov and Borges.

Despite the relative brevity of his career, the complete works of Akutagawa run to twenty-four volumes in Japanese and encompass short stories, novellas, poetry, travelogues, screenplays, essays, journalism, letters and translations. It is dangerous, therefore, to talk of one single masterpiece and yet his 1922 short story "In a Bamboo Grove" surely highlights the genius of Akutagawa and the importance of his legacy.

"In a Bamboo Grove" has a certain familiarity in the West, as the story provided the basis for Akira Kurosawa's 1950 film *Rashōmon,* which, in turn, inspired the somewhat misleading term "Rashomon effect."

In writing the original story, Akutagawa once again drew his inspiration from the *Konjaku Monogatari.* The plot concerns a rape and murder, but Akutagawa retells the story using seven distinct narrative voices, three of which give conflicting accounts of the crimes. In using this narrative technique, Akutagawa may have drawn on "The Moonlit Road" by Ambrose Bierce, whose work he had publicly championed. However, unlike in the Bierce story, Akutagawa refuses to reconcile the divergent narratives thus leaving the reader unable to comfortably "solve" the mystery. As Seiji M.

Lippit has written, "the real horror of the story may be not that each witness is lying, but rather the possibility that each is, somehow, telling the truth."

Now more than ever, this one story seems to predict and speak to our world of collapsed grand narratives, post truths, fake news and billions of competing, vehement subjectivities, all fragmented and adrift.

Off the page, and away from his desk, Ryūnosuke struggled to hold his own life together. He married and had children but, like his father before him, he embarked on a number of affairs, one of which came to cause him profound anguish and regret. He grew increasingly certain he had inherited his mother's mental illness and became addicted to soporifics in order to sleep. His health, in general, never seemed to recover fully from the pleurisy he contracted on a trip to China in 1921. Two years later, the Great Kantō Earthquake struck. Although the family house in Tabata was only slightly damaged, Ryūnosuke's sister and half-brother lost their homes and both looked to him for financial assistance and care. He also repeatedly toured the ruined city, witnessing and then documenting the death and the destruction, and the violence of vigilante mobs against the Korean community. The non- fiction pieces he wrote in the aftermath were all censored by the authorities. In the three years following the disaster, Ryūnosuke wrote very little.

The last year of his life was particularly fraught, exacerbated by worsening health and financial worries: as well as having to provide for his own household, which included his adoptive parents and his aunt Fuki, Ryūnosuke was forced to take on the debts of his brother-in-law, who had committed suicide when charged with bankruptcy, fraud and arson.

Yet that last year of Ryūnosuke's life saw a creative outpouring as diverse as it was prolific and which includes some of his very finest and most enduring work: the deeply personal "Death Register" and

"Winter," the fragile melancholy of "Mirage," the claustrophobic "Villa of Genkaku," the experimental screenplays "Temptation" and "Asakusa Park," the biting bitter satire of the novella *Kappa*, a biography and meditation on the life of Christ, "Man of the West," the hallucinatory nightmare of "Spinning Gears" and, finally, a summation of his own life, reduced to fifty-one harrowing fragments which he entitled "The Life of a Stupid Man."

July 23, 1927, the second year of the new Shōwa era, was one of the hottest on record. Ryūnosuke spent the day finishing a sequel to "Man of the West." And then, his work complete, in the early hours of the next morning, Ryūnosuke took a fatal dose of barbiturates, wished his aunt Fuki goodnight, changed into his favourite *yukata*, and lay down beside his wife, his annotated Bible open on his chest.

*

The suicide of Ryūnosuke Akutagawa was a national sensation, reported even in *The Times* of London. His rambling but typically erudite farewell letter to his friend and colleague Masao Kume was read aloud to reporters at his wake, then printed in full in many newspapers. In the text, Akutagawa declines to give one single specific reason for his decision to end his life, writing instead of living "in a world of diseased nerves" and his "vague sense of anxiety" about his own future. The reasons for and meaning of his suicide have been pondered over, written about and contested ever since. Marxist critics of the time saw it as the ultimate defeat of bourgeoisie intellectualism, others as the most extreme rejection of that very bourgeoisie world. But more so even than the passing of the Emperor Taishō six months before, the death of Akutagawa came to be seen as the end of an era and his "vague sense of anxiety" as a portent of the calamities to come.

Jorge Luis Borges, in his foreword to an Argentinian edition of

Kappa published in 1959, wrote, "Thackeray declared that to think about Swift is to think about the collapse of empire. A similar process of vast disintegration and pain operates in Akutagawa's last works . . ."

The collapse of empires never ends, and the life and work of Ryūnosuke Akutagawa remain as relevant and as resonant as ever.

After Words

Bibliography

The twelve tales which form this novel are inspired and informed by the stories, essays and letters of Ryūnosuke Akutagawa himself, incidents from his own life, and the memories and writings of people around him. I have included a complete list of all the sources used in the writing of this novel but, for anyone who has not read Akutagawa, I would begin with:

Rashōmon and Seventeen Other Stories, trans. Jay Rubin (Penguin, 2006).
Kappa, trans. Geoffrey Bownas (Tuttle, 1971; Peter Owen, 2009).

Both books also include very useful biographical information.

Many of the stories of Akutagawa have been widely translated, over many years, though most collections are now out of print:

Akutagawa and Dazai: Instances of Literary Adaptation, trans. James O'Brien (Center for Asian Studies, Arizona State University, 1988; Kurodahan Press, 2004).
The Beautiful and the Grotesque, originally published under the title *Exotic Japanese Stories*, trans. Takashi Kojima and John McVittie (Liverlight, 1964 and 2010).
"A Bizarre Reunion," trans. Steven P. Venti, in *Kaiki: Uncanny Tales from Japan, Volume 3: Tales of the Metropolis* (Kurodahan Press, 2012).
Cogwheels and Other Stories, trans. Howard Norman (Mosaic Press, 1982, 2015).
"The Death Register," trans. Lawrence Rogers, in *Tokyo Stories: A Literary Stroll*, ed. Lawrence Rogers (University of California Press, 2002).
The Essential Akutagawa, ed. Seiji M. Lippit (Marsilio, 1999).

Die Fluten des Sumida, trans. Armin Stein (IUDICIUM Verlag, 2010).

A Fool's Life, trans. Will Petersen (Grossman Publishers, 1970).

A Fool's Life, trans. Anthony Barnett and Naoko Toraiwa (Allardyce, Barnett, 2007).

"General Kim," trans. Jay Rubin, in *Monkey Business Vol. 3* (Villagebooks, 2013).

Hell Screen and Other Stories, trans. W. H. H. Norman (Hokuseido, 1948).

Hell Screen, Cogwheels, A Fool's Life, trans. Takashi Kojima, Cid Corman, Susumu Kamaike and Will Petersen, with a foreword by Jorge Luis Borges and introduction by Kazuya Sakai (Eridanos Press, 1987).

Japanese Short Stories, trans. Takashi Kojima (Liverlight, 1961).

Kappa, trans. Seiichi Shiojiri (Akitaya, 1947, and Hokuseido, 1951).

Kirishitan Stories by Akutagawa Ryūnosuke, trans. Yoshiko and Andrew Dykstra, in *Japanese Religions*, Vol. 31 (2006).

Mandarins, trans. Charles de Wolf (Archipelago, 2010).

"The Mirage," trans. Beongcheon Yu, in *Chicago Review*, XVIII, No. 2 (1965).

Rashōmon and Other Stories, trans. Takashi Kojima (Liverlight, 1952).

Rashōmon and Other Stories, trans. Glenn W. Shaw (Hara Shobo, 1964).

The Spider's Thread and Other Stories, trans. Dorothy Britton (Kodansha International, 1987).

Tales Grotesque and Curious, trans. Glenn W. Shaw (Hokuseido, 1930).

Three Strange Tales, trans. Glenn Anderson (One Peace Books, 2012).

The Three Treasures, trans. Takamasa Sasaki (Hokuseido, 1951).

"Travels in China," trans. Joshua A. Fogel, in *Chinese Studies in History* (1997).

Tu Tze-Chun, trans. Dorothy Britton, with woodcuts by Naoko Matsubara, and an introduction by E. G. Seidensticker (Kodansha International, 1965).

"Western Man, Western Man Continued," trans. Akiko Inoue, in *Posthumous Works of Ryūnosuke Akutagawa* (Tenri, Tenri Jihosha, 1961).

"Wonder Island," trans. Dan O'Neill, in *Three-Dimensional Reading: Stories of Time and Space in Japanese Modernist Fiction, 1911–1932*, ed. Angela Yiu (University of Hawai'i Press, 2013).

The following texts contain studies of Akutagawa's life and work:

Akutagawa Fumi, *Tsuisō Akutagawa Ryūnosuke* (Chūō Kōron-sha, 1981).

Bates, Alex, *The Culture of the Quake* (University of Michigan, 2015).

De Vos, George A., with Hiroshi Wagatsuma, "Alienation and the Author; A Triptych on Social Conformity and Deviancy in Japanese Intellectuals," in *Socialization for Achievement*, ed. George A. De Vos (University of California Press, 1973).

Fowler, Edward, *The Rhetoric of Confession: Shishōsetsu in Early Twentieth-Century Japanese Fiction* (University of California Press, 1988).

Fukasawa, Margaret Benton, *Kitahara Hakushū: His Life and Poetry* (East Asia Program, Cornell University, 1993).

Hibbett, Howard S., "Akutagawa Ryūnosuke," in *Modern Japanese Writers*, ed. Jay Rubin (Scribner's, 2001).

Hibbett, Howard S., "Akutagawa Ryūnosuke and the Negative Ideal," in *Personality in Japanese History*, ed. Albert M. Craig and Donald H. Shively (University of California Press, 1970).

Hirotsu Kazuo, *Shinpen Dōjidai no Sakka-tachi* (Iwanami shoten, 1992).

Iga, Mamoru, "Ryūnosuke Akutagawa," in *The Thorn in the Chrysanthemum* (University of California Press, 1986).

Ishiwari Tōru (ed.), *Akutagawa Ryūnosuke Shokan-shū* (Iwanami shoten, 2009).

Ishiwari Tōru (ed.), *Akutagawa Ryūnosuke Zuihitsu-shū* (Iwanami shoten, 2014).

Karatani, Kōjin, "On the Power to Construct," in *Origins of Modern Japanese Literature*, trans. Brett de Bary (Duke University Press, 1993).

Keene, Donald, *Dawn to the West: Japanese Literature of the Modern Era* (Holt, Rinehart and Winston, 1984).

Kondō Tomie, *Tabata Bunshi-mura* (Chūō Kōron-sha, 1983).

Kuzumaki Yoshitoshi, *Akutagawa Ryūnosuke Miteikōshū* (Iwanami shoten, 1968).

Lippit, Seiji M., "Disintegrating Mechanisms of Subjectivity: Akutagawa Ryūnosuke's Last Writings," in *Topographies of Japanese Modernism* (Columbia University Press, 2002).

Matsumoto Seichō, *Shōwa-shi Hakkutsu* (Bungei Shunjū, 1978).

Morimoto Osamu, *Akutagawa Ryūnosuke Denki Ronkō* (Meiji shoin, 1964).

Napier, Susan J., *The Fantastic in Modern Japanese Literature* (Routledge, 1996).

Niina Noriaki, *Akutagawa Ryūnosuke no Nagasaki* (Nagasaki Bunkensha, 2015).

Richie, Donald, *Rashōmon* (Rutgers, 1987).

Schencking, Charles J., *The Great Kantō Earthquake* (Columbia University Press, 2013).

Sekiguchi Yasuyoshi (ed.), *Akutagawa Ryūnosuke Shin-Jiten* (Kanrin shobō, 2003).

Suter, Rebecca, *Holy Ghosts: The Christian Century in Modern Japanese Fiction* (University of Hawai'i Press, 2015).

Uchida Hyakken, *Watashi no "Sōseki" to "Ryūnosuke"* (Chikuma shobō, 1993).

Ueda, Makoto, "Akutagawa Ryūnosuke," in *Modern Japanese Writers and the Nature of Literature* (Stanford University Press, 1976).

Weisenfeld, Gennifer, *Imaging Disaster: Tokyo and the Visual Culture of Japan's Great Earthquake of 1923* (University of California Press, 2012).

Yamanouchi, Hisaaki, "The Rivals: Shiga Naoya and Akutagawa Ryūnosuke," in *The Search for Authenticity in Modern Japanese Literature* (Cambridge University Press, 1978).

Yamazaki Mitsuo, *Yabu no Naka no Ie* (Bungei Shunjū, 1997).

Yoshida Seiichi et al. (eds), *Akutagawa Ryūnosuke zenshū*, 8 vols (Chikuma shobō, 1964–5).

Yu, Beongcheon, *Akutagawa: An Introduction* (Wayne State University Press, 1972).

The following texts are of or about the times in which Akutagawa lived:

Bargen, Doris G., *Suicidal Honor* (University of Hawai'i Press, 2006).

Beongcheon Yu, *Natsume Sōseki* (Twayne, 1969).

DiNitto, Rebecca, *Uchida Hyakken: A Critique of Modernity and Militarism in Pre-war Japan* (Harvard University Press, 2008).

Dong, Stella, *Shanghai* (William Morrow, 2000).

Gluck, Carol, *Japan's Modern Myths* (Princeton University Press, 1985).

Heinrich, Amy Vladeck, *Fragments of Rainbows: The Life and Poetry of Saitō Mokichi* (Columbia University Press, 1983).

Irwin, John T., *The Mystery to a Solution: Poe, Borges, and the Analytic Detective Story* (Johns Hopkins University Press, 1996).

Karatani, Kōjin, *History and Repetition*, trans. and ed. Seiji M. Lippit (Columbia University Press, 2012).

Kawabata, Yasunari, *The Scarlet Gang of Asakusa*, trans. Alisa Freedman, with a foreword and afterword by Donald Richie (University of California Press, 2005).

Keene, Dennis, *Yokomitsu Riichi Modernist* (Columbia University Press, 1980).

Kurosawa, Akira, *Something Like an Autobiography*, trans. Audie E. Bock (Vintage Books, 1983).

Lifton, Robert Jay, Katō, Shūichi, and Reich, Michael R., *Six Lives, Six Deaths* (Yale University Press, 1979).

Mansfield, Stephen, *Tokyo: A Cultural and Literary History* (Signal Books, 2009).

Mitford, A. B., *Tales of Old Japan* (Macmillan, 1876).

Ōgai, Mori, *Not a Song Like Any Other: An Anthology of Writings by Mori Ōgai*, ed. J. Thomas Rimmer (University of Hawai'i Press, 2004).

Ōgai, Mori, *Youth and Other Stories*, trans. and ed. J. Thomas Rimmer (University of Hawai'i Press, 1994).

Poe, Edgar Allan, *The Complete Tales and Poems* (Penguin, 1982).

Rimmer, J. Thomas, *Mori Ōgai* (Twayne, 1975).

Saito, Satoru, *Detective Fiction and the Rise of the Japanese Novel, 1880–1930* (Harvard University Asia Center, 2012).

Saitō, Mokichi, *Red Lights: Selected Tanka Sequences from Shakkō*, trans. Seishi Shinoda and Sanford Goldstein (Purdue Research Foundation, 1989).

Seidensticker, Edward, *Low City, High City* (Harvard University Press, 1983).

Seidensticker, Edward, *Tokyo Rising* (Charles E. Tuttle, 1991).

Songling, Pu, *Strange Tales from a Chinese Studio*, trans. John Minford (Penguin, 2006).

Sōseki, Natsume, *Kokoro*, trans. Edwin McClellan (Regnery Publishing, 1957).

Sōseki, Natsume, *The Tower of London: Tales of Victorian London*, trans. and with an introduction by Damian Flanagan (Peter Owen, 2004).

Sōseki, Natsume, *The Wayfarer*, trans. Beongcheon Yu (Tuttle, 1969).

Tanizaki, Jun'ichirō, *Red Roofs & Other Stories*, trans. Anthony H. Chalmers and Paul McCarthy (University of Michigan Press, 2016).

Tietjens, Eunice, *Profiles from China* (Ralph Fletcher Seymour, 1917).

Tyler, William J. (ed.), *Modaniizumu: Modernist Fiction from Japan, 1913–1938* (University of Hawai'i Press, 2008).

Uchida, Hyakken, *Realm of the Dead*, trans. Rachel DiNitto (Dalkey, 2006).

Waley, Paul, *Tokyo: City of Stories* (Weatherhill, 1991).

Waley, Paul, *Tokyo Now and Then* (Weatherhill, 1984).

Yokomitsu, Riichi, *Shanghai*, trans. Dennis Washburn (Centre for Japanese Studies, University of Michigan, 2001).

Acknowledgements

List of illustrations:

Frontispiece: Akutagawa, in his study, 1924. Courtesy of the
Museum of Modern Japanese.

Title page: Kappa drawn by Akutagawa, *c.*1922.

After the Thread: postcard of the Shinobazu Pond in Ueno, Tokyo,
*c.*1910.

Hell Screens: Akutagawa, *c.*1896, 1905 and 1927. Courtesy of the
Museum of Modern Japanese.

Repetition: photographs of General Nogi and his wife on the
morning of their deaths, September 13, 1912, taken by Akio
Shinroku.

Jack the Ripper's Bedroom: a Huntley & Palmers biscuit tin, as
mentioned in *Heart of Darkness* by Joseph Conrad, 1899.

A Twice-Told Tale: *Men's Head* by Kazimir Malevich, date
uncertain.

The Yellow Christ: *The Yellow Christ* by Paul Gauguin, 1889.
Albright-Knox Gallery, Buffalo, New York.

After the War: postcard of the Bridge of Nine Turnings, Shanghai,
date unknown.

The Exorcists: Kappa drawn by Akutagawa, 1927.

After the Disaster: *Saika no Ato* by Ikeda Yōson, ink and mineral
pigments on silk, 1924. Collection of Kurashiki Shiritsu
Bijutsukan.

"Saint Kappa": Akutagawa, 1925. Courtesy of the Museum of
Modern Japanese.

The Spectres of Christ: the *yukata* made from material Akutagawa
bought on his trip to China in 1922, and which he wore on the

night of his death in 1927. Courtesy of the Museum of Modern Japanese.

After the Fact: Akutagawa in death, by Ryūichi Oana, July 24, 1927.
Bare Bones: Akutagawa at his desk. Courtesy of the Museum of Modern Japanese.

*

Certain chapters and sections of this novel were previously published in the following edited or substantially different forms:

After the Disaster, Before the Disaster in *March Was Made of Yarn*, a collection of stories written to commemorate the first anniversary of the 2011 Tōhoku earthquake and tsunami, published in the US and UK by Vintage in 2012.

A Twice-Told Tale, under the title *After Ryūnosuke, Before Ryūnosuke*, in the Japanese literary journal *Monkey Business* in 2013.

After the War, Before the War in *Granta 127* in 2014.

After the Thread, Before the Thread was originally written for *Fantasma*, an Italian collection of the three stories listed above, published by il Saggiatore in 2016.

Finally, parts of *"Saint Kappa"* were written for the twelfth Bridge the Gap? in Genoa, Italy, organised by the Centre for Contemporary Art Kitakyushu, Japan, and presented to the audience in the booklet *After the Crash, Before the Crash* on March 4, 2016.

*

I would like to thank the following people: Ian Bahrami, Stephen Barber, Andrew Benbow, Ian Cusack, Walter Donohue, Didier Faustino, Laura Oldfield Ford, Luca Formenton, Giuseppe Genna,

Jean-Paul Gratias, François Guérif, Jeanne Guyon, Mike Handford, Yuka Igarashi, Kazuo Ishiguro, Jason James, Joan Jonas, Rob Kraitt, Justin McCurry, Sonny Mehta, David Mitchell, Shunichiro Nagashima, Kazuo Okanoya, Anna Pallai, Richard Lloyd Parry, Roger Pulvers, Sukhdev Sandhu, Junzo Sawa, Katy Shaw, Anna Sherman, Motoyuki Shibata, Pelin Tan, Peter Thompson, Paul Tickell, Rirkrit Tiravanija, David Turner, Rob Turner, Kate Ward, Gen Yamabe, and the Peace family, here and there, and finally, Matteo Battarra, Angus Cargill, Hamish Macaskill, Akiko Miyake, and Jon Riley, without whom this book would never have been finished.

David Peace—named in 2003 as one of *Granta*'s Best of Young British Novelists—was born and brought up in Yorkshire. He is the author of the Red Riding Quartet (*Nineteen Seventy-Four, Nineteen Seventy-Seven, Nineteen Eighty,* and *Nineteen Eighty-Three*); *GB84,* which was awarded the James Tait Black Memorial Prize; *The Damned Utd* and *Red or Dead,* which was shortlisted for the Goldsmiths Prize. The final part of his Tokyo Trilogy—to follow *Tokyo Year Zero* and *Occupied City*—will follow *Patient X,* his tenth novel. He lives in Tokyo.

A NOTE ON THE TYPE

This book was set in Adobe Garamond. Designed for the Adobe Corporation by Robert Slimbach, the fonts are based on types first cut by Claude Garamond (ca. 1480–1561). Garamond was a pupil of Geoffroy Tory and is believed to have followed the Venetian models, although he introduced a number of important differences, and it is to him that we owe the letter we now know as "old style." He gave to his letters a certain elegance and feeling of movement that won their creator an immediate reputation and the patronage of Francis I of France.

Composed by North Market Street Graphics,
Lancaster, Pennsylvania
Printed and bound by Berryville Graphics, Berryville, Virginia